Francesca Clementis wa[...] degree in Philosophy from Sussex University, she spent ten years in advertising before becoming a full-time writer. She lives in London with her husband and daughter.

Francesca is the author of *Big Girls Don't Cry* and *Mad About the Girls*, also published by Piatkus. In 2000 she won an Arts Council of England Writers' Award.

Also by Francesca Clementis

Big Girls Don't Cry
Mad About the Girls

Would I Lie to You?

Francesca Clementis

PIATKUS

Copyright © 2001 Francesca Clementis

First published in Great Britain in 2001 by
Judy Piatkus (Publishers) Ltd of
5 Windmill Street, London W1T 2JA
email: info@piatkus.co.uk

This edition published 2001

The moral right of the author has been asserted

*A catalogue record for this book is available
from the British Library*

ISBN 0 7499 3275 9

Typeset in Times by Palimpsest Book Production Limited,
Polmont, Stirlingshire

Printed and bound in Great Britain by
Mackays of Chatham plc, Chatham, Kent

For my godchildren with love: Geraldine Revill, Chester Campbell, Simon Bernie and Michael Elford. With love also to Stephanie Bernie and Matthew Elford.

My warmest thanks to the Arts Council of England for its generous support when it really made a difference.

Chapter 1

Lauren took a deep breath and a deeper swallow of her icy white wine. She hated parties, especially Stella's parties, best friend or not. But there was one advantage for Lauren. In fact there was *only* one in the case of Stella's parties. Lauren would have to focus so hard on not making a complete fool of herself, as was her custom at parties, that she would forget the two questions that were tormenting her, screaming for answers. That was the theory.

Her first lie was surprisingly easy. Hardly a lie at all. Just one of those things somebody says to make somebody else feel comfortable. Careless words uttered without thought for the consequences.

'Great party, Stella!' Lauren shouted above the thudding music. (This wasn't the lie. It was a lie, but not *the* lie. This was just a good guest's courtesy. The real lie came ten minutes later.)

Stella raised her glass in thanks, not even bothering to try and compete with the throbbing bass. The party was a triumph by her own criteria. It was a house-warming and the aim of the party was to cram many more people in than during the house-warming at the previous house. It signalled a bigger house, progress, visible evidence that the owners were movers, constantly edging forwards and upwards. Never standing still. It was exhausting to watch. The mere act of receiving the biennial change of address card made Lauren feel tired.

'It's a huge house!' Lauren yelled, knowing that this was exactly what her friend wanted to hear.

Stella rewarded her with a proud grin. 'Three receptions, five bedrooms, three bathrooms, one en suite, and a conservatory. Of course, it needs masses of work. But it was such a bargain.'

Lauren looked around at the decor. It wasn't difficult to see why it had been such a bargain. The previous owners had evidently subscribed to the *Changing Rooms* Guide to Making Your House Completely Unsellable. Every room had been decorated in a different style, with Moroccan dining room leading into Aborigine living room by way of a hallway that had been feng shuied into a crystal apocalypse.

Lauren no longer bothered asking why Stella and Pete insisted on buying bigger and bigger houses when they had no intention of having children. She understood. The houses *were* their children. Well, Stella's anyway. Pete never talked about it but he seemed happy enough with Stella's housebuying obsession.

'Who are all these people?' Lauren asked, gesturing over the mass of unfamiliar faces. She'd known both Stella and Pete for eighteen years, since university days, and thought she had met most of their friends and acquaintances.

Stella waved her hand vaguely. 'I invited everyone from work, and we asked friends of friends, that sort of thing. You know.'

2

Lauren knew. Stella needed friends by the number. She needed to know that at any time she could fill a room or a pub or a house with people who liked her. Most of all, Stella needed to be liked. By everyone she met. This didn't diminish the friendship she offered Lauren, which was deep and generous. But she also had to have the reassurance of a fat address book and a noticeboard pinned thick with invitations. She judged the achievements of each year on the increase in numbers of Christmas cards received. She only had to meet someone amenable for them to join her computer database. Pete went along with this placidly. He hated conflict and felt fortunate that the only contribution required to keep Stella happy was to open his home to a constant stream of strangers and play the straight man to Stella's well-rehearsed banter.

But this party was something else. It was as if Stella and Pete had gone to IKEA, accosted all those attractive couples in their Gap jeans, persuaded them to drop their flatpacks containing entire integrated living environments, herded them into a coach and lured them into this interior-designed Armageddon with a glass of Pouilly-Fumé. All on a Wednesday night. ('It's the new Saturday,' Stella assured everyone.)

Stella's appearance soared over this frightening buzz of compulsory enjoyment like a firework. She glittered and gleamed from the fresh highlights in her immaculate blond bob right through to her gold eyeshadow, sparkling lipstick, sequinned tunic dress and impossibly high coordinating shoes. Lauren tried not to cover her eyes at this visual onslaught. Only sunglasses would have offered any real protection. But she admired Stella's

3

gift for transforming her essential ordinariness into a shimmering presence.

Only someone who'd seen Stella wearing no make-up and a tracksuit could recognise the enormity of this achievement. Because Stella was essentially plain: there was no other word for her. There was nothing flawed in her features; they just didn't add up to prettiness or beauty or character or any other positive descriptives you could think of. But she was fortunate to have identified and accepted her facial failings early in life and learned to maximise the qualities she had.

She was all style, all glitz, all personality, all froth. The complete opposite of Lauren.

Where Stella was all style, Lauren was all substance. To look at Lauren was to know that she was smart. She had clever eyes. Not wise, but clever. And she had the bearing of a confident woman used to getting her own way without having to flirt.

Where Stella was all glitz, Lauren was all understated chic. As her salary had rocketed, so she had developed a taste and a flair for picking expensive clothes that always looked unique and stylish without ever being wacky.

Where Stella was all personality, Lauren was socially unevolved. She was a businesswoman and could handle herself in all situations. She could deal with the contrasting types she encountered in her varied work. She could talk to anyone on any work-related subject. But at parties she was permanently thirteen, gauche, clumsy. Once she got over the initial hurdle of first encounters she was fine. If she got over that hurdle, rather than trip over her mouth as usually happened.

And where Stella was froth, Lauren was a still pond.

4

At least that's how she appeared at first. As in the calmest of ponds, there were deep waters where all manner of dark life forms threatened to float to the surface. But Lauren was an expert at keeping them down. She was later to discover that it was this continuous effort to suppress her deeper emotions which left her so bereft of the basic social skills.

In this friendship, both Lauren and Stella appreciated the fundamental differences between them. Each found the other amusing, compelling and absolutely incomprehensible. Each waited for the day when the whole point of the other person would reveal itself, when Stella would understand why Lauren took life so seriously and Lauren would find out what Stella was so frightened of.

Lauren also depended on Stella and Pete's marriage. Its longevity and stability was a rock, a sanctuary, a constant. She loved watching them, always the same, never changing.

'Have you made up your mind and have you told your mum yet?' Stella asked over the din.

Whoops. Those were the two questions Lauren had come here to avoid.

She had two weeks to decide. Five years ago, the offer of a job in New York would have had Lauren packing her bags in minutes. There had been nothing to keep her in London, no family, no partner, nothing except a friend who gave terrible parties.

It was the reappearance of her mother that made the situation more tricky. Lauren had only been reconciled with her mother for three years after a long mutually agreed separation. Their relationship had been difficult after the death of Lauren's father when she was only six.

Lauren's mum had never been able to forgive her daughter for being born just when her singing career was about to take off. And Lauren couldn't forgive her mum for not being the one that died instead of her dad. Well, that's what the shrinks would have said. If you asked the two of them, they would have said that they simply irritated the hell out of each other. They drifted apart as Lauren's work took off and she began travelling a lot. The trips home became further and further apart, the phone calls became shorter and more strained.

Round about the same time, her mum revived her own career. She began singing in pubs and clubs, performing songs from musicals and '30s and '40s Tin Pan Alley classics to young audiences who found her style retro and cool. Ironically, Lauren had done her a great favour by forcing a postponement of her mother's career. If Maureen Connor had tried to make it as a singer in the '50s, her lack of genuine talent would have brought her crushing rejection from audiences used to stylish singers like Ella Fitzgerald and Peggy Lee.

But in the new millennium, she was ironic. She was postmodern. She was kitsch. She was practically a star in her limited universe. And as she finally found fulfilment in one area of her life, she felt the need to fill in all the gaps in the other areas. She resolved to make up for thirty years of lacklustre parenting by becoming the earth mother that Lauren had never wanted in the first place.

And as Lauren established her own company and her reputation grew and spread, she too found herself looking at the voids in her personal life. So she and Maureen approached each other tentatively. At least for Lauren it was tentative; Maureen modelled her new mother-persona on Ethel Merman in *Gypsy*, all booming voice, grand gestures, big hair. She was positively scary in her determination to make Lauren like her, love her, forgive her.

What would happen to her if her only daughter was to move abroad? Lauren asked herself.

Stella was getting impatient for an answer. 'Not yet,' Lauren answered. After all, this was Stella. She didn't want to hear about the grey areas. Never had.

Stella smiled approvingly at this correct answer. 'Oh well, as long as it's all sorted out before your birthday. I presume lunch at your mum's is still on? Pete and I are looking forward to it.'

Lauren nodded glumly at the prospect. Then, in the shorthand that their long acquaintance allowed, Stella touched Lauren's arm gently as she rushed off to greet a new arrival at the door.

Lauren smiled weakly at a number of faces who smiled weakly back. It was a standard social courtesy, just in case any of them had met before. She turned back to Stella, who'd disappeared into the Raj-style (with just a hint of Amish puritan) kitchen to check on her canapés. Oh, no. That moment. That party moment when you are the only one not ensconced in a chatty pair or small crowd, not even hovering uninvited on the edge, laughing at in-jokes that you couldn't possibly understand. Alone, standing with a full glass that doesn't need tactical refilling and no buffet to go and raid very slowly.

Two options: bathroom or garden. Having visited the bathroom once already and been unable to relieve herself on a toilet seat consisting of golden insects preserved in resin (Insect-embossed toilet seats – postmodern or just gross? Discuss), she made her way to the garden.

Opening the back door, she felt her muscles unwind slightly. Not because she liked gardens. On the contrary, she found them puzzling. You broke your back planting bulbs and seeds. They grew, looked lovely for about a fortnight, then they died. Then you did it all over again. No, it wasn't for her. If she wanted aesthetic pleasure, she watched *The Sound of Music* or arranged pieces of pineapple on a Hawaiian pizza into a smiley face.

But gardens are useful at parties. Hosts are pleased that you are admiring their handiwork and there is no one to upset or offend, an unfortunate habit with Lauren. So here she was in Stella and Pete's garden.

At least she thought it was the garden. There wasn't a blade of grass, not a single bedding plant or shrub. No dying roses or thriving weeds. No sign of a plastic patio dining set. Just bleached decking weaving in and out of some rather scary sculptures surrounding a water feature constructed from dozens of Marmite jars covered in concrete and painted indigo. What sort of garden is that? An award-winning garden, that's what. One that's been photographed for *House and Garden*. One that cost the previous occupants over £5000 before they finally placed the house on the market, having robbed themselves of their last vestige of good taste.

Having taken a few seconds to acclimatise herself to this sensory wasteland, she realised that she was not alone. Another guest had sought the same refuge as her. Decision time: to turn back and loiter in the kitchen hoping there would be plates of snacks she could carry about, or to speak.

The sound of raucous, vacuous laughter honking from the direction of the kitchen helped her to make up her mind. She would talk to the man. How difficult could it be?

He looked nice enough. About her age. Friendly face. But that haircut. It was perilously close to 1970s footballer with those droopy layers edging towards his shoulders. And the clothes completed the look. Jeans about a hundred years old that probably never had fitted properly and certainly didn't now. And the compulsory black T-shirt. He had to be a social worker or a media studies lecturer in a redbrick university. Something like that. If he was a friend of Stella's, he would certainly be a professional. At the very least he would know somebody famous. Either way, there should be something uncontroversial they could talk about.

It made no difference to Lauren that he was a man. She was capable of dropping comprehensive clangers in the presence of both women and men. Men as such didn't make her nervous, any strangers did. And right now, she was not looking for a partner. Not with the prospect of a move abroad.

Although, that aside, she hadn't been looking for anyone for some time, not since her mother had catapulted herself back into her world. Maureen had not been content with filling the holes left in her daughter's life by her past absence – she was busy drilling new holes wherever she found space and filling them too. Lauren's life was being sucked up by her mum like a piece of kitchen towel. She could hardly sniff without Maureen popping up with a hanky, a bottle of Night Nurse and a homemade shepherd's pie. New York seemed an oasis of privacy and freedom.

No, she didn't have room for romantic complications. No room and no need. So that took the additional pressure off this encounter.

Chris Fallon was thinking exactly the same thing. He was not looking for romance either. Not because he was coming to terms with a crazy mother who wanted to sing duets from *The King and I* with him, nor because he was about to emigrate although he expected to be looking for a new job in the near future. He shook the thought out of his mind. The only advantage of this dreadful party was that the awfulness would distract him from the knife poised behind his back. That was the theory.

A new relationship was the last thing he wanted. He was just out of an intense five-year live-in almost-marriage that had left him bruised and unstable. All he wanted to do for the next six months or so was to read a lot of books, watch a lot of videos, eat a lot of microwaveable chicken korma. And he wanted to do it alone.

But he wasn't rude. So when the girl approached him, he welcomed her with a friendly smile. He would probably have smiled even if he had been rude. People smiled at Lauren. They never knew why. It might have been her boyish crop that only a very beautiful woman could get away with; or the freckles that no amount of industrial-strength foundation could conceal; or the little scar by the corner of her mouth which gave her an attractively lopsided smile. She'd never lost that toddler prettiness that had induced old people in the street to push sixpences into her hand while wiping away an emotional tear. Now they just smiled. Like Chris.

'Chris Fallon,' he said, holding out his hand. Lauren shook it firmly. By acting as if this was a professional introduction, she hoped to avoid her customary ineptitude.

'Lauren Connor.' Keep it simple, she warned herself. Don't say anything rash. Not until I'm safely over the first few fences of self-incrimination. I could be out in the garden for a while. I don't want to scare him off too soon.

Chris had his own fears, his own insecurities. He wasn't good at reading women's intentions. He couldn't tell if Lauren was making pleasant conversation or whether she was thinking that this might be leading somewhere. He didn't want to give her the wrong impression but he didn't know how to broach the subject without sounding presumptuous or foolish. Neither wanted to be the one to make the first mistake. So they blundered on painfully.

After a screaming silence, Chris calculated that it was probably his turn to speak. Think of something safe, he thought. 'So how do you know Pete and Stella?'

'I went to university with them both,' Lauren replied, pleased to be asked a question that didn't require careful consideration. 'I've known them eighteen years now,' she added. She watched as Chris tried silently to work out the implications this had for her age. 'That makes me thirty-six,' she said, laughing.

'No, I wasn't, I mean, I didn't . . .' Chris spluttered before he caught sight of Lauren's amused expression. Then he shrugged. 'OK. You win. I *was* wondering.' His face crumpled into a self-effacing cheeky grin. Lauren allowed her shoulder muscles to unclench. A few more minutes and she'd stop worrying altogether.

She couldn't help what she said next. She was intoxicated by the ease of the contact. It was a long time since she'd handled an encounter with a new person with such relative ease. She was probably also intoxicated by three glasses of wine in thirty minutes on an empty stomach. That was her excuse when she conducted the post-mortem in the bath later.

'You're a Virgo, aren't you?' she blurted out. The question had never caused her any problems in the past. It was standard conversational fodder. And Lauren felt sure-footed talking about this. She was good at guessing people's star signs. Well, she wasn't really, she just believed she was. When she got it wrong (most of the time), she put it down to wilful misinformation. If someone insists on looking like a dreamy Aquarian when they are really a hard-headed Taurean, it's nothing less than fraud.

She had a predisposition towards Virgos. They tended to be nicer, kinder, more sensitive. So, although Chris couldn't know it, she was complimenting him by this assumption.

She didn't get the result she desired. His quirky grin dissolved into an amused, quizzical expression. He seemed to be considering his answer cautiously, which confused Lauren when the question was not multiple-choice.

'Am I?' he answered ambiguously. Lauren interpreted his response as surprise at having his star sign so wrongly guessed. But she wasn't certain. So she began to laugh. To buy some time. She wasn't sure what she had done

12

wrong, but she sensed that her innocent question had not been well received. Damn, she thought. I should have gone to the kitchen and joined the honking laughers. I could have just chuckled and giggled and never had to say a word.

'That's interesting,' Chris said vaguely, mystified as to why Lauren was laughing. Even when he told jokes, people tended not to laugh. Besides, he wasn't aware he'd said anything funny.

Lauren's laugh had degenerated into a weak smile. She was still trying to come up with a witty pay-off to this improvised skit. She contributed one of those non-committal hissing noises that communicates nothing apart from one's continued existence on the planet.

Chris, realising that she was waiting for him to say something, carried on. 'So you're interested in astrology?' That's all he said.

But that's not all Lauren heard. Astrology, he'd said. With *that* tone of voice. At least it sounded to her like *that* tone of voice. She was super-sensitive to everything this man was saying and made the false assumption that he was equally sensitive to everything she was saying. That he was judging her. Without thinking, her hand flew to her necklace and the Pisces pendant that her mother had given her on her twenty-first birthday. So she told a lie. The first lie.

'Not really!'

That was all she said. She didn't deliver a ten-minute diatribe on the logical impossibility of astrology peppered by humorous anecdotes. She wasn't aiming for any higher level of misdirection. She was just trying to edge her way out of a corner she believed had trapped her. That was all.

13

'Not really!' Just the smallest of sentences, as small as a sentence can be, but with an exclamation mark. She consoled herself with the reasoning that maybe an exclamation mark, however convincingly articulated, could be signalling that she was being ironic rather than dishonest. But she didn't believe that herself and it was her lie.

Chris looked at her curiously. She felt her skin heat up, as if he could see the words I'M LYING imprinted across her forehead. 'Isn't that a Pisces fish on your necklace?' he asked.

And although the first sort-of lie had already slipped out, Lauren still had a chance to scramble back up to a position of truth. I mean, what difference did this man's opinion make? She'd probably not see him again until Stella's next house-warming in a couple of years.

But she was flustered. Her face was radiating an alarming red glow. She'd lost her cool and didn't know how to get it back. This always happened and she'd never learned what to do. There was a line somewhere, specifically for occasions like these, a little throwaway where a woman sounds endearingly fallible for making a minor social gaffe. Sadly, she'd never found out what this line was despite reading women's magazines all the way from *Jackie* to *Marie Claire*.

It was her turn to speak. She couldn't run away like Cinderella. So she ploughed onwards, nothing to lose, taking no prisoners. She wasn't a self-possessed businesswoman now, capable of negotiating a competitive contract with the toughest of executives. She was a teenager in a hand-me-down dress at a disco. She wasn't herself. She literally wasn't herself. She was person-at-a-party, trying to make a good first impression. And the thought that she was failing, yet again, was making her a little bit crazy. Yet again.

'This?' she said, fingering the offending pendant casually. 'It's nothing to do with Pisces. It's just a fish design.' And even this might not have proved disastrous if she'd stopped there. But she didn't. She couldn't. Not until she received confirmation that she'd clawed her way back to the level playing field of their kick-off. So she went on, plunging ever deeper into a bottomless pit of mud. 'I'm not even Pisces, so why would I have a Pisces necklace?'

Chapter 2

Yes, of course this was a monumentally stupid thing to say, stupid and utterly pointless. So if you have NEVER said anything so horribly moronic that you instantly wanted to take it back, if you have never wasted hours replaying a particularly imbecilic comment and slapping the side of your head to check that you still have a brain, if you are an absolutely perfect person in complete control of your tongue, then feel free to judge Lauren as harshly as you like. Otherwise just send up a brief, silent prayer that, almost certainly, whatever you said did not set off the catastrophic chain of consequences that Lauren's lie did.

Minutes later, on her way to the bathroom, she beckoned Stella to one side. 'Look, I've been talking to that Chris Fallon. And please don't ask me why, but if you come over and if it comes up in conversation, then I'm not Pisces, OK?'

Stella looked at her stupidly. 'What are you talking about?'

Lauren tutted and waved her hands about. 'Same old, same old. Me putting my foot in it and following through with the rest of my leg.' Without waiting for a reply, she was gone. Stella tried to call her back but Lauren had gone into the bathroom. Which was soundproofed. (Pete and Stella had both shuddered as they tried to decide why anyone would have their bathroom soundproofed.) And she didn't get another chance. So it wasn't Stella's fault that she didn't tell Lauren about the brief conversation she'd had with Chris earlier. That's what she tried to convince herself of as she thought back an hour.

Stella had been busy with the preparations for the party and Chris was getting in her way. She wasn't that keen on him, only tolerating him because she liked his ex-girlfriend Beth so much. He was too unkempt for her and he gave off an aura of unpredictability. She didn't like that. She preferred men like her husband: well groomed, reined in, controlled. To get rid of Chris, she'd been trying to persuade him to go and look at the garden.

'It's amazing!' she'd told him. 'So grand and desolate and . . . existential.'

Chris correctly interpreted this as a warning not to expect trailing petunias. As he obediently walked towards the back door, Stella couldn't stop herself from continuing in her role of perfect hostess.

'You'll probably come across Lauren while you're out there. She always ends up in the garden at my parties. I don't know why. She hates the outdoors.'

'Which one is Lauren?' Chris asked, knowing from experience how Stella liked to categorise her friends. If a serial killer was to gatecrash one of her dinner parties, her first thought would be whether it was best to place him next to a vegetarian or a carnivore.

Without thinking, Stella summed up Lauren as if she was enrolling her in a dating agency. 'Lauren – telecommunications consultant although I've never really understood what she does, very successful, loves old

17

musicals, great cook, Pisces, prefers Virgos, bit strange, very nice.'

She didn't even bother to check Chris's reaction to this introduction before he walked away. It hadn't been important. He and Lauren were completely unsuited. He was so cynical and earthy, she was so . . . well she was a bit fey and awkward, if Stella had to be honest. That's why she'd never had Lauren to dinner parties with Chris and Beth.

But now her casual words ricocheted round her mind as she contemplated Lauren's admission. Should she tell her friend that this man already knew that she was lying? What would be the point? Stella thought. Whatever was going on this evening between Lauren and Chris, a relationship was never going to get off the ground, particularly now that Chris had caught her in a very silly lie. And Lauren would feel such a fool if she knew. Anyone would. Why put her through it? No, she'd leave it.

Pete was refilling two glasses in the kitchen. He spotted Stella standing there wrapped up in herself. It was not like her. Stella rarely took the risk of introspection. He knew that she found it so much more reliable to look outwards for validation. He walked over and put his arm round her. She seldom needed comfort or reassurance from him and he liked being able to provide her with something other than the services of an under-qualified butler.

'What's up? Everyone seems to be having a great time.' He presumed that her only concern could be for the party. He knew her well but this time he was wrong.

Stella cleared her throat. 'Nothing. It's just something

18

Lauren said. I think she might be getting on quite well with Chris.'

'Chris? Which one's that?' Pete found it difficult to keep up with the parade of names that Stella frogmarched through his life.

'Chris Fallon. The Teacher of the Difficult Children.'

'Oh, you mean Beth's ex-boyfriend. So what's the problem?'

Stella looked at him awkwardly. 'It's not a problem as such.'

Stella couldn't tell him what the problem was. Pete hated it when she got involved in other people's lives. (She called it 'involved', he called it 'interfering'.) And he hated her insistence on seeing complexity where he didn't feel there was a need for any. He'd be cross with her and tell her to grab Lauren immediately and put her in the picture. He wouldn't understand. She wasn't sure she understood herself. She was a bit drunk and all these demands on her decision-making processes were too much. But she had to say something to Pete. He already knew something was wrong. So she said the first thing that came into her mind (apart from a few choice swear words).

'It's just that I was talking to Chris earlier and I got the distinct impression that he wants to get back with Beth and I think he might be about to ask Lauren out to make Beth jealous. I simply don't want Lauren to get hurt. You know how she always ends up getting hurt but I'd hate it if I could have prevented it.' The whole thing was untrue but perfectly credible to Pete.

Pete had undergone too many of Stella's autopsies following Lauren's disastrous relationships. For years,

Lauren had presented her friends with a succession of unsuitable men all of whom she had tried to please until they left her for women who pleased themselves. She eventually came to her senses and stopped submerging herself in other people's expectations.

But the exertions of the years had exhausted her. She bought herself a very expensive one-bedroomed flat which she decorated in a style that almost any other human being would find intolerable. She'd woven a cocoon for herself. It was a subconscious gesture to prevent anyone from taking a step too far into her world. And she'd been hiding there for three years.

Pete drew in a breath. 'I thought Chris was the one who broke it off with Beth? Why would he want her back?'

Stella cursed him for remembering this. It wasn't like him to take in the details of their friends' love lives. 'Obviously he's changed his mind!' she snapped. 'They came to the party together, didn't they? Or didn't Beth tell you that in the past hour you've spent talking to her? What have you been talking about all this time, anyway?'

It had been Stella's lie that had made her defensive. It was her defensiveness that made her aggressive. And it was her aggressiveness that made Pete defensive. And it was his defensiveness that made him lie.

'I was letting her cry on my shoulder, if you must know. She's been talking about Chris the whole time.'

The words came out before he'd formed them in his brain and withdrawn them for being senseless. But he felt that he couldn't tell Stella he'd spent an hour enjoying Beth's easy conversation. That they'd talked about big things. Life stuff. The subjects he and Stella didn't talk about because Stella didn't like to. She wouldn't understand, he thought. Would get the wrong idea. And he didn't know the right idea himself at this point. He was feeling a bit . . . distracted, distant.

This house made him uneasy and he couldn't put his finger on the reason. He had a film playing on a continuous reel in his mind, about Stella and their marriage which had consisted of buying houses, renovating houses, selling houses, talking about houses . . . the relentless activity that allowed not a single moment for reflection. It all betrayed a terrible fear of spare time. And the ceaseless acquisitions that bolstered Stella and gave her a sense of stability, acquisitions that felt like a succession of millstones to Pete. Beth understood.

He and Stella didn't talk about things like that. They talked about colour swatches and futons, house prices and mortgage rates, friends' relationships or the FT Share Index. Anything impersonal. It was easier to say that he'd been talking to Beth about Chris; easier and less dangerous. And innocent. And, therefore, justifiable.

Stella looked surprised. Beth hadn't said anything to her and they'd talked quite a lot in the weeks since the break-up. In fact, Beth claimed to be relieved that it was all over. Stella was inwardly furious that her so-called friend should confide in Pete rather than herself. Then it struck her. The answer to her own little dilemma. 'That's it then!' she announced brightly. 'Beth wants to be back with Chris and he, er, wants to get back with her. So let's see what we can do to help them along. That will nip this Lauren/Chris thing in the bud before Lauren gets involved.'

Pete was alarmed at this sudden turn of events. He'd just wanted to close down the subject safely with Stella so that he could get back to Beth and resume their conversation. He didn't want Beth to get back with Chris. Not one bit. And neither did Beth, from what she was saying. But he couldn't say this to Stella. 'I've got to take these drinks over, Beth is waiting,' was all he could say. And he disappeared towards the Aztec-style reception room before Stella had a chance to take this conspiracy any further.

In the time Lauren had taken to go to the loo, Chris pondered Lauren's baffling lie. He understood why she'd done it. When he'd first met Beth, he'd pretended to like French films to impress her. Even before he fell in love with her. If he'd known that he would be moving in with her within three weeks, he would have been more cautious about what he said. He hadn't realised that he'd be spending the next five years watching every major and minor production to come out of France. And there had never seemed to be an appropriate moment to confess his little fib.

There were some people one just wanted to impress. Beth was one; it transpired that he, himself, was another. But he couldn't work out how Lauren intended to impress him by lying about her star sign. It was a mystery. Unless there was something about Pisceans that everyone knew except him. Maybe they were notoriously fickle or prone to violence. He'd ask one of the women teachers at school tomorrow.

The really, really bizarre outcome of this self-questioning was that he found himself warming towards Lauren. She'd become vulnerable in his eyes with her reckless and apparently futile folly. He was puzzled by the turnaround from his earlier firm resolve to avoid new entanglements.

But while he was enjoying being single he was not, by nature, selfish or self-centred. He missed Beth's gentleness, her needs, his sense of usefulness. And Lauren was turning into someone who seemed in need of some care. Against all of his better judgements, he began to think of Lauren as someone he might want to get to know. *Might*. Getting to know a woman was never a casual exercise to Chris. He'd done impetuosity in the past. It hadn't suited him.

He was thirty-seven and happy that his youth was behind him. He'd just about survived the compulsory period of reckless promiscuity that always seems to be the holy grail of adulthood to the adolescent male. There must have been over ten years of going out with girls who drew little hearts over their letter 'i's and found keeping up with the actions to 'YMCA' and 'Agadoo' intellectually stimulating.

And it had all proved a blessed diversion after his stultifying upbringing by two parents who devoted their lives to Wagner. They were without doubt certifiable. Their sole aim as parents was to imbue their two children with the same passion for opera that they shared. They were relentless. As a fifth birthday present, Chris had been taken to Bayreuth and treated to a performance of *Lohengrin*. In German. When he'd actually asked for a chopper bike.

When his sister turned five, she had the good fortune to be hospitalised with acute appendicitis. So he went to Bayreuth in her place. Again. He couldn't recall which opera he saw, but it was very long, very depressing, very German. He never forgave her.

23

So for a long time, he craved the company of girls whose only concept of German civilisation was an appreciation of the Teutonic relationship with beach towels and sunbeds on holiday. And he wasn't left unaffected by this walk on the wild side. He might have failed to inspire any of his girlfriends to switch from Radio 1 to Radio 3 but they bequeathed him a lifelong passion for *Carry On* films and fried-egg sandwiches.

Eventually his mind screamed for mercy and his cultural heritage broke through. He never truly forgave his parents for wearing dirndls and lederhosen when he brought schoolfriends round but he was still unable to shake off the appalling legacy they had cursed him with – good taste. While he never reconciled himself to German opera, he did find himself drawn once more to women who read without dragging their finger along the words. And Beth was a whole lot more than that.

He was surprised to find someone like Lauren so soon after separating from Beth. After a long relationship, a good one, it is hard to conceive that one could meet anyone as right again. And for unidentifiable reasons there seemed to be something potentially right about Lauren. He'd wait until the reasons became clearer before he committed himself any further.

He was pleased with the way the evening was progressing. He'd been dreading the whole thing. In fact he'd only come tonight because Beth was obliged to be here and couldn't find anyone to accompany her. Stella's parties had quite a reputation in South London professional circles and men of otherwise strong character would tremble at the merest suggestion that they might be required to endure one of her enforced fun fests.

After all that, Beth had ensconced herself in a corner with Pete and seemed oblivious to Chris's presence. Great. He couldn't imagine what they were talking about. It would be boring, knowing Pete as he did. Just watching Pete made his muscles tense up. The man was so closed up, it was astonishing he could function among other people. And that haircut. He had that straight swept-back style favoured by men who were preparing for eventual hair loss by choosing a style which would never require much hair. Maybe Beth was offering him beauty tips.

At least when Stella had shunted him into the garden, he had identified the move as the first fortuitous step towards making a sly exit. He'd been seconds away from sneaking out when Lauren had come up to him. Now he was glad he'd stayed.

'I wish he'd just leave,' Stella muttered furiously under her breath. He'd been outside for ages. She wasn't fooled by his feigned interest in the garden. She recognised his ploy to make a dash for freedom. So why was he hanging around now? To give her something else to worry about, that's why, she decided.

She flitted from room to room, kissing all the guests whether she knew them or not. She was trying to find a copy of *Time Out* except she couldn't remember if she'd deemed it a good thing to have on show or an embarrassing telltale sign of her lack of sophistication which needed to be hidden from view. If it was the latter, the magazine could be anywhere. Anywhere except the bathroom: only novelty books like *The Compendium of Bottom Jokes* were acceptable in bathrooms.

She finally located the publication on something that

25

passed for a coffee table, grabbed it, pulled her mobile phone out of her handbag and locked herself in the bathroom to deal with her problem.

'Is Stella all right?' Beth asked Pete in concern.

'Why?' Pete didn't want to talk to Beth about Stella. He was beginning to feel like somebody else, somebody free, with possibilities before him. This brief time with Beth allowed him to consider the outside chance that he might one day be able to reinvent himself. Then the mention of Stella reminded him cruelly that his life was not his own to reinvent.

The last hour had passed too quickly. What had started with polite small talk had somehow become terrifyingly substantial. He replayed those first words, wondering who had taken the first step from the impersonal to the personal.

'Hi Pete.' Beth had made him jump when she'd arrived. He was fiddling with the new sound system that Stella had just bought. He couldn't find a volume switch. Or any switches for that matter. It was just a black and chrome box with eerie flashing lights.

He'd stood up. 'Beth, nice to see you.' He congratulated himself on remembering her name. He kissed her on both cheeks while he struggled to recall anything about her.

'How's things?' he asked. The perfect non-committal opening gambit.

Beth considered this. 'I miss Chris,' she said. 'Five years is a long time to spend with someone. And this was my first serious relationship. I feel . . . almost bereaved and yet I don't regret him leaving.'

26

Pete looked around to see if she had mistaken him for someone else. Someone who looked like a good listener. Because he was lost with this sort of talk. He was fine on blockbuster films, proportional representation and wine vintages. Anything to do with emotions left him floundering. It was the direct result of eighteen years living with Stella. Not his fault.

'I'm sorry,' he replied lamely.

Beth smiled at him. 'You're lucky being married for such a long time.'

Pete couldn't stop himself. 'I don't feel lucky.'

Beth looked surprised. 'Why do you say that?'

It was too late to take the comment back. And he didn't want to. A door that had been straining at the latch for a long time was opening.

That was how it had started. And they had been talking about favourite books they'd read as teenagers (him – *Zen and the Art of Motorcycle Maintenance*, her – *Little Women*, each groaned at the other's choice) when Beth spotted Stella acting strangely.

'She's just dashed into the loo with a magazine,' Beth said, her eyes fixed on the cloakroom door as if the answer to the puzzle might appear in lights when the lavatory was flushed. 'And her mobile phone,' she added.

Pete turned to look at the door as well. Stella never read in the bathroom. She considered it tacky. Pete read on the loo all the time. It was usually the only place in whatever house they were inhabiting that he could be guaranteed any peace. And as for the phone . . .

'I don't know,' he admitted.

The earlier ease that had settled between them fell away at the unwelcome intrusion of Stella's odd behaviour.

They each retreated inwards to come to terms with the hotpot of feelings that was warming up to a rolling boil. And to turn the heat down.

Lauren returned. Chris forced her back on to the subject she'd hoped to change by pleading a need for the bathroom. He was giving her a chance to back down and confess, jokingly, her silly fib. To be kind, get her off the hook. 'What are you then, if you're not Pisces?' Chris asked Lauren with a strange smile that Lauren couldn't fathom. And she didn't have the spare resources to do any more fathoming. All her resources were fully occupied.

She was irritated. 'You seem more interested in astrology than I am!'

Chris flinched at her sharp tone. Lauren noticed and sighed inwardly. This was going badly. She was beginning to think that she should escape now before it got worse. Unfortunately, there was no more honking going on in the kitchen that she could join. Throughout the house, guests were talking. Wherever she went, she would be forced to make conversation. And history had taught her that there was no limit to the number of people she could offend, upset or irritate in one short evening. She resolved to limit the damage to Chris, for Stella's sake. She'd ride this out boldly.

'Sorry. I've had too much to drink. Ignore me.' Realising that she hadn't had too much to drink, but wishing that she had, she quickly finished her glass. She changed the subject before she could bury herself even deeper.

'So how do you know Stella and Pete?' She could feel her heartbeat settle down and cursed herself for not pursuing a safer line of chat like this from the beginning. Chris visibly relaxed and Lauren dared to think that this might be her first successful rescue of a seemingly irretrievable situation.

'As a matter of fact, I don't know them that well. They're friends of my ex-girlfriend Beth. She invited me along for moral support. She finds these things a bit much.'

Now it was Lauren's turn to look confused. 'Did you say *ex*-girlfriend?'

Chris smiled. 'I know. How modern is that! Not just friends with my ex-girlfriend but still happy to go out in public with her.'

'I think that's . . . admirable. I really do.' That's what she said. What she thought was: How weird is that? She had never managed to maintain any kind of friendship with her ex-boyfriends. She preferred her relationships to be neatly compartmentalised and for her acquaintances to stay where they were when they started out in her life. Men who wished to be transferred from her lover box to her good friend box generally found themselves stuffed into the memory box where they occupied precious space with their dead weight.

'So how does Beth know Stella?' she asked Chris, still trying to decide if his continuing friendship with Beth was mature or the sign of a sad absence of any other friends.

'Beth is a doctor, an oncologist, she treated Stella once.'

Then Lauren realised who Chris was referring to. Stella had gone through a cancer scare a few years back. For weeks, she'd talked incessantly of this fantastic doctor who'd wangled Stella to the top of waiting lists for tests which were thankfully to prove negative. Eventually, the doctor had weakened under the onslaught of persistent invitations to join Stella and Pete for dinner. Everyone weakened with Stella in the end. Lauren even recalled mentions of the woman doctor's boyfriend.

'So you must be the Teacher of Difficult Children!' she exclaimed, proud of her good memory.

Chris's mouth tightened ever so slightly. 'That's how Stella described me, I'll bet. She does like to pigeonhole her acquaintances, doesn't she?'

Lauren bristled at the criticism of her friend, however justified it was. 'Not really, she's just interested in people, that's all.'

Chris liked the way that Lauren had defended Stella, however unworthy Stella was of any defence. It all confirmed his growing belief that Lauren was a fundamentally decent person. That mattered to him.

'Anyway, they're not difficult children, they're just challenging,' Chris said with feeling.

Lauren decided that this was another possible area for contention and left it swiftly. She looked towards the house where the party was beginning to spill over into the garden. 'So which one is Beth?' she asked with genuine interest. She immediately picked out two particularly stunning women and placed a silent bet that one of them would be the doctor.

Chris followed her gaze. 'There she is,' he said, pointing to the most beautiful of the two. She was deep in conversation with Pete, Lauren observed. A little too deep, she thought before dismissing what she concluded was a mild case of mid-party overfamiliarity. Stella was approaching the cosy pair looking less than pleased.

'She looks nice,' Lauren said, meaning it sincerely.

Chris looked away from the vision of perfection that was Beth. 'She is nice,' he pointed out.

And then it happened. The realisation struck her that Chris was behaving differently to before, he was looking at her differently. She liked it and responded to it. Not by choice, because it was the last thing she would have chosen, but something in her was reacting to Chris's interest independently of her will.

Lauren was developing a headache. Too much wine, not enough food – the definition of Stella's hospitality. Chris noticed that she was rubbing her temples before she noticed herself.

'Are you all right?' he asked.

'I've just got a bit of a headache, that's all. I've spent too much time in front of the computer probably.'

'So you're the Computer Friend Stella is always talking about!' Chris exclaimed.

Lauren was offended. The Computer Friend. Eighteen years of propping Stella up through some dark days, making up the numbers at some of the world's worst dinner parties, accompanying her to staggeringly boring art gallery showings of young artists Stella wanted to drag into her coterie. Eighteen years and she was the Computer Friend. She was embarrassed by her own indignation at not being described as Best Friend. Surely she was Stella's Best Friend? She was the one invited round when Stella's parents were staying, as if she were one of the family. She was the one whose Christmas card was always put on the mantelpiece with the immediate family's cards and not consigned to the colour-co-ordinated displays in the hall. She resolved never to refer to Stella as her Best Friend again before reminding herself that she had left playgroup over thirty years ago.

'That's me! The Computer Friend!'

'So what exactly do you do?' Chris asked.

She told him exactly what she did. She summarised the development of telecommunications over the last twenty years before explaining her role in introducing backward-looking companies to twenty-first-century technology. His eyes didn't glaze over, which she hoped was interest rather than politeness. It gave her the courage to break the silence that followed her mini sales spiel.

The silence was meaningful rather than painful. They both knew they'd moved on to a fragile footing, quite unexpectedly, but not unpleasantly.

'Oh oh, awkward moment time,' Lauren joked. 'This is where I ask you if you like football to impress you with how laddish I am.' She was surprised by her own flirtatiousness. She hadn't known she had it in her.

Chris let the corners of his mouth sag into a mock-pout. 'It wouldn't impress me. I *loathe* football.'

'Right,' Lauren replied, chastened by the implied criticism of her conversational gambit.

Chris felt mean. 'Don't worry. I was going to ask you if you liked the theatre to impress you with how cultured I am.'

Lauren loved the theatre and was unsure of the correct answer to this question. And she wasn't planning to make any more mistakes. In the end, she didn't get a chance to answer. Stella was coming over to them, dragging a reluctant Pete and Beth with her.

* * *

'What are you playing at?' Pete whispered angrily to Stella.

'You'll see. I've got a plan,' Stella whispered back.

The five of them shuffled into an awkward circle. There were the introductions of Beth to Lauren since Pete, Stella and Chris knew each other. Then Lauren's swift, efficient woman-to-woman appraisal of Beth.

Lauren observed that Beth occupied that vague age zone between twenty-five and forty, where the extremes of living can either add to or subtract from the ageing process. In truth, Beth looked about fifteen. Knowing that she was a medical specialist, Lauren calculated that she had be in her thirties.

She looked fantastic: effortless, low-maintenance fantastic. Everything about her reflected natural beauty. Her body was slim and gently toned, the sign of a healthy, non-obsessive diet and exercise regime; the dark, dark hair fell straight down on her shoulders in a timeless style; her velvet trousers and silky Indian-style tunic top were loosely fitting, the statement of a body-confident woman with nothing to prove. And that pretty face with those blue eyes, looked open, intelligent, humorous, kind.

But looking at Beth's face and the utter absence of experience written across her eyes left Lauren with one overwhelming impression – this wasn't a woman, this was a child.

Bloody hell, thought Lauren, what man wouldn't fall in love with Beth? Lauren immediately wanted to take her home, pour her some Ribena and read her a bedtime story. What on earth could have possessed Chris to separate from her? She was perfect.

She had gone from lack of interest in Chris to mild

jealousy of his ex-girlfriend in the space of ten minutes. What's happening? she wondered.

She was annoyed with Stella for bringing Beth over. If only she'd waited another ten minutes, Lauren and Chris might have established some form of rapport, come to some kind of vague understanding, one way or the other.

Stella appeared oblivious to Lauren's accusing scowl. 'So, Chris, how have you been? We haven't seen you for ages. Where have you been hiding yourself?'

Chris glanced awkwardly at Beth, wondering what on earth she'd been saying. 'Well, I've been busy. And there have been things to sort out, somewhere to live, you know . . .'

He waited for Beth to rescue him from this. Surely she'd told everyone that they'd split up. As if Stella could read his mind, she carried on. 'Oh yes, Beth told us about your sort-of separation. Hopefully it will all work out.'

Now Lauren was confused. Stella seemed to be trying to get Chris and Beth back together. Why would she do that? What did she know that Lauren didn't know?

'Anyway, Pete and I were thinking, are you free on Friday night, Chris?'

Stella's question caught Chris off guard. 'Erm, I think so, I mean, yes, I suppose I am.'

'Fantastic!' Stella shrieked, making them all jump. 'I know Beth's free because she just told me, and I know how much you and Beth love French films, and so do we. Anyway there's a Jean-Luc Godard festival at the National Film Theatre and they're showing *Pravda* on Friday. And they've got tickets. I know because I've checked.' Beth and Pete exchanged a knowing glance.

'What do you say we all go?' she said. 'The five of us,' she added quickly, including Lauren.

Lauren frowned, wondering if Stella had forgotten that she was going to be in Cumbria on Friday and wouldn't be able to get back for the evening. Until she knew what Stella was trying to achieve with this little outing, she couldn't begin to untangle all the subplots.

Pete was simply stunned by his wife's suggestion. Not just because he hated French films. He *really* hated French films. But because Stella was manipulating a happily separated couple into a reconciliation that neither of them sought. And it was partly his fault. He intervened quickly.

'Sorry, darling, we can't do Friday. Mum and Dad are coming down.' (He prayed that he'd be able to explain the necessity for a spur-of-the-moment visit to his parents along with the accompanying subterfuge. They were not the most complex of folk and would be unhappy to take part in any deception of their daughter-in-law.)

Stella gasped. 'Friday? You didn't tell me!'

Pete raised his eyebrows, smiling weakly. 'You were probably too busy pottering about with packing cases when I told you.'

Stella favoured him with an accusing glare, then brightened up. 'Never mind. Chris and Beth can still go. Oh, and Lauren, of course.'

Lauren was still trying to decide what Stella was playing at. The three of them going out together? That was taking maturity a step too far. While she was planning what to say, Beth cleared her throat and delivered a not-very-convincing excuse.

'The thing is, I can't go myself, anyway. I'm on call

35

Friday. One of my patients is having radical surgery and we're not sure what we're going to find. I can't be too far from the hospital and the National is too far.' A totally plausible excuse and totally untrue but Stella couldn't see this, still believing that Beth was anxious to get back with Chris.

Stella's face dropped. She was scrambling about for a fresh approach when Lauren made a decisive move. None of this had made any sense so far but here, finally, was something she understood. No more messing around. 'That leaves just me, then. I'm not doing anything Friday. I *love* French films.' She hadn't any idea where this would lead but surely any decision was better than the mass of dithering indecision that was crippling the lot of them.

Stella almost said something. But she didn't. And luckily for the sake of her friendship, Lauren didn't notice the hesitation.

Nobody spoke for a few moments. Chris realised that all eyes were on him, waiting for him to cast his vote. Like Lauren and Pete and Beth, he had been baffled by Stella's strange insistence that they all have a jolly trip to the cinema (and there was nothing jolly about Jean-Luc Godard, nothing at all). Everything had been going fine, well, reasonably fine, until now.

He was being forced to commit to seeing Lauren again when he wasn't sure, he really wasn't sure. But what could he say? (Plenty, actually, and he thought of at least ten practical objections to this line of action when he was in the bath later that night. Hours too late.)

And so it came to pass that Chris found himself arranging a date to see a French film, which he'd hated each of the five times he'd been dragged to see it before, with an attractive but vulnerable woman at a time when he had vowed to withdraw from attractive, vulnerable women for the foreseeable future.

He had forty-eight hours to decide whether he wanted to take a chance on a new relationship, however casual it might appear at the moment.

Lauren had forty-eight hours to find a way of getting to and from a meeting in the depths of Cumbria that was scheduled to last all day. Oh, and also to discover who the hell Jean-Luc Godard was. Because she hated French films even more than Chris did.

Chapter 3

Lauren looked out of the train window anxiously. She watched the panorama transform from dirty grey to shimmering green and was unmoved. She felt only the stress of the day ahead and the worry of how she was going to cram a full day's meetings into the ninety minutes she could spare before catching the 14.10 back to London.

She asked herself for the thousandth time why she hadn't just told Chris that today would be difficult and suggested that they go and see another incomprehensible French film on a different day. But then she'd also asked herself a thousand times why she'd lied about her star sign. The more she replayed the conversation in her mind, the less certain she was about the tone of voice she thought she'd heard Chris use. And the more foolish she felt. And the less sure she was about seeing Chris again.

If, *if*, this developed into anything, she was going to have to get round the fact that it was her birthday in two weeks. He might just work out that this made her a Piscean.

Look on the bright side, she told herself, I'll probably drive him nuts in the two weeks between now and my birthday. It usually takes that long for me to drive a man away. She resolved to concentrate her efforts on sorting today out before panicking over the tales she would need to tell in the coming couple of weeks. After that, she could well be saying her tearful farewells before leaving for the States. Permanently.

Lauren was an IT consultant. Nobody outside the IT world (i.e. all her friends and most of the world) had any idea what she actually did but she earned more than them all. She was self-employed, hiring herself out on short- and long-term projects to both small and large companies. And Trent Outdoor Wear was as small as they came; a 'chain' of five shops selling specialist sportswear across the Lake District. They needed Lauren's expertise to link the shops up with computers and an internal phone system. It would probably take her a month and would involve staying up there during the week.

She wasn't overly keen on jobs that kept her away from home. It always meant sorting out a whole lot of time-consuming housekeeping details, getting neighbours to keep an eye on her flat, doing bagloads of laundry at weekends, paying bills over the phone, that sort of thing. Also, this didn't promise to be the best-paid of assignments. However, she'd agreed to spend a day with the company's owner, Richard Trent, to hear what he had to say. And a day in Cumbria had seemed an attractive prospect on a rainy Friday in February.

She harboured a faint hope that the change of scene might help her to make her final decision about New York. Although her prospective employers didn't expect her to move immediately, they did want a firm decision in two weeks. Just after her birthday.

Ninety minutes, she thought. Just long enough to get

the necessary information from the man and decide whether she wanted to spend what could be her last month in Britain away from London.

She continued to look through the window as the scenery became ever more beautiful. Why doesn't this move me? she wondered.

Chris looked out of the window on to Tooting High Street. It was seven thirty in the morning and he watched vans pulling up, double-parking in front of colourful shopfronts, unloading fruit and vegetables that seemed permanently underripe. His third cup of tea was finally starting to revive him.

He'd been at work last night until gone eleven, trying to resolve some of the problems that were threatening both the school and, by implication, his career. He hadn't managed to get to sleep until about three o'clock, incapable of switching off his tensions. God I miss Beth, he'd thought, wishing he could have talked to her about his worries.

It hit him then. Why haven't I got any friends? He had colleagues and drinking partners and blokes from college who phoned him when they were attending conferences in London. But no friend.

He'd read Nick Hornby and he'd liked to think he was that sort of liberated man, in touch with his feelings. But he was lacking in like-minded male friends to accompany him through the obligatory bonding process. And now he saw this as a significant gap in his life.

He hadn't needed friends as such before. There had always been staffroom camaraderie to support him during his working life and women to accompany him through his personal life. He'd kept the two aspects of his life happily separate until Beth. Gradually he'd found himself needing everyone else less and less while he loved and depended upon Beth more and more.

I must stop thinking about Beth all the time, he snapped to himself. My best friend was my lover and she's gone. He would choose his next friend with more long-sightedness next time.

While he was beginning to puzzle out the answer to how a grown man goes about finding a friend, the phone rang. He picked it up anxiously, unable to come up with any good reason why someone would call him at this time. At first, when he heard Stella's voice, he found himself automatically looking around for Beth. His telephone conversations with Stella had always consisted of one or two polite exchanges before handing her over to Beth. But this time, she'd phoned him. There were no precedents for this and they were both a bit awkward.

'I tried to call you all last night,' Stella said accusingly. 'You weren't in.'

Chris was so stunned by her nerve that he found himself apologising. 'Sorry,' he said, 'I was working late.'

Stella regretted her harshness and softened her tone. 'Don't be silly. I was just worried that I wouldn't be able to talk to you before you went out with Lauren tonight.'

'Right,' Chris answered flatly.

Stella sensed his coldness and tried to appease him. 'So, how's work, then?' she asked, hoping to get to her point from a more roundabout route.

'Fine,' he answered, certain that she did not want to hear of the twelve-year-old who'd tried to stab him again

41

during English yesterday. The conversation had a very alien feel to him. He would have slammed the phone down but he was too tired to do anything so physical, so he sighed and became polite. He tried to remember what Stella did and failed, so he stuck to the ever-reliable: 'And how are things with you?'

Stella always believed that her friends were being literal when they asked this. Leaving out references to her menstrual cycle, she treated Chris to a thirty-minute summary of the previous day. He switched on his selective hearing mechanism to filter out the irrelevant bits. This left him with information that she could efficiently have communicated in thirty seconds: she'd had a terrible day at her publishing company (although she never mentioned books at any point, which caused Chris to wonder exactly what she did all day), she'd spoken to five people whom Stella assumed Chris knew and she was planning to stencil Lowry-type figures on the newly sandblasted kitchen floor at some stage in the future.

Throughout the monologue Chris went into a mini-coma, emerging during Stella's pauses to interject an appropriately neutral series of comments such as: 'I can imagine,' 'Really?' and 'I know.' At the end, Stella finally got round to her true reason for calling.

'This is all a bit delicate, Chris.'

'What is?' Chris asked, not really wanting to know. Chris didn't like delicate. He liked easy and straightforward, black and white. All of his ventures into grey and tricky and delicate had caused him stress.

'I know you're seeing Lauren tonight. It's about that misunderstanding you had with her.'

Misunderstanding. Good choice of word, Chris thought. Wrong, but tactful.

'What about it?' he replied diplomatically.

'Well, the thing is, I know that Lauren . . . this sounds so silly!'

Chris helped her out. 'She lied about her birthday.'

Stella made an anxious whooshy noise. 'It wasn't a lie, as such, no, she just thought . . . it's just that you gave her the impression that you would not respect her somehow if she admitted she was . . . you know.'

Oh good, he thought, so it was all my fault. That's all right then. He shook his head, aware that the gesture was somewhat futile on the phone but consoling himself with the thought that the most satisfying gestures are usually futile. How had Lauren managed to misjudge him so wildly? He didn't feel that strongly about anything. Except his work, maybe. And his loathing of Wagner, of course. Apart from that, though, he was Mr Amenable. He read the *Guardian*, for goodness' sake.

He even liked most of the kids he taught and they were all convicted criminals. How much more easy-going could he be?

'I don't know what gave her that impression,' he said tightly.

'I think it was the way you said the word "astrology",' Stella answered helpfully.

The way I said the word 'astrology'? Chris thought. He didn't even recollect saying the word, let alone in a particular way. To him, conversation was a means of imparting and receiving information. He didn't have any surplus energy to expend on using the right tone. He aimed to be courteous and tried not to cause offence, something he had evidently failed to do on this occasion.

'She must have imagined it,' he sighed. 'We were just chatting. I probably wouldn't have reacted if she'd said she dabbled in witchcraft.'

Stella groaned. If he was as indifferent as he claimed, then Lauren's lie and all the subsequent panic Stella had gone through were for nothing. Lauren could be working herself up into a state worrying about tonight and all for no reason. It was suddenly vital to Stella that she retrieve this situation and get things back on an even footing for Lauren. It's what friends do.

'Look, Chris, I know you're going to think this sounds crazy, but can I ask you an enormous favour?'

He wanted to say 'no' straight away. He knew that any favour Stella asked would involve him in something complex, something that would bring disorder into the neat universe he was constructing around him.

Three days earlier, he'd vowed that he wouldn't even consider a new relationship for at least a year. And now, not only was he on the verge of a new relationship, but it was one that required mediation, favours and subterfuge.

'What sort of favour?' he asked wearily.

'Well, since Lauren obviously got hold of the wrong end of the stick about you, now she's petrified that you're going to find out she lied, which of course you will if you go out with her for a while because it's her birthday in two weeks—'

'The favour?' Chris interrupted, now in real physical need of a fourth cup of tea.

'Right, yes. So what I was thinking was if you could

44

somehow convey to Lauren that you have completely forgotten what she said, or didn't register it, or something. Then she can forget about it. But don't make it too obvious. Just slip it into the conversation, maybe bringing up the subject in a roundabout fashion, then act a bit dozy or whatever.'

'Is that all? I think you might have mistaken me for Kenneth Branagh,' he pointed out drily.

Stella was losing interest now that she'd said her piece. 'Look, just give her the impression that you're forgetful or that you weren't listening yesterday because you had something on your mind, something like that.'

'I really don't see why I can't just tell her that I know,' he said. 'I mean it's no big deal.'

'You can't!' Stella shouted, causing Chris to pull the receiver away from his ear. 'Then she'll want to know who told you.'

Now it's clear, Chris thought. Self-preservation, the oldest and strongest of human instincts. And from what Beth had always said, Stella was motivated entirely by the craving, a real longing, for constant approval.

'I don't see what the problem is,' he said reasonably. 'It's not as if you gave away some dark, deep secret.'

'I know, but she'll say that I should have told her afterwards.' Stella was getting flustered.

Chris was fed up with this. 'Look, I can't believe you're making such a drama out of this. I've got to go now.'

'So I'll leave you to take care of this, shall I?' Stella tried one last anxious time.

Chris put the phone down. As he replayed the conversation through his head, he was struck by how surreal it all was. The amount of time a group of adults could squander on something so utterly, utterly insignificant. But then he struggled to recall a single moment from recent years when he had squandered time on anything that *was* significant to him.

It was all relative and he had to face the truth that everything in his life outside work was relatively trivial. He concluded that perhaps it was preferable to spend days fretting over small lies than spend one minute facing the big lies that shape our lives.

This thought, the thought of big lies, for a reason he couldn't grasp, made him think of Beth. But before he could work out why she should pop into his mind just then, it suddenly occurred to him that the only person who had his new phone number was Beth. So she must have given it to Stella. Why on earth would she do that?

Richard Trent looked at Lauren quizzically. 'So what you're saying is that you've got to dash back to London shortly to go and see a French film which you'll hate with a man you're not even sure you want to go out with, who thinks you're not a Piscean even though you are but you don't know why you said that you weren't?'

That sounded about right to Lauren. Not right, as in rational, but the facts were essentially correct. Sitting on a bench by a frozen lake, the line between rational and irrational was blurred and meaningless to her.

There was something about this place that released her, permitted her to loosen the chains that kept her from breaking free. And there was something about her new client that encouraged honesty rather than dissemblance. She'd warmed to him within minutes of meeting him.

He'd been serving a difficult customer in the shop when she arrived, which had given Lauren a chance to appraise him without being observed. She watched in fascination as he tried to satisfy the Walter Mitty fantasies of a customer who wanted to be kitted out in clothes suitable for an Antarctic exploration when he was in fact planning to ramble over the common near his Barratt home just outside Morecambe.

Richard Trent was in his forties or early fifties. It was impossible to pinpoint the exact age since he wasn't manifesting any giveaway signs. He had a full head of hair, he wasn't wearing inch-thick bifocal spectacles and his teeth looked real. And while the trousers were appalling, they were not held up by a belt under his armpits. He was attractive, she concluded objectively, impersonally. Then she dismissed the thought.

It was no longer important to her to know exactly how old people were. At some time after her thirtieth birthday, Lauren had lost her knack for guessing ages. In her late teens and early twenties, she'd possessed a cut-off switch in her discernment antennae which instantly located and discounted anyone over forty.

But as her thirties raced towards a close, age became less significant to her. She was no longer afraid of being forty, or even fifty or sixty. She envisaged an unorthodox future, where she would retire early and trek through jungles in Bermuda shorts, Dr Scholl sandals and ankle socks, talking to gap-year travellers who'd find her unworldly wisdom inspirational.

Marriage did not feature in her scheme of things. She neither welcomed it nor avoided it. She'd simply learned that anything involving other people was impossible to control. Mothers left. Boyfriends left. Consequently she looked no further than herself when making plans. Her life was increasingly solitary, apart from her mum who haunted her life like a cheery poltergeist, and she didn't mind. It was the not-minding that worried her a bit.

She learned a lot about her prospective client by monitoring the lines at the corners of his eyes, wrinkling like linen as his customer's requests became more and more ridiculous. She wondered if he could teach her how to use her eyes to communicate like that rather than depending on her treacherous tongue.

His age might have been irrelevant but his clothes were hard to ignore. He was wearing a green checked lumberjack's shirt and black cords that had seen better days. Or at least she assumed they had seen better days – she couldn't believe that this was as good as they got.

As the door finally closed behind the city-dweller who was now ready to face marauding polar bears in the park with his survival gear, Richard Trent turned to face Lauren. He greeted her with a particularly warm smile, and she was a woman who had been on the receiving end of many warm smiles. She was a connoisseur. This was a good one.

'You must be Lauren Connor,' he said, coming forward to shake hands.

'How did you know that?' she asked, surprised since she was early for her appointment. Then she looked at herself through his eyes and saw a suited-up businesswoman who was completely out of place in this rugged casual environment. She laughed self-consciously.

'Don't worry,' Richard said. 'It's my fault. I should

have dressed more formally. It's just the girl who normally works in the shop hasn't turned up yet so I had to step in and a suit can be a bit off-putting to your average mountaineer.'

'No, it's my fault,' Lauren replied. 'I should have realised that this was never going to be the typical workplace and dressed more appropriately.'

'My wife used to tell me to stop apologising all the time. She was American and said that the English seem compelled to take the blame for everything from bumping into strangers to Third World debt.'

'*Was* American? Did she die?' Lauren asked. She immediately wanted to take the tactless question back. But she didn't. Why would she? Why start making life easy for myself now, she wondered.

Richard didn't appear to take offence. 'No. We got divorced a few years ago.'

'Oh, good . . . I mean, it's not good that you're divorced but it's good that she's not dead, I mean . . .' Lauren gave up trying to make it sound better. She was a woman who knew that her skill lay in making things sound worse.

Richard touched her arm reassuringly as he brushed past to tidy up a display of Swiss Army knives. Lauren wanted to ask exactly what all those additional prongs with the knobbly bits were for apart from getting stones out of horses' hooves but she restrained herself. Wow, I can restrain myself, she thought. My evolution into maturity is finally complete.

'Well, now we both feel completely ill at ease,' Richard said lightly. 'What a tremendous start to our business relationship!' He didn't look at all ill at ease. Lauren liked that. She put aside all her earlier reservations about this job and began looking forward to spending the next few working weeks in the company of this man.

They both stood in the shop for a few seconds until they could no longer sustain their smiles. Fortunately for their facial muscles, Maria the store manager arrived in a fluster of excuses and shooed them both over to Richard's office in his cottage next door to the shop.

'Can I get you something?' Richard asked Lauren. 'Tea, coffee, Kendal Mint Cake? Just joking,' he added hastily. 'We're actually quite civilised "oop North", we even have chocolate HobNobs.'

They sat on two battered chairs at a coffee table littered with nature magazines which Richard gathered up and heaped on to the floor. It was not the way Lauren was accustomed to negotiating contracts but she quickly settled into her professional persona as Richard talked her through his ramshackle commercial set-up. Introducing the shops to the twenty-first century would prove quite a challenge. They didn't even have proper tills, just cash drawers and handwritten receipts.

A growing interest in outdoor pursuits had led to a surge in business for Richard's shops and he was forced to contemplate a full modernisation plan to meet the demand.

'Why are you so opposed to change?' Lauren asked, aware of her new client's reluctance to move forward.

'It's just computers, I suppose. I hate them. They are stopping people from talking to each other. The phone is bad enough but at least there have always been some things that have justified face-to-face meetings. Now you can do everything by sending forms electronically, setting up conference calls, even signing contracts by pressing buttons and generating artificial signatures. I like seeing faces, shaking hands, sharing jokes. I can't remember the last time anyone came to this office, hence the mess. And what really bothers me is that eventually nobody will visit shops in person, it will all be shopping over the Net.'

Lauren became defensive. When Richard said that he hated computers, it was as if he'd said that he hated her. Because she loved them. And for all the exact same reasons that he hated them. She hated meetings: the false smiles, the enforced bonhomie, having to drink weak tea and not being able to dunk her biscuits in it. And she liked communicating by e-mail; the delay meant that she could write messages then erase the worst of her stream-of-consciousness observations before transmitting them. She was a woman who benefited from strict editing.

In fact she couldn't help thinking that it might have been helpful to have first met Chris Fallon in an Internet chat room. They could have exchanged all the relevant pieces of information cleanly and concisely then both made an informed decision about where, if anywhere, they wanted to go from there.

And that's how, after signing contracts, she came to blurt out the story of Stella's party to Richard Trent. Along with the rest of her life.

'. . . and my mum is not like other mothers. She was a secretary when I was young and, all through my school years, she used to leave Vesta meals out for me to rehydrate for my tea every night while she went to play bingo. Now she sings songs from *Gypsy* and *Oklahoma!*

51

in South London pubs and gets paid ten pounds and all the Bacardi Breezers she can drink. And she phones me twice a day to make up for all the years when she only called me when she was drunk or watching that bit in *Fiddler on the Roof* when Topol gets all weepy about his daughters. I'm talking too much, aren't I?'

Richard fished a brown paper bag out of his bin. 'Maybe if you breathed in and out into this, it might help.'

Lauren laughed and relaxed. 'Sorry. I'm tense and I always talk too much and too fast when I'm tense. It gets me into a lot of trouble.'

'I'm beginning to see that. So what are you doing in this job? Shouldn't you be in advertising or sales or one of those professions where it's impossible to talk too much?'

'You must be kidding. The telecommunications industry has been a godsend for someone as socially inept as I am. Once I've got through the necessary ordeal of defining the needs of each particular client, then I don't have to deal much with people at all. It's all computers to be linked, engineering problems to be overcome, connections to be fused. Obviously I have to deal with personnel along the way but it's all neat and factual. Nothing I say can cause any damage. That's a great relief both to me and my clients.'

'You have a fantastic reputation. Your name was recommended by all three of the retailers I asked.'

'That's because I'm good at solving concrete problems. I love problems when I know that there is a solution. And in telecoms there is always a solution. I would hate to work in one of those jobs where you have to manipulate public opinion or change perceptions or anything like that. Basically, if the problem can't be represented numerically, my mind shuts down.'

Richard looked at her curiously. 'Can I ask a rude question?'

Lauren clasped her hands together ecstatically. 'I long for people to ask me rude questions! It makes me feel better about all the rude questions I will inevitably have asked them.'

'For someone so grounded in concrete details, so committed to the practical and straightforward, it seems out of character to mention star signs in the first place. You were joking, weren't you?'

Strangely, when Richard spoke like this, she didn't feel under attack as she had done with Chris. 'I suppose deep down I don't take it that seriously. But I quite like the idea that there could be some external influence moulding and shaping us. I like regular patterns, statistical regularities. And why shouldn't the accident of our birth be significant? Just because everything that comes after makes no sense?'

Richard noticed that she was dunking her biscuit so aggressively in her tea that the bottom half had dropped off and was dissolving unappealingly in the cup. Also he'd given her the seat facing the window with a glorious view across the mountains and she hadn't looked out of the window once. She needed his help as much as he needed hers.

'So when can you start?' he asked.

Lauren looked at her watch. 'I'd love to say that I could start now but I've got to catch that train. I wish I'd come up last night. I could have spent longer looking round, going over your books and so on.'

She needs serious help, Richard thought. What sort of person comes to the Lake District and gets excited about going over books?

'I thought that was the original plan,' he said. 'What changed your mind?'

Lauren became distant. 'I just had things to think about. I'd hoped I could make some decisions before I came here. It would have helped me get a clearer picture of what I was doing.'

Richard didn't push her on this. And she didn't give any more details. Yesterday suddenly seemed a long time ago and a long way away. She could barely remember it.

Beth remembered everything about yesterday. Yesterday, she had been sitting on the sofa, leaning into the left-hand cushion that used to be 'her' side. She'd teased herself for behaving so mechanically. There were no sides any more. All of them were hers now. She shifted into the centre of the sofa but it felt wrong, unmoulded, unfamiliar. She moved back to her side.

She looked around at the changes since Chris had left. The half-empty bookcases, the pale geometric shapes on the lemon walls where his prints of Shakespeare productions and *Carry On* posters had once sat side by side in glorious contradiction. She had tried to move her own pictures around but that had merely exposed new shadows.

The marks bothered her. They were like scars. And although she knew that she could paint them over, that somehow seemed like cheating. She felt that she ought to get used to them before she allowed herself the luxury of erasing them.

Memories flitted in and out of her head, uninvited, random memories. She suddenly had a picture of Chris's parents before her. Chris could never get used to the fact that Beth envied him his mum and dad. 'At least they wanted you,' she used to say to him wistfully as he cringed at his mother's latest purchase – hair extensions woven into long blond plaits or souvenir beer tankards shaped like Rhine maidens.

There was no arguing this point. While Chris's parents were incontrovertibly mad, Beth's were just distant. They had been stunned to find themselves parents when they were both forty-four. Neither had wanted children and neither could explain how the pregnancy had happened. They were both academics and maintained only the faintest connection to the real world. Thus when Beth arrived they didn't know how to go about incorporating her into the exclusivity of their lives.

They did their best. They drew up charts so that they would remember to feed her. They read her Virgil and Homer and dressed her in miniature versions of their own clothes. They encouraged her to invite friends home who would then be tested on their mental arithmetic by Beth's mother before being allowed anything to eat. Nobody came twice. At school, she looked like a freak and it was only her startling good looks that just about saved her from being destroyed by bullies.

The only jokes she knew had Latin punchlines and were meaningless to any of her peers. To teenagers who want nothing more than to be exactly the same as everyone else, to conform in every possible respect, Beth's originality was anathema. But at medical school, she found herself the centre of attention. Uniqueness is a much-prized quality to students and Beth achieved the pinnacle of individuality without having so much as to dye her hair red.

But she wasn't interested. She was focused on her studies. Medicine was something she could do, that she was good at, that didn't need her to be anything other than what she was. With minimal effort she excelled at all her disciplines, hence her subsequent swift rise to the post of registrar.

And then Chris turned up in casualty with a broken arm while she was helping out during staff shortages. He caught her when she wasn't working towards any other particular career goal. She was distracted, not thinking straight. Before she knew what she was doing, she'd moved in with him, clueless as to whether this was right for her or not. Unlike Lauren, Beth hadn't read any women's magazines.

And as she wrote the story of her own life, making it up as she went along, her parents were little more than footnotes, doggedly making their presence felt, as was right and proper, but always reminding her that she was not the same as other women and couldn't expect the same things. Even if they'd known what women of Beth's generation wanted. She'd become dependent on Chris to teach her what she should expect, what she was entitled to need.

She was now thirty-five and they were seventy-nine. But they had always been old and she had always been an outsider. Until Chris brought her in from the cold.

Then he left her. After he'd taught her to make fried-egg sandwiches the way he liked them, to laugh at Sid James, to make small talk with people she didn't like, to share and compromise. He left her. And she wasn't as devastated as she felt she ought to be.

Which was why she was very susceptible and confused when Pete phoned her.

Chapter 4

'Why is it me who has to phone her?' Pete asked Stella for the third time.

'Why don't you listen to me?' Stella replied, exasperated from dealing with difficult builders on the phone all day. Her business partners were becoming increasingly unsympathetic about her problems, or at least about the amount of work time she seemed to spend on the phone. And there were limits to how much interest they could show in a catalogue of Art Nouveau fireplace surrounds.

'I'm busy trying to get everything in order before your mum and dad come to stay and I need to get Chris's new phone number. I want to talk to him about Lauren before they go out tomorrow.'

'But Beth's *your* friend. I hardly know her.'

Stella looked him impatiently. 'I don't know how you can say that after last night. I could barely prise the two of you apart.'

It was fortunate for Pete that Stella was too worried about the pinoleum blinds she had ordered in the wrong shade of burnt orange to notice that he was turning fiercely red. Besides, it never occurred to Stella that another woman might find Pete's company anything more than . . . well, companionable.

'I already told you, she was—'

'Yes, yes, I know, crying on your shoulder,' Stella interrupted. 'So now you've got a good excuse to call her up. Find out how she's feeling today. Seeing as how you're suddenly in touch with your feminine side,' she added sarcastically.

'And what am I supposed to say is the reason for your sudden interest in Chris when you made it so patently clear that you never liked him in the past?' Pete snapped back, finding Stella very annoying today.

'Why do I have to think of everything?' Stella mumbled under her breath, just loudly enough for Pete to hear.

'Because you're the one who knows everything,' Pete mumbled, not quite loudly enough for Stella to hear.

They'd both had so much to drink at the party that, by this morning, they'd forgotten all the details of the various stories they'd told to each other and to their friends. But Stella remembered all too clearly omitting to tell Lauren that her little lie was in the open.

As she stared at her face in the bathroom mirror, startled by the extra ten years a hangover adds to one's skin, she experienced a rare moment of insight. All she could think of was the unimaginable prospect of Lauren being angry with her, over nothing of significance. It shouldn't have caused her more than a second's consternation before being dismissed from her schedule of daily concerns, but it refused to go.

She worked hard at her friendships. They defined her. They were precious, dynamic organisms that needed nurturing. Like any living thing, they could die of neglect. And Stella simply would not, could not allow this to happen. Therefore, she was the one who initiated and perpetuated all contact. It didn't bother her at all that hardly anybody called her, so certain were all her friends that she would be calling *them* very soon.

She was assiduous in remembering birthdays along with all the relevant and not-so-relevant details of her friends' lives. She knew all about everyone's families, she knew the jobs of their in-laws, the pets of their step-families, the food preferences of their neighbours. She had a vast collection of greetings cards in her desk drawer ready for every occasion and for every person. Job interview? Dead cat? Bad flu? Stella would send a card immediately. She had cards with musical themes for her concert-going friends, cards with fish for fish-lovers and beautiful fine-art cards for new friends she was still trying to impress.

And Lauren was right. Stella did regard her as her Best Friend. So if Stella happened to consider that making Lauren cross with her was about the worst thing that could happen to her at this particular time, at any time, then maybe it wasn't so surprising, even if it was out of all proportion to the real problems of people living in a less egocentric world.

'Just do it, Pete. Please,' Stella said, wanting to be rid of this problem so that she could concentrate on the terrazzo floor she was having laid in the dining room the next day.

Maybe that's what Pete had wanted, the decision to be made for him, so that he could feel completely innocent when he called Beth. Even though he had wanted to do little else since he'd woken up.

* * *

'Hi, Beth, it's Pete, Pete Lynch,' he added unnecess-arily.

'This is amazing! I can't believe you phoned at the exact moment I was thinking of you.' Beth's words came out easily. They were the words of a sixteen-year-old with a crush. Or a woman who had never read *Cosmopolitan*. She was less experienced in guile than most of her female peers, having had only one relationship in her life – and that was with a man who only knew how to deceive himself.

'Really?' Pete was surprised. He was not very good at guile himself and despised the tricks and ploys that Stella and her friends discussed. He recognised the rarity of a spontaneous comment and it heightened his aware-ness of the difference between Beth and his wife. He quenched the feeling of disloyalty that this thought pro-voked in him.

'It was wonderful talking to you last night,' Beth said. 'I've felt so isolated since Chris and I split up. He was my best friend as well as my partner and although I was quite relieved when he went after the problems we were having, I've missed his company more than I could have anticipated. And at the same time, I haven't missed him as much as I should. And I was glad in a way because we probably wouldn't have spent so much time chatting if Chris and I had been together.'

Pete was overwhelmed by her warmth but slightly alarmed by the note of neediness and desperation that she was not bothering to cover up. He'd intended to make the call a quick one, a few minutes of polite chat, acknowledging the distance they'd travelled the night before and then efficiently getting to the reason for his call. But he found himself responding to Beth's implied invitation to resume their intimacy. Once more, his words slipped out before he could stop them. He didn't want to stop them, he realised.

'You're lucky, Beth. I still have my partner and I still feel isolated. Stella stopped being my best friend a long time ago.'

'Whose fault is that?' Beth asked.

Pete had never given the question any real thought. 'I suppose I've always assumed it's her fault. But now I think of it, I stopped talking to her properly quite a few years back.'

'Why?'

This was not how it was supposed to be. Pete was uncomfortable with all this emotional confrontation. Especially since Stella was upstairs. 'Look, do you mind if we don't go into this right now? It doesn't feel right, somehow.'

'Oh I'm sorry, Pete!' Beth was mortified. 'I wasn't thinking. I wasn't trying to make you find fault with your own relationship. I'm in no position to do that with my track record. And I'm not trying to come between you, it's just I think we could become real friends, not just fake ones like . . .' She stopped herself from finishing the sentence but Pete knew that she was going to mention Stella and her quantitative approach to friendship.

Pete felt himself being sucked deeper and deeper into Beth's world. He needed some time to consider whether or not this was something he should do. But there was no time. Beth didn't give him any. Besides, Stella had come downstairs and was now hovering by the phone hissing,

'Get the phone number from her quickly, I want to catch Chris in case he goes out!'

So when Beth asked him if he'd like to meet up, for a coffee or lunch or something, just as friends, he found himself quickly agreeing. If he'd prevaricated, Stella would have wondered what he and Beth were talking about that required such deep deliberation. It wasn't his fault. None of this was his fault.

He coughed nervously. 'Oh Beth, the reason I called was, er, I wondered if you could give me Chris's new phone number.'

Beth couldn't mask her disappointment. Or her curiosity. 'Oh right. What do you need it for?'

Stella was gesticulating wildly beside him. He couldn't be sure but he thought she was trying to make sure he knew that he was not to mention her part in this conspiracy. 'Oh, it's just that, er, I was going to ask him if he'd like to meet up for a drink, or a football game or something.' He cringed at his own lack of conviction.

'That's funny,' Beth said, 'I always got the impression that you didn't like Chris.'

Pete glared at Stella across the receiver as he dug himself further into a place he didn't want to be. 'No, not at all. I never got to know him very well, that's all. But last night, he mentioned that he wouldn't mind meeting up at some point.'

Beth thought this was odd since Chris had always maintained that he couldn't stand Stella or Pete. But she gave him the number anyway, which Pete wrote down in relief that this ordeal was almost over.

'I have to speak to him myself later on, I'll let him

63

know you're going to be phoning to invite him out,' Beth added.

Thank you so much, Stella, Chris cursed silently. Now I'm going to have to spend an evening with the man. Why do I feel that my life is spiralling out of control?

'Great!' he said with as much sincerity as he could muster. 'Anyway, Beth, it was nice talking to you again.'

'Same here. So why don't you give me a call on Saturday? I've got the afternoon off, we could meet,' Beth said with childlike eagerness. 'If Stella doesn't mind, of course,' she added quickly.

'Er yes, that would be great,' Pete said, glancing awkwardly at Stella, pressing the receiver tight against his ear so that she wouldn't hear the other end of the conversation. Now he had to find an excuse to get away on Saturday afternoon – and that was normally Stella's time for dragging him round markets looking for beautiful pieces of furniture to scumble-glaze into yet more possessions.

'What would be great?' Stella whispered.

Pete shook his head to try and convey that nothing of consequence was being agreed. He managed to finish the call without saying anything else that might sound compromising. As he turned to face Stella, she looked at him strangely. 'Why are you sweating so much?'

He guiltily brushed his hand over his damp face. 'Why do you think? Making me lie like that! Now I've got to go out for a drink with a man I can't stand! Can you do your own dirty work in the future please?' And with that, he stomped off, thus avoiding having to recount the entire exchange to Stella. I'm getting good at this evasion business, he thought. But this gave him no sense of pride. Quite the opposite.

As he walked through the house towards the room that was laughingly designated as his study (DIY disaster meets Mad Max), he stopped to look at himself in the floor-to-ceiling mirror in the hall.

Like everyone, he didn't see himself the way others did. He only saw what he thought were the bad bits. He saw his slight build with small, well-concealed pockets of flab, which betrayed a complete disdain for diet or exercise. This made him wary of any man (or woman!) who produced a muscle when lifting a glass. He saw irredeemably ordinary brown hair that had remained in the same inoffensive style since he was sixteen. He wouldn't have known what else to do with it. He saw a face which had none of the attributes that women seemed to swoon over in the cinema: blue eyes, but not piercing like Brad Pitt's; strong chin but no dimple; straight nose but his wife thought Jimmy Nail was lovely; own teeth, OK so this might not have been of interest to anyone apart from his dentist but, hey, if it made him feel better about himself, let him enjoy this accomplishment.

And he wore glasses. There, that's got that out of the way. He'd tried contact lenses but his eyes couldn't tolerate them. And, yes, he knew that Michael Caine wore glasses and that Robbie Williams even wore plain glass spectacles but that was different. Everyone who wore prescription glasses knew that. Pete had worn them all his life. He'd been teased at school and overlooked by girls until he hit the sixth form and moody sixteen-year-olds decided that glasses made him look seriously intellectual.

So when he saw himself in the mirror, he saw the bloke with glasses. And that's how everyone described him, he knew.

The upside of his anonymity was that he could, if he chose, commit an armed robbery in broad daylight and get away with it, because no witnesses would ever be able to describe him accurately or produce a photofit picture. He looked like everyone's brother or cousin or that doctor with glasses in *ER* who isn't George Clooney or his Croatian replacement or the young handsome idealistic one.

Most of all though, he didn't look like a husband contemplating betrayal. He didn't know what one of those looked like, but he was sure they would have stronger facial features.

In the ensuing forty-eight hours before he met Beth, he managed to persuade himself that he was beyond any doubt a victim of extraneous circumstances. That it was Stella who had forced him into the position where he had agreed to meet up with Beth. Alone.

But he wasn't unhappy. He had no idea what the future held for him. And he liked the feeling. He felt that the promises of the past had sadly let him down.

'I think there's something wrong with me,' Pete had once complained to Stella in days when he still thought it was worth talking to her about non-essential subjects.

'What?' Stella had frowned, not liking references to anything being wrong.

Pete had organised his face into a parody of angst and trauma. 'I actually like my parents. Even worse, I like their way of life. I want to be like them. That must make me in need of a shrink.'

Stella had misinterpreted this as a subtle dig at her own parents who, while not abusive, were still not people she wanted to emulate. 'Very funny, Pete,' she'd replied, making her feelings plain.

But he hadn't intended it to be funny, despite his comical expression. He'd meant it. His parents had brought up five children with no money but a bucketload of humour and love. They'd bequeathed a library full of memories to them all: the Friday nights playing Monopoly; the week's break each summer in a four-berth caravan in Lyme Regis; the Sunday afternoon teas where their mum would make sandwiches for all seven of them with a Wonderloaf and a single jar of sardine paste; the in-jokes.

It was a good life. Little surprise then, that all of the children should be so keen to get married and carry on the tradition. More of the same could only be better, surely.

And for Pete's four sisters, this had proved to be true. The extended family extended at a staggering pace and the happiness grew with similar speed. Until Pete, the youngest of the five, made the one big mistake of his life. He married a girl totally unsuited to him, in the misguided belief that marriage would have a positive, transforming effect, turning Stella into someone else, a wife, a mother, a sandwich-maker and Monopoly-player.

But Stella came from a different type of family. One where the parents argued and the three siblings were indifferent to each other. Not bad, just unmemorable, uninspiring.

And Pete omitted to alert Stella to his expectations.

So while she loved Pete's parents and was touched by their warm acceptance of her into their family, despite their disappointment at her reluctance to have children, she did not want to be like them. Theirs was the exact opposite of the life she craved.

And Pete was too decent to hold his hands up and admit he'd made a mistake. The mistake was his fault. He should have made his hopes clear before he married Stella. As she certainly had. But he'd paid no attention to her, thinking she'd change. His fault.

So the dreams had been filed away under U for Unobtainable. But as he contemplated meeting Beth tomorrow, he found himself reaching for the dusty file. He pulled back in shock.

I'm not that kind of man, I'm not that kind of man, he repeated, desperately hoping that, if he repeated it often enough, he might believe it.

Richard drove Lauren to the station to catch the train back to London. They hadn't had time for a proper lunch but Richard had insisted on taking her up the hill behind the shop to look at the spectacular scenery across the Lakes. He pulled some fresh bread and some very smelly blue cheese from one of the many pockets in his battered jacket. They shared a bottle of water and Lauren wiped the soggy crumbs from her lips with her sleeve.

They'd sorted out the formalities of the planned work schedule in a matter of minutes and spent the rest of the short time left chatting about themselves. Lauren almost regretted having to leave so soon, even with the prospect of her date with Chris that night. Especially with the prospect of the date with Chris. But she would be seeing Richard again on Monday when she began her assignment.

'Oh, I nearly forgot, can you fix up somewhere for me to stay during the week?' she asked. 'Just a room in the local pub or that sort of thing will be fine.'

'Nonsense,' Richard answered briskly. 'I've got a self-contained flat attached to the cottage. You can stay there. It will be more convenient for you and I'll be on hand to help out if you have any questions.'

She should have said no. She knew that things could get messy if there wasn't a clearly drawn line between business and social commitments. And she would be in Tendale from Monday through to Friday. That meant a lot of out-of-work hours to fill.

But Lauren had made a career of not saying the things she should (and saying even more things that she shouldn't). So she agreed.

On the train home, she automatically took out her laptop and switched it on, ready to write up the details of her meeting while they were still fresh in her mind. But her fingers hovered over the keys, limp and useless. Her eyes were fixed on the world outside the train window. It was exactly the same moving picture that she'd ignored on the way up but to Lauren it looked different. Greener, whiter, starker. She wanted to pull the emergency cord and get out so that she could smell the air.

Frankly the thought unnerved her. She was a town girl. A successful businesswoman. She'd selected her career and other life choices very carefully to minimise emotional upheaval. New York was a natural progression in her pursuit of anonymity within the safe confines of twenty-four-hour crowds and noise. The countryside had

69

always left her cold with its capricious changes and random pleasures and torments. Yet suddenly it was drawing her in.

And she couldn't work. The propositions, the numbers, the calculations, they all seemed dull and grey. She closed the laptop down. I'll do it later when I'm back in London. When I'm back in my real world. As she sat back and lost herself in the hills, she remembered what she had been thinking about before she got her computer out.

As the train had pulled away, she'd watched Richard's face get smaller (he'd insisted on seeing her on to the platform and wryly presenting her with a bar of Kendal Mint Cake for the journey). She'd smiled to herself as she went over the seed of the idea that had been planted in her during her time with him. He could be the answer to all my problems with my mum, she thought. He is such a good, decent man, full of compassion, full of fun and character. She ought to marry again. It's been far too long since Dad's death. Someone new would make her happy, give her someone else to focus on. Someone other than me.

As the train had pulled away, Richard had watched Lauren's face get smaller. He didn't know what she was thinking of but he'd suspected it might be the coming evening. By all accounts the omens for that were not good. That pleased him, although he was not a malicious man. He'd smiled to himself as he dwelt on the thought that had been preoccupying him throughout his time with her. She is such a vibrant, complex woman, full of possibility, full of wit and intelligence – I like her. A lot.

Chapter 5

The film seemed endless. Even with the subtitles it was hard to follow the plot. Chris found it easier since this was the sixth time he'd seen *Pravda*. He'd endured five subsequent post-mortems with Beth, who'd tried gamely to explain the motifs without ever managing to convey what it was actually about. He hoped that Lauren wasn't going to want to talk about the film afterwards. He knew that he would have to slap her if she so much as mentioned the word 'deconstruct'.

Lauren was trying to keep up but she was distracted by the prospect of dinner afterwards. She kept feeling nervously at her throat where she had taken off her Pisces necklace. She'd worn it continuously since her twenty-first birthday and she felt very strange without it. It was made of a thin gold plate and needed constant polishing to stop it from looking tarnished. But it was one of the very few presents her mother had ever given her and she treasured it. It seemed like an act of betrayal or even infidelity to remove it for such a deceitful reason.

On the train back from the Lakes, she'd formulated a plan for sorting out the problem of the lie. It was not very convincing but involved blaming it on drunkenness along with an elaborate tale of bluff and pretence that was entirely Stella's fault. The narrative was to be delivered with great wit and masterful comic timing. The outcome was to be that Chris would not understand a word Lauren was saying but he would be in doubt as to her correct star sign and impending birthday. A result indeed.

Chris had a similarly convoluted plan to get her off the hook. He too was going to pretend that he'd been drunk. And stupid. And forgetful. Whatever. The whole thing was preposterous and he just wanted to get it out of the way so he could relax with Lauren and see what developed when they didn't have to watch what they were saying.

That was the plan. The reality was different, as so often seemed to happen in Lauren's life. All was going well for both of them as they walked over Hungerford Bridge towards Covent Garden, until they started discussing restaurants. Lauren had agreed with Chris's choice of a sushi bar. She was allergic to shellfish so she preferred to avoid all fish restaurants but, not for the first time, she was anxious to please so she sacrificed her good sense for what she perceived were good manners. She said that she loved sushi, sure that she would be able to find something unthreatening on the menu.

The place was very modern. It was decorated in a minimalist style, in other words, not decorated at all. It didn't even look very clean but she assumed that it was supposed to look dirty and was probably scrubbed to the point of obsession by the vacant-looking staff.

The menus arrived and Lauren scanned the descriptions optimistically, hoping to find something that would not trigger off her allergy to shellfish or her aversion to anything slimy. Her optimism was thwarted. They might just as well have handed her some antihistamine tablets and a sick bag as soon as she walked in. And a paper bag to put over her head when her skin erupted.

'What are you going to have?' Chris asked. 'Everything here is fantastic!'

Stella coughed delicately in her most Jane-Austen-heroine-like fashion. 'I've never been a big eater.' (MAJOR LIE, ONE NOT TO BE RECOMMENDED UNLESS YOU WANT TO BE CONDEMNED TO A LIFETIME OF SMALL MEALS AND NO SNACKS.) 'I think I'll just have some rice and some of the . . . vegetable thingies.'

Lauren picked up on Chris's crestfallen face. She took one more desperate look at the menu again. 'Well, maybe we could share one of the specials?'

Chris cheered up and promptly ordered plateloads of slimy and allergen-full stuff. It seemed a good moment for Lauren to embark upon the dramatic explanation of her slip of the tongue. She had demoted her transgression from the category of lies after watching a party political broadcast and discovering what real lies are like.

She was just about to start her speech, honestly she was, when she noticed that Chris was watching someone behind her. She turned round to see a woman striding towards them.

She was six feet tall and as thin as a person can be without rumours of eating disorders circulating. She had a fiercely short haircut and the most incredible bone structure which either made her utterly beautiful or mirror-breakingly ugly, depending on the sensibilities of the observer. Lauren found her plain scary and had to stop herself from holding up her hands in the shape of a crucifix as this life force approached.

73

Chris's face had dissolved into the most joyous smile and Lauren had the awful feeling that this was another ex-girlfriend to reckon with. How mature was this man?

'Izzy! What are you doing here?' Chris asked, jumping up to kiss her on both cheeks.

'The same as you, I expect.'

'Are you with someone?' Chris looked behind Izzy to see if she was being accompanied. Lauren had already looked. There was no-one.

'I'm meeting up with some friends at a club later so I just thought I'd grab something to eat first. And since this is our favourite place, I knew there was a chance I'd find you here.'

'Then you must join us, mustn't she, Lauren?' Chris appealed to Lauren who really wanted to say that Izzy absolutely must not join them. The woman would terrify her into saying something dreadful and, so far, Lauren had managed to restrain her natural tendency to self-destruct. But she was too polite to be honest. So she just nodded and pressed her lips tightly together to prevent immediate disaster. The woman looked puzzled at Lauren's odd expression.

'Aren't you going to introduce us properly, Tristan?'

Tristan?

'Of course, sorry! Izzy, this is Lauren Connor; Lauren, this is my sister Izzy. Isolde.'

Sister. OK. Tristan and Isolde. No, no, no.

Chris looked sheepish. 'Don't say it. We've heard it all before. At least you can understand why I call myself Chris. And can that be the last time we refer to it, please?'

Lauren understood entirely and liked him all the more for his embarrassment. His vulnerability moved her as hers had moved Chris at Stella's party.

Izzy sat down at the table and looked Lauren up and down unashamedly. 'So Lauren, how long have you known our Tristan?'

'We only met a couple of days ago.'

'You're a fast worker, Tris. You only split up with Batty Beth a couple of weeks ago. I would have thought you'd need at least a few months to get your sanity back before stepping out again.'

Chris looked uncomfortable. 'I wish you wouldn't call Beth that. She wasn't batty, she'd just had a difficult upbringing and it made her a little off-kilter.'

Izzy turned to face Lauren. 'Trust me, the woman is completely round the twist. Do you know, in all the five years she was living with Tris, she never once told her parents. They didn't even know she had a boyfriend, let alone that she lived with him.'

Lauren considered this. It was decidedly weird, there was no doubt about it. 'But didn't her parents ever come round to the flat?' she asked Chris.

Izzy answered for him. 'Oh yes, and Tris had to bundle up all his stuff and hide it round at my place. He had to take down all the photos which had him in them, remove all the books which were obviously not Beth's, clear out the bathroom, everything. Then he had to walk the streets until they'd left before he could move back in.'

Chris was squirming at this revelation. 'It wasn't that bad, Izzy, you're exaggerating.'

Izzy shook her head. 'No, I'm not exaggerating. She

was terrified that her mad, senile parents would find out that their little princess was not living in a fairytale fortress, untouched by human hands.'

Chris raised a finger in objection. 'It wasn't like that. She was waiting for the right time to tell them. They were elderly. A bit old-fashioned. In fact, she was planning to tell them when she went to stay with them last week.'

Izzy sat back in astonishment. 'You didn't tell me that. So after five years, she finally decides to come clean. And then you dump her. What does that say about you, Tris?'

Lauren wondered the same thing. But neither she nor Chris (she couldn't think of him as Tristan, not seriously) had a chance to take this thought further because Izzy hadn't finished.

'Oh well, it's probably for the best. I mean, you could never have trusted her, not when she was so good at hiding things like that. I once sat there in the flat while she was on the phone to her mum, or Mother as she had to call her, and she was spouting a whole stream of lies, bold as brass, no hesitation. I used to say to Tris, if she could lie like that to her mum and get away with it, she can do the same to you.'

Both Lauren and Chris were thinking the same thing – this was bad, really, really bad. They were both intending to dabble in a little harmless playacting to undo a silly conversational mishap but Izzy's damning judgement on the perils of dishonesty had thrown them off-balance.

The food arrived and things got worse. At least they did for Lauren, who managed to swallow a few mouthfuls of innocent-looking food before she felt her skin begin to prickle ominously.

'Are you all right, Lauren? You seem very flushed and a bit, I don't know, blotchy.'

Thank you, Izzy, Lauren cursed silently, I really needed to have that pointed out to me. 'I don't feel very well, actually. I think it must be something I ate earlier.' Now was not the time to bring up her omission to mention that she was allergic to shellfish and, therefore, everything she was eating.

Chris leaned forward in concern. 'Let's get you home then before you get any worse.'

Things can't get much worse, Chris, Lauren thought. She was wrong.

'Surprise!'

Chris and Lauren jumped back in horror as the door was flung open by Lauren's mother.

Maureen Connor took one look at her daughter's puffy face and pulled her straight into the flat. 'Oh my God! Look at you! What have you been doing? You haven't been eating—'

Lauren didn't let her finish the incriminating sentence. She threw her arms round her mum, which was very perplexing for Maureen since neither of them were huggy people. But it achieved the desired effect of stopping the woman from saying the wrong thing at this delicate stage.

'Mum! How lovely to see you. What a . . . a surprise! Erm, do come in, Chris. Mum, this is Chris. Chris, this is my mum.'

Chris stayed where he was. Having never met Beth's parents in five years of living together and being secretly happy with that state of affairs, he was not overly keen

on meeting Lauren's mum after one not very successful date.

'Listen, now that I know your mum is here to look after
you, I'll be on my way. I've got some work to catch up
with at home.'

Lauren was relieved. She wanted the evening to end
as much as he did. Especially since she knew what her
mother was like. She talked too much and too quickly.
Words shot from her mouth like bullets from an automatic
rifle – the sheer quantity ensured that some of them would
always land in unexpected places and cause maximum
damage. Lauren had inherited this particular gift from
Maureen. If she could have chosen a hereditary quality,
she would have preferred her mum's narrow feet.

'Of course, I understand. Thank you for a lovely
evening,' Lauren said cheerfully.

'Are you sure you're OK?'

'I'm fine,' Lauren replied gratefully. 'Honestly.'

Chris didn't appear convinced. 'Well, I suppose if
your mother is here, then . . .' He let the sentence drift
off. 'I'll call you tomorrow,' he said, 'to see if you're
feeling better.'

'That would be great,' she replied cheerfully. And if
she'd shut the door straight away, the evening could
have been salvaged. But she lingered a second or two,
wondering if she dared slip in a jokey reference to
birthdays to clear the air once and for all. And before
she could reach the conclusion that this was a bad idea,
her mum had taken charge.

'Don't be so silly. You can't let the young man go
without inviting him in. I've seen *Ally McBeal*, I know
what you young people do. He has to have a cup of coffee

and listen to some of your CDs. Come on in, don't just stand there. I won't be in the way, you won't even know I'm here.'

She effectively dragged the poor man into the flat and guided him forcefully towards the sofa. For one horrible moment, Lauren wondered if her mum was going to offer him a packet of condoms. Unlikely though it sounded, she wasn't going to take any chances.

'Can you give me a hand in the kitchen, Mum?' Lauren borrowed her mum's strongarm tactics and yanked her away from the CD cabinet where Maureen was searching for the soundtrack to *Seven Brides for Seven Brothers*.

'He seems very nice, love. Should I start saving for a hat?' Maureen was oblivious to Lauren's tension as they reached the kitchen and shut the door behind them.

Lauren started to whisper, constantly flicking nervous glances towards the door. 'Mum, just listen to me. I haven't got time to go into it, but don't mention my birthday or my necklace or my star sign or that I'm allergic to shellfish and always said I'd rather die than eat sushi.'

Maureen screwed up her face in confusion. 'I don't understand. Have you lied about your age or something? There's nothing wrong with that, your father thought I was younger than him until we got married and he saw my birth certificate. By then, it didn't matter, so I—'

'Mum, I haven't lied about my age, why would I? That would be stupid. No, I just told him . . . I just had the impression that he thought . . . well, he looked at my necklace in a funny way. Oh, look, you'll just think I'm mad. And you'd be right. But I'm sorting it out. Just

79

don't say anything. Especially not that my birthday is coming up.'

Maureen shrugged cheerfully. 'OK love. So does that mean you aren't going to invite him to your birthday lunch in a fortnight? That seems daft. It's always such a lovely occasion and it would have been a nice thing to invite him to.'

'I don't even know if I'm going to see him again. Just leave it, Mum,' Lauren warned. But Maureen didn't leave things. Leaving things implied neglect and she had been a neglectful mother for too many years. She was a doing mother now.

Lauren tried to work out what her mum was thinking but didn't have the time. Or the will. 'Can you just make some coffee, Mum? And add some cold water to it so it's not too hot – I don't want him to stay too long.'

She escaped from the kitchen before Maureen could ask more perfectly reasonable questions which Lauren did not feel like answering. Back in the living room, Chris was doing what people always do when they go to someone's house for the first time: he was scrutinising the books on the shelf and flicking through the record collection.

Lauren watched his attention focus on her extensive shelves of glossy books about Broadway and Hollywood musicals. And she detected the hint of a smile on his face when he saw the endless film and show soundtracks that reflected her musical taste (or absence of musical taste, as previous boyfriends had pointed out).

'Do you like musicals?' she asked him, moving away from the kitchen where her mum was making more noise than a simple coffee-making job should generate. Please don't let her be reorganising my cupboards, Lauren thought. That's always a sign that something is up.

Chris considered the question. 'Not really. I suppose I find it a bit strange when grown men and women suddenly burst into song in the middle of a perfectly ordinary situation. It jars with my sense of reality, makes me feel uncomfortable.'

Dead on cue, a piercing high note came flying from the kitchen as Maureen began to sing 'Everything's Coming Up Roses' as if an MGM audition was on offer. Lauren cringed for a second before observing that her mum's voice was getting really good.

'I quite like this one,' Chris said, holding out a CD soundtrack of *West Side Story*. 'It's more gutsy than the others.'

'You mean guns, knives and boys hanging out in gangs?' Lauren asked, amused by his conventional choice. She put the CD on and waited for that evocative two-tone whistle that always transported her to a New York where pure love could overcome the most entrenched racial hatred and everyone knew the words to everyone else's songs. That was what she wanted. Someone who knew the words to her songs.

She pulled herself back from the impossible dream. 'I was thinking about the other night,' Lauren began awkwardly. 'I don't know about you but I was a little the worse for wear.'

'Me too,' Chris echoed encouragingly, hoping she was about to clear things up. He was prepared to accept whatever explanation she offered, however ridiculous. Unfortunately, he didn't get a chance.

'Coffee's ready!' Maureen announced as she burst into

the living room carrying a tray, three cups of coffee (oh no, thought Lauren, *three* cups) and a box of Jaffa Cakes. 'I don't know if she's mentioned it,' Maureen said, 'but Jaffa Cakes are Lauren's favourites, Chris. She never buys them for herself so I like to treat her to them when I come and visit.'

Now Lauren knew what all the noise had been. Maureen had been rearranging all the shelf space in the kitchen to accommodate twenty-four boxes of Jaffa Cakes. The sad thing was that Lauren hadn't liked Jaffa Cakes since she was fourteen when she'd gone through a very brief addiction to them. When Maureen reinvented herself as the perfect mother a few years earlier, she had dredged up some happy memories, or any memories, of her daughter's childhood that she could replicate as proof of her own redemption. See, I still remember the things you always liked best, the gestures implied.

Jaffa Cakes were one of these things. Historical romances, Neil Diamond LPs and pink pearlescent nail varnish were some others. Lauren didn't have the heart to tell her mum that she'd long since grown out of these fads. And now that it had gone on so long, she couldn't tell her the truth. It would make Maureen feel deceived for all the occasions when Lauren had beamed joyfully to receive the totally unwanted offerings.

She picked up a Jaffa Cake with what she hoped was a look of happy gratitude and sank her teeth into the squidgy soft orange jelly that always reminded her of when she was sick after drinking half a bottle of Cointreau as a student.

Conversation had dried up completely. They listened to the Jets sing joyfully of how they were going to rid

82

the streets of the immigrant punks who threatened their wholesome apple pie way of life. Ahh, the American Dream.

'So where is this lovely restaurant that Lauren's just been telling me about? I love sushi but there isn't much call for it in Watford.'

Chris explained where it was, grateful for such an uncontroversial question to answer. He and Maureen discussed the merits of various fish dishes before the ominous silence descended once more.

Lauren wondered if she was ever going to get the opportunity to deliver her speech. Chris was wondering the same. While they were wondering, Maureen was about to fire another woefully inappropriate salvo into the conversational desert.

'So Chris, I hope Lauren will be bringing you to visit me soon. I'm sure you'd love to see all the photos of her when she was a young girl. Not that she's old now, of course,' she added hastily, trying to remember exactly what Lauren had said about the age business. 'Actually, we're having a little lunch party in a couple of weeks' time.'

Lauren pleaded with her eyes: DON'T DO THIS! Maureen winked at her and shook her head slightly. I know what I'm doing, the gesture said.

She didn't know what she was doing. Or saying. That was the kindest way to look at it. She just felt compelled to help her daughter out of a sticky spot. That's what mothers do, real mothers, give their children a helping hand whether they want it or not.

'I'm sure Lauren will tell you what it's all in aid of. In time.' And then she winked again, proudly. There,

83

she thought. Now Lauren will have to sort this nonsense out. If I hadn't forced her hand, it could have dragged on indefinitely.

Why couldn't you have just left the crate of Jaffa Cakes outside the door? Lauren thought bitterly. Why couldn't you have just stayed at home and practised your scales? Or even just stayed in the kitchen? What am I supposed to say now? How can I make it all sound spontaneous and flippant when my mum has made an official pronouncement to Chris that I have something specific to tell him?

Chris ached for her. He knew about difficult parents. He and Izzy had both coped in different ways. He'd punished his mother and father by playing Monkees records in his bedroom at full volume all day.

Izzy, meanwhile, had embarked upon a journey of self-mutilation that bewildered Mr and Mrs Fallon without actually causing them any suffering. Even when she escalated her campaign, they humoured her in the single wise act of their parenting lives. She started off modelling herself on Morticia from *The Addams Family* which was the first programme she ever saw at a friend's house – the Fallon home didn't have a television. After that, she recreated herself regularly – she was currently mid-image change from Joyce Grenfell to Tina Turner. To her parents' disappointment, she never went through a Rhine maiden phase even when they brought her a winged helmet and a trident back from the Bayreuth Festival one year.

She had begged Chris not to leave home until she finished school. 'Mum and Dad are completely bonkers, Tris. If you leave me with them, they'll make me start

wearing my hair in long, blond plaits or something.'
So Chris stayed at home until he was twenty-one and
Izzy was eighteen, by which time his parents were both
wearing bizarrely embroidered smock tops over shorts.

The result of this was that Izzy owed Chris a massive
debt of gratitude. She was still waiting for an opportunity
to repay him. That time was not far off.

Chris gulped down his (almost undrinkable) lukewarm
coffee and left swiftly without giving Lauren a chance to
remedy her mother's blundering interventions. He said
he'd call her, which he meant. But Lauren didn't know
that he meant it. She was convinced that her mum's
performance had put him off for good. Not that she was
overly bothered by his departure. The evening had gone
nowhere towards persuading her that Chris was someone
worth giving up New York for. Or even Cumbria.

But she was so furious with her mother for turning up
without an invitation that she decided to make Maureen
feel bad by blaming her for scuppering the start of a
major affair.

Well, that's that, she decided. It was three o'clock in
the morning. Her mum had finally gone after some
unpleasant words. It was standard mother-and-daughter
stuff; starting off with the specific: (Lauren) Why did
you have to say that? (Maureen) Why didn't you just
tell him the truth in the first place? Then on to the more
general: (Lauren) Why do you always have to ruin my
relationships? (Maureen) Why do you always have to
ruin your own relationships? Then finally on to the sheer
nastiness that always provides the climax to such scenes:
(Lauren) I think I preferred you in those thirty-odd years

when you didn't care – at least you stayed out of my life. Maureen said nothing to that. It's a maternal gift, if not a necessity, to be able to absorb your child's resentments and frustrations without reflecting them back.

Needless to say, Lauren felt bad about her harshness after Maureen had gone. That is, after spending three cathartic hours thinking vicious thoughts of her mother to the taped accompaniment of Stephen Sondheim's appropriately complex music.

How can I leave her? she asked herself over and over again. How can I stay? she answered herself.

Then, as she lay in bed willing herself to go to sleep, she stopped contemplating the decision she had still not made to ask herself a perplexing question: What on earth was so important that my mum felt the need to turn up uninvited on a Friday night? Because, in the heat of the argument, Lauren had forgotten to ask.

Chapter 6

It was lunchtime on Saturday and Pete had still not summoned up the courage to tell Stella that he was going out. He'd already decided that he couldn't tell her he was meeting Beth. She would get the wrong idea if there is such a thing as the wrong idea when the right idea hasn't been defined.

Although Stella did appear to be in a particularly good mood. She had been relieved to get the call from Lauren saying that she was going up to Cumbria today rather than Monday after a unmemorable evening with Chris. She hadn't gone into detail about what had happened; the call had to be kept short because there wasn't a very good reception on Lauren's mobile with the mountains all around. Stella had made all the right sympathetic noises and they'd agreed to catch up when Lauren was back in London.

Pete's parents had agreed to come down for the weekend at the last minute, not very happy at having to go along with the story that it had all been planned a while ago.

'The thing is, Pete,' his dad had said, 'your mum and I don't hold with secrets between man and wife. Now I don't know what's going on between the two of you, but get it sorted before things get out of hand.'

They were not very good actors and, from the minute they arrived, Stella was concerned that something was wrong.

'Pete, are your mum and dad OK? They seem . . . strange.'

'You're imagining it,' Pete said irritably, wanting the weekend to pass as quickly as possible so that he could return to his humdrum, predictable existence.

'I don't think I am,' Stella muttered grimly, determined to find out what was going on with some subtle investigative stratagems.

'So what's going on?' she demanded firmly, cornering Bill and Ann in the conservatory where they were shocked to find explicit pornographic drawings stencilled all over the radiators. They jumped up and tried hard not to look guilty. They were not successful.

Bill took the lead. 'We were just er, admiring the radiators. Very . . . unusual.'

Stella shook her head irritably. 'I'm not talking about the radiators. And, by the way, you don't have to worry, we didn't put those stencils on, it was the previous owners.'

Bill and Ann looked relieved at this. They'd wondered if the application of pornography to household appliances was yet further evidence of marital disharmony. Their relief didn't last long.

Stella was unstoppable. 'I know that something is up. You may be able to hide it from Pete but you can't hide it from me. You've been behaving strangely ever since you got here. So what is it? Please. I'm worried about you. I'm not moving from this spot until you tell me what it is.'

Now they felt terrible. They loved her like their own daughter and they were lying to her. They struggled to find something, anything, to say that would pacify her.

'I've just had a few heart pains, that's all,' Ann said.

'We've just got a few money problems, that's all,' Bill said.

They spoke at the same time then turned to face each other in astonishment. Stella rushed to comfort them both. Her effusiveness was overwhelming and her in-laws flinched at the group hug she initiated. Stella could not see the wary looks that Bill and Ann were exchanging. Nor could she have understood them, even if she had.

'I had no idea!' she exclaimed. 'Why have you kept all these worries to yourselves? Pete would have wanted to know.'

Ann left it to Bill to get them out of this. He seemed to be finding this charade a lot easier than she did, in her opinion.

Bill cleared his throat. 'Well, you see, Stella, we didn't want any of our kids to know that we were having any problems. And they're not serious, just little blips,' he added reassuringly.

'I don't see how heart pains can be little blips,' Stella said doubtfully. 'And money problems are always serious.'

'Well, anyway, we're on top of them now and we just think it's better if Pete doesn't worry about anything. I mean, he's got enough on his plate with everything going on at work.'

Stella stepped back. 'What do you mean? Nothing's going on at work, is it?'

Bill was horrified. He'd assumed that Pete told Stella

everything. He and Ann had no secrets from each other – apart from Ann not mentioning heart pains to him before and his omitting to share his concerns about their finances.

Pete had confided in them during their last visit. The consultancy he worked for was being taken over and redundancies were being threatened. Bill had tried to reassure him. 'You don't have to worry though, Pete, it'll be the old ones they get rid of, not the young blood like you.'

Bill would never forget the sad look Pete had given him. 'Dad, I *am* one of the old ones. I'm not that far off forty. That's old in this business.' At that point, Stella had come into the room waving a baguette precariously and Pete had stopped talking. Weeks later, Bill now realised that Pete hadn't wanted his wife to hear what they were discussing.

He began to bluster. 'Maybe I've got the wrong end of the stick. You know what a daft idiot I am, always getting my wires crossed.'

Stella wouldn't be swayed. 'So what has he actually said to you about his work? He hasn't said anything to me.'

Ann couldn't hold herself back. 'When did you last ask him how his job was going?'

Stella recoiled as if she'd been punched. 'What do you mean by that? Pete and I are always talking. We tell each other everything.'

Bill and Ann said nothing. They had spent enough time in their son's many houses to know that Stella's idea of 'always talking' worked on a strictly one-way basis. It had taken them a few years to accept that Pete

90

was happy, or at least content, to be the silent partner in the marriage. Stella needed a silent partner or at least a very quiet one.

Within hours of meeting them for the first time, she had talked her future in-laws through her mother's recent hysterectomy, her father's overdraft, the horror her parents had felt when one of their sons dropped out of college (drugs were alluded to but never acknowledged openly) and her own difficulties with the Pill. They'd found her strangely appealing in her openness but did wonder whether Pete could survive her domination.

They'd never seen Stella and Pete talk as such. They'd seen instructions being relayed, information being exchanged, schedules being confirmed. But talking? The upside of this was that they never saw them arguing.

It was a strange marriage in their eyes, but one that appeared to work. Well, they were still married after fifteen years.

Their worry had always been that Pete had married Stella because he felt sorry for her. He used to compare her family to his own. 'They're great pranksters, her mum and dad,' he told them. 'They consider the height of sophisticated humour to drive down quiet streets with car windows open, screaming: "Pants!" at the top of their voices.' Bill and Ann had exchanged glances.

Pete had tried to understand Stella's parents. 'They just want to be fun, to have fun. It's relentless.'

For many years, Stella had resisted the family's pull into the life of incessant merriment. She'd been clever and hardworking, shutting herself away in the bedroom to study while her mum and dad crooned drunkenly to Showaddywaddy records downstairs.

But while her two brothers' academic achievements were greeted with mystified delight, her own results were received with suspicion. 'A girl like you ought to be going out, enjoying yourself,' they'd said. As if she were letting herself down. Letting them down by behaving like the boys. Clever sons were one thing. Clever daughters were unnatural.

And then one Christmas, when she was fourteen, she'd been persuaded to have a couple of Babychams with dinner. It had made her tipsy and she'd joined in the traditional singalong with her parents' Elvis compilation tapes. They'd clapped and cheered, even her brothers. 'Go on, girl!' they'd shouted. 'We always knew you had it in you!' She felt noticed, warm, a sense of belonging for the first time in her life. And after that, Stella had never stopped performing, she never stopped entertaining.

As a plain girl, she learned that she had to go that bit further, try that bit harder, just to keep up with her peers. She never took anything for granted, she felt entitled to nothing. She learned to cook to please her brothers and, subsequently, her boyfriends. She learned to kiss on first dates and vowed to marry the first man who didn't try to change her.

'I think you're very beautiful,' Pete had said that first night in the Freshers' disco. He was drunk. She knew he was drunk but even drunks had not found her beautiful before. 'I think you're very . . . lively,' he'd said when he sobered up and she'd asked him what he thought of her. 'You're very different to my last girlfriend,' he'd said when he was thinking about splitting up with Stella. 'You're very different to everyone,' he'd said when thinking about marrying her. He was nineteen.

He'd only had one girlfriend before. He didn't know what he was doing, what he was saying.

They got married after graduation. Bill and Ann were concerned that he was more in love with the idea of marriage than the woman he was marrying. But he seemed happy. Or he didn't seem unhappy. They had lots of friends, gave lots of parties. They had no children but this was a joint decision. That's what Stella said. Pete never discussed it. Bill and Ann discussed it a lot.

Now Stella was worried. She clung to her status quo like a security blanket. She didn't like deep, personal discussions with Pete because she was always afraid of forcing him to say something that he might not be able to unsay.

But Pete had obviously said something to his parents and not to her. That had implications for her marriage, which scared her. And annoyed her. Why hadn't he said something before they committed to this house? He'd agreed that it would be fun to buy a house that needed everything doing to it. Rather, he hadn't disagreed, which amounted to the same thing. If he'd had the slightest inkling that his job might be in jeopardy, he should have said something so they could have stayed where they were.

That's what she was thinking. But she didn't say anything. She did what she always did when she had something serious on her mind – she drew up a shopping list.

Bill and Ann tiptoed out of the room as they watched Stella get geared up for some seriously conspicuous consumption. As they made their way quickly to the safety of their bedroom, there was a definite tension between them.

Bill expressed his tension by picking up a newspaper and reading it intently. Ann sat in a chair and watched him, silently seething. This went on for a while. And it wasn't easy sitting still for any length of time in a room decorated in baroque style with a hint of nineteenth-century lunatic asylum.

Ann broke the silence first. 'So was that just a lie about us having money problems, something you said to fob Stella off, or is it true?'

Bill sighed and put his paper down. 'I shouldn't have said anything. It's nothing, honestly. It's as I said to Stella, just a blip, minor cashflow thing, that's all.'

Ann shook her head, puzzled. 'I don't understand. Our mortgage was paid off years ago, we're on a good pension, we've got savings, how can we have cashflow difficulties?'

Bill tried to sound confident. 'It's nothing to worry about. I lent some money to Pete a few months back. He said he'd pay us back when the sale of the other house went through. Only thing was, he and Stella didn't get as much as they'd hoped. Still, he should be able to pay us back when he gets his annual bonus.'

'But what if he doesn't get a bonus what with the takeover that he was worried about? And why didn't you tell me?' Ann's voice was shaky.

'It was Pete who insisted I didn't tell you. He knew you'd get in a lather. Anyway, there was no point, it was just a temporary loan. What was the point in you getting in a tizzy over nothing?'

Ann looked at him as if he were a stranger. 'How many other things have you kept from me over the last forty years?'

Bill stood up angrily. 'What about you? How long have you been having heart pains?'

Stella waved her arms impatiently. 'They're nothing! Just twinges. The doctor said—'

'You went to see a doctor?' Bill interrupted. 'It was bad enough to see a doctor but you didn't think to tell me about it? So what did the doctor say about these "twinges"?'

Ann turned away. 'He said that it could be nothing but that I'd need some tests. They'll probably show that there's nothing wrong with me. So what would have been the point of telling you? You'd have been all concerned over nothing.'

The mutual deceit, so small, so innocuous, hung between them like a steamed-up window blurring all the clarity that had previously illuminated their solid marriage. Only the sound of the front door being slammed shook them from their preoccupation.

They went downstairs to find Stella shouting at the door. 'Fine! Go and get some fresh air! Find yourself! Do what you like!'

'Stella, what's the matter?' Ann was unaccustomed to any extreme displays of emotion in this house. It alarmed her.

Stella stared at the door in confusion. 'I don't know, Ann, I truly don't know.'

And she didn't. She couldn't work out how it happened. One minute she was asking Pete his opinion on an asymmetric dado rail, the next he was storming out of the house. What had she said or done?

'What do you think about painting the rail cerise with a rag-rolled effect?' was all she'd said.

He practically went berserk, that was the only way she could describe his response.

He started circling the room. 'Why ask me?' he said. 'Do what you like. You always do anyway.'

Stella remembered what Bill had said about Pete's job situation. She wondered if things were serious and if this was the reason for Pete's strange mood.

'Your dad was telling me that you've got something going on at work?' she said tentatively.

Pete exploded. 'He had no right to tell you anything!'

'You've got to be kidding! How do you think I felt to learn about my own husband's career problems from my father-in-law?'

Pete stared at her. 'I am sure you managed to console yourself with a quick flick through the Heal's catalogue and a comforting fondle of your American Express card.'

Stella gasped. 'I don't know what's up with you but you don't have to take it out on me!'

'Do you want to know what's up with me?' He didn't wait for an answer. 'I'll tell you. There's a good chance that I'm going to be out of a job in a couple of weeks' time. I'll get the statutory minimum redundancy payment, which will pay my share of the mortgage for three months by which time I will have to have found another equally well-paid job. But what is really up with me is that I have been worried sick for a long time now and you haven't noticed.'

Stella was stunned by his outburst. So stunned that she didn't notice his nervous check at the time on his watch.

'You let us go ahead with buying this house, knowing

that you might be losing your job? How could you have done that without saying anything?'

'I didn't know anything. I thought it would all blow over and then I would have worried you over nothing. And you were determined to move. You were getting all restless and I knew you wouldn't be happy until you found something else to focus on.'

Stella snorted at this. 'So now I know what you really think of me. Thanks a lot.'

At this Pete walked towards the door, grabbing his jacket on the way. 'This is getting us nowhere. I'm going out for some fresh air.'

And as he slammed the door, Stella suddenly realised that he was wearing his blue and white jumper, the one she had to nag him to wear when they had people coming round. The one that she always said was her favourite. That's funny, she thought.

Maureen loved Sainsburys. She was a born-again shopper, a supermarket fetishist. It was two weeks before Lauren's birthday lunch but there was a lot to prepare. She was aware that she had not been the best of mothers while Lauren was growing up and she had been making up for it since her rebirth as earth mother.

Up and down the aisles she went, referring constantly to her shopping list. She was planning a lavish spread, particularly in the light of the new man in Lauren's life. She liked the look of this Chris chappie. There was that funny business about all the things she wasn't allowed to say, but now Lauren would have to sort it out. She'd seen to that, she thought proudly. It was probably all a silly misunderstanding anyway. Once they had a chance to sit down without an interfering mother in the way, Lauren would be able to explain it all away. They'd have a good chuckle about it when the truth came out.

True, he'd left in a bit of a hurry and Lauren had been convinced that it was the last she would see of him, but Maureen thought otherwise. She'd spent a couple of hours trying to convince her daughter that he would probably call her the next day but Lauren wouldn't listen. It all got nasty and personal, the way most of her attempts at maternal influence ended up.

'So that's why I didn't tell her,' she had said finally to the man lying next to her later that night.

Eddie Knight sat up and stroked her hair affectionately. 'You're going to have to tell her soon. She'll be here in two weeks and I've got no intention of moving out.'

Maureen liked the way that sounded. He's nothing like my late loser of a husband, she thought gratefully. Thank God. She was only glad that her mum had never seen the man she married.

'Where did she get her voice from?' Elsie used to ask her husband in awe of their prodigious daughter. 'She's amazing!'

'Stop going on about her, you'll give her a big head,' her husband would reply. 'Maureen, here's a bottle of Tizer and a bag of crisps,' he'd say, 'you just sit outside the pub and be a good girl while your mam and I have a little drinkie.'

Maureen was adored by her mother and ignored by her father all her young life. When they were killed in a car crash, three days before Maureen's seventeenth birthday, she was left with an inflated opinion of her own singing talent, courtesy of her mother, and an utter absence of personal self-worth, thanks to her father.

She'd married Jim Connor because he was captivated by her voice, her youth and her vulnerability. She was overwhelmed by his charm, his big talk, his crazy promises. She married him before she found out that he hadn't been sober once since she'd known him.

'You could be as big as Dusty,' he'd said in the early days before they got married. 'You're getting a bit on the big side,' he slurred in disgust towards the end of her unplanned, difficult pregnancy.

But he'd changed after Lauren's birth. Stopped drinking. Got a steady job. He was besotted with his daughter, intoxicated by her smile. 'You changed your dad with your smile,' Maureen used to tell Lauren. But the compliment was to become a double-edged sword. The six happy years she had with the reformed Jim after Lauren's birth made his death all the more difficult to accept. She then blamed Lauren for raising her expectations as well as ruining her burgeoning singing career.

Thirty years later, she met Eddie. She'd been getting her relationship with Lauren back on track, and her career was taking off at the most astonishing rate. She didn't expect any more blessings after a hitherto less than blessed life. Things were already looking so good.

He was lovely. She wasn't sure she deserved him. In fact, she knew she didn't deserve him. Eddie was an ordinary, reasonably successful salesman with no neuroses, addictions or Freudian/Oedipal hang-ups to blame on a tragic youth. She'd met him at a pub where she was singing. He'd been captivated by her voice, her experience, her vulnerability. Just like Jim. And that was where all similarity ended.

'Do you know you've got a voice like Ethel Merman?' he'd said.

'At last, a man who knows who Ethel Merman is!' she replied.

Lifelong love affairs have been built on far less than a shared passion for Ethel Merman and Maureen and Eddie had a whole lot more going for them. As soon as they'd overcome the hurdle of introducing Eddie to Lauren.

Lauren's birthday lunch was going to be the first time the two would meet. Maureen had planned to tell Lauren about Eddie in advance on Friday, give her time to get used to the idea. That's why she'd gone to see her on impulse. But, well, it didn't work out like that.

'Don't be daft, Eddie,' Maureen said, 'you won't have to move out, it won't come to that! It's not as if we've got anything to hide! It's just a delicate situation.'

Eddie smiled indulgently. 'Sweetheart, we've been living together for six months and your daughter doesn't even know I exist.'

Maureen looked sheepish. 'The timing just hasn't been right. I always stay with her over Christmas and I could hardly ask her if it was all right for my boyfriend to come as well.'

'I don't see why not, I'm great at Scrabble, I know all the words to "Have Yourself a Merry Little Christmas" and I don't mind the hard centres in a box of Quality Street. That makes me the perfect festive season guest!'

Maureen laughed and kissed Eddie fondly. 'Maybe, but Christmas is always a bit emotional. Lauren's father died on Christmas Eve and I didn't want her to be upset over the course of the holiday. It didn't seem an appropriate moment to introduce her to what she would see as her father's replacement. Don't worry, I'll get round to telling her on her birthday.'

'Well, I'll leave it in your hands. But I can't help thinking you should have told her yesterday.'

'What are you doing here today?' Richard asked her, surprised but pleased to have his Saturday plans interrupted by Lauren's arrival. 'I wasn't expecting you until Monday.' He relieved her of her suitcase, which was pulling her arm down to the ground.

Lauren rubbed her arm muscles, noting how easily Richard lifted the heavy bag. As a single woman, she was overly impressed by a man's capacity to do the simple things that caused her to struggle. But Richard was particularly muscular. His strength came from living the outdoor life.

He showed her to the annexe where he hadn't finished making the preparations for her arrival. It was a complete mess. Lauren smiled at the piles of books and boxes of photos heaped on the bed. The floor was a sea of clothes, mainly women's, and odd objects that she assumed were pieces of mountaineering equipment.

Lauren bent down to help him with the clearing operation. She picked up a woman's thermal vest. 'I presume this belonged to your ex-wife or is there something you'd rather not tell me?'

Richard grabbed it and stuffed it in a bin liner with the rest of the clothes, avoiding eye contact. Lauren regretted her flippancy immediately. 'God, I'm really sorry. I've done it again, haven't I? Why don't I keep my big mouth shut? It's just, picking up a woman's vest in a new client's bedroom, it's like stepping into a parallel universe. I'm more used to discussing the wine list and murmuring politely when he shows me a picture of his two labradors. I just had this sudden image of you coming in from a walk on the mountains, deranged with oxygen deprivation, and putting on your wife's clothes by mistake.'

She stopped abruptly, wishing she'd been able to do so three sentences earlier. 'You're wondering if you can legally get out of our contract on the grounds of unprofessional behaviour, namely that I'm accusing you of wearing women's clothing,' she said.

Richard stood up finally. His eyes were crinkled. Lauren exhaled in relief. He's smiling inside! How strange that I should be able to read his moods when I hardly know him, she observed. He cleared his throat and placed his finger on his chin in mock contemplation. 'What I'm wondering is, how have you managed to get to your age, to this stage in your career, without being assaulted or institutionalised or serially fired?'

Lauren laughed. 'That's the point! I manage by keeping contact on a strictly professional basis. Now if we were in a boardroom and you were in a suit and I was wearing my reading specs, you would be stunned by my senior managerial presence. I would trust that woman with my life as well as my business, you'd say.'

Richard suppressed a smile. 'But with my former wife's underwear in your hand, all professionalism slips away?'

Lauren's eyes narrowed suspiciously. 'Are you making fun of me, Richard?'

Richard mimicked her expression. 'I certainly am,

102

Lauren. So why don't we get this done as quickly as possible then I'll put on a suit, you can put on your reading specs and you can show me some of that senior managerial presence.'

Lauren tilted her head to one side. 'Are you making fun of me *again*?'

Richard laughed out loud. 'You make it too easy!'

Lauren blushed. She was about to ask him why his ex-wife had left her thermals behind but, fortunately, her subconscious had fulfilled its quota of indiscretions for the day. She swallowed the offending question efficiently and looked around for something safe to touch.

Richard smoothly grabbed as much of the stuff as he could and chucked it all on to the landing outside. 'Sorry about this, I was planning to clear it all out tomorrow.'

'Don't apologise, it's my fault. I came up on impulse. I would have called first to say I was coming but I left at six o'clock this morning and I didn't think you'd appreciate being woken up that early on a Saturday.'

Richard raised his eyebrows. 'You wouldn't have woken me up. I'd already been up for over an hour at that point. At the weekends, I always get up early and drive to one of the mountains. Maybe you'd like to join me tomorrow?' Lauren's face betrayed her feelings. Richard laughed. 'I take it you're not a crack-of-dawn woman.'

'Definitely not,' Lauren said.

'So what got you up so early this morning?' he asked.

'Bad night,' she replied curtly. There was a silence while Richard waited for her to expand on this. When no expansion was forthcoming, he tactfully changed the subject.

'Well, you're here now, so what did you have in mind for the rest of the weekend? You weren't planning on starting work immediately, were you?'

Lauren shook her head. 'I thought it might be nice to see some of the countryside while I have the time to appreciate it. Once I get started, I'll be stuck in front of the computer for much of the time.'

'That's great!' Richard said. 'I'd love to take you on some of my favourite walks. And I promise that the views are just as beautiful after nine o'clock in the morning.'

Lauren smiled gratefully, suddenly looking forward to the rest of this weekend.

Richard thought he understood her smile. The fact that his first marriage had ended because of his astonishingly consistent ability to misinterpret everything his wife said or did didn't dent his confidence to get it right this time around. It was obvious that the date with the man-who-didn't-know-she-was-a-Pisces didn't go well. Her speedy journey up to Tendale could only mean one thing: she wanted to see him before their business relationship became established, to build a personal bond, to get to know him.

Of course, like most impulsive gestures, this one had more than one interpretation and, sadly, Richard had chosen the wrong one. Lauren's uncomfortable night had ended with her worrying about her mother. Like Richard, Lauren thought she understood human nature quite keenly and she had come to an equally false conclusion about why her mother had dropped in unexpectedly. She was obviously painfully lonely.

Over Christmas, Lauren had noticed that her mother

had been a bit tense, preoccupied. The pub singing was going well and Lauren was pleased for her mum but it was clearly not filling the immense gap left by her husband. She must have felt absolutely desperate to drive down to London on a Friday night, just for some company.

And it was this aching sense of pity that brought Lauren to Tendale. She had been horrible to her mum, and all the woman had tried to do was help her out of a hole in the best way she could. Well, now it was Lauren's turn to help *her*. She was going to introduce the idea of her mother to Richard Trent so that he would be half in love with her when he finally met her. OK, maybe this was primarily for Lauren's benefit but Maureen would still be a winner.

There was no time to waste. They were both busy people and she needed some time alone with Richard to sow some seeds.

Then, once the problem of her mother had been addressed, she could decide whether she was going to move to New York. But she hadn't thought about New York for twenty-four hours. Odd, Lauren thought, then dismissed her concern. I've had other things on my mind, she reassured herself.

There were two weeks until her birthday and the big lunch party her mum had planned. Lauren was going to invite Richard. Her mother would be thrilled, she knew she would.

Chapter 7

Pete had popped into a pub for a quick drink before meeting Beth. His head was throbbing from the confrontation he'd just had with Stella. Mostly he felt guilty at having manipulated the scene so that he had a reason to storm out. But he believed he knew Stella well enough to predict that she would have forgotten all about it once she had a bucket of emulsion in her hand.

What am I doing? he asked himself. Skulking around, meeting another woman and not telling my wife about it. This isn't me. But he didn't like the 'me' he used to be. He was scared at the possibility of losing his job. He had always been happy to be defined by his work, having stoically accepted that his marriage was never going to contribute much to his personal growth.

And now he was going to lose the only thing that gave him the strength to cope with the draining demands of his ever-acquisitive wife. That ridiculous party was the last straw. All that fuss about Lauren and Chris and everyone not telling something to everyone else. He wouldn't even be here now if Stella hadn't forced him into a corner from which he could only escape by prevaricating (another useful euphemism for 'lying', popular with people in denial). It was too much for Pete, too tiring. And now he was part of it. Drawn into an unfamiliar universe where people say one thing and mean another. He felt like the only real flesh-and-blood character in one of those Japanese cartoons that aren't remotely funny.

As he walked into the tea shop where Beth was waiting for him, reading the *Guardian*, he felt instantly calmed by her presence. He quickly ran through all the things he had to remember not to say to her. There were none. She knew he was married. She probably knew more about his marriage than he did, judging by the amount of time Stella spent on the phone to her. He could say anything to Beth and this knowledge took his breath away.

'Hi!' he said, as he sat down opposite her. Beth folded her paper and smiled widely. Pete felt sadness wash over him like a hot flush as he found himself reluctantly playing the 'what if' game.

There are two versions of the 'what if' game. There's the futile one, played by us all in times of weakness or depression, where we replay every bad decision we ever made and substitute the ones that hindsight reveals to be right. This game is best played alone, late at night, when you are drinking that blue liqueur you brought back from Spain a few years ago (the only alcohol in the house) and listening to Janis Ian or Leonard Cohen. Maybe that's a generational thing; younger players of this game might listen to Joy Division but the very name is offputting to a depressive.

Then there's the optimistic version of the game. Where you take a possibility, maybe distant but always real, and fast-forward to the idyllic life that grabbing the chance might offer.

Pete was playing both versions simultaneously, while also pretending to scrutinise a tea trolley filled with home-made cakes and fruit breads. He even managed to choose something, although he didn't know what it was. Something with cherries on top.

While the waitress painstakingly cut a slice from his chosen cake, he wondered what his life might have been like if he hadn't married Stella. If he'd married someone who didn't feel the constant need to prove herself. Someone who was not searching hopelessly for a candyfloss lifestyle that never threatened to penetrate her surface and hurt her. Someone who acknowledged that *Friends* was a TV programme and not a government-sponsored model of how modern people should be living.

And then he wondered what his future would be like if he left Stella right this minute and spent the rest of his life with Beth. He knew that these were the thoughts of a madman and that he would soon be going home to Stella with a bunch of overpriced lilies and a promise to sand down a door as atonement. He would spend a companionable, but occasionally strained, hour in this twee little backwater with Beth. Then they would both acknowledge that their meeting denoted a lapse in concentration, that they'd both taken their eye off the ball when they should both have kept moving in a linear progression towards their own particular destinies. And if they were both dissatisfied with what they saw in the distance and craved a detour, well, they would have to go and take an evening class or find religion like other people floundering in a life that wasn't of their choosing.

'What are you thinking?' Beth asked him.

Pete jumped. He looked down at his plate and realised that he'd eaten the cake without thinking. It must have been the drink he had in the pub. It was only a double scotch, but on an empty stomach.

What am I thinking? I'm thinking that I haven't been asked that question for many years. Not unless Stella wanted approval for a new purchase. It was so long since he'd talked about his thoughts with Stella (he strained to recall if he ever had), that he couldn't think of an innocuous, glib reply.

So he answered honestly. Honesty is the best policy, they say. But not when emotions are teetering on the edge and there's nothing at the bottom to catch them. Don't say it, Pete! You won't be able to unsay it!

He said it. 'I was thinking about my life with Stella. And about what I'm doing here with you. And why I didn't tell Stella I was meeting you.'

Beth instinctively reached her hand over to cover Pete's. He left it there. 'Pete, I'm really sorry if I'm making trouble for you. I mean, I was so grateful for our talk the other night. One of my patients had died and it had shaken me up.' Pete removed his hand to scratch his eyelid self-consciously. 'Oh no, not you as well,' Beth said disappointedly.

'What's that supposed to mean?' Pete said, on the defensive.

Beth shrugged. 'Chris used to do that whenever I talked about my work. Avoid looking at me, develop a sudden fascination with his thumb or a cushion or something. Anything to change the subject.'

Pete couldn't find any words to refute the accusation. 'I'm sorry but I happen to think it's perfectly understandable to find talk of death very discomfiting.' He was now picking cake crumbs up with his little fingernail.

'Maybe it is, but then who am I supposed to talk to when the subject arises in my life? Which it does rather regularly,' Beth asked, almost pleading. 'My parents would prefer I worked in orthopaedics, fixing broken bones. They never ask what I'm working on. People like Stella only want to hear about miracle cures or really old people who'd probably have died soon anyway. And Chris spent five years changing the subject. I thought you might be different, Pete. I could really do with a friend.' She suddenly appeared very young, very small.

Pete should have left then. Before what was left of his resistance was overwhelmed by the surge of pity, empathy that he was experiencing for this woman. But he didn't leave. He wasn't the leaving type. This made him think reluctantly of Stella.

'I just feel that I'm being disloyal,' he said, not needing to say any more, to say Stella's name.

Beth leaned forward earnestly. 'I honestly wouldn't think about doing anything that would upset Stella. But you're right. I'm obviously not thinking properly. Of course it's not right for us to be doing this, however innocent it all is. Stella would feel jealous that I'm talking to you rather than her, let alone the other implications.'

They both went quiet at the thought of 'the other implications'. Beth regretted her words and tried to find something that would get them back to the pleasant state of companionship they'd enjoyed at the party.

'Did you phone Chris?' she asked brightly.

Pete screwed up his forehead. 'Why would I phone Chris?' he replied. Then he remembered the lie he'd had to tell Beth to get Chris's phone number for Stella. He hit his head in a gesture of oafishness. 'Sorry, what am

I thinking of! No, I mean I tried to call him straight after I spoke to you but he was engaged.'

'That was probably my fault,' Beth said apologetically. 'I had to phone him about having some post forwarded and then I mentioned to him about you and him arranging to meet up.'

I bet he was thrilled to hear that, Pete thought wryly. 'I'll give him a call later,' he said.

'He'll be out later,' Beth said, 'he's got some meetings on at school and then the staff are all going out together.' She looked at her watch. 'But you should catch him if you call now.'

Pete went pale. 'That's all right, there's no hurry. I'll catch up with him in the week.'

'Don't be silly!' Beth said. 'You may as well phone him now. You've got your mobile with you,' she added, pointing to the mobile phone which Pete instantly wanted to consign to oblivion. 'Besides, he doesn't get a lot of spare time with all the extra-curricular stuff going on at school. So it's best to fix something up as soon as possible. Pass me the phone and I'll dial the number for you.'

And without waiting for Pete to come up with his next excuse that the battery had run out, Beth had grabbed the phone and dialled Chris's number. She handed the phone back to Pete and sat back, grateful for a few moments to compose herself. This was all proving too stressful for her. She knew how naive she must seem to Pete. But she genuinely hadn't intended anything apart from building a friendship with him. Maybe deep down some other feelings had stirred but, if they had, she wasn't aware of them. Until Pete started talking about his marriage and about her in that strange way.

'Hello?'

Damn, thought Pete, he's in. 'Oh, er, hello Chris. It's Pete here, Pete Lynch.'

Damn, thought Chris. He'd hoped Beth had got the wrong end of the stick when she told him that Pete would be calling him. 'Hi Pete, how's things?'

'Oh fine,' Pete answered, 'and you?' I've got nothing to say to this man.

'Busy, busy,' Chris said, 'you know how it is.' Maybe if I waffle a bit, he'll have to dash off before we actually fix up a time to meet.

'Certainly do. So, er, did you enjoy the party the other night?' Pete asked, getting more and more desperate. I wish I'd paid more attention to Stella's interminable phone conversations where she prattled on about nothing for hours on end. I'm not very good at this small talk.

'Yeah. Great! You and Stella really know how to entertain!' Oh my God, don't tell me Stella's got him to phone me up and plead Lauren's case. I really don't need this.

Pete had come to the end of his entire repertoire of polite chat which was why he looked up in despair. He noticed Beth's eyes widening. He followed her glance towards the window where Stella was standing, peering through with her hands over her eyes to shield them from the reflected glare. At that exact moment, Stella saw him. And Beth.

He had to get off the phone as quickly as possible. But natural good manners stopped him from shouting a hasty goodbye and hanging up. He cursed his parents for bringing him up to be so polite.

He began speaking very quickly, calculating that it would take Stella a couple of minutes at the outside to negotiate her way through the arcade to the door of the tea shop and then squeeze through all the tables that were squashed together to maximise trade.

'So Chris, anyway, we were going to get together, so when are you free? This week? Next weekend? When?'

The man is determined to see me, Chris thought. I can't imagine why. Beth said I'd told him at the party that I'd like to get together. I must have been drunker than I thought. Still, I can't get out of it. Without being rude. But natural good manners stopped him from claiming a full diary until the twenty-second century. He cursed his parents for bringing him up to be so polite.

He couldn't think of anything worse than sitting in a pub and having to talk to Pete for a whole evening. Then he remembered that Beth had said something about football. Personally he hated football but at least he wouldn't have to talk to Pete during the match.

'How about going to see a match next Saturday?' he suggested without much enthusiasm.

Personally Pete hated football but had a vague recollection of his fumbling suggestion of a football match during the strained phone call to Beth. It had just seemed a suitably manly thing to suggest since he was determined not to go and sit through a French film with Chris. At least he wouldn't have to talk to Chris during the match. And Pete couldn't think of anything worse than sitting in a pub and having to talk to Chris for a whole evening.

'Great idea!' he said, speeding up as Stella walked through the door of the tea shop.

'I'll get the tickets,' Chris offered, wanting to ensure that they were sitting with the noisiest, most partisan fans who would render all conversation completely impossible. 'So who do you support?'

Who do I support, thought Pete frantically, trying to remember the names of any London teams. Stella has seen us. She's walking more quickly. Who do I support? He saw a bus pass the window. It had TOTTENHAM on the destination board.

'Tottenham,' he blurted out. 'I support Tottenham.' Stella had reached the table and was pulling up a chair purposefully. 'Look Chris, I have to dash. I'll leave the tickets to you then. A football match! Great! I can't wait! Thanks. We'll talk next week to arrange where we're meeting. Bye!' There was no more time left for politeness. He terminated the call without waiting for Chris to say goodbye.

Chris looked at his phone in astonishment. The man is completely round the bend, he thought. I've got to go to a football match which I will hate with a man I hardly know who sounds as if he's gone totally insane.

He decided to have another go at phoning Lauren, who hadn't returned his call from this morning. He wanted to make sure she'd recovered from whatever had made her face erupt like that. And he also felt bad about leaving in such a hurry. The evening hadn't been a great success but he was a decent man. He'd promised to call and he believed in keeping promises.

He dialled Lauren's number but hung up when the answering machine clicked in.

'Stella, what are you doing here?' Pete said, jumping up

to kiss Stella and beckoning to the waitress with what he hoped were inoffensive hand movements.

'That's funny, I was about to ask you the same thing. I came looking for you, of course. You didn't take the car so you couldn't have gone far. Fancy seeing you here, too, Beth. And since when did you like football, Pete? And how long have you supported Tottenham?'

Too many questions and not even tea and cake to distract her, Pete thought.

'Let me go and grab that waitress and get you sorted. Won't be a sec.' He dashed off towards the waitress who was precariously carrying five plates of buttered malt loaf over to a table consisting of four children who were pouring sugar on to each other's hair and one woman who looked Prozaced into submission.

The waitress was not impressed by this man who was getting in her way and disturbing her momentum. 'I've seen you already! Go and sit down and I'll come over and take your new order when I've dealt with this table!'

'Let me help you,' Pete said in a blinding moment of inspiration. He grabbed the plates from the protesting girl and stumbled over to the table of junior hooligans. He looked back over his shoulder at Stella and gave her a helpless shrug as he presented himself as a victim, roped in to help a girl in need. When he got to the table, one of the kids flicked sugar all over his head. He laughed maniacally, grateful for any diversion that kept him away from Stella for a bit longer.

'What on earth is he doing?' Stella said, more to herself than to Beth.

'I think he's trying to be helpful,' Beth suggested, feeling awkward and sweaty at being alone with Stella.

She wondered if it might look a bit odd if she also got up and started helping the waitresses out. Because she was very uncomfortable sitting where she was.

'So, Beth, what's with the secret assignation with Pete? Not planning a wild, passionate affair with my husband, I hope!'

Despite her naivety, Beth understood that Stella was joking. That she could not conceive of anyone wanting a wild, passionate affair with her husband. That the very thought was ridiculous. This insight into her friend's marriage made her very sad for Pete, and for Stella too.

In the absence of Pete, it was up to her to explain what she and Pete were doing here. 'We just bumped into each other in the street. I sort of dragged Pete in here. He wanted to get back home to you.' It was exactly the right thing to say. Actually, for someone as apparently innocent as Beth, she was a most accomplished deceiver. She'd spent years convincing her parents that she lived alone in a suspiciously spacious flat, coming up with endless excuses to get out of family holidays and keeping parental visits to the barest minimum.

Stella had given up watching Pete now that he had become embroiled in a full-on sugar fight with the four children who were shrieking with laughter. She didn't often see Pete with children but it always unsettled her to observe how easy he found it. And pleasurable in a way that she found incomprehensible.

It had never been a conscious decision but Stella tended to cull friends from her address book when they had children. Wherever she lived, she made their home as child-unfriendly as possible, presenting terrified parents with a massive array of breakables and valuables all at child height.

They seldom returned. And, once more, Stella had to ask herself whether this was a unilateral decision. Whether Pete might have liked more kids coming round. Or to have kids himself.

But now wasn't the time to go into disturbing subjects like this. She remembered that Pete had told her about how unhappy Beth was and how she longed to get together with Chris. She put on her most sympathetic expression and extended her hand to Beth's.

'Pete told me about how miserable you've been over Chris. What a pig!'

Beth was confused. 'I'm not sure exactly what Pete said but—'

Stella interrupted, an annoying habit which on this occasion was to save Beth from the embarrassment of landing Pete in trouble. 'I know what it's like at parties. You have a few drinks, get maudlin, then need someone to offload all your troubles on. Poor you, you got saddled with my husband, not the most compassionate of souls.'

Beth wanted to defend him but stopped, realising that it might be tactless. 'He did his best,' she said ambiguously, wishing that Pete would return as quickly as possible. She too had noticed how much fun he was having with the kids. It made him appear more attractive to her and she wondered what this said about her own unresolved feelings about having children.

Pete finally concluded his messy game and slipped a five-pound note to the waitress when he thought no one was looking, to cover the extra work that would be needed to clear up all the mess. Stella noticed. And

Beth noticed. Without realising it, the little distraction that he'd undertaken to avoid the confrontation between the two women had left both of the women with a fresh appraisal of the man they'd thought he was. If he'd known that it would cause even knottier tangles, maybe he'd have stuck to plan one and pretended to choke on a currant.

He sat back down nervously between Beth and Stella. There was no blood and neither of them seemed about to tip tea over his head. Whatever had been said had clearly not compromised him. He was inordinately grateful to Beth but saddened that, yet again, Stella had prevented them from finishing what they were talking about.

It's not my fault, he thought. I'll have to see her again, just to make sure that we're still friends and that Stella didn't say anything to upset her. Not because I want to. OK that's a lie, it's because I want to. But if Stella hadn't turned up, Beth and I might have said all we needed to say and then bid one last platonic farewell. So it's all Stella's fault.

Beth swallowed the rest of her tea, which scalded the back of her throat, and stood up. 'Well, I'd better be on my way. I can't hold you up any longer. Thanks for lending me your husband, Stella. I don't know what I would have done if I hadn't bumped into him on the street. I desperately needed someone to talk to and he saved the day.'

Thank you, Pete mouthed silently to Beth while Stella wasn't looking, appreciating her deft method of conveying roughly what had been said to Stella in their defence. He then lifted his hand to his ear, signalling that he would phone her. It seemed like an act of sheer collusion to him, purposely excluding Stella, and was perhaps his biggest betrayal so far. Even if it was all Stella's fault, he repeated to himself in a not very convincing attempt to deflect the blame.

After she'd gone, Pete turned to Stella. 'Stella, about earlier, I'm sorry and—'

Stella waved her hand to tell him that it didn't matter. She appeared to have forgotten his outburst earlier. In fact, it was not forgotten, but Stella hadn't liked where the argument was leading so she was applying diversionary tactics.

'That isn't important. Well it is important, but we can talk about that later. Actually I was pleased for an excuse to get out of the house. I think your mum and dad have had words.'

Pete frowned. That didn't sound like his parents. 'What about? They seemed perfectly happy this morning.'

Stella quickly remembered that Bill and Ann had asked her not to say anything to Pete. 'Oh I'm sure it's nothing. Your dad left his glasses somewhere and it took your mum ages to find them.'

'He's always doing that,' Pete said affectionately. Then his expression became more serious. 'But why would mum get in a bother about that? I hope nothing's up that they're not telling me about.'

Back at Stella's house the phone was ringing. Bill and Ann were sitting in the conservatory (Inuit minimalism with a hint of Scottish crofter's cottage) not talking to each other.

After the fourth ring, Bill finally spoke wearily. 'Should we answer that?'

119

'What does it matter what I think? Since when have you sought my opinion before making decisions?' Ann replied in typical wronged-wife style.

Bill refrained from turning this into another rally of accusations and recriminations. He pulled himself up from the chair (he thought it was a chair; it was in fact a sneakily disguised drinks cabinet and he'd been leaning on a button that had been producing ice cubes for the past hour).

He spent another four rings looking for the phone. It turned out to be a perfectly flat oblong of metal with two tiny holes. He picked it up apprehensively, held it in front of his mouth and spoke nervously into both ends until he worked out which was the earpiece.

'Hello?' he said.

'Who's that?' the voice at the other end demanded. This is the most annoying thing that can be said on the phone. What are you supposed to say back? If they've got the wrong number then is there any need to give them your name?

'It's Bill,' Bill replied, not knowing what else he could say.

'Bill who?' the voice asked suspiciously.

'Bill Lynch, Pete's dad.'

This did the trick. 'Oh, that Bill! Hello Bill, it's Maureen, Maureen Connor.'

'Hello Maureen, how are you?' Bill asked, having no idea who Maureen was. Ann was the names one in the marriage. He was the drinks pourer and the garden show-arounder and the washer-upper. Names weren't his thing.

'Very well, Bill. Listen, I was wondering if I could have a word with Stella.'

'Sorry, Maureen, she's out at the moment. Pete is, too. But you can give me a message if you like.' He didn't bother looking around for a pen and paper. In this house, it would probably be hanging from a chandelier somewhere. He pulled out an old receipt and the stub of pencil he used to put his bets on down at the bookie's. Something else he hadn't told Ann about. And never would.

'That's kind of you, Bill. It's about Lauren's birthday lunch. It's only two weeks away and I wanted to make sure that Stella and Pete would be coming. They came last year and the year before but I wasn't sure if they could spare the time with the new house needing all that work right now.'

Lauren's mum! That's who she was. Bill felt happier now that he knew who he was talking to. 'I'll get one of them to call you back when they're in.'

'That'll be lovely.' Then she hesitated for a second. 'I'll tell you what. Do you know what I'm thinking?'

Bill didn't. Ann was the thinking one in the marriage. He was the earner, the provider, the giver. He found ceaseless comfort in the rigid roles that a long marriage throws up.

'What's that, Maureen?'

'I was thinking about all the times Lauren has talked about you and Ann and how kind you've been to her since she's known you.'

Then Bill remembered some more. This was the mother who didn't want to know her daughter for years. Ann had taken Lauren under her wing, listened to her, complimented her, shown an interest in everything she did.

'Are you still there, Bill?' Maureen asked anxiously.

121

Bill wasn't very good at listening and thinking at the same time. 'Sorry, Maureen, I was in another world.'

'Well what I was thinking was, that I think it would be really nice for Lauren if you come too. It could be a surprise. She loves you both dearly and I want to make this birthday extra-special for her.' While this was true, she also saw the advantage of having extra guests there to diffuse any potential tension between Lauren and Eddie.

'That sounds lovely, Maureen. In two weeks, you said?'

'That's right. I'm going to make a proper party of it. Her new young man, Chris, is going to be there, so it'll be nice for him to see Lauren surrounded by all the people who love her.'

'I'll do that, Maureen. I know Ann'll be chuffed to meet you. We're both fond of Lauren. We'd give anything to see her happy.'

'Well, if all goes well, she should be happy soon,' Maureen added enigmatically before saying goodbye.

Ann wasn't chuffed. Not chuffed at all. 'I'm having my tests two days before the party. I don't know how I'm going to feel.'

'How was I supposed to know that? I'm not a mind-reader.'

Then they had the 'mind-reader' fight so popular in marriage, which ran along predictable lines, commonly started by the husband but always ending with the wife.

They stopped arguing when Stella and Pete got back and were both relieved to see that they had got over whatever it was that was bothering them. Bill passed on Maureen's message.

'That's great! I'd completely forgotten about Maureen's party for Lauren. We could do with a party, couldn't we Pete?'

Like a mallet over the head, thought Pete miserably. 'Haven't you forgotten the party we've just had? I haven't. We'll be paying for it for the next couple of months.'

Stella groaned. 'Don't be such a miseryguts. It'll do us good. And your mum and dad, too,' she added, knowing that would sway Pete after what she'd told him about their earlier altercation.

Once she'd said that, Pete had no choice but to keep quiet. Now was not the moment to tell her that they might not have much to celebrate in two weeks' time. On the day before Lauren's party, he had a meeting with the board of the company that was taking over his firm. He would learn then if he had a job or not.

'It's going to be a lovely party!' Stella exclaimed happily.

Everyone else looked doubtful.

Chapter 8

Chris was having a bad day. He'd given up leaving
messages on Lauren's phone and didn't know what to
do next. He vaguely remembered her saying that she'd
be out of town during the week; perhaps she'd planned
to go up today. He wished he'd had the foresight to get
her mobile number. He could always phone Stella to ask
her but, knowing his luck, it would be his new 'best mate'
Pete who answered and he'd end up having to discuss
whether Tottenham would field the four-four-two or the
five-two-three on Saturday or something equally macho.

So he decided to wait until next weekend and then try
again. He didn't think she was necessarily avoiding his
calls. She'd seemed friendly enough when they'd been
out and was certainly trying to clear the air between them
before her strange mother breezed in and invited him to
Lauren's birthday party. It was obvious, even to a man as
unversed in subtlety as Chris, that it *was* a birthday party.
So Lauren must have said something to her mother in the
kitchen to give her the impression that she was intending
to see him again.

He was still ambivalent. It was hard for him to think
objectively about Lauren without being reminded of all
the entanglements into which she had inadvertently led
him. And if he could turn back the clock, he might well

not have bothered to agree to see Lauren in the first place. At least he wouldn't have to go to a football match on Saturday.

But she had a certain unusual appeal. There was a neediness in her that she obviously didn't know she possessed. Rather like Beth. Yes, he concluded. I'd like to see her again.

If I could get hold of her, he thought drily. He'd gone over the evening in his head and, as far as he could recall, he hadn't done anything wrong. So she would have no reason to avoid him. The poor, dear, sweet man had no idea that what he had done was irrelevant. It always was. It was what he was *perceived* to have done that had provoked Lauren into launching an all-out assault on her mother. And running off to the Lake District.

He was blissfully unaware of all these frenetic activities but this didn't help to disperse the unease he was feeling at the abrupt halt in communications. And it came on top of a growing crisis at work.

Chris had been drawn into teaching by the noblest of motives. He believed absolutely that education was the only equaliser. He had enjoyed the privileges of private school and only at college was he finally exposed to the true picture of education available to the general population.

In those days, private schooling was not so widespread. Everywhere he heard the same thing. The luck of the draw that had taken a few good teachers into dead-end schools. Teachers who had gone on to inspire and motivate the lucky children who could so easily have slipped down the academic plughole under a more indifferent teacher.

He'd had no idea that opportunity was such a hit-and-miss business.

He started looking at the defeated expressions on the young faces of the unemployed coming out of the social security office or whatever the government was calling it nowadays. He wondered how many of them could have been reached, touched, picked up and propelled by the right teacher at the right time. And he decided that he would be that right teacher. That he would reach, touch, pick up and propel as many no-hope kids as he could towards a future which offered even the faintest glimmer of hope.

It had seemed inevitable when he found himself in a school for children who had been excluded from other schools. The ones the teachers refused to teach. He relished the challenge. And he wasn't unrealistic in his expectations. He didn't for one minute believe that the belligerent faces of his pupils, barely managing to contain the anger that boiled underneath, would one day wear doe-eyed smiles of adoring appreciation. That all the thugs would become lawyers and vicars and ask him to be godparent to their children.

He just wanted to rescue them from futility, to keep them out of trouble until they had found their feet and could survive or, preferably, do better than survive. And some of his students had gone on to get jobs, a heroic achievement for them. Some had stayed out of prison and, in those cases, that was a positive result too. But the rewards trickled through. Chris loved this work passionately.

Now it was under threat. While the successes had been modest, the failures had been dramatic. Recently, two of

Chris's pupils had taken part in an armed robbery where a bank clerk had been shot. It wasn't something that looked good in an Ofsted report. It came after a long line of pupils' offences which had escalated in seriousness.

It had been decided by the local council that, if one more incident of this kind should happen, they would seriously consider closing the school. The more persistent offenders would be transferred back to the young offenders' institutions to which they'd been sentenced before being thrown the lifeline of this unique school.

The rest would be returned to the mainstream schools which had been unable to handle these boys (and few girls) in the first place. If this happened, and it was looking fairly certain that it would, Chris had been told he could either look for similar work in special units in other boroughs or he could be given a job in one of the many struggling local schools that were crying out for teachers of his ability.

All of the kids were aware of the situation and Chris could only hope that this threat would be enough to halt the slide.

He'd planned to talk to Lauren about it last night but the evening didn't quite go according to plan. He needed someone to talk to now. He immediately thought of Beth, but she was gone. It still took him by surprise when he realised that he no longer lived with Beth. She had played such a big part in his life for such a long time that she had become an automatic response to any need that arose. They had developed their own rhythm, their own way of being together that suited them both. They knew how to talk to each other and how to listen. They'd moulded each other into true partners and it was like an amputation to lose her.

'Well, you didn't exactly lose her, you dumped her,' Izzy pointed out acidly. Chris had phoned her up and asked her to meet him for dinner. Izzy knew that she would always only be his reserve, called upon when the first choice was not around. She didn't mind this. She was deeply fond of Chris and still grateful to him for staying at home all those years ago until she could get away herself. She needed him still, to share in the madness of their childhood and their parents, to replay their common experiences until she could make sense of them. Looking at Chris, professional, well adjusted, socially acceptable, gave her hope that she too could one day shake off the eccentricity that she had reluctantly inherited.

It had started with the name and gone downhill from there. She sometimes believed that her parents had only had a second child because it seemed ludicrous to have a Tristan without an Isolde. At least she never had to wonder if they would have preferred a boy. She always felt wanted.

'You are magnificent!' her daddy had said. 'Such presence, such passion!' Mummy had said. She waited in vain for them to call her pretty or sweet. Then came the disappointment when she realised that it would never happen because she was neither sweet nor pretty.

From that moment, she became determined to avoid ever being judged by conventional standards. She embraced the extreme possibilities of altering her appearance so that she would always shock, intrigue, disconcert. Nobody would ever ask themselves if Izzy was pretty while they were too busy wondering if it had hurt to have butterflies tattooed behind her knees.

When she was eighteen, her brother moved to London and she hoped that he might ask her to share a flat with him there. He didn't so, to spite him, she chose to go to university in Scotland, as far away from him as she could. As she was only eighteen, she didn't know that such acts of spite are seldom acknowledged or taken personally by men unless signposted and explained in big letters.

She then spent three miserable years missing her brother and blaming him for every bad decision she made. She took her misery out on her hair, subjecting it to outrageous colour changes. It never survived and she was left with only a sparse covering of brown fluff on her head in her thirties. She made it into a statement.

'What are you doing with your life?' Chris had asked her periodically as she flitted in and out of jobs, relationships and towns.

Izzy avoided such questions. She was a drifter looking for answers. She had lovers, many lovers. They lasted from between one night and a few weeks. Seldom more. She always left them before they began to judge her.

'You could be an actress!' they would say. 'You could be a dancer!' 'You could be a model!'

And she tried them all, achieving no fame but a reasonable income. Everyone she met envied her such an apparently glamorous lifestyle. It couldn't satisfy her but she didn't know if anything could.

She harboured a secret yearning to be ordinary but she never had the courage to explore it. She longed to be conventional but didn't know how. She was currently a professional dog-walker, dragging as many as twenty dogs to the park twice a day. It was surprisingly lucrative and she found that dogs were not as judgemental as most people.

It was Chris who kept her sane, gave her hope. She watched him meticulously, wondering how someone with the same upbringing as she'd had could end up so normal. One day when the time was right, she was going to ask him how he did it.

Tonight, as they had done on so many other occasions, they got drunk together and began performing duets from *The Ring* until the pub landlord chucked them out. They were drowning out Britney Spears on the jukebox and that would never do.

They staggered back to Izzy's flat nearby where Chris decided to sleep on the sofa rather than attempt to get home on the bus. Izzy left her bedroom door open so they could talk while they were both in bed.

'We used to do this all the time when we were kids, do you remember?' Izzy asked sleepily.

'I remember you refused to go to sleep and you kept talking until Mum or Dad came and shut both our doors.'

'I hated it when they did that, didn't you, Tris?' Izzy asked.

Even in his drunken fog, Chris sensed that disagreeing would not go down too well. Izzy had driven him crazy when they were kids. He'd known that she was not happy and had tried his best to help her, letting her tag along sometimes when he was out with his friends. But she was just too weird. He was embarrassed by her.

And at night, he wanted to concentrate on the forbidden radio under the covers. Sometimes, he just let her ramble on, not bothering to listen, occasionally popping his head out to utter a sympathetic grunt. He hadn't known at the time that she was indulging in some of her more extreme flights of fancy and she took his neutral responses as approval. He often wondered if she might have avoided some of her wilder life choices if he'd told her not to be so ridiculous in those early years.

So now, although he desperately wanted to go to sleep, he forced himself to keep the conversation going for a little longer. For Izzy's sake.

'So what are you going to do about Lauren?' she asked. They'd spent most of the evening talking about his job and his fears that one more student crime would close the school. She had huge respect for his integrity and envied him for feeling so strongly about anything. Or anyone. He'd mentioned Lauren in passing and she wondered if it was a touchy subject.

Chris thought about Lauren. Again. 'I don't know, Izzy. I like her but frankly I don't know if it's worth all the hassle.'

'What sort of hassle?' Izzy asked.

Chris hesitated. He hadn't told his sister the whole preposterous story about the Pisces necklace and the lie and the rest. It was all seeming more and more ludicrous as the time dragged on, making resolution look less and less likely. Also it seemed disloyal to Lauren. Izzy was very loyal to Chris and would not think too kindly of Lauren for causing her brother any kind of anxiety. And if he was to continue seeing Lauren, he wanted Izzy to like her.

'Oh, nothing much. I'm just having trouble getting hold of her. She's out of town and I forgot to get her mobile number. I just wish I could talk to her, to make sure she's OK after last night.'

This was the last thing he managed to say before he fell asleep. Izzy gave this some thought. If that's all that's giving him grief, I'm sure I can help him out. I'll get him the mobile number.

On Sunday morning, after Chris had staggered off home to do some marking, she called Beth. I mustn't call her 'Batty', she repeated silently to herself as she waited for the phone to be picked up.

'Hello?' Beth's voice whispered.

'Hi Beth, It's Izzy. I hope I haven't woken you up.'

'You have actually. I've been on call all night and I only got to bed an hour ago. And I've got to be back at the hospital in a couple of hours' time.' At least I don't have to be polite to the witch now that I've split up with Chris, she thought.

Izzy ignored the hostility and put it down to fatigue. Besides, she had a mission and she would not be swayed by Beth's stroppiness.

'Sorry about that, Beth,' she said, not sounding at all sorry. 'Anyway, I've got a bit of an emergency myself. I need to get in touch with the people whose party you went to last week with Tristan. Stella and Pete, I think they're called?'

Beth became fully alert at the sound of Pete's name. 'Why do you need to speak to them? You don't even know them.' She didn't know why she was suspicious. She thought it might be to do with the growing unease she experienced whenever she thought of Pete. They hadn't done anything wrong, not by the most puritanical

132

standards, but she had come away from the tea shop absolutely consumed by the what-if game.

She couldn't stop thinking about him. It was even interfering with her work by keeping her awake. She'd lied to Izzy. She'd been in bed for hours, she just hadn't been able to get to sleep. She knew she was being foolish. She was a doctor, she could discern facts from fantasy. The facts were simple: 1) Pete was married and showed no signs of wanting to be otherwise, however dissatisfied he was with his marriage; 2) she had just come out of the first and only serious relationship of her life. She knew that she could not make sensible decisions so soon after Chris's departure; 3) she was still trying to come up with number three – two facts didn't seem enough.

And now Izzy was stirring her up again. She assumed that Izzy was acting on Chris's behalf and that it had something to do with the girl at the party, the one who'd been so keen to go and see *Pravda* with Chris. She'd been surprised at the pang she'd experienced when she saw Chris with someone else. Was it jealousy? It made no sense to her since she'd been so relieved when Chris announced that he was moving out.

Beth's greatest asset in dealing with modern life was that she'd never read women's magazines or watched soap operas. She hadn't got a clue about conventional reactions to emotional upheaval. She didn't know that she was entitled to feel traumatised at the end of a long live-in relationship, however happy she was to be living alone again. She didn't know that the Yellow Pages was stuffed with hundreds of names of counsellors who earned a living from lapping up the pain of people in Beth's position.

In her years of medical practice, she had never come across anyone dying from a broken heart and consequently she had no place for it in her personal index of suitable responses. She had felt detached when he'd left, sad, a bit lost but not devastated, which she read as evidence that she probably hadn't loved him. But then she also recognised that her instant attachment to Pete Lynch was totally out of character. She hadn't worked that out yet.

But now she thought about it, she wondered if her confusion was linked to seeing Chris look at another woman the way he used to look at her.

She was tired. Her eyes were sore. She loathed Izzy and her affectations that Chris had always defended as endearing characteristics. This was the last person she wanted to talk to when she had so many difficult questions to answer. She gave her Stella's number and put the phone down without saying goodbye. That gave her pleasure.

Izzy looked at the receiver with dislike. What's got you? she thought, unsympathetic to Beth's claim of tiredness. She'd always thought Beth was a waste of space (apart from being a life-saving doctor which she grudgingly admitted was a fairly worthwhile use of her time) and not worthy of Chris. More to the point, she wasn't worthy of Izzy. Because Izzy was looking forward to having a sister-in-law one day. She'd never been very good at making friends for herself and had relied on Chris to supply them. She knew she was abrasive and lacking in the more basic girly skills that female friendships seemed to require. But she liked to think that other women might begin to warm to her after a compulsory prolonged exposure.

And it seemed that this would only happen through Chris.

After the long list of vacuous, smiling airheads that Chris had introduced to Izzy for years, she'd been excited to hear about his new doctor girlfriend. The first meeting had been a disaster. Chris was obviously infatuated with Beth and it didn't take much to work out why. Beth was beautiful. And clever. And nice. And successful. And loved by a good man.

Throughout that first evening, Izzy had waited for Beth to strike up conversations, to show an interest in Izzy, to open up about herself. And Beth had just sat there, smiling beatifically at Chris. It was creepy, in Izzy's opinion. And there was no excuse for it, what with Beth's professional status. Surely she spoke to her patients?

Beth had not actually been feeling beatific and would have been surprised to hear that Izzy so misread her expression. She simply hadn't known what to say in the face of this astonishing woman about whom she'd heard so much from Chris. All the prior knowledge in the world could not have prepared her for the reality of Izzy.

'Don't be put off by her appearance,' Chris had warned her.

Yeah, right. It was like meeting someone with a disfigurement and trying not to stare at it. Except that Izzy's disfigurement was self-inflicted and all-encompassing. She was going through her Adam and the Ants phase (over ten years after it was fashionable) and she was dressed and made up entirely in black and silver. If there was anything underneath that stark exterior, Beth didn't get a chance to discover. The smile had been her only way of preventing herself from betraying her

135

sense of astonishment that Chris should have such a sister.

The great tragedy of Izzy and Beth was that neither of them possessed a sufficiently developed social awareness to recognise how alike they were. Both had felt alienated through their unconventional upbringings. Both had trouble forming friendships and both badly needed a good friend. They were being thrown together through Chris and had a great opportunity to forge a cautious bond, comparing notes on how they each dealt with life as an outsider in a world that demanded conformity.

And if Chris had not wasted so many years with women who, in an attempt to please him with their passivity, had taught him nothing about the complexity and fragility of female consciousness, he might have been able to bridge the gulf between the two.

Five years of tense contact followed between Beth and Izzy. They were at their most civilised when Chris was about, competing to be the most polite and tolerant. But when Chris was out of the room, guards were lowered and snide comments were exchanged as each woman came to learn the other's weak points.

From what Izzy had seen of Lauren, she at least seemed to have a bit of life in her. And she seemed normal, a very admirable quality indeed in Izzy's eyes. Maybe if Chris had told her of Lauren's crazy lie and the equally crazy reasons for it, Izzy might not have gone to so much trouble to facilitate the romance on her brother's behalf.

But he didn't so she did.

'Hello? Is that Stella?'

'No, this is her mother-in law. I'm afraid Stella has gone out. Can I give her a message?'

'Perhaps you can. My name's Isolde Fallon. My brother Chris used to go out with Beth Savile, who used to be Stella's oncologist, and they were both at the party last week.'

Ann waited for Izzy to go on. She'd got lost before Izzy reached Beth's connection with Stella. She had other things on her mind and could not handle labyrinthine messages. 'Oh er, right then, Isolde, I'll get Stella to phone you when she gets back.'

'No, no,' Izzy said irritably. 'I don't want her to phone me, she doesn't even know me.'

Ann was regretting answering the phone in the first place. 'Then what is the message?' she asked, sounding as irritable as Isolde.

Why is everyone so tetchy? Izzy asked herself. 'I just need to get hold of the mobile phone number of someone else at the party. Lauren something, I don't know her last name.'

Ann hesitated. She felt a bit uneasy giving out someone else's phone number. But Bill was standing in front of her, waving his arms about. 'Come and help me, the smoke alarms are all going off and I can't even see them in this madhouse. Where the hell are Stella and Pete? How long does it take to go and get the Sunday papers?'

So Ann quickly rummaged around until she found Stella's address book in a kitchen drawer. She found Lauren's entry and picked up the phone again.

'Sorry, there doesn't seem to be a note of Lauren's mobile number. Just her home number and her mother's home number.'

Izzy remembered that Chris had met Lauren's mum. She sounded crazy. That was fine. Izzy knew all about crazy. 'If you give me her mum's number, I can call her and get the mobile number from her.'

'Well, I'm not sure I should . . .' Ann didn't know what to do. Bill was now waving his arms even more dramatically and the noise from the smoke alarms appeared to be getting louder.

Izzy had an idea. 'I understand how you might not want to hand out numbers. So how about you phoning Lauren's mum and getting the mobile number and calling me back?'

Ann would have felt much happier doing this but she couldn't leave Bill to deal with the alarms by himself any longer. He wasn't very good at emergencies. That was her department. 'Oh I'm sure it will be all right. I'll give you Maureen's number and you can ring her yourself.'

So she gave the number to Izzy and rushed off to help Bill. In all the chaos, she completely forgot to mention it to Stella.

'Chris's sister!' Maureen exclaimed in delight later that night when Izzy finally got through to her. 'How nice! Lauren mentioned that she met you. And your brother is such a lovely man! It was great to meet him the other day!'

'He liked meeting you too,' Izzy replied in a rare moment of social aplomb. It's amazing how pleasant and conventional I can be when I'm acting on somebody else's behalf, she thought.

'So what was it you said you wanted, Isolde?' Maureen asked Izzy.

Izzy hadn't thought this through. It was going to sound strange that she needed Lauren's mobile phone number for Chris when Maureen clearly thought that Lauren and Chris were as good as engaged.

'Oh, well it's a surprise I'm planning for Chris's birthday. I wanted to talk to Lauren about it when Chris isn't there. So I need her mobile phone number.' She was very proud of this lie. It was unrehearsed and yet utterly plausible. Maureen agreed.

'Oh what a thoughtful girl you are! Here's the number then. Have you got a pen ready?' As she read out Lauren's mobile number, Maureen had an idea. She was having lots of ideas at the moment. And she gave in to all of them, good or bad, to make up for all the ideas she didn't bother having while Lauren was growing up.

'I was just thinking, you mentioning birthdays,' she said to Izzy. 'I don't know if your brother mentioned it, but we're having a little party for Lauren in a couple of weeks' time. Normally it's just us family and close friends, but this year I want it to be special so I'm inviting some of Lauren's other chums along. So seeing as how you've met Lauren and she and your brother are, well, whatever, why don't you come along too?'

Izzy was startled by this invitation. But she couldn't think of a good reason to decline. She'd used up all her imaginative faculties. 'Oh, well thanks. That's very kind of you. I'd love to come.'

'Another one for the party!' Izzy heard Maureen call to someone in the background. Unless Maureen was talking to herself, something Izzy was partial to. 'Now you give me your address and I'll send you directions. Lauren will be so pleased when she finds out what I've done! Oh and don't tell Lauren if you see her. Let's make it a surprise!'

Izzy agreed.

After putting the phone down, Maureen turned to Eddie. 'Isn't that lovely! Our Lauren's young man's sister is coming to the party. And she told me that it was Chris's birthday coming up too. We'll make it a double celebration and surprise them both!'

'Is his birthday on the same day then?' Eddie asked Maureen, knowing her well enough to be unconvinced by her interpretation of vague pieces of information.

Maureen thought about this for about a second. 'I'm not sure but it must be round about then because she was planning a surprise for his birthday and she wouldn't do that if it wasn't really soon.'

Eddie was not so sure. 'Not necessarily. If she was planning something very complicated it might take months.'

Maureen wasn't paying attention to him. She was already flicking through her book of novelty party cakes looking for something appropriate for a teacher who was in love with a telecommunications consultant. 'Maybe I'll just do a big cake with two hearts and their initials.'

'Mo, love, didn't you say that your Lauren had only just started going out with this chap? Isn't it a bit premature for hearts and joint cakes?' Eddie's role had become that of the voice of reason within days of meeting Maureen. Unfortunately, his voice was not yet loud enough for Maureen to hear him clearly.

Maureen smiled at him patronisingly. 'You forget that I'm her mother and I know her. I saw them together. He's the one, I'm sure!'

* * *

I don't need the phone on, there's nobody I want to hear from, Lauren thought. She switched off her mobile in a grand gesture. The gesture was essentially futile since reception was practically non-existent on Scafell Pike. But it was meaningful to Lauren. She was removing herself from the things that chained her to London. She hadn't put on any make-up and her hair was scooped into a tight ponytail and tucked under a bobble hat. She was blissfully relaxed and enjoying the sensation of speaking freely without concern for what Richard thought of her. Turning off the phone was cutting off the last link to her other life.

She wasn't even wearing her own clothes, being woefully understocked in anything thermal, waterproof or otherwise suitable for climbing a snowy mountain in February. Richard had opened up the shop and kitted her out in the most up to date outdoor clothes.

She'd looked in the mirror and wondered who the woman in the reflection was. It wasn't her. It was someone younger and fresher, someone natural and unspoiled, someone straightforward. Not her at all. She was wearing a yellow jacket made of a fabric apparently tested on an Antarctic expedition – it was good to know that if she should be buried under a collapsing igloo, she would not die of hypothermia. She also wore red trousers made of a thin material that rustled when she walked. Her hat and gloves were black and thick. Her boots, solid yet light. She felt sexless. That in turn was liberating.

She felt guilty that, in the twenty-four hours that she'd been here, she hadn't once switched on her computer. No, she didn't feel guilty at all. She felt wonderful. But she felt that she ought to be feeling guilty. She'd fully intended to do some preparatory work on her project over the weekend, especially since she hadn't done anything on the train on Friday afternoon. This wasn't like her at all. She'd always been the queen of preparation. It tended to minimise the possibility of careless mistakes. And when you are a careless person by nature, that possibility has to be considered at all times.

Richard gave her a whistle, a sachet of dehydrated food and something that looked like a tinfoil roasting bag.

'What's all this for?' she asked, alarmed at the implications of the words 'survival bag' printed over the tinfoil.

'It's just in case we get separated or something happens to me.' If the aim had been to persuade Lauren to move closer, he could not have said anything more effective.

'Like what?' Lauren asked.

'We're moving across some slippery paths. It's easy to fall, and there are some quite steep drops up there.'

Lauren took hold of his arm. 'Listen, if you fall anywhere, I'm going to jump after you. I'm not good at heroic acts of solo endurance on mountains.'

They both smiled in sudden mutual understanding. They liked each other.

After an hour of gentle walking up the slightest of inclines, Lauren thought that her lungs were going to implode. 'Can we stop for a while, do you think?' she asked, bending over to relax her spine which was crying out for mercy. She collapsed on to the grass without dignity.

Richard suppressed a laugh. 'I thought you businesswomen worked out at gyms and had personal trainers. You're not very fit, are you?'

Lauren tried to slow her breathing down so that she

could get a sentence out without hyperventilating. 'I'll have you know that I can hold my own in any aerobics class. And if you happened to have some 70s and 80s disco tracks on you I could dance around my rucksack until night falls. But walking up sheer slopes like this is unnatural. And there's something about this air. It must be the greenhouse effect or something that makes it unbreathable.' She stopped and looked at Richard, who was staring at her in amusement.

'Now what are you thinking?' she asked.

'I'm wondering if you're delirious in which case I should get you stretchered off the mountain before your toes and fingers start dropping off, or if you are just deranged. In a very attractive way, of course.'

His eyes sparkled as he gently helped her to her feet and encouraged her to continue. My mum is going to LOVE him, Lauren thought as she felt the warmth of his body supporting her over the more difficult sections of the path.

'It's my birthday in two weeks' time,' she blurted out when she had recovered her breath sufficiently to speak normally.

'Is that a hint?' Richard replied, finding it hard work keeping up with the increasingly mercurial switches in conversation.

'No, no. You've already given me hundreds of pounds' worth of clothes—'

'Which you will not be able to wear anywhere in London without looking ridiculous,' Richard interrupted.

'And you barely know me. In fact I forbid you to buy me a present. Or a card or anything.'

Yes, Richard thought. She's deranged. And the crazier

she gets, the more attracted I am to her. I suppose it's inevitable after Cindy.

Cindy was not crazy. She exuded common sense, down-to-earth, matter-of-fact grounding. Exactly the sort of woman he'd expected to marry. Apart from the fact that she was American, which to him made her a cultural loose cannon after a life spent entirely in one village.

His parents had met while walking the Pennine Way. After years of saving, they managed to buy their first shop, three months before Richard's birth and ten years after his sister Anita's birth.

'At last we've got a son. He'll be able to take over the business one day,' his father used to say.

'If he wants to,' his mother pointed out.

'Of course he'll want to,' his father would retort, 'his sister won't be able to run a business.' This was a long time ago; don't judge them by today's standards.

Of course he was instantly resented by Anita who had always assumed that she would one day run the business that her parents had talked about all her life. He tried hard to win her forgiveness for being born but he failed. She was the first of a series of women he tried to please. Like Lauren, he wasn't very good at pleasing others. He decided to save his passion, his deepest feelings, for the mountains that never demanded apologies.

Out of loyalty to his parents, Richard never mentioned his dream of travelling the world and climbing the big mountains. When they died within weeks of each other, he left college and moved into the shop straight away, not as a matter of sacrifice, but because of who he was.

He was a good man, paralysed and defined at the same time by his rigid sense of obligation.

Anita showed her resentment at being ousted from her inheritance by marrying the first man who wasn't put off by her muscular calves. In their wills, her parents left Anita their collection of antique climbing paraphernalia including some historic crampons. What she did with them is unrecorded. But she took them with her when she left Tendale and Richard never heard from her again.

When Cindy walked into his shop, he had been running and building up the business for two years. She was a graduate on a walking holiday in the Lake District and pitifully unprepared for the winter when she asked Richard to recommend a full kit. Then she asked him if he would act as her guide. Then she asked him to marry her.

'I know about you Englishmen, I've seen *Brideshead Revisited*,' she said once. It was not meant as a joke. Before she came to England, she was already half in love with the idea of marrying someone called Sebastian or Hugh. Richard represented a deviation from her plans but she saw his potential.

She mistook his lack of ambition for weakness. She intended to provide him with her strength. She mistook his cavalier approach to business as inexperience. She intended to provide him with a schedule of proposed sweeping changes to his working practices, courtesy of her MBA. She mistook his devotion to the outdoors for a sad response to loneliness. She intended to provide him with constant company. And as for children – there were no misunderstandings there, they never talked about it. Until they'd been married for six years.

'Do you regret marrying me now you know I can't have children?' Cindy had asked him.

'No, not at all,' Richard had reassured her. And this was true. Her inability to have children was the least of it. He regretted marrying her because she'd mistaken him for somebody completely different and couldn't mask her disappointment when she discovered the truth.

After ten years, she resented Richard, hated him, for not changing into the man she'd intended him to become. After fifteen years, they were completely indifferent to each other. She left Richard for a widower with a dicky heart but a very healthy fortune.

Richard credited her with the expansion of his shops into other villages. He continued running the business, as his parents had always expected him to do. He rediscovered the joys of walking without the accompanying nasal New Jersey twang of Cindy giving a running commentary on his failings as a man, husband and empire builder.

When she left, she made a point of leaving all her outdoor clothes from her Gore-Tex jacket to the thermal vest that Lauren had thrown at him earlier. 'I won't be needing these,' she said icily. She tossed the rest of her belongings into the car she'd rented and drove off very, very quickly.

That was five years ago. He became aware of Lauren waving her hand in front of his face. 'Earth to Richard!' He shook his head to shift himself out of his reverie. 'Sorry,' he said. 'I was just thinking.'

'What about?' Lauren asked. She knew that this was a controversial question and she didn't care. Must be the oxygen deprivation, she thought. I've never not cared about anything before.

He smiled. Sadly? Lauren couldn't be sure. 'About all the stuff I cleared out today.'

'Your ex-wife's underwear?' Lauren asked. She and Richard exchanged mischievous glances. Now they didn't just like each other, they understood each other.

Richard didn't say anything. No need. What a wonderful feeling that was.

They carried on walking. 'How old are you, Richard?' Lauren asked at the peak of Scafell Pike. She must be worrying about the age difference, he concluded, when he saw her lost in thought. He was right, but it was the age difference between him and her mother that was on her mind.

Forty-eight he answered, watching carefully for her reaction. She seemed to be doing some kind of mental arithmetic.

'Right,' she said vaguely.

'Why did you want to know?' he asked boldly.

Lauren shrugged. 'Just wondering. I haven't said anything tactless for at least half an hour and I didn't want you to start getting used to this new, discreet me. I thought a nice inappropriate reference to age was overdue.'

'Thank you for the reassurance,' Richard said. 'I was getting a bit concerned. For a moment, I thought you might actually be relaxing.'

Lauren poked her tongue out at him. 'Thank *you*.' She stared at the vast expanse of beauty and stillness that surrounded her. I wonder if there are views like this in New York? she asked herself. She didn't bother trying to come up with an answer. I'll think about it later, she decided. Tomorrow, the weekend, soon.

'So will you come to my party, Richard?' she asked.

'I mean, it won't be anything big, not even a party, just lunch with my mum and a couple of friends. But I'd really like you to be there.'

'I wouldn't miss it for the world,' he replied.

Chapter 9

Pete and Stella walked back from the newsagent in silence. It wasn't a comfortable silence. It took Pete a few minutes to work out why. In all the years he had known Stella, it had always been her responsibility to initiate and maintain conversations between them. And for every hundred words that she spouted, he would be expected to respond with five. It hadn't been planned or written into the wedding ceremony; it was just the way it had worked out as it did for so many married couples.

He thought they'd resolved the tension from yesterday. She had forced him to expand on the subject of Beth and her apparent obsession with her ex-boyfriend. In an unconscious act of self-defence, Pete had ended up exaggerating Beth's need to talk to him, portraying Beth as a would-be stalker, deranged from being rejected, unable to think or talk about anything except Chris.

Stella had shaken her head in disbelief. 'It's a good thing you're going out with Chris next week. It'll give you a chance to talk it over with him.'

Pete looked alarmed. 'I'm only going out with him because you made me say that it was something we'd talked about. You forced me into it.'

'Whatever. Anyway, it's all worked out for the best. You'll probably have a great time. Did I ever tell you

149

I went out with a Tottenham fan when I was younger?'

Only a million times, Pete thought uncharitably. 'I think so,' he answered.

'Every single girl in my class wanted him to ask them out but it was me whom he asked,' she said, still proud of her first conquest at the age of sixteen. Pete had never let on that he'd heard the rest of the story from her brothers. Apparently, she'd discovered that the boy was a Tottenham fan. She'd taken most of her savings out of the building society and spent it on the full supporter's gear. She then took to walking casually past the youth club near to closing time in her blue and white regalia.

When he emerged, she ignored him, conscious of his admiring gaze following her down Balham High Road.

He'd run after her. 'I didn't know you were a Spurs fan,' he'd observed, clearly impressed.

She'd blinked coolly. 'You never asked.'

He was her first love and, although he treated her appallingly, her confidence shot up at the acquisition of so desirable a boyfriend in the eyes of her peers.

This set the tone for the rest of her life as she learned to wear whatever uniform was necessary to win over an unenthusiastic audience. She became the queen of disguise. In fact when Pete first woke up and saw Stella in her Winnie the Pooh nightshirt and scrubbed face, he experienced a moment of panic that he'd seduced her younger sister.

Stella was rummaging around in one of the hundreds of packing cases that littered the house. 'I think I might even have some of the gear somewhere. Hat, scarf, that sort of thing. You won't look so out of place then.'

'Why should I look out of place?' Pete asked, finding everything that Stella said intensely annoying.

'Well, you've told Chris you're a fan so you can't exactly turn up in your Paul Smith trousers and M and S jumper.'

'It's February. It will be freezing cold. Knowing my luck it will be snowing as well. I will be wearing six layers of my thickest clothes and I won't care if I look like a complete pillock. Can we drop the subject please?'

Stella had dropped the subject but she hadn't pushed it out of her mind. It was the only thing she could think of. Because she knew that Pete was hiding something from her.

Pete had never indulged in more than the most cursory of polite chitchat with any of her friends. She used to moan about the fact to Lauren. 'I sometimes think he comes across as rude but he's just shy. I do wish he'd make a bit more of an effort, though.'

Even with Lauren, whom he'd met at the same time as Stella at university, conversation was kept to a superficial level. He was genuinely interested in her job, the only person Lauren knew who was, and occasionally cut out articles on telecommunications that he thought might interest her. But he could never talk to her for more than five or ten minutes, until the subject turned to him, in fact. Then he would revert to his role of mine host, topping up glasses, smiling reassuringly at Stella, rescuing the furniture and carpets from squashed tortilla chips.

And when someone refuses to open up about themselves, it's very hard to take an interest in them. There's a massive difference between being enigmatic and being anti-social. Pete veered strongly towards the latter personality type.

Stella found herself thinking back to the party. At the time, she'd been too preoccupied with the mini-drama of Lauren's fib to give Pete's attention to Beth any serious thought. His excuse had made sense. Perhaps Beth was upset about Chris leaving her. But then she thought back to when Beth had arrived at the party. She and Chris had seemed relaxed. He'd gone off to dump their coats in a designated bedroom and got lost. So she'd had a few minutes alone in the kitchen with Beth.

What had they talked about? Stella had asked herself. How had Beth seemed? The truth was that Beth had been absolutely fine. A little vague about what she would do next after such a long relationship. But her work was so involving that she had decided to concentrate on that for a while. If she'd had unhealthy obsessions festering away, wouldn't a sign of this have slipped out in front of Stella? They were friends, for goodness' sake. And Beth had been her doctor! She'd seen her through the most terrifying experience of her life. I mean, why would anyone keep secrets in such a close friendship? Stella thought.

And more importantly, why would she decide to unburden herself to Pete, a veritable Vulcan of suppressed emotions? Stella even called him Mr Spock sometimes, when he was being particularly reluctant to discuss anything apart from the FTSE Index or the electricity bill. Admittedly, she was sometimes less than keen herself to talk about the emotional issues Pete on occasion raised, but then he always chose the wrong time and the wrong subject. She didn't like being put on the spot like that so she tended to steer the conversation into safer waters.

No matter how many ways she played the scene in her imagination, Stella simply could not imagine how Beth and Pete had ended up in a soul-searching exchange worthy of Oprah Winfrey.

And then bumping into each other in the street like that? The explanation had been perfectly reasonable. But afterwards, when Stella was stripping an armoire down and the rhythmic sanding motion had focused her concentration, she went through the events leading up to the fortuitous meeting in the High Street: Pete's 'tantrum', the small fact of his imminent redundancy that he'd not got round to mentioning, storming out of the house, which he'd never done before. It was all painfully calculated. And suspicious. And it could only mean one thing.

Pete must have a serious health concern that he wanted to discuss with Beth, since she was the only doctor friend they had. And she was an oncologist. The 'c' word.

As they walked home with the papers, Stella was trying to come up with a way of encouraging Pete to tell her what was on his mind. He was so ready to lose his temper at the moment that she knew she had to be subtle in her approach. And she could do that because she entirely understood why he was doing this.

After all, the reason she'd become friends with Beth was because Beth had been so understanding about her own health problems. And in the beginning Stella hadn't discussed that with Pete either. She'd wanted to get the facts clear before she burdened Pete with her fears. Maybe that's not how married couples should carry on but it was how Pete and Stella did things. And marriages didn't come much stronger than theirs, everybody said so.

Also, she had to hide all her suspicions from Pete. She had to go along with this stupid story of Beth and her hysterical separation anxiety. If Pete suspected that Stella was on to him, it could make things worse. She knew how it felt to be scared of cancer. How you look for any excuse to retreat into denial. Whatever was wrong with Pete, at least he was doing something about it. Even if it was just an off-the-record discussion with Beth. She didn't want to push him into denying and burying his symptoms.

But Stella was scared. If Pete was ill, she wanted to know what she was up against. She couldn't ask Beth, because Beth was too professional to betray Pete's confidence. And she couldn't ask Pete because he would just shout at her and deny that anything was the matter.

Then she had a brilliant idea. Chris Fallon! He and Pete were going to that football match next week. She could ask him to try and sound Pete out about his health. He would understand her concerns, surely.

Yes, that's what she would do, she would meet up with Chris before next Saturday and plead her case. In the meanwhile, she resolved not to let on that she was aware of his little deception. If he was worried about himself, the best thing she could do for him was distract him by getting him to worry about someone else.

She took Pete's arm and looked at him warmly. 'I was miles away there! I've been thinking, Pete. I'm worried about your mum and dad. They told me not to say anything but I think you have a right to know.'

*   *   *

154

'Why didn't you tell me, Mum?'

Ann glared at Stella, who blushed at being on the receiving end of such ferocity. 'It's just as I told your father, there didn't seem any point in worrying anybody about anything until I got the results of the tests.'

This didn't appease Pete and it looked as if it was going to set Bill off as well. Stella decided to intervene swiftly. All this talk about secret symptoms and tests made her think of Pete and his own health crisis. Anxious to protect him from a subject that was already causing him such distress, she quickly moved the discussion on, taking the opportunity to display her own sympathetic standpoint to such an attitude.

'I can understand that, Pete, can't you? Besides, maybe it's the money side of things we ought to be talking about. It's not as if we can do anything about your mum until she's been to the hospital but surely we can help out financially.'

Bill snorted, also angry with Stella for betraying their trust. Both Bill and Ann had forgotten that it was their agreement, albeit reluctant, to go along with Pete's deception of Stella in the first place that had forced them to reveal their own secrets.

'I hardly think you're in a position to help us out financially, Stella, since it's only because of you and Pete that we're in this position at all.' It was Pete's turn to glare this time. 'It's no use looking at me like that, son, I told you at the time you should tell Stella what the situation is.'

Stella looked from face to face, trying to make one of them, any of them, meet her eyes. 'What situation? Can somebody kindly tell me what is going on?'

Nobody spoke for a few seconds. Then Pete realised that he couldn't rely on anyone else to rescue him. He cleared his throat awkwardly. 'I should have told you Stella. I'm sorry. It was when we sold the last house. We were a few thousand short, more than a few actually, and we needed a bridging loan to get this house. And I was going to go to the bank but I knew that they would check with my company and they'd hear about the takeover and turn us down so I went to Dad.'

Stella stood there staring at her husband, who was becoming more alien by the minute. 'Without telling me? You borrowed money from Dad that you KNEW you might not be able to pay back so that we could buy a house with an astronomical mortgage? Even though you could be on the dole in a few months' time? I don't . . . I can't . . .'

She was building up to a devastating tirade for which Pete, Bill and Ann all braced themselves. Then something inside her seemed to go 'pop'. She visibly took some deep breaths and composed her face into a grim smile. This was even more worrying to the others. They had a ghastly fear that she might be having some kind of breakdown.

Pete spoke to reassure her. 'Stella, I'm so sorry. But it still might all turn out OK, really it might. I might not lose my job and, even if I do, I might get a good enough pay-off that we won't have any money problems. I didn't want to burden you with all this until I had all the facts and knew what we were up against.'

Stella looked at him lovingly. Poor Pete, she was thinking. It's exactly as I thought. He wants to protect me. As if I give a toss about the money when he could be seriously ill. Or the house, for that matter. She longed to throw her arms round him and tell him so. Since considering the possibility that she might lose Pete, her love for him had been revitalised, raised to a level that it had never attained before. She no longer saw him only as a companion or the provider of fifty per cent of all the possessions she so treasured or the straight man to her comic turn.

She looked at her husband and, for the first time since she met him all those years earlier, she saw the one person, the one thing she could not bear to be without. And she couldn't tell him. Not now. He'd know that something was up. She felt unfamiliar tears forming in the corners of her eyes and didn't move quickly enough to stop them from dripping down.

Pete was horrified to have made Stella so unhappy. He'd never seen her cry and hated the first time to be caused by his own selfishly reckless behaviour. He rushed over to her and held her tightly. 'Stella, I promise you it will all be all right. We'll manage, I promise. I won't let anything happen to you or this house. And we'll pay Dad back. He knows that.'

Bill was cringing at the sight of this raw emotion. He wanted to hide behind a newspaper or go and pull up some weeds or something. Anything to get out of this intensely private moment. Ann felt the same but she was also moved. They're going to be OK, she thought. She hadn't been sure for some time, but seeing them together like this in the first real test of their marriage comforted her.

Stella allowed herself to sink into Pete's hug. She didn't trust herself to say anything. I love this man. I love this man. I will not lose him. I can give up everything else but I will not lose my husband.

*   *   *

157

Chris came out of the head teacher's office on Monday morning barely managing to contain his anger. He turned to confront the raw aggression radiating out of the sullen teenager sitting outside the head's door. 'I don't know how I did it, Ryder, but I just bought you one last chance. And that goes for the whole school as well.'

'Thanks for nothing, sir,' the boy sneered. His complete lack of regret for the consequences of his action deflated Chris totally. He sat down next to Dean Ryder and looked at him as if the boy were a newly discovered life form.

'I don't get it, Dean. I mean, I really want to understand you, that's all. I've given up trying to help you, since you're so clearly hell-bent on self-destruction, but I'm genuinely interested in why you seem so determined to take the whole school down with you. What have any of us done to make you hate us so much?'

Dean looked straight ahead of him, deliberately avoiding his teacher's face. 'Don't flatter yourself. I don't care enough about anyone here to hate them. Not even you, sir.'

'You're not stupid, even though it would be difficult to persuade a judge of that fact after your latest stunt. You must have known that you could have had this school shut down. Your final warning made it very clear. One more criminal offence and that was it. And stealing the caretaker's car? Why did you do it? I know none of us can stop you from joyriding since you plainly want to die before you're eighteen, but couldn't you at least have done it miles away from here where you might not have got nicked? You were caught on the school CCTV, for God's sake!'

Dean grinned. It was not a nice thing to see. 'Maybe I was doing it for attention, poor deprived kid like me from a broken home,' he said in mock-innocence.

Chris lost his temper. 'I've just spent the best part of half an hour persuading the caretaker not to press charges. He's agreed since you didn't do any damage to the car.'

Dean snorted. 'Poxy car couldn't go fast enough to cause any real damage.'

Chris shook his head. He was defeated and he knew it. 'Because charges are not being brought, the head has decided that he is not obliged to let the authorities know about this incident. You know that, if the Department of Education had got wind of this, that would have been the end of the school.'

'Yes, sir, you told us last week and, like you said, I'm not stupid.'

'And then what would happen to you?' Chris asked, still searching for any way to get through to the boy.

Dean shrugged. 'I'd be sent somewhere else. I still wouldn't pass any exams. I still wouldn't get a job so I'd start pinching stuff and end up like my old man, in and out of prison, doing this and that.'

'And that's the sort of life you want for yourself?' Chris asked in amazement.

Dean stood up and looked at Chris in disgust. 'It's the only sort available. Save all your do-gooding for someone who's impressed by your look-at-me-I'm-one-of-the-lads haircut.' Then he walked off.

As Chris left the school that afternoon, he glanced

in at some of the classrooms as he passed them. The homework clubs were compulsory but the atmosphere was kept more relaxed than during the rest of the day. To look at the children bending over their books, you would not have guessed that the cream of South London's young career criminals were being educated here. Contrary to public perception, the school managed to maintain a surprisingly high level of discipline. The classes were small and represented the first personal attention some of these kids had ever received. Of course deterrents were used, the most effective being related to food. It never ceased to surprise Chris what these kids would do for pizza and chips.

If the school closed, then over ninety per cent of the pupils here would revert to crime within weeks. They would be immediately ostracised at whatever school they were placed in and would react the only way they knew how, with violence or any other kind of anti-social behaviour they happened to embrace.

Chris had prevented this from happening today but he knew that it was just a matter of time before it happened again. And when it did, he would probably not be able to save the day.

His depression grew as he drove home and he very nearly didn't answer the phone that was ringing as he opened his front door. But there was the fleeting chance that it was Lauren calling from the Lake District. He threw his bag down on the floor and picked up the receiver with a degree of eagerness.

'Hello?'

'Oh hi, Chris, it's Stella again, Stella Lynch!'

Chris sometimes wondered what British society would

be like if we had the same liberal gun laws that the Americans enjoyed or endured. On occasions like this, he was grateful that weapons of such instantaneous and deadly effect were not available because he would surely shoot this woman if she were standing in front of him right now.

He blamed Stella entirely for the whole mess with Lauren. It was perhaps irrational and unfair of him to do so, but people were killed for irrational and unfair motives all the time in the USA. He'd seen *NYPD Blue*, he knew this to be a fact. Stella had, from the outset, been an irritation to Chris in her consistent dedication to everything that was shallow and superficial in the world. When he was drawing up a mental list of reasons why he should or should not leave Beth, the first item listed on the 'should' column was 'never having to see Stella Lynch again'. And now she was phoning him once more.

'Hi, Stella. What can I do for you?' He'd learned from their last conversation not to be sucked into the 'how are you' line of questioning.

'I need your help, Chris.' Stella sounded subdued and Chris was instantly worried that something had happened to Beth. He'd never heard Stella like this before. She was always so relentlessly cheerful that he'd been led to wonder if she was on drugs.

'You sound serious, Stella. What is it? It's nothing to do with Beth, is it?'

'In a way. It's about Saturday. You're going to a football match with Pete, aren't you?'

Chris unclenched his muscles at the news that it was something utterly trivial, as he'd expected. 'I meant to call Pete about that. You see—' Stella didn't give him a chance to finish. He was trying to tell her that Tottenham were playing Manchester United this coming Saturday and the seats had all been sold out weeks ago. It had been the best bit of news that he'd heard for ages.

'Look, Chris, I can't talk right now. Can I see you tomorrow? Just for ten minutes. I wouldn't ask if it wasn't really, really important.'

'Can't you give me some idea what this is all about?' Chris asked, exasperated by Stella's vagueness. 'I'm really busy at school right now and it's not easy to get out during the day.'

'Then I'll come over to you. We can just talk by the gate or something. Please!' She lowered her voice to a whisper. 'I can't talk over the phone. I'm at the office. And obviously I can't talk at home.'

Chris wasn't interested in all this melodrama. He'd had a bad day and had found it difficult not to pick a fight with every little delinquent who challenged his authority. He was prepared to argue all evening with Stella if necessary. But he heard his mobile phone ringing in his briefcase. He'd left the number on Lauren's answer machine. Maybe she'd picked the message up. He started rooting frantically through the briefcase trying to locate his mobile phone. He had to get rid of Stella immediately and the easiest way of doing that was giving in to her demands. 'OK. Look. If you drive into the school car park at about twelve thirty, you'll find plenty of spaces. It's the beginning of the lunch break. I can see you for about five minutes, no longer.'

'That will be perfect. Chris, I can't begin to tell you how grateful I am. And I know you'll understand when I tell you what this is all about. Thank you so much . . .'

She carried on thanking him for another five minutes, not realising that Chris had cut her off.

Chris had found his mobile. His optimism was thwarted yet again when he saw Izzy's number on the caller display. 'What is it now, Izzy?' he snapped.

'That's absolutely charming after all I've done for you.'

'Izzy, I'm not in the mood for cryptic conversations. If you're expecting me to guess what you're talking about, you can just hang up now.'

'You're lucky I know you. Anyone else might be offended at such a lack of warmth.'

'Izzy, get to the point,' Chris warned.

'I just thought you might be pleased to know that I've got hold of Lauren's mobile phone number.'

Chris didn't know what to say. Mainly because he didn't know what she was talking about. He didn't remember asking Izzy to get hold of Lauren's number. Why would he? 'Izzy, I know I was drunk on Saturday night and I wasn't much better in the morning, but I don't recall even mentioning Lauren's mobile phone number to you.'

Izzy had expected floods of gratitude. This was not going as well as expected. She sighed.

'You said that you needed to talk to her, to clear something up, but she was out of town all week and you didn't have her mobile phone number, so I called Beth and she gave me Stella's phone number and I called Stella and—'

Chris interrupted before she had a chance to explain that it was actually Stella's mother who'd spoken to her. 'You called Stella?' He couldn't believe it. Stella again.

She was at the centre of all the chaos in his life. She was like a malign spirit that he'd accidentally woken from an eternal slumber a few days earlier and was now saddled with for ever.

'What's your problem, Chris? You wanted the phone number. I got you the phone number. Now shall I give it to you or not?'

Chris didn't dare ask what she'd had to say to get Lauren's phone number out of Stella. His biggest fear was that Stella's sudden impassioned plea to see him was somehow linked to Izzy.

'OK, Izzy.' He wrote down the number without much enthusiasm.

'So are you going to phone her?' Izzy asked eagerly. Now that she'd been invited to the big family party, she was keen to move this romance forward. She had a good feeling about Lauren.

'I don't know, Izzy. The more I think about it, the less real it all seems, the less real she seems. I'm beginning to get the impression that it was never meant to be. In fact, I know I shouldn't say this, but I'm even missing Beth. Life was so much more straightforward with her.'

Izzy was alarmed at this. If he was contemplating going back to Beth, he must be depressed. And that meant only one thing. He needed Izzy's help.

That evening, he sat in front of his marking looking up frequently at Lauren's phone number pinned on his noticeboard. He was reluctant to phone her until he'd heard what Stella had to say. Just in case there were further complications to this whole sorry saga that he needed to understand before he said or did something else wrong.

Izzy was wrong. She was right that he was depressed but wrong that he wanted Beth back. It was just something he said. What he wanted was to turn back the clock to the party and replay that first conversation with Lauren. He wanted to talk with her like normal people do, then go out like normal people do, tell each other about their lives, find points of common interest or not, have a good time or not. They'd either hit it off or not. That's what he wanted. No more games. And as soon as he spoke to Lauren, he was going to say precisely that. After tomorrow.

Chapter 10

Lauren was in trouble. She couldn't concentrate. She couldn't focus on the job. She couldn't even type properly. She was still struggling to finish her preliminary report for Richard, outlining what she planned to do with timings and costings. She should have finished this on the train after their first meeting so that she could start work first thing on Monday morning.

But it was Tuesday, it was eleven thirty, she was on her fifth cup of tea and she was staring at the word 'preliminary' and wondering if it was correctly spelled. Perhaps staring was the wrong word. She was making an effort to keep her eyes fixed on the word in a sheer act of will to avoid looking out of the window.

It was all because of Sunday. What had started out as a ramble with a client had ended up as the most exhilarating experience of her life. She'd walked through a forest and felt thrilled by the sinister oppression of the densely over-hanging trees. She hadn't known that nature could evoke any feelings other than boredom. She'd clomped through heather, amazed to find roughly carved steps among the pinks and purples popping up through the snow. She'd almost sunk in a bog in an overly zealous attempt to protect her modesty, searching for a place to relieve herself that offered some cover. 'Didn't you hear me shouting?' Richard asked her in exasperation as he heaved her out. She hadn't heard him. She'd been listening to the silence of the mountains.

She'd never heard silence before. That is the sad legacy of the child brought up entirely in town. She'd always assumed that she wouldn't like silence so she'd made a point of avoiding it. She took holidays in bustling resorts, chose homes on busy streets, worked with the television on, slept with the radio on.

And now she'd tasted the drug, she couldn't get enough of it. When they reached Wastwater Screes Top, ten miles later, she was a born-again walker. The pain in her lungs, the stitch in her side, the throbbing ache at the back of her calves – all proof that she was alive, fully, joyously alive. She made the discovery that what she had always thought of as contentment with her life was nothing more than a powerful, self-administered anaesthetic.

Richard watched her as she drank in the lakes and dales like someone released from an underground prison. Her eyes widened as beauty unfolded upon beauty. She took off her woolly hat to loosen her hair from its sweaty hold on her scalp. She was totally unaware of her appearance, of the propriety of this life-changing trip with a business client. She didn't care what she said or did at this point. All that she could think of was the absolute, utter rightness of being in this place at this time.

She broke away from her contemplation after what seemed like an age but was more like ten minutes. Richard didn't avert his gaze and she blushed furiously at his attention.

'You must think I'm such an idiot, acting as if I've never seen a mountain in my life,' she said.

'And have you?' Richard asked.

'Have I what?'

'Ever seen a mountain in your life? And seeing one on television or through a window doesn't count.'

'I'm embarrassed to say that I haven't.'

Richard laughed. 'Don't be embarrassed! That makes you very lucky. I know people who've lived around here all their lives who've never seen the mountains. I mean, they see them every day but they've never opened their eyes and looked at them. You, on the other hand, have been able to see them with the eyes of someone who's been deprived of the opportunity of taking such magnificence for granted.'

'Am I the first person you've ever seen react so extremely to this view?' she asked, wanting to believe that what she was going through was unique.

'No you're not,' Richard replied honestly. 'I see it a lot. It's one of the reasons I've held back for so long from modernising the shops' operations. Anything that stops anyone from coming here is a bad thing, from that point of view. I mean, in a couple of weeks' time, if you need to do any business with me, you'll be able to do it at night while you're looking out on a dank London street with the smell of kebabs and cigarette butts wafting through your window. You'll never need to come here again.'

And it was this awful prospect that was stopping Lauren from making any progress with her modernising of Richard's obsolete operation.

Stella closed her car window to block out the smell of kebabs and cigarette butts wafting off the dank streets that led to the school where Chris worked. She unconsciously locked all the doors and slid her handbag out of sight under the seat. She turned into the car park and found a space as far away from the building as possible. The noise emanating from the school was daunting. It sounded as if a riot was in progress, which was not far from the truth since the deep-fat fryer had broken and there were no chips for lunch.

Chris had been delegated the task of pacifying the pupils who were threatening to smash up the dining room. In an act of desperate surrender that was immediately effective, if philosophically unsound, he phoned up the local fish and chip shop and arranged for seventy large portions of chips to be prepared and collected.

After delivering this news to the militant students, he ordered them to amuse themselves in the most undestructive way possible until the food arrived. He then gave the cook a free hand with disciplining any unruliness, short of third degree burns or broken bones, while he dashed out to see Stella.

He banged on the car window, causing Stella to jump in terror. She had been sitting with her finger pressed on the four on her mobile phone, having already pressed the first ten digits of the nearest police station's number in readiness for any assault. Fortunately she was prevented from summoning an armed response unit by dropping the phone in shock. She put her hands over her face defensively and screamed for help.

'Stella! Stella, you silly cow, it's me! Stop screaming!'

Stella stopped screaming and peeked through her fingers to check that it was indeed Chris and not a juvenile serial killer with good imitative skills. She unlocked the car doors and let him into the front seat, immediately locking the doors again as soon as he was in.

'Why did you sneak up on me like that?' she asked furiously.

'Stella, I walked directly in front of the car from the building, wearing a red jumper and waving both arms. I could not have been less sneaky if my approach had been announced by a dozen bugle-players.'

'Well there's no need to be so sarcastic. This isn't the most relaxing place for a woman to be alone.' Stella was now scrambling about for a dignified fallback position after her less than dignified introduction.

'Stella, it wasn't my idea to meet today. You insisted, if you remember. Now, as you can hear, this is not a good time for me. I can't leave the dear little children to their own devices for too long. So what's so important that couldn't wait and couldn't be discussed on the phone?'

Stella became instantly subdued. She quickly told Chris about Pete's cancer fears and Beth's involvement. She invented a few additional details to make the whole story sound less speculative. This didn't seem deceitful to Stella. She knew she was right in her conclusion and knew that she had to get Chris on her side. Therefore she had to be convincing in her communication of the situation and the necessary action that she was going to require of Chris.

Chris sat back in his seat, taken unawares. He too had been surprised at the amount of time Pete and Beth had spent together at that party. If he hadn't been so entranced by Lauren's arrival, he might have had to confront the fact that he felt jealous to see another man enjoying Beth's company so soon after he'd split up from her.

Not that he'd wanted her to be unhappy, of course, but such a speedy recovery did suggest that her feelings for Chris might not have been that deep or genuine.

So he was only too willing to accept Stella's interpretation of the evidence. God, Pete having cancer. It wasn't as if they were friends or anything but he and Pete were about the same age. The thought made him very uncomfortable.

Beth had never talked about her work at home but he could always tell when one of her special patients had died. He was grateful to her for not insisting on sharing her grief with him. Well, she'd tried but he'd made his feelings on the subject plain. He didn't handle talk of death very well. It was an issue he'd been able to ignore throughout his life simply by being blessed with long-living parents. In fact, he'd never lost anyone close to him, a statistic that astonished her when he first told Beth.

'But what about your grandparents?' she asked.

'All died before Izzy and I were born,' Chris answered.

Beth shook her head in disbelief. She wondered how Chris would react when he was finally forced to confront the prospect of the death of a loved one, or even just an acquaintance.

And it looked like the time could be approaching. His aversion to the subject under discussion had the effect of blunting his faculty of discernment. He just took in what Stella was saying without question. He accepted his mission – to find out what was wrong with Pete, without Pete guessing that he was acting on Stella's instructions – because he didn't know how to refuse.

To his horror, Stella then burst into tears and leaned

towards him for comfort. He was forced to hold her, which was not easy to do in the bucket seats of a BMW. Stella had ended up half sitting on his lap and their legs had become entangled. It was only the spectre of cancer hanging over them that stopped the scene from descending into physical farce. Eventually, Chris managed to pacify her. He was quite impressed by his achievement, never having thought of himself as an empathetic man.

As he walked back to the school, he heard Stella's car drive away. He'd been so shocked at what she had to say that he'd forgotten to point out that he hadn't been able to get tickets for the match on Saturday. Then he heard the cacophony of adapted football chants come screeching through the dining room as seventy delinquents sang in perfect harmony of exactly what the cook could do with her macaroni cheese.

He didn't know that he was smiling as he increased his walking speed purposefully. Of course, he thought. Where else does one go to buy tickets to a sell-out football match? Somewhere in this prime cross-section of the criminal tendency there must be someone with access to unofficially obtained tickets.

The other thing he didn't know was that he had been watched from the minute he left the school building by Dean Ryder. Dean always knew when a new car was in the car park. Coming from a large and illustrious family of car thieves, he was genetically programmed to sense the presence of an executive motor from five miles away.

In the beginning he'd watched the scene being acted out with interest. It was obviously Mr Fallon's wife. It was apparent that they were not going to be getting up to much apart from a clumsy grope. Shame, he thought. Once he'd worked out that they weren't going to be leaving the car unattended, Dean turned his attention to the other motors in the car park, looking for his next hit.

'Dean Ryder. What are you doing out of the building?'

'Trying to decide which car to steal next, *sir*.' Chris cringed. Only Dean Ryder could make 'sir' sound offensive.

'Very funny, Ryder,' Chris replied. 'You know it's against the rules to leave the building during lunch break. If you go straight back now, I won't report you.'

'You are a saint, sir.'

Chris decided that at the next staff meeting he'd suggest a rule should be introduced to make irony a punishable offence in students. But he swallowed his annoyance. He needed a favour.

'Dean, let me ask you a question.' He kept his tone brusque, not wanting the boy to know how desperate he was for some help.

'What do you want to break into?'

'It's not that kind of question, Dean.' But not far from it, he thought. 'How would someone go about getting two tickets for the Manchester United / Tottenham match this Saturday?'

It was the first time Dean had ever been lost for a quick comeback. There was a lesson in there for Chris as a teacher. He'd think about that when he'd got through the torture of the football match with Pete.

'I never had you down as a football fan,' Dean said curiously.

'I'm not really,' Chris replied. 'But I've got a friend who's very ill and I've sort of promised to take him on Saturday.'

'Well if you don't mind my saying so, sir, that was a pretty crap sort of promise.'

Thank you, Dean. 'None the less, that's the situation. So what do I do?'

'How much do you want to pay?' Dean was getting interested now. This could be good business and it didn't do any harm to have a teacher owing you a favour.

Chris was aware that he was setting himself up to be taken for a ride. He was out of his depth and Dean knew it. 'Just tell me how much they cost and I'll tell you if it's acceptable.'

Dean upped the price by another twenty pounds on hearing Mr Fallon's uncertainty. 'And will you be needing transport on one of the supporters' buses or will you be making your own way up to Manchester?'

Chris's face must have betrayed his shock. 'What do you mean, Manchester? Isn't the match going to be played at Tottenham?'

Dean sneered. 'You're going to see a match and you don't even know where it's being played? A real fan, are you, sir?'

'It didn't occur to me to check. I just phoned up the ticketline at Tottenham and they laughed at me, told me the match had been sold out for ages. They didn't say anything about where it was being played.'

'Well, they wouldn't. They'd assume you knew that if the match details say "Manchester Utd v Tottenham Hotspur", that means that it's an away match.' Dean was enjoying the teacher's discomfort.

Chris rubbed his temples. He had been fighting a permanent headache since Stella's party six days ago. He asked himself if it was possible to be allergic to a person. Because if it was, then that would explain the throbbing pain that attacked him every time he heard her voice.

'OK, so now we've ascertained that I am a moron, can you give me a straight answer?' Chris was getting weary.

'Let me get this right, sir, you want me to get you two tickets for the match?'

'That's right, Dean. Can you do it?'

'No problem. All you had to do is ask. Stay there while I make a call.' He whipped out a banned mobile phone from his pocket and walked away to ring someone, Chris didn't want to know who.

Once the transaction had been concluded, Chris wondered if Pete had realised that the match was in Manchester. Saturday was going to be a long day. Am I mad? he asked himself. It's one thing to do someone a favour but this looks as if it's going into three figures. And I'll probably be unemployed soon with Dean Ryder holding my career in his grubby hands.

But while Stella was talking about Pete, a little seed was germinating in Chris's head. It was the vaguest, wildest possibility that Pete might turn out to be the friend *he* needed. That the favour might go both ways.

And while it might have been cheaper to stick an ad in the *Guardian* for like-minded men for bonding, this seemed more unforced, more natural. A footie match, what men *wouldn't* bond there?

*   *   *

Izzy's main problem was having too much time on her hands. Even when she was walking her clients' dogs, she had nothing to distract her. She dialled Lauren's mobile phone number for the tenth time that day. Wherever Lauren was, there was not much of a signal.

She hadn't decided precisely what she was going to say to Lauren if she did ever get through to her. Just when she'd made up her mind that this was a bad idea, she got a ringing tone.

'Hello?' Lauren's voice was very crackly but just about comprehensible.

'Oh hello, Lauren. It's Izzy here. Chris's sister. We met on Friday.'

'I can hardly hear you. Hold on a second.' Lauren drove round the bend ahead and pulled into a lay-by. Richard had lent her his car and it wasn't the easiest vehicle in the world to handle. Izzy listened to some choice expletives which, unlike the more mundane conversation, penetrated the static very clearly.

Lauren was driving over to one of Richard's other shops and had offered to switch the phone on so that Richard would be able to contact her if necessary. She always made herself available to clients twenty-four hours a day when she was on assignment. It was the sort of accountability that set her apart from other consultants.

He'd found this very amusing. 'I can't think of a single thing that might happen during the two hours you'll be in the car that couldn't wait until you got to the other end. Then I could call you at the shop on an ordinary phone. So please don't bother with it on my account. Better still, chuck the bloody thing into the lake!'

Lauren was no longer baffled by his Luddite attitude towards technology and was beginning to feel sympathetic to his viewpoint. When the phone had rung in the car, it startled her. She hadn't realised she'd even switched it on. It must have been a reflex action on getting into her car. She felt a pang of sadness that she wasn't as distanced from her past as she'd thought.

The reception was appalling but at least the voice on the other end was audible. What the hell was Chris's sister doing phoning her up here? Where did she get her number from? These were just two of the questions that got lost in the ether of static between Cumbria and Tooting.

Then the line became relatively clear for a few moments and the two women spoke as quickly as they could while they could make sense of what the other was saying.

'Has something happened to Chris?' Lauren shouted.

'No,' Izzy shouted back, improvising wildly. 'He's fine. I just wanted to speak to you because I'm organising a surprise for Chris this weekend and I know he'd want you to be there.'

'Is it his birthday?' Lauren asked, surprised that Chris hadn't mentioned it. Then again, it hadn't been a dream date.

'Sorry, it's a bad line,' Izzy yelled, almost deafening Lauren. The line was perfect but it was a great excuse for avoiding a question. 'Listen, will you be back on Friday?'

Since Izzy was shouting, Lauren felt obliged to shout back. This wasn't a problem for Lauren who was sitting in a car in the middle of nowhere. But as Izzy was walking twenty dogs on Tooting Common, she was looking seriously deranged as she yelled into a phone then held the receiver at arm's length while everyone within a mile's radius heard Lauren's every word.

'As a matter of fact I was going to stay up here this weekend.'

'You must come, Chris would be really upset if you weren't there!' Izzy screamed.

Lauren had been planning to spend the whole weekend walking with Richard. She had persuaded him to take her on some of the more ambitious paths. And she never missed an opportunity to sing her mother's praises to Richard. Her aim was that he would be half in love with Maureen before he was introduced to her at the forthcoming party.

Now the bizarre Isolde was trying to entice Lauren back to London at the weekend so that she could humiliate herself in front of Chris again. She hadn't even thought about him for the last two days. Until now.

It was as if the very act of switching on and picking up the phone had undone the spells that the mountains had cast on Lauren. All sense of calm was seeping out of her and vanishing into the distance. And she wanted it returned. She wanted to be back at Richard's shop, watching him work, seeing how many times she caught him sneaking glances out of the window. He did the same for her. They'd got into the habit of meeting up for tea breaks to compare scores.

'I saw you take seven peeks including one trip outside during a completely redundant visit to the store room to get stock that was already on the shop floor,' Lauren had said, sitting back in victory this morning.

Richard was not so easily defeated. 'I saw you take

five peeks BUT you left the office four times and I could swear I heard the front door open on each occasion.'

Lauren raised her eyebrows in mock indignation. 'Are you suggesting that I was skiving outside, Mr Trent? I'll have you know that I am cursed with a weak bladder and every one of those excursions was a physical necessity.'

'Liar, liar, Miss Connor.'

She'd never dealt with clients as informally as this before and it was all evidence to her of the transforming power this place was wielding over her. But the magic was dissolving.

Chris Fallon insinuated himself back into the front of her mind once more. She remembered the party. Meeting him. Talking to him. Saying the wrong thing. Then a dozen more wrong things. Then he gave her the impression that he liked her a bit. And this made her like him a bit.

And it had been a wonderful distraction. She forgot about her mum, forgot about New York and deadlines. For one night. But then she woke up and nothing had changed. So she ran away. And suddenly, after one single weekend away from normality, she was venturing out in a completely new direction. Away from her mum, away from New York, away from Chris, whoever he was. What was she thinking of? The distraction had turned into yet another complication, another variable in the decision-making process. Maybe she needed to step back, simplify, streamline.

Going back to London would be a start to acknowledging her situation. It would be the grown-up thing to do.

A car came tearing round the corner, clipping her wing mirror as it passed. 'Pig!' she shouted.

'What did you say?' Izzy asked, assuming she'd mis-heard Lauren.

'Sorry, I wasn't talking to you. Some idiot on the road.' Lauren felt her shoulder muscles harden as the old stresses took hold once more. At this point, the line really did begin to break up. 'Look, are you sure Chris would want me to be there?'

'Positive!' Izzy replied enthusiastically. 'Why don't we meet at the sushi restaurant we all ate at last week? Shall we say seven o'clock on Friday?'

Lauren didn't get a chance to decline the invitation or to protest at the choice of venue. There was nothing but white noise on the line. She ended the call and gazed out the window beyond the lay-by. Skiddaw dominated the horizon. That's where she was supposed to be heading with Richard this coming Sunday. Now everything was changing.

On impulse she got out of the car and threw the phone violently into the lake below. As it flew in a perfect arc through the air on its final journey into the water, it began to ring. But Lauren didn't hear it. She was already enjoying listening to the silence of the mountains again.

Chris listened to the ringing tone on the end of the phone then it went dead. It had taken him all day to get through to Lauren and then she cut him off. She must have seen his number on the caller display and decided not to speak to him. That was it. He gave up.

Chapter 11

'You've got to be kidding,' Chris said. 'Three hundred pounds?'

Dean raised his hands. 'That's for the pair. It's a special rate I got for you. To anyone else it would be three hundred each.'

'Don't expect me to be grateful, Dean. We both know that you earn more from your various scams in a day than I earn in a month. So please don't try and pretend that you're doing me a favour.'

'These are the best tickets you can get, sir. Your friend will be dead impressed.'

Chris snatched the tickets out of Dean's hand, gave him an envelope with the agreed money and walked away, proud that he hadn't slapped the smirking youth. But despite feeling well and truly ripped off, he was relieved to finally have the tickets in his hand. It was Thursday and he'd been dreading having to tell Stella that he wouldn't be able to meet up with Pete on Saturday.

He heard Dean calling after him. 'Oh, there was one other thing, sir!'

Chris closed his eyes. What now? 'Go on, Dean.'

'You know about the big demo in Manchester this Saturday?'

Chris didn't. Why should he? He lived in London.

'Well, they've known about it for three weeks so they decided to play the match earlier.'

'How much earlier?' Chris asked.

'Kick-off is at ten thirty in the morning.'

Chris shrugged. 'So we'll have to get up earlier. It's a pain but not a major problem.'

'That depends, sir. You won't be able to go up by train or coach at that time. There are only a couple of early departures and they were fully booked ages ago.'

'So we can drive.'

Dean shook his head. 'You won't be able to get near Manchester. The approaching roads will be cut off to all traffic except public transport. The police are trying to keep the rent-a-mob crowd out of the demo.'

Chris held the now-useless tickets up in defeat. 'So you've sold me two tickets to a match that is impossible to get to? Thank you so much.'

'It's not impossible to get to. You'll just have to go up the evening before. Anyway, must dash, sir, cars to thieve, mugs to rip off.'

He ran off, laughing. Chris placed the three hundred pounds' worth of tickets in his inside jacket pocket. They were the most expensive items he possessed after his car and his flat and he didn't want to make them easily accessible to the den of pickpockets in school.

He made his way back into the building, which had gone ominously quiet. The silence gave him time to meditate on how something had taken over his life. One minute he was going to a party he hadn't wanted to attend, then before he could say 'fickle finger of fate', he was on his way to his first football match with a man he barely knew who might or might not have cancer. And he had to travel up the night before.

That brought him up short. The night before? That's tomorrow. I need to tell Pete.

He had the afternoon to get used to the idea before phoning Pete in the evening. Once he'd stopped agonising over the indignity of having his life organised for him by an unknown force, he began to look forward to the whole adventure. Not the football, of course, although even that had a certain macho attraction.

It was the prospect of having a friend that had finally really begun to appeal. And why shouldn't Pete become a good friend? Providing he wasn't going to drop dead in the immediate future, obviously. It would be a bad omen if his first foray into male bonding should end in premature death. Still, right now Pete was the only candidate on the list.

Pinning the precious tickets on his noticeboard where Lauren's phone number had once been affectionately placed, he dialled Pete's number.

Stella answered. Chris tensed up at the sound of her voice. He hadn't heard from her in two days and he was daring to hope that the hex had passed. The handover of the phone to Pete passed without incident, intervention or any requests that he would not be able to decline. Life was looking up.

'Hello?' Pete didn't sound too enthusiastic but Chris remembered what Pete was going through and this stopped him from taking offence. He doubled his efforts at 'cheerful bloke' mode. This only served to confirm to Pete that Chris and he had nothing in common.

'Good news, Pete!'

The football season has been cancelled? You have a rare tropical disease that will confine you to quarantine for the next five years? Pete was confident that Chris's definition of good news would not be the same as his. He was right.

'What's that, Chris?'

'I've got the tickets for Saturday!'

Whoop-de-doop, Pete thought. 'That's wonderful. So, I expect you've phoned to make arrangements.'

He must be very ill to react so miserably to the news of tickets to Tottenham's biggest match of the season, Chris thought.

'Yes, well it's not as straightforward as I'd imagined. You didn't tell me that they were playing away this weekend.'

'Away?' Pete asked. 'Away where?'

Chris laughed. 'Away where! You know where. Manchester. The big one. Man U!'

Oh my God, Pete thought. I've got to go to Manchester with this man on Saturday. I'll have to talk to him all the way there and all the way back. This defeats the purpose of choosing a football match so that we wouldn't have to talk. It's all going wrong. Desperate measures were called for.

'Look, Chris. I'm terribly sorry, but I hadn't realised the match was going to be played in Manchester. I just don't think I'm going to be able to make it. I've been feeling under the weather . . .'

He felt a fraud for lying like this but he couldn't think of any other excuse.

Chris was having none of it. 'I know how you feel.

184

I've been feeling a bit jaded myself. And I have the answer.'

Oh no, thought Pete. An answer.

Chris went on. 'I don't know whether you were aware of the big demo in Manchester in Saturday?'

Pete didn't know. Why would he? He lived in London. And unless it meant that he didn't have to go to the football match, he wasn't interested.

'Well, to cut a long story short, the match is going to be earlier than usual, in the morning, and the only way we can get there is to travel up the night before.'

It took a few seconds for this information to work its way into Pete's consciousness, so unreal did the whole situation appear to him. Then he frowned. Stella, who'd been watching him nervously throughout the call, moved closer. 'What's the matter?' she whispered. Pete shook his head at her.

'Sorry, Chris, I don't understand. Are you saying that we have to go up to Manchester tomorrow? And stay there overnight?'

'That's right! It was a bit of a surprise to me as well but, when I had time to get used to the idea, I thought it might be fun. And I knew I wouldn't be able to speak to you before tonight and I was worried that everywhere would be booked so I took the liberty of provisionally booking a hotel for us. It sounds a great place with a swimming pool and a gym and a jacuzzi!'

Now Pete knew that this man was insane. Unless Chris was the victim of suppressed homosexual tendencies that were oozing to the surface at the prospect of a testosterone-abundant football trip. Either way it was beyond a joke. 'Look, I'm sorry, Chris, but . . .'

185

He was distracted by Stella gesticulating wildly in front of him. 'Hold on a second, Chris.' He put his hand over the mouthpiece. 'What do you want?' he hissed at Stella irritably.

'I think you should go. It would do you good to get away for a night. I know you've had . . . matters on your mind. And you've been taking it out on me. Maybe we could both do with a night apart. *I* certainly could. Don't turn this down out of hand.'

Pete knew that he'd been impossible to Stella for the last couple of days. But she'd been driving him nuts. Watching him when she didn't think he was aware of it, tiptoeing around him, agreeing with everything he said. It just antagonised him. And he knew that it was all down to him. She hadn't done anything apart from stay the same person for twenty years.

It wasn't her fault that she wasn't Beth. But it *was* her fault that he had been forced to speak to Beth again and then see her. And now it *was* her fault that he had to make the decision not to speak to Beth again or see her. He had no choice after Stella's outburst on Sunday.

He'd been shaken by her tears. They drove him to a realisation he would have preferred to ignore: that she needed him to stay the same, for their marriage to stay the same, for the rhythm and structure of their whole life together to stay the same.

Stella was not a brave woman. Her only act of courage consisted of moving house. She was only strong if all the elements in her life were suspended in perfect equilibrium and any kind of threat sent her running for cover. He'd known that when he married her and he'd allowed her to take his acquiescence to her needs for granted for all these years. Therefore he had to accept his responsibility to stay in his place, where he'd always been. For her sake.

But it was hard. Beth had woken him from a stupor and it was bloody hard to get back to sleep. 'Hello? Are you still there, Pete?' Chris was yelling down the phone. Stella was pleading with her eyes. They both wanted him to go. Neither of them cared what he wanted. Why should he care himself?

He swallowed hard and smiled grimly at Stella. 'Sorry Chris, I just had to think things through. Yes, that sounds fine. It was just all out of the blue. But, yeah, it sounds just fine.'

Chris put the phone down, sweating horribly. His attempts to convey enthusiastic bonhomie had not come easily and he was aware that he must have sounded like an over-enthusiastic adolescent trying to persuade a reluctant girl to go and see *Nightmare on Elm Street 6*. That was the problem with spending the majority of one's working hours in the presence of over-enthusiastic adolescents. Still, he'd achieved what he'd set out to do.

He was pouring himself a beer when the phone rang. He cursed himself when his first thought was that it might be Lauren. Why can't I get that woman out of my head?

It was Izzy. Again. He was beginning to find her as irritating as Stella. She was remorselessly cheerful.

'Hi, Tris! How's it all going?'

'Exactly the same as the last time you phoned me. Except the school is that much closer to shutting down, I'm three hundred pounds worse off . . .'

'What's happened, Tristan?' Izzy sounded concerned.

Chris closed his eyes and tried to sound upbeat. He shouldn't take his preoccupations out on Izzy. Even if that was the primary function of a younger sister. 'Sorry, I've just had a bad day. So how's the dog-walking business?'

'Not brilliant. One of the Jack Russells broke off his lead and killed a goose.'

'Is that bad?' Chris wasn't being argumentative, he just hated geese, as does any normal person who has ever visited a park with geese in it.

Izzy shared his feelings. 'It wouldn't have been bad had the Parks Police not caught up with me and accused me of harbouring a fugitive from justice.'

'How did they know it was one of your dogs?' Chris sat down and took a long drink of his beer. He was enjoying himself now. It was always good to hear of someone else's trouble. Not serious trouble, just a minor offence, one that would not go beyond the magistrate's court.

'They followed the trail of blood and feathers,' Izzy replied miserably.

Chris would never eat goose again. 'So apart from that, how are things?' he asked, hoping that she had managed to encounter some degree of normality at some point in the last forty-eight hours. For Izzy, that would be an achievement.

'Well, I've got some good news. It's more of a surprise, actually.'

'That's great, Izzy! What is it?'

'Ah, well, it wouldn't be a surprise if I told you now! You'll have to wait until tomorrow night. Shall we say seven o'clock at Sushi Soho?'

'Oh Izzy, I'm sorry. I can't do tomorrow night.'

'Don't be silly, of course you can. You didn't say the other night that you had anything planned.'

Chris went into long-suffering older-brother mode. 'That was then. Now I do have something planned.'

Izzy was furious. 'Well, what are you doing? Can't you do it some other night? Any other night?'

'No, Izzy, I can't. I'm going up to Manchester with a friend. We're stopping overnight then going to see a football match on Saturday.'

'Tris, you hate football. You always said it was all Nobby Stiles and Bovril.'

'That's when it was all Nobby Stiles and Bovril. It's different now. More intelligent. More . . . Italian. Besides, Pete who I'm going with is a real Tottenham fan. This is more his idea than mine. Although now I've got used to the idea, I'm quite keen.'

Izzy would have laughed if the carefully planned reunion between her brother and his would-be girlfriend was not now in jeopardy. 'Why can't you go up on Saturday morning?'

'Does nobody know about the big demo in Manchester on Saturday?'

Apparently not.

Izzy dialled Lauren's mobile number, stabbing the numbers viciously, pretending that she was poking her brother in the eye with each prod. The line was dead. Not even out of range. Dead. Well, that was that. She would be travelling back to London on Friday, tomorrow, for a celebration with Chris. Except that Chris wouldn't be there. And she had no way of contacting Lauren to let her know.

Looks like it'll just be the two of us, Izzy thought. I hope Lauren has a sense of humour.

Lauren was losing her sense of humour rapidly. It was her fourth day on this project and it was going badly. While a chain of shops working to nineteenth-century accounting and communications procedures appears very romantic to a passing rambler, it is a nightmare to a management consultant.

Richard had given her a comprehensive description of all of his shops, each place revealing further anachronisms that defied all attempts at modernisation. Eventually, she had to visit the sites in person.

She had also reluctantly reached the decision that she needed to take on somebody else to help her with the initial set-up legwork. In most of her jobs, she employed a team of 'techies' to deal with the on-site technical problems. With this job, she'd originally thought the small size of the operation would not justify any other personnel. But she hadn't banked on the sheer scope of the problems ahead, namely the obsoleteness of the current equipment in the shops. When she got back to London, she was going to ring round some old colleagues to find someone cheap and flexible to give her a hand.

Her first call on the whistlestop tour of Richard's shops was in Ambleside. The shop was run by an old lady who claimed to be Richard's aunt (although he was vague about the actual relationship). She had thought that the answering machine Richard supplied ten years earlier was the devil's own invention. She had refused categorically to use it despite Richard's insistence that it be switched on while the shop was closed. Every time he visited, he switched it on. On his subsequent visit, the tape would be full of unplayed messages.

'Has business fallen? Have there been complaints? No. So let that be an end to this nonsense,' she'd said when he confronted her. She was the village Girls' Brigade leader and would have preferred to communicate with Richard by standing on the roof of the shop and using semaphore.

Lauren had taken Richard's advice and dressed in her walking clothes to meet her. Before she got out of the car, she checked her face in her mirror. Not a scrap of make-up, again at Richard's recommendation. She was struck by her cheeks. They were red. I have ruddy cheeks, she thought, savouring the unfamiliarity of the words. Less than a week out of town and she was turning into Heidi.

Still, the lethal assault on her epidermis was worth it. Auntie Joan, Richard's self-professed aunt and manager of his smallest shop, welcomed her as if she were a favourite daughter returning from a successful but dangerous attempt on Everest.

She bounded towards Lauren like a gazelle, all lean, wiry and wizened. She was somewhere between sixty and 160 but her eyes were those of a wise child. Her lustrous grey hair was braided into an impressive French plait. Lauren analysed her features, looking for a family resemblance to Richard. The only similarity was the glint of fun in the upturned mouth and deep, deep laughter lines.

'Ooh, you look half dead with the cold. Come on through and warm yourself. I'll make you a cup of tea.' Joan turned the sign on the shop door to CLOSED and led her by the hand through to the office.

Lauren looked back at the shop in confusion. 'Should you be shutting up the shop like that?' she asked.

Joan bustled about with a battered old whistling kettle and a teapot with a lid that didn't match. 'The world won't come to an end just because you can't buy a woolly vest in Ambleside for half an hour. Now, I'm going to put a few sugars in this to warm your blood.'

After three mugs of tea, a pile of the most delicious buttery shortbread she had ever tasted and the entire unedited history of the Trent family, Lauren realised that she had not opened her laptop yet.

'So, Joan, I suppose Richard told you why I was coming over?'

'I don't listen to him when he goes all silly on me. I said to him, "Richard, you're talking to me on the phone, what more do we need? If I want anything, I can phone you or write to you or even put on my walking boots and hike over to you in an afternoon. I've worked in this shop for over fifty years. I keep copies of everything and I can work out exactly how much of everything I'm going to sell in any week of the year. What do I need computers linked to centralised stockrooms for? You save your money, I said to him!" Then he told me all about you. Ooh, I thought, grand! A young girl! That's nice. Well, we'll take a look at her and see what she's like, then. Show her some Cumbrian hospitality. So here you are!'

Lauren mentally reran every course she had ever attended on interpersonal techniques. She'd slogged through role-play sessions where she had always excelled at adapting to the unconventional client approaches. She could deal deftly with gropers, fascists, sexists, perverts, weaklings and men who wanted to be mothered by her.

But nowhere had she been taught how to deal with little old ladies who used your state-of-the-art personal computer as a coaster for a cup of tea and a saucer of biscuits.

She wagged her finger at the charming old lady. 'Joan, Richard warned me about you! I know what you're trying to do but I can be just as cunning as you.' She gently removed the tea paraphernalia from her computer and began preparing for her informal presentation to Joan.

Joan crinkled her eyebrows. 'I doubt that, still you can have a go if you want to. But you'll have to wait for now, I've got to open the shop. We can't have you going back to Richard and telling him that the senile old woman is letting the business fall to rack and ruin, can we?'

But Lauren had the measure of the woman. She picked up the laptop and followed her through to the shop. She spent the rest of the day shadowing Joan as she went about her work.

Joan spent an hour making painstaking notes in a pocketbook itemising shelf contents and checking stock-lists against the carbon copies of handwritten receipts clipped together in a metal cash box. After she'd finished the task, Lauren showed the computer screen to her. 'Once you're on line, you won't have to do any of that. It will be done automatically.'

'I can't be doing with all that. Not at my age.' Lauren wouldn't have been surprised if Joan had pulled out an abacus. Still she persevered, offering an alternative vision for the laborious administration that dominated Joan's day.

'You don't have to do all this, Joan.'

Joan's face hardened. 'And what would I do instead,

then?' she asked. 'Stay at home and make cakes for the Women's Institute? Knit? Prune my roses?' Her voice was trembling. Lauren sensed her fear of being rendered obsolete and she felt obliged to apologise on behalf of the dehumanising technology that she was reluctantly representing.

'You would do exactly what you already do but without all the crap.'

Joan's eyes narrowed at the jarring word. It offended her but it pacified her at the same time. It mirrored her own anger and frustration at being forced to accept change where she didn't think change was necessary. She listened more carefully.

Lauren continued. 'You would still be working in the shop, all day and every day if you choose, but you can spend all that time dealing with your customers, the people. You can chat to them. You can even make them tea and biscuits in the time you'll be saving on admin! You can show them your photos from when you climbed all around the world in your youth. You can look at *their* photos. It's the way you always wanted to work but never could. You never had the time. I'm offering you the time.'

Joan glanced at her appraisingly. 'Richard was right about you.'

Lauren was curious. 'Why? What did he say about me?'

Joan was about to answer then shook her head and smiled. 'Nothing at all. He'll tell you himself if he wants to. Now, you tell me what I have to do to get all this time you've promised me.'

Yes! thought Lauren. Richard said I'd never win her

round and I did. But the victory was short-lived. When Lauren sat down with Joan and talked her through the new cash register, computer and phone that would be installed, Joan stared at her. 'Sorry, love, I think I misunderstood what you were saying. I thought you just put all these things in and switched them on and then they looked after themselves. I didn't know I'd have to be touching them myself. I'm far too old for all that.'

'But Joan, don't be silly, a bright woman like you . . .'

It was too late. Joan was on her way to put the kettle on, still tutting at Lauren's foolishness.

Great, thought Lauren. Richard's either going to have to sack his aunt or the system will just have to bypass this particular shop. Lauren couldn't know that she was going to encounter similar obstinacy at all the other shops too.

Sitting on the train back to London, she thought about Chris and the coming evening. Suddenly, she longed for people she understood, who talked her language. She and Chris were going to sort out the little hiccup that had dogged their first two meetings and then they could see where things went from there.

The story of Chris and Lauren was playing in her head like a film running on an old projector. Sometimes the images crackled so badly, she couldn't see what was happening or hear the voices. Then the film would whirr to a halt. But just as she was about to pick up her Payne's Poppets and leave, the picture would flash back in vibrant clarity. And that's how it was now. Clear and compelling.

It was a world that made sense to her, not challenging her or making her cheeks ruddy. She opened her laptop and concentrated on her work, not stopping to look out of the window until the train pulled into Euston.

Chapter 12

Izzy got to the restaurant at seven o'clock, wanting to have a drink by herself before Lauren arrived. She asked for a table for two and sat back to indulge in a spot of people-watching. It was the usual crowd. Mainly young, definitely fashionable, partly oriental. They were drawn by the food, the reputation and the possibility of seeing someone famous. It certainly wasn't the prices that attracted custom.

Izzy was amused to see an older couple walk into the restaurant looking bemused. The woman was what Izzy would describe as a brassy blonde who might have seen better days – although that wasn't definite. She must have been in her fifties and was dressed like a drag queen. She could even have been a drag queen.

Her escort was roughly of a similar age but was as restrained and understated in appearance as a man had to be when he was accompanying Shirley Bassey.

Izzy sat back in delight. These were her kind of people. She wondered how they were going to cope in this foreign environment. Not well, it seemed. They were sitting by a window and enjoying the bustle of Soho folk rushing to cinemas and theatres, pubs and restaurants, on a Friday night. Then an anaemic waitress handed them a menu and their visible sense of pleasure abated.

Izzy felt sorry for them. They'd probably looked through the window, seen how stark the decor was and assumed it was a cheap and cheerful café. They were of a generation that equated the scale of charges with the degree of ostentation. No waiters in black suits lifting golden domes dramatically from Spode plates laden with the finest beef – how expensive can it be?

Very expensive, was the answer. The couple were whispering awkwardly to each other and Izzy longed for them to get up and leave – she couldn't bear their discomfort much longer. It was all too reminiscent of the many occasions when she'd felt an outsider. Not for financial reasons but from the sheer misery of knowing that she was the wrong sort of person.

But the man had taken the women's hand firmly and was smiling at her. He loved her. That's what the gesture and the smile said. And the familiar enemy of envy stuck its knife into Izzy once more.

She longed for someone to take her hand and be absorbed in her, her alone. But she didn't want to wait as long this woman. She couldn't. Not if she was going to have children. Ha, ha. Izzy having children, she imagined acquaintances sniggering. Shouldn't be allowed. Poor kids. But at the back of her mind was this delicious notion that mothering might be what she was always supposed to do. She clung to the possibility ever more desperately as if it were a life raft with a slow puncture.

She focused her attention back on the mysterious couple. The woman was returning her partner's smile and then directed her attention to the menu more assuredly. The whole scene had only taken a couple of minutes but Izzy had already finished her first drink. She was reminded of all the articles she'd read on excessive drinking. It shouldn't have bothered her but it did.

Still, this was not the right time to attempt restraint. Get through tonight, then reform tomorrow. She ordered another drink, sat back and planned what she was going to say to Lauren when she arrived.

She was halfway through her fourth hypothetical scenario when she was distracted again by the couple at the window. The woman was becoming agitated. She was looking out of the window and drawing back quickly, as if she couldn't believe what she was seeing. Whatever it was, it was the last thing she'd expected.

Then she turned to her companion and started talking quickly. The man was not happy with what was being said. His face was thunderous. The woman was pleading with him, grabbing his hand and stroking it frantically, all the while looking through the window, where Izzy could just about see the reflection of a taxi.

Finally the man got up and left the restaurant, slamming the door behind him and almost shattering the glass panel. The woman sat back in relief for about three seconds. Izzy couldn't take her eyes off the door, fully expecting Arnold Schwarzenegger to burst in with a twenty-third-century laser weapon targeted on the drag queen.

So when the door opened and Lauren walked in, she was taken aback.

Lauren had spotted Izzy immediately. Of course she had. Even in this most bohemian of settings, Izzy stood out like a rare bird in a budgie cage. But Lauren felt

198

that Izzy had toned her appearance down slightly. Only slightly but significantly. Her hair was red, but it was a warmer shade of red, not too far from chestnut. And her make-up, while still striking in its contrasting colours, actually complemented her magnificent bone structure rather than camouflaging it. She was even wearing a dress. There wasn't much of it, but it was still a dress as opposed to a swathe of material bunched around her skeletal frame in random pleats.

Her appreciative appraisal must have been reflected on her face for Izzy found herself blushing at Lauren's warm greeting. She stood up, conscious of her towering height, and bowed her head slightly to compensate. Lauren took this as an invitation to kiss her, which she did. Izzy recoiled slightly from this unfamiliar intimacy and they bumped noses.

Tears came to their eyes from the collision but it had the happy effect of relaxing the stressful moment. They both sat down, rubbing their heads and laughing.

'Sorry!' they both said at the same time.

Laughter over, silence descended upon them like a raincloud. Neither of them was much good at idle chat but Lauren could at least assume her professional persona and initiate a conversation as if Izzy were a client.

'So, have you been waiting long?' she asked, looking around for a waiter. She needed a drink. It had been a long journey and the buffet car had been closed. She was thirsty after quickly eating two bars of chocolate from a machine on the station platform. She was not going to repeat the mistake from last week. Tonight she was going to plead a stomach upset and just nibble on some plain noodles or rice.

'I only just got here myself,' Izzy said, not mentioning that she was on her second drink.

Lauren caught a waiter's eye and ordered a gin and tonic. She had a sudden memory of Richard's Auntie Joan sitting in her shop looking at the photographs of new cash registers that Lauren was showing her and reacting as if they were radioactive. 'Can you make that a double?' she called after the waiter.

The first sip of the long, strong drink was enough to restore her strength and she allowed her shoulder and neck muscles to uncoil. 'So,' she said to Izzy. 'Where's your brother and what are we celebrating?'

Izzy took a deep breath and prepared to deliver her speech on why there was a radical change of plan for the evening. But before she had a chance to speak, she saw that Lauren was staring at the woman by the window. Grateful for the postponement of her explanations, she leaned forward eagerly. 'I know, she's amazing, isn't she? I've been watching her for a while. Do you think it's a man or a woman?'

At this, Lauren turned to face Izzy with an odd expression on her face. 'Oh, I don't have to speculate on that one, she is definitely a woman.'

Izzy looked again, wondering what clues she'd missed. 'How can you be so sure?'

Without taking her eyes off the woman, who was now getting up and walking towards them, Lauren replied: 'Because she's my mother.'

'What are you doing here?' Maureen asked, not sounding

very maternal for a mother talking to her daughter. 'I thought you said you were staying up in Tendale this weekend?'

'I was but there was a last-minute change of plan,' Lauren answered.

'You didn't say when we spoke yesterday,' Maureen accused.

'I didn't know that I had to account for all my movements, Mum. Anyway, what are you doing here? It's a long way from Watford.'

'I've got a gig not too far from here,' Maureen replied cheerfully.

Lauren squirmed at the word 'gig'. Her mum was going to be singing songs from the musicals accompanied by a bad pianist in a rundown pub in front of an audience who wouldn't listen. That was not a gig, it was a scene from an Alan Bennett play.

'What, in Soho?' Lauren asked.

'No, not exactly. Bethnal Green actually. But I remembered you talking about this restaurant last week and thought it might be fun to come here first. You know how much I love to try new things.'

That was one of the few things that Lauren did know about her mother. While she was growing up, her mum's restlessness had known no boundaries. She was constantly searching for something to interest her or challenge her or give her a sense of purpose. She'd drifted from bingo to tap-dancing to cake-decorating to creative writing.

In every case, she started off fired up with enthusiasm. Once the novelty wore off, which it always did, she would blame her dwindling attendance on the demands of motherhood and 'having to be there for Lauren'. It was a lie, they'd both known it, but Lauren had gone along with the lie, feeling that she had to compensate for her father having died while loving Lauren more than Maureen.

This was one of the many unspoken subjects that bubbled beneath the surface of Maureen and Lauren's relatively new relationship.

Still, sushi? Then Lauren realised what struck her as so strange. 'But what are you doing here by yourself? I thought you hated going to restaurants on your own.'

Maureen sent a swift glance towards Izzy, hoping that her eyes were expressive enough to convey that she didn't want Lauren to know that she had not arrived alone. Izzy was too intrigued by the news that this woman was Lauren's mother to want to get involved in this rather tense mother/daughter exchange. She'd thought that no parents could be as weird as hers. But, on re-evaluation, she decided that Lauren's mum was worse. At least her own mum and dad looked normal when they went out in public. They might have bored for England on the subject of Wagner, but they only dressed up at home. She was overwhelmingly grateful to Lauren for indirectly diminishing her own feelings of bitterness and embarrassment towards her parents.

This was all the more reason to encourage a union between her and Chris. Damn Chris for not being here tonight! she thought.

She listened to Maureen lying with ease about her lone presence here. 'I remembered you saying that you met Chris's sister here last week, that she'd come by herself.'

'Yes,' Lauren said, 'and that's when you said that you

couldn't understand any woman walking into a restaurant and eating all alone. You said it wasn't right.'

She'd forgotten that Izzy was sitting across the table listening to this discussion. 'Sorry, Izzy,' she said.

'So you're Izzy?' Maureen said enthusiastically. 'How lovely to meet you! I love your hair! I was going to have mine that colour but I thought it might look a little cheap.'

Izzy was too amused to be offended. And she knew that Maureen had not meant the comment to be taken personally. Izzy had been on the receiving end of so many insults in her time that she could differentiate between the deliberate and the accidental barbs.

Lauren was pulled up short by the reminder that she was arguing with her mum in front of Izzy without going through the requisite introduction. 'Isolde Fallon, this is my mother, Maureen. Mum, this is Isolde, Izzy.'

Maureen shook hands with Izzy warmly. 'I've met your brother, Izzy. He's such a charming man!'

Izzy caught on that they were not going to mention the telephone conversation in the week. It hadn't been discussed but clearly her attendance at the party next week was to be a surprise. None of which went to explain why she wasn't telling her daughter about her escort who'd been shoved unceremoniously out of the door on Lauren's arrival. And to think Izzy had assumed that Lauren was an utterly conventional woman with a deliciously grey upbringing! They were practically soul sisters with their mad parents.

'So Mum, this is still not making any sense. You didn't answer my question. What are you doing here by yourself?'

Maureen was saved from fabricating an answer by Izzy's gasp of recognition as yet another familiar face appeared at the door.

'What's she doing here?' Izzy exclaimed.

Both Maureen and Lauren turned to see who it was. It took Lauren a few moments to place the face. It was Beth. Chris's ex-girlfriend.

She immediately wished she'd stayed in Cumbria. There were too many surprises here, too much to absorb and compute. She was slightly mollified by Izzy's reaction. She was as surprised as Lauren. It meant that Beth was not expected to join the celebration. Whatever the celebration was. Speaking of which, where was Chris?

Beth looked unhappy to see Izzy and even more unhappy to see Lauren with her. However she had no choice but to do the right thing socially and come over. She was with a very handsome man who was touching her arm in a rather desperate gesture of ownership.

'Hello Isolde, what an unexpected surprise.' Her use of Izzy's full name grated on Izzy as Beth knew it would.

'I don't see why it should be a surprise, I come here enough, as you know.'

'Yes but I thought you only came when there was a chance of bumping into me and Chris,' she said, and ruining our evening, she thought.

'Not at all,' Izzy replied tightly. 'I frequently came by myself or with friends. It was just a coincidence that we all met up so often.'

'Really?' Beth observed disbelievingly. She decided not to continue the acrimony. There were too many other emotions churning up inside her to waste precious energy on scoring points off Izzy. She turned to Lauren.

'Hi, Lauren, how are you?'

'Fine, Beth, and you?'

Beth smiled warmly. 'The same.'

Maureen was straining to be introduced so Lauren did the honours, even though she wanted to cut this meeting short at the first possible opportunity.

'Er, this is my mother, Maureen, and this is Beth Savile, Mum. She was Stella's doctor a few years back when she had that bit of bother, do you remember?'

'Oh yes, I do! Stella said you were wonderful, getting her to the top of lists and the like.'

'I didn't really do anything special,' Beth said, not wanting to explain that Stella had been one of those appallingly demanding patients that doctors bust a gut for, simply to get them out of their consulting rooms. 'Besides, it wouldn't be ethical to break the rules for some patients and not for others.'

'Well that's not how Stella told it,' Maureen pointed out admiringly.

Lauren knew exactly why Beth had gone to such trouble for Stella and sympathised. 'Well Mum, you have to take what Stella says with a pinch of salt.'

Maureen sniffed. 'Maybe, but I know that if I ever have any bother in that department, I'm going to come looking for Beth here to see me right!'

Beth's eyes widened in horror at the idea of Maureen bringing any of her problems to her. Lauren spotted her fear and decided to rescue her. It was one of the jobs frequently required of daughters with embarrassing mothers.

'It doesn't work like that, Mum. If you ever did get ill, you couldn't choose who you saw, it would depend on where you lived.'

Beth looked at Lauren and smiled gratefully. Maureen wasn't convinced. 'Listen, I've worked all my life. I've paid my stamps. If, God forbid, anything happens to me, I am entitled to see the best doctor in the land and I will sit outside Beth's office until the Health Service acknowledges my rights.'

Beth decided that a trip to church was in order to offer up a serious prayer for the health of this woman. Lauren read her mind. Beth knew that her thoughts were transparent and she enjoyed a moment of co-conspirators' silence with Lauren.

Beth's handsome escort was hovering behind them. Beth introduced him as another doctor from her hospital. Izzy and Lauren both noticed how he looked at Beth. He clearly had more than friendship on his mind. That was good news for Izzy. Lauren was uninterested.

Beth and the lovely doctor made their way to a table in the back section of the restaurant where they were thankfully out of sight. Only Maureen seemed disappointed to see her go. She was planning to discuss a few of the minor ailments that she couldn't be bothered to take to her GP.

Their eyes were all drawn to the window where a storm was now hurling vertical sheets of rain against the glass.

'We were lucky to get here before that started,' Izzy observed.

Maureen was about to agree when she spotted Eddie's drenched face peeping through the edge of the window. She'd completely forgotten that she'd told him to wait round the corner while she spoke to Lauren. The poor man! She jumped up.

'Anyway, I must go! Got to warm up before I go on stage.'

'Where exactly are you singing?' Izzy asked. 'Perhaps we can come and see you later?'

Maureen hesitated, thinking of how Eddie would feel about sitting by himself in a pub while she entertained her daughter and friend. He'd just about accepted her pleas to wait until the party next week before being introduced to Lauren. But she didn't want to push her luck.

'I'll tell you what. I'll get Lauren to let you know when I'm doing a big show in one of the clubs and we can make a proper night of it.'

She swiftly pecked Lauren on the cheek then did the same to Izzy. That was twice Izzy had been kissed this evening. So much affection was making her head spin.

Then she was gone. Lauren watched her leave with an increasingly puzzled expression. 'She didn't have anything to eat. What on earth was all that about?'

Izzy decided to assume the role of Maureen's defender. 'Actually, I think she'd just finished when I arrived. Speaking of which, I hope you're hungry. I ordered the special for us to share. I know you didn't get much of a chance to enjoy it with Chris last week before you felt unwell.'

Lauren managed a weakly polite 'thank you' before emptying her glass in one long swig and ordering another. Another double.

Maureen snuggled up against Eddie in the taxi, trying to warm him up after his soaking in the shower. 'I'm ever so sorry, love. But you do understand, don't you? Anyway, only one more week. It'll be so much easier if she meets you in a crowd, I know it will. I know it was just going to be a small lunch but it's turning into a proper party. And the party's getting bigger all the time!'

Because Maureen had spotted the complicit exchange between Beth and her daughter and filed it away in her head. They are obviously good friends, she thought. I'll have to get her to Lauren's party next week!

Lauren and Izzy nursed their drinks, both sipping continuously to pass the time. Izzy knew that the moment had come to break the news about Chris.

'I tried to call you yesterday,' she said with a hint of mild accusation.

Lauren shuddered when she thought of yesterday. 'It wasn't a good day for me.'

Izzy couldn't recall the last time she had a good day so she wasn't overly sympathetic. 'So did you have the phone switched off then?'

'Do you mean my mobile?'

Izzy nodded.

Lauren giggled. Oops, she thought, I'm getting drunk. I only giggle when I've had too much to drink too quickly. 'Actually, I threw my mobile phone into a lake. Derwentwater, to be precise.'

Then Izzy giggled. Oops, she thought, I'm getting drunk. I only giggle when I've had too much to drink too quickly. 'Why did you do that?'

Lauren hadn't bothered to ask herself that question. 'Good question,' she said. 'I think it was just after I spoke to you the other day.'

Izzy raised her eyebrows. 'Is that a compliment or an insult?'

Lauren shrugged. 'Neither. I just decided I didn't need it any more. And the lake was very beautiful.'

'So you threw it in.' It was a statement not a question. The action seemed quite logical to Izzy in her increasingly hazy state.

'That's right,' agreed Lauren. 'I threw it in.' Then she giggled again.

'Well, that was a bit of a problem because I tried to call you yesterday,' Izzy repeated.

'So you said,' Lauren replied. This triggered off a coughing fit in them both. The waiter brought their food over very quickly. The manager had spotted the two women getting drunk and resolved to get them served and out as quickly as possible.

Izzy crammed some pretty rolls of fish and vegetables into her mouth in a not very successful attempt to sober herself up. She swallowed too fast and had a choking fit. That sobered them both up.

'It was a fantastic feeling when I watched the phone fly away from me,' Lauren said wistfully. 'It had become part of me, like a third arm. But it had added nothing to my life.' She looked at Izzy. 'Have you got a mobile?' she asked.

Izzy nodded. 'Of course I have.'

Lauren slammed her hands on the table, attracting more attention. 'You see, you said it. You said "of course". As if the very idea of not having a mobile phone were absurd.'

Izzy found her hand sliding down to her bag where the phone nestled on the top for easy access. 'I'm not that bad. It's just a convenience, that's all.'

'You're wrong,' Lauren said to her glass. 'Every single

time you talk into a mobile is a wasted opportunity for silence, for thought, for just looking out of the window. You're never alone, you're always accessible. That's a bad thing. Makes you afraid of being alone. Makes you do anything to make sure that never happens.'

Izzy said nothing. She never talked about loneliness or being alone. Just living it was bad enough. When she had finally found someone to talk to, she wanted to pretend that the subject had no relevance for her. If chucking your mobile phone away made you more introspective, more prone to analysing the gaps in your life, then she was never going to let hers out of her hand.

Lauren was roused from her reverie by Izzy running her finger around her glass. If it was an attention-seeking device, it worked.

'So why did you phone me?' Lauren asked.

'You're going to be so annoyed with me,' Izzy said, preparing Lauren for the worst.

'Why? What have you done?' Lauren asked.

'Well, it wasn't my fault. It's that bloody brother of mine. He didn't tell me but he's arranged to go and see a football match with Pete, your friend Stella's husband.'

'What on earth for? I didn't know they were such good buddies.'

Izzy shrugged. 'I don't know, he was very mysterious about it. It's apparently a proper lads' outing. The match is tomorrow but they're going up tonight because of some demo in Manchester.'

Lauren was disappointed. All the soul-searching she'd gone through before deciding to come to London. She could be eating shepherd's pie with Richard in front of the window, watching the sun go down, not speaking.

All lovely but escapist, irresponsible for a woman in her transitory position.

She'd come here to find some solid ground. She had it all planned. Friday evening with Izzy and Chris, she'd get on well with Chris, they'd have a pleasant evening on Saturday, just the two of them, then on Sunday she could reflect. This was how life could be if she stayed in London. Pleasant times with pleasant men. Was it enough to keep her from New York? She only had a week to decide.

But once again the plans had gone wrong. She shook her head. 'I can't imagine how he persuaded Pete to go to a football match with him. Pete absolutely hates football.'

Izzy shook her head. 'You're wrong. The only reason they're going is because Pete is a real Tottenham Hotspur fan.'

Now it was Lauren's turn to shake her head. 'No, you're wrong. I've known Pete for nearly twenty years. Nobody hates football as much as he does.'

Then she and Izzy gazed out into space as they absorbed the implications of this news. They both knew that Chris hated football. Izzy had always known it and Chris had said as much to Lauren when they first met. Lauren had replayed that first meeting so many times in her head, that every detail had become embedded firmly in her memory.

So what were two men who hated football and were not good friends doing on a lads' football weekend away?

By ten thirty, the two men were on their fifth pint each and were eating a ferociously hot curry.

'I can't remember the last time I did this,' Pete said, relishing the burning sensation as the searing piece of chicken made its destructive way down his throat. He swallowed half a pint of lager to numb the pain.

Chris sniffed unattractively. His eyes were watering from the food and his nose was running. It was much hotter than he was used to but he hadn't wanted to appear a wimp in front of his new best friend.

'If I'm honest, I'm not sure I ever did this. I've not been much of a man's man as such. I've always preferred female company.' He sounded apologetic, uncertain if this was something to be confessed or boasted. 'What about you?'

'I've definitely never done this. I met Stella so early that I never really had the chance to be wild and reckless. Not that I feel I've missed out on anything,' he added, not wanting to betray the slightest dissatisfaction with his marriage.

Neither of them was seriously drunk. They might have been unaccustomed to beer and curry binges but they were both seasoned drinkers. Endless sequences of dinner parties had rendered their systems immune to alcohol damage. But the drink was loosening their tongues without their realising it.

'Me neither,' Chris agreed. 'I can see why men like to do this though. It's nice not having to force yourself to make conversation which you have to do when you're with a woman.'

'Is that what it used to be like with Beth, forcing conversations over dinner?' Pete asked, looking down at his food, not trusting himself to let Chris see the inordinate interest he had in the answer.

It didn't take much to bring Beth back into Chris's thoughts. Since finally ridding himself of all memories of those two insane evenings with Lauren, there had been a hole in his life. He'd made a tiny space for Lauren, space that he hadn't intended to make so soon after Beth, and so far, she'd made no serious attempts to fill it. He knew that he should revert to his original plan which was to live alone for some time, concentrate on his work, sort out what he was going to do with his life if the school closed.

None of this appealed. He wasn't used to making decisions alone. He'd always slightly envied his single colleagues who made impulsive choices, knowing that they had nobody else's needs to consider. But now that he was single, he'd developed a theory that this was a fallacy, put about by lonely people so that no one would pity them. Because if nobody is affected by anything you do, then your very existence on the planet is essentially superfluous. If you're not loved, then you can't be missed.

He wanted the entanglement back again. And after the untidy experience with Lauren, who could blame him for yearning once more for the safe simplicity of life with Beth?

Which brought him back to Pete's question. 'What was life like with Beth? It was wonderful. It was calm and exciting and predictable and a bit tricky and comfortable. I miss her. She's the one person in the world I need right now and I sent her away.' He wanted to take the words back. He'd never talked about his feelings to anyone apart from occasionally with Beth after a fight. And he always regretted it. He wasn't ready to spill his heart over another man's curry just yet.

But this openness triggered a similar need to unburden himself in Pete. He hadn't been able to talk to anyone about his situation and Beth's ex-boyfriend was the worst person to choose for the role now. But there was no one else. He would probably never get another chance. So he had to select his words very, very carefully indeed.

'If it makes you feel any better, I know how you feel. I'm in a similar situation myself.' He cleared his throat self-consciously, uncertain of exactly how much he dared to say without giving the game away.

Chris sat up, trying to conceal that he was paying special attention to whatever Pete was about to tell him. So far, he'd been unsuccessful in getting Pete to talk about his health. There were only so many ways he could bring up the subject without it appearing contrived. So he'd decided to sit back and see what effect the drink had on bringing deeper worries to the surface. It had worked for Chris – he'd been perfectly content before he started drinking, now he felt suicidal.

'I've had something on my mind for a short while now, something I haven't been able to talk to Stella about.'

'Right,' Chris said, non-committally, guardedly optimistic that Pete was going to open up. 'That must be tough. Having no one to talk it over with.'

'Well, there is someone,' Pete said quietly.

Now we're getting to it, Chris thought. Softly, softly. 'And is this . . . person able to help?'

Pete smiled sadly. 'This person is both the cause of my trouble and, at the same time, the only one who can help. What kind of mess is that?' He didn't care that he was more or less admitting to Chris that he had feelings for another woman. He needed some advice.

It was fortunate that he didn't care. It would have been a redundant worry since Chris hadn't a clue that this was what Pete was confessing. He was fairly sure that Beth was the woman Pete was talking about, unless his life was more complicated than anyone could have imagined. But he assumed that Pete's dilemma was that Beth could confirm his suspicions about his symptoms and was also the only person who could put his mind at rest. He had to tread very carefully here.

'So, this er, trouble – how serious is it?'

Pete pictured himself with Beth. He imagined Stella's face if he left her. 'As bad as it gets,' he said, swallowing hard.

Oh God, thought Chris. Stella was right. He ached with the burden of responsibility that was on his shoulders now.

'So where do things stand at the moment?' he asked with what he thought was a light touch.

Pete emptied his glass and shook his head. With firm resolution, he raised his eyes to meet Chris's. 'I've already made up my mind. I'm going to ignore it. I was OK before. I'll be OK again. I'm strong, I'll get over it.'

Chris couldn't conceal his alarm. Stella's worst fears were coming true. He was going to ignore his symptoms, go into complete denial. He had to do something fast. 'Are you sure that's a good idea? I mean, troubles don't just disappear if you ignore them. You have to face up to whatever is bothering you, deal with it, then you can put it behind you and get on with your life.' The strain of keeping his words ambiguous was making him sweat. Unless it was the curry.

Pete didn't look convinced. 'But I'm worried about what this person will say if I see her again.'

Her. There. He'd dropped the final pretence. He felt lighter. It was like taking off a heavy coat in a warm house.

Chris was encouraged that he was letting more and more details slip through. He longed to grab Pete by the collar and shake him. 'Go and ring Beth now, you stupid idiot! Get yourself checked out properly before it gets worse!' That's what he wanted to say. But he wasn't drunk enough. He still had some self-restraint left.

'Whatever she says, you need to hear it. You can't open something up without facing what comes out of it before you close it again.'

Pete didn't know what that was supposed to mean. Neither did Chris. The need for subtlety was proving too much. He was becoming so obscure that he was of no earthly use to Pete.

'So what are you saying, Chris?' Pete asked, wanting somebody else's advice since he had no confidence in his own take on the situation.

'I'm saying that you have to see her again. You have to.'

Pete thought of little else as he drifted into a restless sleep after two more pints.

Chapter 13

Stella wandered around the house, finding it impossible to get interested in any of the mammoth decorating tasks that faced her. Last night had been the first she'd spent apart from Pete since they'd met. She couldn't get to sleep and had ended up downstairs watching a black-and-white war film till three o'clock in the morning with Ann.

Bill and Ann had come to stay for another weekend at Pete and Stella's insistence. They had been reluctant to accept the invitation. Hostilities between them were only just beginning to ease after their mutual confessions of the week before. Bill had spent the week watching Ann constantly, always on the alert for a sign that she was ill. If she so much as took a slow, deep breath, he pounced on her.

'Are you OK? Is it your heart? Shall I call a doctor?'

Ann had just about managed to stop herself from screaming at him in frustration. She knew that he was worried and had apologised for not telling him about her problem earlier. In fact, she was now less concerned about her heart and more bothered about their finances.

They'd both been prudent with money throughout their married life. They'd never had credit cards or HP. The only debt they'd ever allowed themselves was a mortgage. If they wanted anything, they saved until they could afford to buy it outright. It was how they both liked to live having grown up with wartime deprivation and insecurity.

So to face the fact that their savings were decimated frightened her terribly. She didn't blame Bill for lending money to Pete, she'd probably have done the same herself if asked, but she hated the fact that he'd concealed what he'd done. He knew how important she felt financial security was and he'd jeopardised that without even consulting her.

They were rebuilding their broken trust gradually and could have done with some more time alone to come to terms with this rift. But Stella and Pete had both sounded desperate.

Pete didn't want to leave Stella on her own while he went to a football match in Manchester with a friend.

'What friend?' Ann had asked Bill. 'He doesn't even like football.' Bill wasn't much help; he just accepted the facts at face value and left Ann to fret over them and look for hidden meanings where probably there were none. He never asked questions. He felt that this made life simpler whereas Ann believed that only an adequate supply of information offered any hope of enlightenment.

Pete had been worried about Stella after her tears. She was vulnerable at the moment and he accepted that it was his fault. The coming week, leading up to the meeting where his future would be decided, was going to be hard for her. He wanted to provide something to occupy her so that she wouldn't have too much time to brood over all the worries that she would not want to talk about.

And he was worried about his parents too. If only he hadn't made the firm decision not to contact Beth again, he would have loved to talk over his mum's symptoms with her. He knew that Beth wasn't a heart specialist and he knew how doctors must hate friends bringing all their sundry health questions to them but he felt sure that Beth wouldn't have minded. Not in his case. Still, it was a moot point since he wouldn't be seeing her again.

He was off to Manchester to keep Stella happy. At least that's why he thought he was going. The more he looked back at his conversation with Chris, the vaguer he was about why he'd agreed to the trip.

Things seemed to be happening in an arbitrary manner recently. He kept hoping that some kind of pattern might emerge and form some recognisable symmetry that he could cling on to. But since their house-warming party, swirls of chaos seemed to be leaving whopping great punctures in his neat linear existence. He hoped that a night away might break the spell that was engulfing him.

When he woke up on Saturday morning with a fuzzy head, his first thoughts were for Stella and his parents. They were all together. He didn't have to worry about them. They would look after each other.

'What are you doing, Stella?' Ann asked gently.

'Nothing,' Stella answered. And she was telling the truth. She was doing nothing. She wasn't painting or cleaning or rearranging or stencilling. She wasn't even flicking through one of her favourite catalogues looking for things to buy.

For someone who believed that the only acceptable life to look back on was one crammed to overflowing with activity, Stella didn't handle inactivity well. She didn't read books, she wasn't much of a television watcher. Stella could only do four things: she could work, entertain, shop and do up houses. That's how she defined herself and she wasn't unhappy with the definition.

And now that she had paralysing concerns about Pete, about their marriage and future, she had no outlet for dealing with her fears.

She couldn't work because it was Saturday and she'd never taken her career seriously enough to bring it home at weekends.

She couldn't entertain, not with Ann and Bill staying in the house, particularly when they were all so miserable. The three of them living under the same roof was like starring in their very own Woody Allen film.

She couldn't go shopping, not now that she knew about the threat of Pete losing his job.

That left doing up houses. She couldn't do any work on the house, not with Pete away. He would have denied it, but Stella didn't do anything without getting his approval first. It was her way of showing continued commitment to their partnership. Practically the only way. And completely the wrong way to have any impact on Pete. Throwing away her hostess trolley would have impressed him more deeply.

Still, she'd done her best to involve him. But Pete had never known this. He'd always assumed that she was paying lip service to him, inviting his approval in exchange for fifty per cent of the capital outlay.

She couldn't even tell Bill and Ann about her fears, not with all they had on their plate. She sat down, walked about, sat down again. She wandered from room to room, wondering how she could have seen any potential in this house. It was a mess and all the money and work in the world would just paper over the cracks.

The truth was, it was not and never would be a home. Stella and Pete had realised lucrative investments, pushed back the frontiers of interior design, slept on bare floorboards and on £3,000 Danish beds. They'd turned hovels into highly desirable residential opportunities. They'd spent every penny they'd ever earned on making their surroundings habitable.

But they'd never made a home.

Stella had always sneered at their friends who married, had babies and then allowed their houses to degenerate into a cosy squalor. She saw hand-woven silk tapestries splattered with Ribena, Chinese carpets with Cheesy Wotsits crushed irremovably into the pattern. She walked through front doors and could not see a single conceivable path into the house that did not involve treading on something sharp and plastic or warm and wet.

Mentally, such families were instantly crossed off her list of acquaintances. The very act of knowing people with such little respect for material possessions meant facing the suggestion of them bringing their destructive tendencies into Stella's immaculate world.

And frankly Stella resented the implication that her values were somehow shallower because she valued things above children. As if children were not little more than acquisitions themselves to many of the parents she knew.

This house had represented the pinnacle of years of hard work to reach a standard of living that she could only have dreamed of in her youth. She and Pete had done it together. True, she'd taken the creative lead and made most of the decisions but that was the way in any partnership.

And yet this night apart from Pete had seriously unsettled her. It wasn't just the possibility of him being ill. It was the more unbearable possibility that his illness wasn't the real problem. She thought back to the house-warming and Pete's distinctly cool attitude to the whole event. It might have been that he was preoccupied with the thoughts of redundancy or tumours.

But then she went back further. To when they were looking at this house and deciding whether or not to buy it. She'd interpreted his declaration of surrender to her will as a display of love. Now she wondered if it was apathy.

And she went back further. To the house before. To the moment when all the work they had done, she had done, was complete. Five years of lavish renovations had seen the price of the Victorian house double. He'd bought champagne and they'd walked round the house, marvelling at the transformation. And when they reached the top of the house, Stella had turned to Pete with shining eyes and said, 'We'll be able to buy a detached Edwardian house with the money we get for this! I've checked the prices around here and we can take our pick – there are some complete dumps on the market that would be perfect for us!'

And it wasn't until the next day when the cleaner came across the unfinished bottle of champagne that Stella had realised the celebration had ended with those words.

She didn't dare look back any further. It was too frightening. She'd placed all her hopes, hers and Pete's, in creating their dream home. And all of a sudden she had to face the truth that, every time they'd come close to achieving the dream, she had yanked it away before the home part had a chance to materialise.

This house. What was she thinking of? Right now, at this precise moment, she longed for it to be a home, one for Pete to come 'home' to. Because she now believed that this was what he wanted. She'd been so willing to accept that he shared her vision that it had never occurred to her to ask him if he had a vision of his own.

Still, it wasn't too late. She could remedy the situation. Obviously they had to fix this house up. They could never sell it on in its present condition. Only someone with Stella's lunatic aspirations and a limitless budget would take on such a white elephant. But she'd keep the work to a minimum. Paint the whole bloody house magnolia, if necessary, then sell it and buy a home with Pete. For them both.

She needed to talk to someone. To have this decision validated. She needed to talk to Lauren. She dialled her home number. No answer. She dialled the mobile. No longer in existence. Stella frowned. It was nine o'clock on a Saturday morning. Where was Lauren?

'I think I'm going to die,' Lauren groaned as she crawled back from the bathroom. She'd been sick most of the night, mainly from the sushi that she'd eaten in an act of drunken recklessness, but also from the drink. She'd lost track of how much she and Izzy had got through. In fact, she'd lost track of the entire evening after arriving at a bar called The Funky something or other and ordering a hideous long pink drink that belonged in the '80s.

'Who said that?' Izzy called from her bedroom in alarm. She staggered into the living room and stared at Lauren for a few seconds before her addled brain could compute who this was. 'Oh, it's you,' she said. 'Do you feel as bad as I feel?'

Lauren looked at her. 'Perhaps a better question would be: "Do I look as bad as you look?" Have you seen yourself in the mirror yet?'

Izzy walked over to the full-length mirror in the hall and had to take a step back at the apparition before her.

Overnight she had turned into the Ghost of Christmas Yet to Come. The spectral pallor of her skin was highlighted by some spectacular streaks of bronze eye shadow, blue glittery mascara, cerise blusher and blood-red lipstick. She must have tossed and turned a lot on her pillow in the night because it looked as if some jovial practical joker had crept in while she was sleeping and smeared trifle across her face.

The effect was completed by still being dressed in yesterday's clothes. Except that her beautifully cut dress was now a tea towel, creased, damp and marked with ominous stains. Izzy had woken up with hangovers before but this was the worst. Since her appearance had always been the one aspect of her life that she could control, it was mortifying to see herself looking like Edna the Inebriate Woman.

'Oh my God,' she finally managed to choke out. 'I'm going to have a shower immediately.' Then she sank into a chair. 'As soon as I can stand up for more than five seconds without feeling dizzy, that's when I'm going to have a shower.'

The two women sat in a state of companionable suffering for about fifteen minutes. Lauren eventually dragged herself to her feet and moved very slowly towards the kitchen. 'Shall I make a cup of tea?' she whispered, not wanting to make her headache any worse, although that didn't seem possible.

Izzy nodded slightly.

By ten thirty, they'd both managed to keep some tea and dry toast down. They'd even managed to shower although that had been a painful experience requiring much aspirin. It had taken some time for Izzy to find any clothes that would fit Lauren. After several soul-destroying attempts to squeeze into trousers the width of pipe cleaners, Lauren settled for some tracksuit bottoms and a baggy jumper.

With their faces scrubbed clean, Izzy and Lauren looked like teenagers (if you squinted and ignored the fine lines and war-weary eyes). They sat in armchairs facing each other, totally wiped out by the effort of showering and dressing. They were replaying the previous evening, going over the details of what each had learned about the other.

Their revelations had become more exaggerated and more obscure as the night progressed and the glasses were refilled. Izzy talked about Wagner a lot, using some less than operatic language, and she gave Lauren a garbled CV which encompassed some of the most bizarre jobs that a middle-class girl could take on. Apparently Izzy had, for one mad week, strutted around the circus ring in a shimmering thong, smiling and pointing as acrobats and trapeze artists risked their lives in the foolhardy pursuit of making children clap.

And she'd been a foot model, or more precisely, a toe model. A photograph of the big toe on her left foot was on the front of every box of corn plasters sold in south-east Asia. She'd even taken off her shoe in the sushi restaurant so that Lauren could inspect the prize specimen through Izzy's fine stockings. 'Are you making this up?' Lauren had asked doubtfully, mistaking Izzy for someone with a sense of humour.

Izzy had been indignant. 'Of course I'm not! Anyway, why are you so surprised? You must have seen photos of toes before in adverts, did you never wonder about whose feet they were?'

Lauren looked blank. 'I can't say I have. But I'll always give foot pictures my full attention in the future.' And the absolute absence of irony in her comment was the final proof that Lauren had gone past the stage of being pleasantly tiddly and was now entering into the completely soused phase.

After the lengthy monologue entitled Every Job I Have Ever Done, Lauren had asked Izzy about her personal life. She felt that they had become intimate enough for such a question to be acceptable – after all, they'd gone to the ladies' together and passed toilet paper under the cubicle partitions.

Izzy had become subdued at this point. If Lauren had been sober, she would have recognised that this was a sensitive issue and changed the subject. But she wasn't and she didn't.

'Come on, Izzy. I mean you must have men falling over themselves to get to you. You look like a model and you're all . . . I don't know, you're all . . .'

'Different,' Izzy said flatly. 'I'm all different, that's

the word you're looking for. And do you know what men want? They want women who are not different. They want women who are the same. And I don't blame them. I don't like different myself. I like normal, conventional, boring, predictable.'

'Sorry if I'm being thick, Izzy, but why do you present yourself like this if you don't want to be different? You know, the hair, the make-up, the clothes.'

Izzy pressed her lips together. It was a defence mechanism she'd perfected that prevented her from crying on inappropriate occasions, i.e. whenever other people were around. 'Well, work it out for yourself, Lauren. Look at me, I mean really look at me.'

Lauren didn't think she needed to look. Izzy was so in-your-face that an observer's eyes would be drawn to her from just about any location in any room where she was standing.

'I have looked, Izzy. You're tall, slim, you've got fantastic bone structure and every woman in the world who meets you must hate you with a vengeance.'

Izzy closed her eyes at the predictable response. 'You have no idea. Lauren, I am the original Scary Spice. I'm genuinely terrifying. People actually say that to me, thinking I'll see the funny side.'

Lauren felt herself going red as she recalled that her initial reaction to Izzy had been exactly the same. 'I'm sure they don't mean to be hurtful. I think they're just struck by your . . . awesome presence.'

'I don't want to have an awesome presence!' Izzy was raising her voice now and the restaurant's other customers were looking up. 'When you look like me, you have two choices: you can go the "awesome presence" route and

227

scare the hell out of everyone you meet or you can try and play down your natural attributes.'

'Have you tried that?' Lauren asked, genuinely curious as to what Izzy would look like unadorned.

Izzy snorted. 'Of course I have. Then, instead of being a tall, thin, bizarrely dressed freak, I look like a tall, thin, plain freak. Either way, people avert their eyes. I am simply not the sort of person who strangers instinctively want to approach for an unthreatening chat.'

Lauren didn't know what to say because she had to agree with Izzy's assessment of herself. She had recoiled from Izzy on their first introduction. And she'd been quick to judge her as abrasive and cold. But now she was seeing a different, deeper side to the woman.

Izzy had asked her about what was going on between her and Chris.

'Why? What has Chris said?' Lauren had asked curiously.

Izzy shrugged. 'Nothing. Well, nothing that makes any sense. Just that you'd had a few communication problems. He didn't go into details.'

Lauren was grateful for Chris's discretion. And she could have preserved the mystery, if she hadn't been in a particularly voluble mood. So the whole story came out.

Izzy listened in amazement. 'I don't quite understand. What do you mean, there was something in the way he said "astrology" that made you lie about your star sign? As far as I know, Chris has no feelings about astrology one way or another. You must have been imagining it.'

Lauren laughed to herself. She'd already considered this and Izzy's statement merely confirmed her suspicion – that she'd lied for nothing, that she'd wasted precious time worrying about it, that she'd wasted an opportunity to get to know a good man in the limited time she might have left in the UK. It was farcical, and utterly irrelevant now. She consoled herself with the thought that no harm had been done.

Izzy felt sorry for Lauren. At the same time, she was thrilled to discover that even normal, pretty women could experience social disaster. Right now, she was enjoying a rare moment of superiority because she had never lied to impress anyone in her life. She couldn't see the point, although at a later stage in their friendship, Lauren was to explain to her how a little judicious deceit can be a very effective ploy in making people feel comfortable, making them like you. She did it in business situations all the time.

But for now, her position on the moral high ground allowed her to be magnanimous in her sympathy. 'Don't give up on Chris, Lauren. I know he's still keen so you should go ahead and try undoing all these tangles. I'm sure that is what he wants.' It's what I want, she wanted to say, but didn't. She wasn't that drunk.

Lauren wasn't listening. Chris was a long way from her thoughts. Just talking about that first meeting had released Chris from the little box in her head labelled 'unfinished business'. While she preferred events that she could control, she was quick to acknowledge a firm shove from fate. She felt very dense for not having realised sooner that she was never meant to be with Chris. She'd finally taken the hint.

But instead of being released to think about New York, she found herself thinking of Tendale. And yesterday. She'd been sitting on a stool in the shop watching Richard arranging a display of ski suits. A ridiculous idea had been creeping into her consciousness for a couple of days and she'd been reluctant to mention it. But it slipped out anyway.

'I can see how easy it was for your wife to fall in love with this place and not want to leave.'

Richard laughed out loud. 'I don't know where you got that impression. She didn't fall in love with this place. She fell in love with a dream, a vision of how she imagined her life in this place could be. She arrived here in May and we were married in September. I should never have married her before she'd experienced winter here. It's hard and cruel.'

Lauren looked doubtful. 'It's winter now and I love it.'

Richard followed her gaze out of the window. The snow had settled everywhere, muting the occasional sound of traffic, dazzling with its unbroken whiteness. 'You've been here a matter of days. And you know you're not staying. There's a difference.'

'But you love the winter, you told me,' Lauren pointed out.

'That's because this is my world.'

Lauren watched him staring out of the window, wondering if he was truly different to her, if this could ever be her world. Wondering how she was supposed to find out.

'What are you thinking?' Richard asked her, without averting his eyes from the view.

Lauren spoke softly. 'That I could sit here for the rest of my life, on this stool, in this shop. Looking at the view, making tea, tutting when your displays were wonky, actually noticing the weather change from autumn to winter. I could live this life, I really could. I'd never have to wear make-up again or eat tiramisu or go to parties.'

Richard glanced up from the shelf. Yes! he wanted to yell. Stay! Live here with me! I'll take you up every mountain and around every lake. I'll help you to forget the men who hurt you and the mother who ignored you and the father who died. You'll be able to say anything, become whoever you want to be. Stay!

He should have said it. Not saying things we want to say can be as destructive as saying things we shouldn't say. Lauren might have laughed at him. Or been embarrassed. Or she might have opened her eyes to him as she had to the mountains.

Still, he left these thoughts unspoken. 'You'd miss it after a few months. I see townies here every week. They come here, all shiny-eyed, talking about how they're going to sell up, throw in their banking careers, open a tea shop or a B and B. "See you soon," they say. They never return. And when you go back to London tomorrow and you're eating sushi with your glamorous friends, you'll cringe at the memory of wanting to give all that up to work in a shop.'

Lauren had been strangely disappointed at his lack of enthusiasm. Not that she'd expected him to invite her to become his business partner. But she'd hoped for an indication that their friendship was more than a month-long contract. That he'd tell her to come back for weekends and holidays, take her up every mountain and around every lake.

She totally forgot that she was contemplating emigrating in a few weeks' time. That had become unimportant.

Richard was the closest she'd had to a proper friend since Stella. And she couldn't swear that her friendship with Stella would have lasted as long as it did if it hadn't been for Stella's commitment.

She couldn't think about the mountain side of her life while she was in London. But the effects had lingered and she'd brought a bit of the 'countryside Lauren' back with her this time.

For the last hour or so, she'd been talking with Izzy in a way that she hadn't done with anyone for a very long time, apart from Richard. With Stella, her conversations were less direct, less honest. It wasn't Stella's fault. Her natural exuberance meant that she could not restrain herself from telling Lauren every single trivial thing that had happened to her since their last talk. There was no time for anything else to get a look in.

If Lauren tried to get Stella to talk about herself, about how she was feeling with all that was going on in her life, Stella merely took this as an invitation to reel off the list of all her latest acquisitions, along with their place of purchase and price.

Stella, however, was always diligent in asking Lauren to unburden herself of all her own personal concerns. She soaked up Lauren's angst like a Freudian sponge, squeezing out dozens of interchangeable responses to each dilemma that Lauren might present. And there was no doubt that Stella truly cared about her friend's happiness. She just couldn't see that it was hard for Lauren to feel close to her when there was nothing of Stella given back.

She had wondered if perhaps Stella was so happy with her lot that she'd lost the concept of discontent altogether. Or maybe Stella was so thick-skinned that no pain could penetrate her resolute cheerfulness. Lauren's last boyfriend, Peter, had said that Stella wasn't thick-skinned, merely thick. Lauren had risen to her friend's defence, claiming that Stella's first-class honours degree in psychology disproved that theory.

'You don't get it, Lauren,' Peter had said. 'You can be a brilliant academic and still be fundamentally stupid. And frankly, for Stella to have a degree in psychology while having no idea that her own psyche is absolutely empty speaks for itself.'

It had been a shame that, by the time Lauren and Peter were having such interesting discussions, relations between them had reached the point of nastiness and every comment was loaded with unpleasant baggage. Because Peter was right.

Lauren thought it disloyal to be feeling more comfort-able with Izzy than her best friend. But she was drunk, so the disloyalty was soon superseded by nausea.

She was surprised to reach the conclusion that Izzy had the makings of a really good friend and she felt sad that Izzy's qualities had gone unappreciated for so long. She decided that she was going to take on the challenge of finding a way to make Izzy presentable, to help her over the first social hurdle of her actual appearance so that people would have the opportunity of getting to know her.

And as she sat in Izzy's living room feeling achingly sorry for this woman who didn't know what to do with herself, she saw a way of helping her and helping herself at the same time.

'I may have got this wrong, but did you say something last night about losing your job?'

Izzy laughed. 'It's not quite as dramatic as that. I wasn't fired or anything, it's just that I decided dog-walking wasn't for me.'

Lauren remembered the story of the Jack Russell and the goose which had reduced her to tears of laughter in The Funky whatever. 'I don't know, I think that a dead goose is fairly dramatic.'

Izzy raised her eyebrows. 'Maybe. I'm still out of work.'

'What are you planning to do?' Lauren asked.

'I don't really know,' Izzy replied. 'I don't need to earn a huge amount. I own this flat outright so I only need living expenses.'

Lauren was surprised. The flat was beautiful and must have been worth over £150,000. 'How did you manage to buy this place?'

Izzy pointed to a framed print on the wall. It was the picture of a toe with a corn plaster on it.

Lauren's mouth dropped open. 'I don't believe it! You made enough money from putting your toe on corn plaster packets in Asia to buy a flat?'

'Partly. But not just that. I was the Dr Scholl model in Australia and the "official foot" of the American Podiatrists' Association from nineteen ninety to ninety-five.'

'Show me your feet again,' Lauren demanded, fascinated to learn what Izzy's toes had that her own didn't.

She peered at them and couldn't discern any true aesthetic merit. They were just very long, as you'd expect from someone of Izzy's height. She looked down at her own feet. Not bad, she thought. A bit squashed and curved, a few stray hairs, nails the texture of a rhinoceros horn but nothing that couldn't be covered up by some good retouching.

'I'm in the wrong business,' she said in wonder.

'You don't mean that,' Izzy replied. 'Your job sounds fantastic. You make things happen, solve problems, you travel around, people respect you. I think it sounds great.'

Lauren leaned forward, letting her substandard toes fall to the ground. 'I'm glad you said that, Izzy, because I've got a proposition for you. How would you like to come and work for me for a few weeks?'

Chapter 14

'She's completely unemployable, that's the trouble with
Izzy,' Chris said to Pete, stamping his feet on the ground
in the false hope that it might help restore the circulation.
Having covered the history of their lives, they were now
on to families. Pete had taken Chris through his large
family, glossing over Bill and Ann's recent problems.
Chris responded with the tale of a dysfunctional pair
of parents and two children who had so far managed
to escape committal to an institution. Although, to Pete's
ears, Izzy sounded completely round the twist.

They were waiting for the match to kick off and were
chatting happily as you'd expect of two men who've
become best friends after sharing a hotel room while
both suffering with the worst case of post-curry diar-
rhoea ever.

Throughout the evening, Chris had wondered at what
point the male bonding he'd read so much about could
be said to have started. Lying on twin beds, holding
their stomachs which were emitting whiney screeches
in perfect two-part harmony, they'd somehow survived
a long night with almost no sleep. They'd talked about
things that neither had shared with anyone else before. It
was like being on a desert island with no hope of rescue.
They both had many things to say before they died.

And even though they didn't actually die, they felt like survivors in the morning. They even considered writing a book about their night. Nobody would buy it but they would feel great.

The bonding experience, the moment of pure synchronicity, of absolute union, did in fact occur when they discovered that they were blessed with the identical superabundance of that marvellous quality that generally sets men apart from women – a staggering degree of hypochondria.

Not for them the stoical acceptance of the after-effects of a dodgy curry. No, for these two musketeers, each visit to the bathroom confirmed their suspicions that they had been struck down by a lethal virus unheard of in the Western world, let alone Manchester. And since there was no woman to give them a glass of Alka Seltzer and tell them to stop being so pathetic, their fantasy about the superbug became more and more plausible to the two deluded creatures.

And as the night wore on and sleep was impossible, they shared their medical histories: the almost fatal doses of flu that their partners had scathingly referred to as colds, the back pains that indicated serious damage from suitably masculine over-exertion which undertrained GPs dismissed as a bit of a strain, the rashes which indicated rare allergies, the bowel movements of menacing variability. Chris and Pete went through the lot.

Chris encouraged the discussion, happy that they'd found a legitimate reason to discuss medical symptoms. Unfortunately, Pete seemed to have so many symptoms that Chris couldn't discern whether any of them were real or imagined. Maybe he was suppressing the worrying ones. Because everything that Pete had, Chris had too, down to the clicking knee and the over-hairy back.

There were only two possible conclusions to draw from Pete's outpourings: either he wasn't seriously ill at all or he was seriously ill, in which case Chris was seriously ill too. Chris didn't get very far beyond this disturbing observation; he was too preoccupied with his own terrible stomach cramps.

They'd managed a few hours of fitful sleep and felt dreadful when they were woken up by an alarm call at seven-thirty, but not too dreadful to stagger downstairs to the restaurant. If Lauren and Izzy had seen them downing an enormous full English breakfast, they would have railed against the cosmic injustice that is men's tolerance of food and drink abuse.

They were in high spirits when they reached the ground and made their way to their stand. 'These are good seats, Chris,' Pete said.

'Are they?' Chris asked, not sure what constituted good seats at a football match.

'I think so,' Pete replied, now feeling less positive on hearing Chris's doubtfulness. He hadn't a clue himself whether they were good seats but he'd felt that it was the polite thing to say. Besides, Chris was a real football fan and wouldn't buy duff seats, surely.

He looked around the rapidly filling ground. Streams of red and blue were pouring in from opposite ends. It was a freezing cold February morning and Pete had been very grateful that Stella had forced him to take her old Spurs accessories.

'I am not wearing that,' he had insisted when she pulled out a bobble hat, scarf and gloves from a chest in the loft.

'Don't be so silly,' Stella had said curtly. 'Everyone wears them at football matches. You'll look out of place if you're not wearing the gear. And Chris will expect it.' She was amused at Pete going through the act of being a Spurs fan. Amused and relieved at the same time because she wouldn't herself have relished maintaining the charade for so long.

Her husband and friends might have been surprised to learn this. They made the assumption that her determination to march through her life with a permanent anti-serious filter switched on was proof of her self-delusion. But Stella was being absolutely true to herself. Unlike the others who were dithering about dreams and decisions, she knew exactly what she wanted and needed. She never wavered or hesitated. She was essentially the same person she had been at eighteen and couldn't understand why others would make life so difficult for themselves by evolving.

Finding her old Spurs clothes brought back memories of her youth. At thirty-seven, she knelt on the floor (stripped boards arranged in a spiral that triggered off a migraine if you stared at them for more than a second) and fingered the faded woolly cockerel of the Spurs badge. She tried to feel fifteen again but failed. She closed her eyes tight and tried to picture herself dancing gracelessly around her bedroom to Kate Bush's 'Wuthering Heights'. No, that image was lost too. And the girl who pretended to like football to make Dave Pinner fancy her? A stranger.

She didn't like this at all. The break in continuity affected her sense of security. And she needed to get her balance back to deal with what was happening now.

Recently, she'd been experiencing the sensation of their life as an old film with Stella doing all the acting and Pete dubbing the soundtrack – except he couldn't get the synchronisation right. His words always came a split second before or after Stella moved her lips. It was just a minor matter of timing but it could ruin the picture.

No, she didn't like where this train of thought was heading. She slammed the chest shut and thrust the souvenirs at Pete. 'Take them. Trust me, you'll be grateful for them.'

And now he was grateful. For all of five minutes. Then he noticed that Chris was shifting in his seat and glancing nervously at the hat.

Pete fingered the hat, thinking that maybe he looked more ridiculous than he thought. 'Why do you keep looking at me like that? I know it's a bit small. It was Stella's when she was fifteen.'

Chris shook his head. 'It's nothing to do with the size.'

'Then what is it?' Pete asked.

Chris inclined his head slightly. 'Haven't you noticed?' he whispered.

Pete looked about. 'No,' he answered, baffled by Chris's edginess.

'Have a look at everyone sitting around us,' Chris hissed, then sat back, not wanting to draw any more attention to himself.

That's when Pete understood. His blue hat with the jaunty yellow bobble was located at the epicentre of an unbroken ocean of red. They were sitting bang in the middle of the Manchester United supporters.

Now Pete wasn't a football fan and neither was Chris. But on the other hand, they were both *Guardian* readers. They knew what it meant to be wearing the wrong colour gear in a crowd of football fans. Sociological unrest – or in English, the threat of a good kicking. These were not the sepia days of old when rival Rovers and City fans from every town would sit side by side, applaud their opponents' free kicks and share Spam and pickle sandwiches and some hot soup from a flask.

Despite the sophisticated security checks, some of the people glaring at them with unconcealed hostility would be carrying weapons. In many cases, judging by the sheer size of the men in question, their hands would make perfectly effective weapons against two soft white-collar workers whose only battle experience was persuading a churlish fishmonger to bone the trout for a forthcoming dinner party.

Pete sat up rigidly. 'What should I do?' he asked Chris frantically.

'Take the bloody hat off, you idiot!' Chris hissed between clenched teeth.

Pete whipped it off and stuffed it in his jacket pocket along with the scarf and gloves. 'I'm freezing cold now,' he mumbled miserably.

Chris kept his eyes fixed ahead, deciding his best plan would be to disassociate himself from Pete. 'At least no one's watching us any more,' he muttered out of the corner of his mouth.

He was wrong.

Chris couldn't make up his mind whether a football match was better or worse than a French film. At least he understood what was going on in the match. Well, sort of. The only important thing he felt he needed to remember was that he must jump up and shout whenever the Manchester United fans did. But no matter how hard he concentrated on the action, his timing was never quite right.

It seemed that jumping up and shouting was obligatory at random intervals. When certain players got the ball in a brilliant tackle and then, minutes later, when they missed an open goal or broke the nose of an opponent for just existing, he would be expected to jump and cheer with exactly the same level of enthusiasm.

Pete, on the other hand, was mesmerised by the game. He had never watched a full football match from start to finish and now he understood how grown men could be reduced to childlike fanaticism as he witnessed the two teams nearly massacring each other over possession of the ball. It was the closest he'd come to a warlike situation. It offered all the benefits of indulging in gratuitous displays of aggression without anyone getting seriously hurt. That was the theory, anyway. He kept up a one-sided commentary to Chris, pointing out pieces of brilliance, heinous examples of injustice and funny haircuts. He was too engrossed in the action to notice that Chris was paying no attention to him.

The only reason Pete was not more worried about the position he and Chris were in was his lack of detailed knowledge of the average football hooligan. Chris, on the other hand, taught football hooligans. He recognised the type and was not ashamed to be terrified of their threat. He kept a pleading eye on the clock, trying to will the hands to move faster. He wanted the game to be over as quickly as possible so that he and Pete could get far away from here.

Throughout the match, he repeated one silent prayer, over and over again: Please do not let Manchester United lose. Please do not let Manchester United lose.

Manchester United lost 1–0.

The referee blew his whistle and Pete sat back clapping, his eyes shining with his new-found obsession. 'Wasn't that the most fantastic thing you've ever seen?' he said to Chris.

Chris was glancing left and right, trying to find the quickest exit through the least menacing-looking fans. 'Shut up and let's go,' he said, pulling Pete to his feet by the sleeve and moving off swiftly.

Pete yanked his sleeve out of Chris's hand.

'What are you doing?' he asked angrily. He wanted to stay till the very end, to listen to the music blaring out of the loudspeakers and read the advertisements for trainers and computers which flickered on and off the electronic hoardings. He wanted to read all the birthday greetings for people called Wayne and Iqbal and Little Freddie that travelled across the base of the scoreboard. He wanted to immerse himself in the total football experience.

Chris wanted to get home alive. 'If we don't get out of here, NOW, we are going to find ourselves in the middle of a very nasty fight.'

Pete was chastened and bowed to Chris's superior knowledge of both football protocol and the criminal tendency. 'What are we waiting for, then?' he said, feeling as if he'd just had a whole puberty-load of testosterone injected into him.

Keeping their heads down, they moved slowly towards the overstretched exits. They stuck to family groups, hoping that their wholesomeness would rub off on them and deflect attackers.

To their amazement, they made it out of the stadium without anything more physical than a shove and a dirty look. They exited from a different part of the stadium to the door they'd entered by. It took them a while to get their bearings. 'How are we getting back to the hotel?' Pete asked, having elected Chris team leader without telling him.

'I think we're going to have to walk,' Chris replied. 'All the public transport will be up the creek now the demo has started.'

So they started the long walk back. In the beginning, there was quite a festive atmosphere as the hordes of fans all moved as one throng towards the city centre. Despite the result, there was still a great sense of camaraderie and Pete loved the sense of belonging to this massive like-minded crowd.

Gradually, the crowds thinned out as individuals and groups drifted in different directions. Chris and Pete increased their pace as a hint of unease crept over them. They didn't have the breath to talk to each other, so intent were they on getting back to a comforting urban sprawl with lots of people to guarantee their safe passage.

The roads were unpleasantly, unnaturally quiet. The police cordon around the city had worked well and there were no cars on these roads leading to the heart of the demo.

But the silence only served to highlight the distant chant that was getting louder and closer with each passing step. Pete and Chris strained to hear what was being sung, aware only that it was not from *The Sound of Music*.

It was Chris who heard it first. He didn't want to believe it so he waited for Pete to confirm his interpretation. Pete's panicky cough seemed to indicate that he'd heard it too.

'Er Chris, are they singing what I think they're singing?'

'What do you think they're singing, Pete?'

'Well, I'm hoping that I'm mistaken. I thought it was Oasis' "Don't Look Back In Anger", but now it's closer, I can just about make out the words and they sound suspiciously like: "You're going to get your heads kicked in." What do you think?'

He'd left out some of the chant's more colourful words that enabled the lyrics to scan. That didn't matter. Chris had heard the song many times before in school. He knew it by heart.

There was no time for a witty reply. Because the chants were now right behind them. Pete and Chris turned to face the gang of red-clothed and red-faced assassins running at them like a scene from *Braveheart*. They turned to each other and in one scream, shouted 'RUN!'

And, possessing none of Mel Gibson's heroic qualities and not being fortunate enough to have stunt doubles, they ran.

Pete and Chris sprinted at full speed, although they kept looking back to see how far behind their hunters were. In fact, they looked back so often that the boys in red started looking back themselves, wondering if there was something interesting going on behind them.

'Stop! Wait a minute!' Chris grabbed Pete's arm and pulled him to a standstill. Pete looked at him in horror. 'Are you mad? They're not that far behind.' He looked back to where the pursuers seemed to have come to a halt themselves. 'In fact, they've stopped running. Fantastic! We're safe. Let's get away from here before they change their minds.'

But Chris wasn't listening. He was walking back to where the red swarm of would-be terrorists seemed to be teeming around a bundle on the ground. Except it wasn't a bundle. 'Pete, they're kicking somebody!'

Pete considered this for a second. 'Yes, but it's not us, come on, let's be on our way.'

'Don't be so callous!'

Pete looked at Chris evenly. 'You obviously don't know me very well, Chris. I'm not callous, I'm a spineless coward. Maybe you're different, but I'm not good at fighting, never was, not even when I was a kid. You may have noticed how good I am at running – that is the result of a childhood spent running away from fights. The only difference is that I am no longer ashamed of my cowardice. In fact, I've come to see it as a sign of intelligence. I mean, only a fool would find any honour in offering himself up as a sacrifice to a howling mob of yobbos.'

Chris was peering at the scene before him. 'I think I know him.'

Pete tried to follow the line of Chris's gaze. 'Who do you think you know?'

'The boy on the floor. I think he's one of my pupils.' Chris began walking over to them. Pete followed, hoping to dissuade him from this folly.

'Look, Pete, he's up now and fighting back. I think he can take care of himself.'

Chris walked more quickly. 'I'm as much of a coward as you, but I can't leave a kid by himself to face those thugs. I couldn't live with myself.'

Chris began to run as the scrummage became more animated. The boy looked as if he was handling himself well.

Pete knew that he was supposed to cast off his craven weakness and storm in with Chris like Rambo. But he just couldn't. He was too scared. Unfortunately, he hadn't brought a white flag or a feather with him to communicate that there was no point in beating him up because he had already surrendered.

And when Chris yelled: 'Hey! Leave him alone!' the yobs all stopped what they were doing and turned their attention on Chris and Pete. As one, the hooligans moved forwards. There was no point in running. Well, there was a point, Pete could probably outrun them all. But he could hardly leave Chris behind. And now, as if by proxy, he seemed also to have responsibility for an unknown youth wearing a Tottenham supporter's colours.

And before he could say: 'Don't hit me, I'm a management consultant!', he was embroiled in a brawl which bore no resemblance to fight scenes in *The Bill*; it was all gritty and messy and unstaged. And not much damage was inflicted since they were all doing their best to avoid getting hurt. No wonder the boy had managed to get up.

There was some blood, some low-grade pain, a lot of swearing and bluff and bravado. At one stage, time appeared to stand still while Chris and the boy made eye contact. Pete watched the exchange with interest as he staved off some ineffectual blows. He just about heard them acknowledge the other's existence.

'Dean Ryder!' Chris said in exasperation.

'Hello, sir!' the boy answered.

Then the police arrived.

The three of them were put in the same cell. Protesters were being arrested all across the city and every cell in every police station was filling up.

'How long are we going to be kept here?' Chris had asked the arresting officer.

'We've all got to get back to manning the demo route in town. So there's only one sergeant on duty here. You've got a long wait on your hands.'

'But we've got to go back to London. Someone's coming to collect us,' Pete said anxiously. He didn't know if it would be Stella or his parents. Either way, it wouldn't be a pleasant drive home.

The police constable looked at him with disgust. 'Maybe you should have thought about that before you picked a fight. You thugs make me sick, especially you professional types, you've got no excuse!'

With that, he slammed the cell door shut.

Pete sat on the bench and put his head in his hands. 'This is a nightmare. I can't believe I've been arrested for brawling. We could end up on that register, you know, the one with all the violent football hooligans that the Home Secretary is always banging on about.'

Dean Ryder snorted. 'In your dreams! You have to do a lot more than slap a few Man U fans to get on the register. I should know, my brother was one of the first names on it.'

His pride was unmistakable.

Chris sighed. 'Dean, I hardly think that is anything to be proud of.'

'Well, that's where you're wrong, sir. You see, everyone knows him. He's really somebody. He can go to any town in Britain, in Europe even, and he'll find people who know him.'

Chris stared at him in exasperation. 'Yes, Ryder, police officers who want to arrest him and other sociopaths like himself who want to kick ten kinds of hell out of him. Is that really your idea of fame?'

'It's the only kind I'm ever going to know,' Dean said sulkily. 'Anyway, what else were we all going to do after the match?'

Pete screwed up his face to come up with the answer to this tricky question. 'Oh, I don't know. Let me see. Your teacher and I could have gone back to our hotel, picked up our bags, caught the train back to London, gone home to a nice warm house, maybe watched an *Inspector Frost*, had a few drinks, something edible to eat and gone to bed without having to apply TCP to our wounds or sleep on our backs to spare our bruised ribs. Something like that.'

Dean was unimpressed. 'And that's the reward for living life on the straight and narrow? Pack me off to Parkhurst right now, it's got be an improvement on your lives.'

Chris was not impressed by his pupil's articulate thesis on the advantages of a life dedicated to crime. 'Dean, we're not in the mood. Because of you, we nearly got ourselves killed and we did get ourselves arrested.'

Dean jumped up. 'Excuse *me*, but I think you got that the wrong way round.'

'What are you talking about?' Chris said.

Dean spoke slowly so that these two dense men grasped what he was saying. 'I spotted you when you left and I could see that those blokes were coming after you. Especially your pillock friend with his Spurs hat.'

Pete reddened with humiliation. Dean went on.

'And I knew that you wouldn't be able to look after yourselves, so I followed behind to give you a hand if you got into bother.'

'So how come they turned on you and not us, if that was what they were after?' Pete asked, anxious to find flaws in Dean's argument. The idea of being beholden to this little hoodlum made him feel quite queasy.

Dean turned to face him. 'When you kept stopping and turning round to look at them, they turned round as well and saw me. And they know me from a bust-up at Aston Villa last month. So they changed their minds and started in on me.'

'And that's when we piled in to save your backside!' Pete said, expecting a thank-you at the very least.

'Perhaps you were watching a different fight. Because if you'd seen me, you would have noticed that I was on top of them. They were just a bunch of Northern jessies, the only reason they came after you was because they knew they could take you.'

Chris and Pete found themselves bristling as their male pride came under attack. 'So are you saying that you didn't need our help?' Chris asked indignantly.

'I'm saying more than that,' Dean said. 'I'm saying it's all your fault we got arrested. If you'd just minded your own business, they'd have run off as soon as I started fighting back and then we'd have all been out the way by the time the police drove by.' Then he sat back and seethed in that moody, belligerent way that only teenage boys can do effectively.

Chris and Pete looked at each other embarrassedly. Neither of them dared speak. Pete wanted to hit Chris for landing them in this trouble. It was entirely his fault, according to what Dean was saying. And he believed the boy. Even Pete, in his ignorance, had been able to see that Dean had been looking after himself perfectly adequately. It had been Chris who'd insisted on piling in.

Meanwhile Chris was uttering silent curses at Pete. It had been Pete's idea to go to a football match in the first place. Chris would rather have sat through all of Wagner's *Lohengrin* than spend ninety bitterly cold minutes (plus fifteen minutes in the interval) watching twenty-two Neanderthals kicking a ball about. Now, he would probably lose his job and the school would close down. Christ! What a disaster.

'Dean, what exactly were you doing at the match? You didn't tell me you were going to be there.'

'You didn't ask. I wouldn't have missed it, always a good chance of a fight in Manchester.'

Chris was confused. 'And you saw us? In a crowd of fifty thousand or something?'

Dean pitied this man who understood so little about the real world. 'I was sitting right behind you, me and my brother. We got the tickets at the same time as yours.'

'You can't have been. We were the only ones in blue in the entire stand.'

Dean tutted. 'You're not very bright for a teacher.

We'd nicked some Man U gear. Unlike you, we didn't intend to attract a kicking. When we want a fight, we pick it ourselves.'

It was another world to Chris and one that he was grateful to be leaving behind him.

Pete got up. 'I've had enough of this,' he said and banged on the cell door. 'Excuse me, can you hear me? I want to make my statement and get out of here. You can't keep us here indefinitely.'

Nobody answered. Pete sat back down defeated. Chris suddenly thought of something. He was reluctant to mention it but this was a desperate situation. 'Er, Pete, there is one way we might get some attention.'

Pete didn't look optimistic. 'Is this going to involve me throwing myself on the floor and pretending to have an epileptic fit or some such ruse?'

Chris looked strained. 'Not exactly. But if you were to have a health-related condition, something serious, then they would have to get you medical attention and that could speed up our release.'

Pete looked confused. 'That's a great idea. Or it would be if I had a health-related condition, or any condition, but I haven't. Unless you think the police might be sympathetic to the sorry saga of our curry from last night?'

Chris changed his approach. He became the you-can-tell-me-anything best friend, hoping to build on their unifying experience of going into battle together. 'Are you sure you don't want to think about this? I mean I know there are some things that we don't like talking about, but this is not the time to be reticent. Of course, I understand—'

Pete raised a hand to shut Chris up. 'What are you jabbering on about? I haven't got anything wrong with me. What made you think I did?'

Chris assumed an expression of hopeless stupidity. It was time to retreat before he forced Pete into a corner from which he refused to come out.

It didn't work on Pete. 'It's no use grinning like a village idiot. Now I *know* that something is up and I want to know what it is.'

'Yeah, come on sir, tell him what's up.' Dean was enjoying the performance and revelling in the opportunity for some audience participation.

'Shut up, Ryder,' Chris said.

'Don't tell him to shut up. Even he can see that you're concealing something.' Pete was grateful for any ally to hand.

Dean looked indignant. 'Why did you say "even he" like that? I'm not stupid, am I?'

Chris sighed. 'No you're not stupid. That's the great tragedy of your life.'

This had a sobering effect on Dean who sat back in another sulk, leaving Chris to deal with Pete, who was still waiting for an answer.

'I was just thinking of last night, that's all. You know, you talked about not being well . . .' It was weak and he knew it. So did Pete, who took offence at the implication that he was some kind of hypochondriac.

'You can talk,' he said. 'Anything I had, you'd had twice as bad, twice as often.'

Chris raised his hands in mock defeat. 'You're right. Sorry. I was not thinking straight last night, the Delhi belly and the lager and everything. I just thought you had something more serious on your mind.'

He was thinking of the oblique references to Beth. So was Pete, who regretted ever mentioning the subject.

'I didn't. It was just the booze talking.'

Damn, thought Chris. I've put him on the defensive.

'Well, this is great,' Dean said. 'Blokes talking about their personal problems. You'll be hugging soon. This is worse than *Brookside*.'

They ignored him. The three eased back into their respective patches of buff concrete and went over the events of the day in their heads. It was impossible to know how long they were sitting like that before the heavy door was swung open. 'Well, gentlemen, you're in luck, somebody is here to bail you two senior citizens out.'

'What about me?' Dean asked anxiously.

'We're still trying to get hold of your mum,' the police officer replied.

The boy looked as if he was going to burst into tears. Chris took pity on him. 'Don't worry, Dean, I'll get you out.'

It was a gruelling three hours before Chris and Pete were able to go. They were let off with a caution. It was made clear to them that they were very lucky to be arrested today. With the immense pressure on the police, they were saving the time-consuming charges for the most serious cases.

Pete and Chris tried to feel lucky and failed. They stepped out of the police station to see Stella attempting a tricky eleven-point turn to weave her way past the police vans that were double-parked and full to overflowing with noisy protesters. She'd driven all the way up there as soon as the police had called her. It was now the evening and she was exhausted. She was also furious with both men, not interested in hearing how they were innocent victims and none of it was their fault.

The arresting officer had made it clear on the phone. Her husband and his friend had been caught throwing punches. She was not amused by the tiniest hint of pride that crept over Chris and Pete's faces when she related this. They would deny the charge of pride vehemently when she accused them later, but she knew what she saw.

When she spotted the men, she nodded her head curtly to acknowledge that she'd seen them. Dean walked out a minute later. For a moment, Chris thought the boy was going to shake his hand. But that was *Tom Brown's Schooldays*. Dean nodded almost imperceptibly as he swaggered over. 'Thanks,' he mumbled. 'I suppose you're going to expect something in exchange?'

Chris sighed. 'I'm not sure that kind of debt is much use to me any more. I won't be asking for any more football tickets and I can't see the school surviving this little incident, but thanks anyway.'

'You need to sign something, Mr Fallon.'

'OK.' Chris turned to Pete. 'Tell Stella I'll be as quick as I can.' He dashed back into the station, leaving Pete on the steps with Dean. They watched Stella's parking manoeuvre with barely suppressed amusement.

'She's a terrible driver,' Pete observed, not looking forward to the long drive home. And he knew that she was not going to let him drive – that would be his punishment. He could tell how upset Stella was by her lack of make-up. She looked gaunt and old and he was moved by her vulnerability.

Dean couldn't take his eyes off the car and driver. 'She's not much of a looker, either. You'd have thought someone like Mr Fallon could do better for himself.'

Pete turned his head abruptly. 'What makes you think she's married to Chris, I mean, Mr Fallon?' His tone was not aggressive, he was just interested in Dean's assumption.

Dean adopted his best man-to-man pose, and nudged Pete knowingly. 'I saw them together in her car. Not that there was much to see, just some kissing and cuddling, but still . . .'

Chris was in Stella's car? Kissing her?

Chris pushed through the door and bounded down the stairs, patting Pete on the back as he passed.

'Come on then, let's hit the road!'

Pete said nothing all the way home. He had a lot on his mind.

Chapter 15

Lauren drove back to Cumbria very early on Sunday morning. She hadn't been able to sleep and had given up round about four a.m. and jumped into the car. She would have gone yesterday afternoon but was worried about her blood alcohol levels after Friday's binge. Izzy was going to take the train up on Monday morning to join Lauren.

Taking the car to Tendale was a sign that she was not just a passing visitor. Like many modern working women, wherever she left her car was home. And London didn't feel much like home at the moment. Stella was there. But friendship with Stella was equally sustainable on the phone.

That was about it. No other ties. A bit pathetic, she thought, after fifteen years in a town. Although the man in the video shop would probably miss her. She always forgot to return her films and ended up paying astronomical fines.

Heading up the M1, she tried to ignore the signs for Watford. She had the birthday lunch looming on the coming Saturday. That was all a bit vague. She had a hazy recollection of her mum inviting Chris but how they'd left it wasn't clear. Still, obviously he wouldn't be able to go; he didn't know where Maureen lived. And even if he did, the fate fairy would see to it that his car was clamped or he was kidnapped by aliens or something equally credible.

She tried to concentrate on the prospect of getting Richard and Maureen together. Originally her only motivation had been to distract her mum so that she would be free to accept the job in the States without feeling guilty. But she wondered if she had other reasons.

Maybe she loved her mum and wanted her to be happy. Am I that good? Lauren wondered. I've never thought of myself as being particularly decent and altruistic. But perhaps I am. This was a cosy thought to meditate upon as she approached the M6.

She had to put her headlights on as the dark oppressive clouds impaired the visibility. Damn, she thought. I hope this weather isn't settling in for the duration. She had called Richard from a service station to let him know that she was up for their scheduled walk on Sunday, albeit a little later than planned.

Her hangover had left her yearning for the head-clearing powers of mountain air. London had smelled different to her yesterday: grimy, putrid, unedifying. She wanted to smell snow and frozen mud and scrunched-up grass. She wanted to drink cocoa and hear nothing except her soothing slurps and the occasional birdsong. And most of all she was looking forward to seeing Richard. How odd to be making friends with a client, she thought. And he was a friend, no question about it.

But while she was still firmly fixed on her intention to introduce Richard to her mum, she was having little nagging itches in her mind about the whole plan. It was as if the closer she grew to Richard, the less convinced she was that he and Maureen would be compatible. At least that's what she thought was the problem. But that was crazy. She would have expected to be reassured as she got to know Richard and found so much in him to like.

But also when she'd bumped into Maureen at the sushi restaurant, she'd been struck with further doubt.

She didn't often see Maureen dressed up for her shows. No wonder Izzy had mistaken her for a drag queen. The very idea of Richard being attracted to her when she was dolled up like that was laughable. He was an outdoors man. He thought make-up was a stupid artifice that served no purpose but to stop the sun and fresh air from nourishing the skin.

She hoped that Maureen was going to dress a little, no a lot, more casually for Saturday. Maybe she'd drop some hints. Because when Maureen was just wearing trousers and a jumper and her hair was freshly washed and hanging loose, she still looked young. Without make-up, her face was lined but not ravaged. She appeared full of hope, not scarred with the finality of all the disappointments of her past life.

In full battle gear, right down to the dazzling chandelier earrings that announced her arrival minutes before she actually got anywhere, she was simply somebody else. And this might have been the person she preferred to be but it wasn't the person Lauren wanted her to be.

She felt happier now that she'd solved the problem of why she'd been having reservations about Richard and her mum. Yes, she thought, her mum's appearance. It was the physical incompatibility, that must be it. It didn't really soothe her qualms but it was something.

She would call Maureen, drop some very subtle hints. In fact, she'd do it now. She couldn't really call her from Richard's. Even though there was a private phone she could use in the little flat, the walls were paper-thin and she didn't want him to hear her priming her mum.

She pulled into another service station and found a phone box. Why did I chuck my mobile away? she screamed at herself. Great gesture. Very inconvenient outcome. She dialled her mum's number. Engaged.

'Hello?'

'Oh hello, this is Maureen Connor, Lauren's mum. Is that Stella?'

'No it's Ann, her mother.'

'Ann! How lovely to talk to you. I had a nice chat with your Bill the other day.'

Ann groaned inwardly at the memory of Bill agreeing to go this wretched lunch party on Saturday. 'Yes, he said.'

'Anyway, is Stella there, love?'

'Not exactly,' Ann said carefully.

Maureen picked up on her caution. 'Is something wrong, have I called at a bad time?'

Ann wondered what she should say. Stella and Pete were in the wasteland they called a garden having a most uncivilised fight. She wasn't sure what it was about, but suspected that it had something to do with having to bail Pete out of jail yesterday. And the little prang with the car on the way home.

'Er, well, she and Pete are . . . tied up right now. Can I get Stella to call you back or is there a message I can give her?'

'Maybe you can help me, Ann. I'm trying to get hold

of the phone number of one of Lauren's friends, I believe she used to be Stella's doctor. Beth Savile?'

'I know who you mean, yes. Well, hold on a second.' She put the handset down and pulled the curtain back to see if Stella could reasonably be summoned to the phone. At that precise second, Stella's arms were flailing about and she was crying. Pete was sitting on the awful Marmite jar statue with his arms folded and a stony expression on his face. Probably not a good time, then.

'I'll tell you what, Maureen, I can see Stella's address book, let me see if Beth's number is in it.' The book was still left out from when Bill had been looking for Lauren's number for Izzy. Maybe if our money problems get out of control we can get a job as a husband-and-wife team with Directory Enquiries, thought Ann grimly.

'Here it is.' She gave Maureen the number as well as the address which Maureen also asked for. 'I hope it was all right for me to give it you,' she said as an afterthought.

'I'm sure she won't mind. I'm going to invite her to Lauren's party on Saturday. It's going to be such a surprise!' Maureen added cheerfully.

Ann was going to tell Stella about the call but she took one look at Stella's fierce frown and changed her mind. It'll be a nice surprise for her as well, she decided.

'Who were you on the phone to?' Lauren asked irritably. Like all daughters, she believed that mothers should be instantly available twenty-four hours a day. As long as they didn't expect the same from their daughters.

'Ah, never you mind!' Maureen answered mysteriously. This sent shivers coursing through Lauren's body.

Her mum was probably planning some horrific surprise. She was probably going to put on her most glittery frock and head for the shopping mall. Maureen had told Lauren that Michael Barrymore was scheduled to be appearing there this week. Lauren had seen his programmes. He would be looking for awful sopranos singing 'My Love Will Go On' and missing all of Celine Dion's high notes. There would be dozens of overweight children dancing to S Club 7's latest record and middle-aged men in toupées juggling while telling jokes that were last told on *Sunday Night at the London Palladium*.

All in all, it would be right up Maureen's street. In a supreme act of filial devotion, Lauren restrained herself from screaming: 'DON'T DO IT, MUM! TAKE UP NEEDLEWORK INSTEAD!'

'That's nice,' she said, not knowing what else to say.

Maureen squirmed with pleasure at managing to keep the surprise to herself. 'So what did you want, Lauren?' she asked.

'Why should I want anything?' Lauren replied, bristling at the implication that she only phoned when she wanted something.

'Because you only phone when you want something,' Maureen said simply.

Lauren didn't bother with the 'oh-no-I-don't'/'oh-yes-you-do' script that she was tempted to pursue. She had an inkling that her mum was right and didn't want to accept this, so she did what she always did when confronted with one of her own failings: she changed the subject.

'Whatever,' she said briskly. 'Mum, I'm calling about Saturday.'

Maureen panicked. 'There's nothing wrong, is there? You can still come? We've had this planned for weeks.'

'Yes, yes, Mum, don't get worked up. Of course I'm going to be there.'

'Thank God for that!' Maureen exclaimed. Lauren thought this was a rather extreme reaction. It was just lunch they were talking about. Just Maureen and Stella and Pete. Her mum would cook something she'd seen on *Celebrity Ready, Steady, Cook* but which wouldn't turn out quite right. Then they'd have a Viennetta with a candle in it. It would be pleasant but strained as all occasions involving Maureen demonstrating her mothering skills tended to be.

'The reason I'm calling is to see if it's OK for me to bring someone along?'

Maureen was confused. 'But you're already bringing someone along. That Chris is coming, isn't he?'

Lauren closed her eyes. 'Oh right, Chris. Well that's all a bit up in the air at the moment,' she said, not wanting to go into the details right now. She'd never get to Tendale if she started this story. 'We've had a few . . . communication problems.'

Have you indeed? thought Maureen. I'll sort that out. She had been impressed by her recently discovered flair for solving communication problems.

'So who would this someone be?' Maureen asked.

Lauren was relieved that her mum didn't argue with her. She'd anticipated Maureen insisting that she bring Chris. She wouldn't have put it past her tracking Chris down, twisting his arm into a half nelson and dragging him single-handedly to Watford.

'It's my client, actually. But he's really nice. And he

263

lives by himself in the Lake District and doesn't get out much. I thought it would make a change for him to come down south. And your lunches are always special. I think he'd appreciate your home cooking.'

Maureen was pacified. She'd had a momentary thought that this was yet another new boyfriend. But this man sounded like Compo out of *Last of the Summer Wine*. She hoped he wouldn't feel out of place at a sophisticated southern lunch party. She made a mental note to buy some milk stout. He'd probably appreciate that.

'That would be lovely, dear. And if he's your client, I'll push the boat out, show him how proud I am of my successful daughter.'

'No!' Lauren shouted, causing Maureen to pull the phone away from her ear. 'Sorry, Mum, I didn't mean to shout. It's just that I don't want you to push the boat out. The opposite, in fact. He's a very low-key man. I think he'd be embarrassed if you overdid things. You know, dressed too formally or whatever,' she said carefully.

Maureen was offended. 'I wasn't going to dress too formally, I haven't even got any formal clothes. I was planning to wear one of my dresses, one of my nice ones. It *is* your birthday after all.'

'That's what I mean, Mum. I would have loved to see you all glammed up, but I think Richard would be rather overwhelmed. He sells walking clothes, I think he might find your sequins a bit over the top. And I do want to impress him. He could be the opening to a whole lot more business if this job goes well.'

There, she'd said it. Now she had to wait. Maureen was miffed. Saturday was going to be a momentous occasion for her, what with the big introduction to Eddie and the surprise party. And now Lauren was telling her to look all mumsy. That was asking a lot and Lauren knew it.

Lauren could tell what Maureen was thinking. 'Mum, I know how important it is to you to look . . . your best, but can you just play it down for my sake? Just this once.'

That was below the belt, sounding all self-pitying, dredging up memories of all the years when Maureen did nothing for her daughter's sake. Lauren felt guilty but she was doing this for her mum. Eventually Maureen would see this and thank her. Eventually.

Maureen agreed and, after putting the phone down, went to her wardrobe to find something suitable to wear. She was blinded by the curtain of glitter and sparkle that faced her and wallowed in the thrill that she always experienced when she looked at her working clothes and all they represented about her new fulfilling life. This was going to be a challenge, she thought.

The good thing about a big house is that there is always privacy. Stella was in one of the upstairs spare rooms (Turkish brothel with the merest hint of terracotta) calling Chris on her mobile phone. Pete had gone out for the papers in a strop. Bill and Ann were downstairs watching something religious on BBC1. They weren't religious themselves but they loved Harry Secombe and there was always a fair-to-middling chance that Harry would be singing on a Welsh mountain on a Sunday morning. Besides, having the TV on meant they didn't have to talk to each other and Stella had felt the tension between them.

'Hello?'

'Chris, it's me, Stella.'

Oh God. Her. I knew it was too good to last. This is going to be the last time I talk to her. 'Hi, Stella. Listen, thanks for yesterday. And I'm really sorry about the car. I don't think it was really your fault, whatever that policeman said.'

'Well, my insurance company weren't so loyal. Bang goes my no-claims bonus. As if Pete and I haven't got enough to worry about.'

'Speaking of Pete,' Chris interrupted, wanting to pass on his information and close this episode down.

'Yes,' Stella said with a little more enthusiasm, though not much. 'The way I feel right now, I don't know why I'm bothering to care about him, but I do. So what did you find out?'

'Not a great deal, I'm afraid. You were definitely right that he's got something on his mind. But as soon as I tried to probe exactly what it was, he shut me out and I couldn't push him, he was already suspicious. I'm sorry if I let you down.'

It was as Stella had feared. 'Don't apologise. He was the same with me. I tried to get him to talk to me today. I mean, fighting in the street is so out of character for Pete. Ever since I've known him, he's always been someone who avoids any kind of confrontation. As soon as I heard he'd been brawling, I realised that it was down to his bottling up all his problems. I'm ashamed to admit that I never used my psychology degree after college or I might have foreseen something like this happening and done something to prevent it. I of all people should have seen the signs.'

Chris was glad that he was on the phone so that Stella didn't have to see him going red. He was about to confess that Pete had been all in favour of avoiding this particular confrontation and that it had been Chris who'd dragged him into the fight. But Stella didn't give him the chance.

'And I'm really sorry that Pete dragged you into it. He told me about the situation at your school. You could lose your job over this. I feel terrible.'

He was *definitely* going to put her straight. He couldn't let her blame Pete and, indirectly, herself for all his troubles.

'Look, Stella, it wasn't—'

'I've got to go,' Stella hissed and cut him off.

Chris stared at the phone. What was all that about, he thought.

'Pete, you're back soon,' Stella said, hiding the mobile under a cushion and scratching the floor tiles as if scraping a mark off.

Pete had seen what she was doing with the phone. 'I ran there and back. I needed to clear my head after yesterday. And this morning.'

'I'm sorry about that. I was upset about the car. And about you getting arrested. It's all right, I don't blame you, I know you must have had your reasons for getting into a fight, I just wish you'd talk to me.'

'Stella, I told you everything there was to tell. I didn't "get into a fight", it all happened around me and I got pulled in. You know I hate anything like that.'

'I don't know anything about you at the moment. You don't talk to me any more.'

'You've had twenty years to ask me to talk to you, why wait till now?' Pete said coldly.

Stella stormed out of the room, not trusting herself to respond.

As soon as she'd gone, Pete retrieved the phone from under the cushion. He pressed the last number redial button.

'Hello?' said the voice at the other end. Pete immediately cut him off. It was Chris.

'You took your time,' Richard said to Lauren accusingly. 'I was expecting you two hours ago. It's nearly eleven o'clock.'

'Sorry,' Lauren apologised, 'there was an accident on the motorway and I got stuck in the middle of a traffic jam.'

'I was worried something might have happened to you,' Richard said quietly.

Lauren smiled. 'If I'd had a mobile phone, I could have called you. But I was so impressed by your little speech on the evils of too much communication that I threw it away. So it's your own fault.'

Richard was amazed that he'd inspired her to such drastic action. Amazed and touched. He pondered on what this meant.

'So are we too late for our walk?' Lauren asked eagerly.

Richard looked out of the window and up at the overcast sky. 'Well, I'm not sure we should attempt it. It's later than we'd planned. We can only do this climb when it's light so we'll have to get up quite a speed. I'm not sure you'll be able to keep up.'

'Please!' Lauren pleaded. 'I really need this walk today. I've been looking forward to it for ages. I'll keep up, I promise.'

'I'd rather leave it. I know how quickly the weather can come down around here.'

'But I need some air! I've had a bad weekend. You whetted my appetite with all your talk about the view from the top. You can't let me down now. Please!'

He should have said no, he knew that. He'd been so dismissive about the ridiculous lie she told to that man in order to win his approval. He'd been so patronising with his little lecture on why all relationships should be based on honesty. And here he was, reluctant to look like a wimp in front of her by refusing to take her for a walk. He was ashamed of himself. But he gave in anyway.

'How about we do a shorter walk today and save High Crag for next weekend?' Richard suggested as a compromise.

'It's my lunch party next weekend, if you haven't forgotten,' Lauren reminded him.

'But that's on the Saturday, isn't it? We can still do it on the Sunday.'

'Where else can we go?' Lauren grumbled, 'you said that High Crag was the climb you really wanted to take me on.'

'And so it is. But there are plenty of others that we can complete before it gets dark. Especially in this kind of weather. I don't want to take a chance that we're going to get stranded somewhere that's completely inaccessible.'

By four fifteen, they were stranded somewhere completely inaccessible.

'This is my fault, isn't it?' Lauren said gloomily.

Richard shifted to make his ankle more comfortable. 'No, it's my fault for listening to you. I knew that the weather was going to be bad. I knew that it was going to get dark early. I should have stuck to my original decision and insisted we stayed at home.'

'But it's my fault you twisted your ankle, isn't it?' Lauren said, anxious to take some blame for this catastrophe. Richard was being so kind about all this and she couldn't bear it. If he didn't say something harsh to her soon, she would have to rip off her scarf and start beating herself across the back with it.

Richard was in too much pain to be bothered with Lauren's feelings. If she insisted on taking the blame, then so be it. 'Put it this way, if you hadn't insisted on climbing up that scree slope to find a bush to pee behind, then you wouldn't have fallen down and landed on top of me. So yes, it's your fault I twisted my ankle. Are you happier now?'

'Much,' Lauren said, steeped in misery. It's all my fault, she repeated silently to herself, over and over again.

They sat quietly for a moment while Richard waited for the paracetamol to kick in and deaden the pain in his throbbing foot.

'Mind you,' Lauren said, 'it's your fault that we haven't got a mobile phone.'

Richard laughed. 'You're absolutely right. So are we even now?'

'I suppose so,' Lauren conceded. 'So what's the plan of action?'

'We can't do anything until I can walk. Hopefully, in

a short while, you'll be able to help me hobble back towards the main footpath. Then you can leave me there and follow the path back to the village and get help.'

'Why don't I go and get help now?' Lauren asked, anxious to find a way of redeeming herself.

'Because you'll get lost. The mist is coming down and it's too easy to take a wrong turn up here. No, you'll have to be patient a little while longer.'

Lauren had never been very good at patience so she was surprised to find herself doing what Richard told her and settling back on the grassy slope. She sensed that Richard didn't want to talk. She was right and he appreciated her tactful silence.

He needed silence to do some thinking. He'd taken the painkillers thirty minutes ago and the ache was not easing at all. And, to his expert eye, his foot was swelling up. He thought it might have a fracture.

Eventually he had to share his conclusion with Lauren. She was devastated. 'Oh my God, you've broken your foot and it's all my fault!' she cried.

'Lauren, it's not actually very helpful to keep blaming yourself. What's done is done and we have to get through this as best we can.'

Lauren resolved to stop moaning and become a strong and obedient lieutenant to her leader through this ordeal. 'Sorry,' she said, 'just tell me what I have to do.'

'Well the first thing you have to do is face a rather difficult fact. I'm afraid it looks as if we might be stuck here until tomorrow morning.'

Lauren gasped. 'Tomorrow morning? But it's still the afternoon! Surely we can do something before the night falls.'

Richard shook his head. 'I'm afraid not. No one in their right mind will set out up here today, not now. We'll just have to make ourselves comfortable and keep warm and dry until it gets light again. There'll be people along here tomorrow, for sure. Or, if the mist clears, you might even be able to see your way to the path.'

Lauren was devastated. The novelty of her love affair with the great outdoors had just come to an emergency stop. She'd anticipated that she and Richard would be hiking through mystical countryside, communing with nature, sharing intimate secrets, while Lauren sowed little seeds of her mother into his subconscious. Then they would march ruddy-cheeked back into the local village where they'd find a little pub with an open fire and eat home-made steak and kidney pie and drink draught cider. That was the plan.

She rubbed her hands together and stamped her feet to try and warm up. Now that they'd stopped walking, she was getting very cold. It would be even colder in New York.

'Did I tell you that I might be moving to New York?' she said abruptly, unaware of the words until they slipped out.

Richard sat very still. 'I don't think you did,' he said carefully. 'I think I would have remembered.'

'I've been offered a job out there. Fantastic opportunity, heading up my own team on a five-year development project. Great money, relocation expenses, company apartment in Manhattan.'

'Sounds wonderful,' Richard said without enthusiasm.

272

Lauren looked up sharply. 'You can't tell me you've had no desire to travel, to see the rest of the world?'

Richard looked out over the darkening mountains. 'I'd always planned to travel, to climb the big peaks, maybe set up as a walking guide in Asia.'

'So why didn't you?' Lauren asked curiously.

'My parents died and I had to take over the business.'

Lauren looked unconvinced. 'You didn't *have* to. You chose to.'

Richard smiled indulgently at her. 'Nothing is that straightforward. None of us exists in isolation. We're all part of families, communities, networks of people. We can't make decisions without considering the implications they have for others.'

'I don't know,' Lauren said. 'It seems to me that people do exactly that all the time.'

'So why haven't you decided just to get up and go then?' Richard asked shrewdly.

'I have to think of my mum,' she said simply. She realised what she had said and smiled back at Richard. 'OK, I take your point, I don't *have* to.'

'So will you go?' Richard asked quietly. Very quietly.

Lauren didn't answer for a while. She couldn't think properly. Her mind was a jumble of pictures and images, mountains, open space and wide expanses of sky. Richard was in lots of the pictures. Taking up valuable thinking space.

'I don't know,' she said. They both settled back into silence, each trying to imagine what life would be like if Lauren moved to New York. Neither felt happy with the prospect at that moment.

She looked very small and frightened. Richard held

out his hand. 'Come over here,' he said. 'You look frozen.'

Lauren shuffled across to him and let him envelop her in his arms. It was the most wonderful feeling she had ever known. Even though they had about twenty layers of clothes between them, she felt that they were fused together. The warmth slowly permeated her being until her shivering slowed down to nothingness.

And her warmth did the same for Richard. She was no longer cold or afraid or guilt-ridden or any of the other negative emotions that she'd taken upon herself. She was happy to be where she was right now. She was glad Richard had broken his foot or they would be sitting opposite each other in a pub instead of huddling together for protection and comfort.

They stayed like that for – how long? Lauren couldn't tell. It got darker and colder. They moved even closer. Every so often Lauren felt Richard tense up with the pain in his foot. She would squeeze his hand and say nothing. Richard was weak with gratitude, overwhelmed by the utter intimacy.

Neither of them wanted to be the one to pull apart first but they were getting hungry and thirsty. Richard had come prepared as he always did when hill-walking. He had plenty of water and food in his rucksack and Lauren leapt upon the Mars Bars she found in one of the side pockets.

They finished the chocolate in four swift bites before the cold began to make itself felt again. Without a word, they came together again. Lauren pulled out a couple of the tinfoil blankets that Richard had folded into her jacket pocket. She wrapped one carefully around the lower half of Richard's body to protect his legs. The she pulled the other one around them both and eased Richard back on to the grass.

'Can I ask you something, Richard?'

'Mmm, you have a captive audience in me. Now's your chance to ask anything you want, in the safe knowledge that I can't escape!'

'Why haven't you married again? Or even got a girl-friend at the moment? There are single women coming through the shop all the time. I mean, that's how you met your wife. But you don't seem interested.'

Richard reflected on his life since Cindy left. Yes there had been countless girls, countless women who had passed through. He'd accompanied some of them on walks. Even slept with a few. But he didn't invite any of them to stay.

'I suppose it was because of my marriage that I've been wary of going down the same path again.'

'Yes, but mistakes don't necessarily have to be repeated. The whole point of mistakes is to learn from them so that you don't fall into the same traps.'

Richard looked at her fondly. She was still very inno-cent for someone who appeared to have taken quite a battering during her life. 'There are some mistakes which are unavoidable, the ones that you only recognise with hindsight.'

'Like?' Lauren prompted.

'Like falling in love with the wrong person. By the time you have, you can't un-fall in love however doomed the relationship may turn out to be.'

'So what's the solution?' Lauren asked.

'It's not really a solution, but as a temporary stop-gap,

you can stop yourself from taking the first steps that might lead you into the trap.'

Lauren held a finger up. 'Aah, but that doesn't allow for one possibility.'

'And what would that be?' Richard asked.

'Falling in love with someone before you have even considered the possibility. Then it would be too late.'

Richard didn't answer. She was right. He was thinking about Lauren. Lauren was thinking of her mother. Both were optimistic.

They lay there for a while looking up at the stars. The mist had blown away by now and the sky was black and endless.

'Why didn't you have children?' she asked, emboldened by their closeness.

Richard didn't answer and she thought he might have fallen asleep. But he was just trying to recollect his stock answer to the common question.

'Cindy couldn't. Well, she said she couldn't. She didn't want to get it checked out. Besides, she liked our life the way it was. The shops, the walking. Eventually, she even loved the winters. She spent weeks drawing up business plans, crazy expansion schedules, pure fantasy but she enjoyed it. And it gave me time to be by myself. It was enough for us. And then, when it wasn't enough, it was too late.'

'Did *you* want kids?' Lauren asked.

'Yes,' Richard replied shortly, then he spoke more gently. 'But not getting what you want is not a tragedy.'

Lauren looked doubtful. 'Then what is?' she asked.

Richard considered this. 'A lifetime of getting too many things you don't want. It means you are depriving someone else of their fair share of happiness and not getting anything out of it yourself. Waste. That's the tragedy.'

'I know about waste,' Lauren said bitterly. 'Having my mum waste her time on me now when I don't want her – I wanted her thirty years ago. And my dad dying just when he had learned how to be a decent husband and father. That's waste.'

Richard gently tightened his hold. 'What about you, Lauren? Would you like children?'

Lauren didn't answer and he thought she might have fallen asleep. But she was just trying to recollect her stock answer to the common question. You know, the usual stuff about waiting for the right man, establishing her career. But she felt protected by the dark and spoke the truth.

'More than anything in the world. And now you'll ask me why I haven't settled down, a nice girl like me.'

'I wasn't going to say anything like that. You can make your choices, set your priorities, but you can't make them happen. I should know.'

Which was exactly how she would have answered him. And that was that. They felt different. As if they'd kissed.

More silence.

'Do you want to hear something funny?' Richard said.

'Well, if you can make me laugh while you have a broken foot and I am succumbing to frostbite, that would be quite an achievement.'

Richard pointed up at a cluster of stars to the left of the sky. 'You see that constellation there?'

Lauren squinted to follow the line that Richard was tracing with his finger. 'Just about,' she said.

'Do you know what that is?' he asked.

'The Great Bear,' she replied doubtfully, referring to the only constellation she'd heard of.

Richard turned to face her. There couldn't have been more than a few inches between them. 'It's Pisces,' he said.

Lauren looked up at the sky again and then back at Richard. His face was closer now. She thought, for one deluded moment, that he was going to kiss her.

Then she got the joke. 'Pisces!' she chuckled. She was still smiling when she fell asleep, locked in Richard's arms. And Richard was smiling too, sometimes sadly, sometimes hopefully, as he watched her drift away. Until he too fell asleep.

Chapter 16

Izzy arrived in Tendale early on Monday afternoon. The taxi pulled up just as Lauren and Richard were being dropped off by the ambulance.

'Oh my God, Lauren, what's happened, are you OK?'

'I'm absolutely fine. Not quite defrosted, but fine. Izzy, this is Richard Trent, our client.'

Richard was walking with difficulty on crutches. His foot was plastered up to his knee. 'Forgive me if I don't shake hands. Nice to meet you.'

'What have you done to your foot?' Izzy asked, wondering why Lauren had not mentioned that their client was so handsome.

'It's a long story,' Richard replied apologetically. 'One that I will not be able to tell until I've had at least three cups of tea.'

In fact, it took three cups of tea and an early dinner down at the local pub (Lauren finally got her steak and kidney pie) before he at last got through the whole story.

'So you spent the whole night together on the mountains? How romantic!' Izzy declared, wondering where this left her brother in Lauren's eyes.

Lauren and Richard both blushed. 'It was hardly romantic!' Lauren said. 'We huddled together for warmth, but it was about survival more than romance. Wouldn't you agree, Richard?'

Richard wouldn't agree but he inclined his head neutrally. Izzy saw the disappointment in his eyes and the way he looked down so that Lauren wouldn't notice. But Izzy noticed. He's in love with her, she thought. And she hasn't got a clue.

Later on when she and Lauren were getting ready for bed in the flat that they were now going to share, she broached the subject casually.

'He's very attractive, isn't he?' she said.

'Who is?' Lauren said. She wasn't being obtuse, she genuinely didn't know who Izzy was referring to.

Izzy widened her eyes at Lauren's denseness. 'Richard, of course.'

'Oh, Richard. Yes, he is attractive.' Lauren was daubing on great dollops of prescription-strength moisturiser to try and soothe her dry skin. A night exposed to the elements had left her face red, flaky and sore.

'I'm surprised you didn't mention it,' Izzy said. 'You told me all about his shops, his car, his senile Auntie Joan, but you left out the bit about him looking like Harrison Ford.'

Lauren stopped rubbing and turned round. 'What are you talking about? Harrison Ford? Richard is in his late forties. He told me so.'

'Lauren, Harrison Ford is fifty-eight at least.'

Lauren thought about this. 'He can't be, Izzy. He was only in *Raiders of the Lost Ark* a few years ago.'

'Twenty years ago. What's the matter with you?'

What *is* the matter with me? Lauren asked herself. But she knew. She'd manoeuvred herself into that position where she thought that time had stopped moving a long time ago. She watched old films and believed that the actors hadn't grown old. She looked in the mirror and thought she was still twenty-two. And she did it because she was scared to face the possibility that it was too late for her. That she'd left it too long to get things right. She'd put a halt on her mental clock until such time as she could resume living a life worthy of her.

This isn't good, she thought. Because if Harrison Ford is fifty-eight, then I'm thirty-seven, I really am. And that has got to be a mistake. Because I haven't done enough to be thirty-seven, not proper things anyway. I haven't had babies or got married or planted trees or bought furniture on five years' interest-free credit, nothing that implies any faith in a future. I know I'm not supposed to care about any of those things, but what have I got instead? Shouldn't I have decided what I want by now and taken at least a few steps towards achieving it?

And if Harrison Ford is fifty-eight and Richard is even younger than Harrison Ford then – what? Was she supposed to look at him in a different way? As something other than a potential partner for her mother? What was Izzy getting at? The nagging itch turned into a nagging voice whispering directly into her head. But she couldn't hear what it was saying. It was something important, the knot in her stomach told her that, but she couldn't decipher the message.

That's when the cliché struck her. Old enough to be your father. Nobody had said it to her so where did it come from? That only applies when you are looking at a man from your own point of view. And until now she'd only ever seen Richard as someone for her mother.

She'd spent the night with a man, in his arms, talked about children, without once thinking of him as anything other than a friend. Weird? Perverse? Deluded? Good thing or bad thing? Which of these applied? She felt weak.

'I'm so tired, Izzy. I barely had a couple of hours' sleep last night.'

'Get to bed then. And stop rubbing that cream in. You're making your skin even redder!'

Lauren stopped rubbing. Izzy was right, little flakes of skin were all over her fingers. She gave up. 'Thanks,' she muttered to nobody in particular and for nothing in particular.

Izzy had known exactly what Lauren was thinking. She'd opened a window to a place Lauren didn't know existed and Lauren was puzzled by the view. Izzy wanted to slam the window shut and shout: DON'T LOOK! THE VIEW IS BETTER WHERE YOU WERE BEFORE! She'd created a wonderful imaginary future where Lauren married Chris and became a sister to her. It was selfish and she wasn't proud of it, but Izzy was not someone who could afford to be generous when it came to friends. She wouldn't go so far as to sabotage any romance between Lauren and Richard, but nor was she going to buy a Barry White CD and tell them to have a nice evening.

'By the way,' Izzy said, 'have you heard from that brother of mine?'

Lauren frowned. 'Chris? No, but I wasn't expecting to. I think I've come to the conclusion that the fates have been against us from the start. It's time to accept defeat gracefully.'

'But you mustn't give up!' Izzy said, hoping she

was concealing her fear. 'Not yet. It hasn't run very smoothly but I have this very strong feeling that it could all still work out fine. I know you both and I know that you might be right for each other!' There. She'd said 'might', not 'would'. It was a subtle distinction but one which made her feel she was behaving honourably.

Lauren didn't want to discuss Chris any more. Not until she'd established where Richard fitted into the hazy picture. But not tonight. She was too tired.

Izzy got into bed and lay there brooding over Lauren's defeatist attitude and the presence of the magnificent Richard. For the first time in her life, Izzy knew what she wanted. She was starting a whole new job which excited her with its potential for achieving success without the need for an abundance of social skills. And she had a new friend, the first proper friend she'd ever had. But she didn't have enough self-confidence to believe that she could sustain this level of achievement on her own merits. Chris was the lynchpin that would hold her new life together. If he and Lauren got together, stayed together, then all three of their futures would become inextricably linked.

The party on Saturday. Everything would be decided on Saturday when they all got together and slugged it out over civilised dialogue and warm Lambrusco. Lauren was the only person who did not realise that this was going to happen.

Lauren crawled into bed and collapsed blissfully into the soft mattress with its ice-cold crisp sheets. This is what heaven will be like, she thought.

Which is what Richard had been thinking all night as he

had held Lauren on the crisp ice-cold grass of a deserted mountain.

Beth was sleeping badly. In the five years of living with Chris, she'd become dependent on his continual physical presence. Having been brought up in a home where affection was expressed by the provision of essential utilities such as clothes and educational toys, it had come as a surprise to her to be hugged and held and stroked and kissed for no apparent reason other than that Chris loved her.

Initially, she'd tensed up when Chris touched her. It was too strange, unfamiliar, and she didn't know how to respond. Then she began to crave Chris's touch. She was like a baby who had been picked up when crying for the first time. It was a miracle, someone responding to your need like that. And the miracle for Beth was that she hadn't even known that she was crying, that she had any needs.

Now she could curse Chris for awakening her to the love that normal people took for granted, only to take it away when it became an addiction. She wasn't certain if it was Chris she missed or just his body, holding her tight, bringing her tea when she was working, correcting the steering on the supermarket trolley as she pushed it. She'd never had someone and lost them before so she didn't know if this feeling of grief was normal or if it would ever pass.

The only time she'd felt whole again was when she was with Pete. She might have felt the same with any man who'd spent time with her at this stage in her life. But she was wise enough to know that this was a lie. It was Pete. Something about him. She didn't know what it was and now she never would, because she would never see him again. She turned over and tried to get some sleep before she went back to the hospital to check on a patient. She had just dropped off when the phone rang.

'Hello,' she mumbled sleepily.

Maureen projected her voice down the phone line like Barbra Streisand. 'Beth! Hello! I do hope this isn't a bad time, I know how busy you must be.'

'Who is this?' Beth asked irritably.

'Oh I am sorry! Normally people recognise my voice instantly so I don't have to say who I am. It's Maureen Connor, Lauren's mother.'

Lauren who? Beth had been about to ask when the evening at the sushi bar came back to her. She shuddered at the memory of bumping into the appalling Izzy and the girl from the party, Lauren. She'd been shocked at how jealous she'd felt at seeing Izzy being so chummy with Lauren. However much she'd despised Izzy and however badly Izzy had behaved towards her, Beth had always comforted herself with the justification that it hadn't been anything personal, that Izzy would hate any woman who was Chris's girlfriend. She couldn't stand anyone or anything taking her precious brother away from her.

Seeing Lauren and Izzy giggling like sisters had brought home a painful truth: it *was* personal. Izzy had taken a personal dislike to Beth. And Beth had never been disliked before. She'd been ignored, misunderstood, mocked, left out of the rounders team every break throughout school, but never disliked. And it hurt.

Which was why she'd got drunk and slept with the doctor who'd been with her that night. She was glad she

285

had. Because it taught her a lesson that would help her in the future – that sleeping with someone you barely know doesn't make you feel more likeable. Doesn't make you forget. Doesn't make you feel better and, when the man has gone, makes you feel a whole lot worse.

And Lauren's mother was another face in the scenario that she was reliving without pleasure right now. She vaguely recalled some frighteningly blond hair and a mask of make-up that perfectly concealed any natural attributes the woman might possess.

'What do you want?' she asked crossly, not caring that she was being rude.

'I've woken you up, haven't I, I can tell,' Maureen said like a mother to a child. 'I'm ever so sorry. So I won't keep you. Just a quick thing. I'm throwing Lauren a surprise party on Saturday, well it's not really a surprise because she knows about it but it will be a surprise when she sees all her friends there. So what do you think?'

'What do I think about what?' Perhaps I'm dreaming, Beth thought. Either that, or this woman is quite mad.

Maureen laughed indulgently. 'You must think I'm quite mad! What I meant to say was that I'd love you to come! And I know that Lauren would love it too.'

'I'm sorry, Mrs Connor, but I really don't think—'

'Now don't say anything now, not while you're all sleepy. Get yourself back to bed and then, when you wake up, have a look at your calendar and see if you're free. I'll pop a map in the post so you'll know how to find us. All right, my love?'

'But I can tell you now . . .'

'Bye bye then. See you Saturday!'

Beth slammed the phone down. She was so angry at

being woken up by the wretched woman that she couldn't get back to sleep. And she needed to. She lay down and concentrated on her breathing, using the same techniques she advocated in her patients who were having difficulty coping with the pain.

In, two, three, four, hold, two, three, four, out, two, three, four, in . . . The phone rang again. This time it was her mobile. She ignored it but the the caller was persistent. She picked up the phone and looked at the number displayed. It was Pete's number. She quickly pressed the button. 'Hello?' she said breathlessly, abandoning her efforts at control.

'Hi, Beth, it's Stella, I do hope this isn't a bad time, I know how busy you must be.'

Why does everyone say that and then phone me anyway? Beth thought, hating Stella for making her think she might be Pete.

'You've woken me up, Stella, and this is the second time today,' she said abruptly.

Stella didn't take offence, which was annoying since Beth had meant to give it.

'Oh dear. Well, I won't keep you. I was just wondering if you could pop round for lunch tomorrow?'

Without hesitation, Beth began to make her excuses, 'I'm sorry but—'

Stella didn't let her finish. 'I took the liberty of checking with your secretary to see what your diary was like and you haven't got any clinics tomorrow afternoon.'

Beth was astounded at Stella's nerve. No, she wasn't, it was perfectly typical of Stella. Whatever, she wasn't going to be browbeaten into this. She had resolved never to see Stella again, if only so as to avoid bumping into Pete. That would be too painful to bear.

'I'm sorry, Stella. What I was going to say was that I have other plans. Since Chris and I split up, I've had a lot on my plate. I'm trying to sell the flat and buy somewhere smaller, and I have to get it done up if I'm going to get a good price.'

Stella's voice brightened considerably. 'Then it's lucky I called! That's my speciality. We can talk about it.'

Beth was not going to weaken. 'Look, Stella, I know you mean well, but I want to do this by myself. As a kind of therapy.'

She listened to Stella breathing, waiting anxiously for the next line. When it came, it was a winner. 'OK, I give in. I wasn't going to do this but I'll tell you the truth. I need to see you. It's a real emergency. It's about Pete.'

Beth held her breath. Stella spotted this. 'I can tell that you've got an idea what I'm talking about. Look, I don't know what's going on, but I'm going crazy with worry. If you don't talk to me, then I'll have to ask Pete right out and then he'll just run away and that never solves anything. Unless you're being chased by rampaging football hooligans, of course, in which running away solves everything, but that's another story.'

Beth didn't pay attention to the subsequent rambling. She was still trying to take in what Stella was saying. What did Stella suspect? She didn't seem to think Beth was involved or she wouldn't be acting so friendly. Beth wished she'd had more sleep so she could think more clearly. But it was no use. She had to come to a decision now.

'OK, Stella,' she said wearily, 'I'll be there. But I don't know what you want to hear from me.'

'Just be there, that's all I ask of you, Beth.' Those were Stella's last words. As she put the phone down, she exhaled loudly. That's the first part of my plan sorted, she said to herself.

Chris looked at his watch for the umpteenth time. He was due to see the board of governors in ten minutes. He'd been so optimistic this morning. Monday had passed without incident. There had been no call to the head's office, no ominous deliveries in the internal mail. He dared, he actually dared to hope that the events of Saturday might have got lost in the system.

But he had been kidding himself. While he had been going about his usual duties, trying to induce a modicum of literacy into a bunch of kids who just wanted to steal his watch, hurried meetings had been taking place behind closed doors all day.

The police had been obliged to inform the school of Dean Ryder's arrest as a condition of his probation agreement. And the officer concerned had taken great pleasure in passing on details of the involvement of a certain teacher in the aforementioned fight.

The wheels of officialdom had spun into action at this astonishing news. The Department of Education had been informed and no fewer than five civil servants had spent the better part of a day looking for precedents to this situation. Only two things were certain: Dean Ryder would be sent to a young offenders' institution where he would acquire new skills to take into adult life such as how to conceal a weapon, how to break into an alarmed vehicle and what to do with 5,000 Martine McCutcheon CDs that he might steal by mistake. And the school would close.

Chris walked slowly towards the boardroom knowing only too well where this was going to end. And as he sat before the long table of ten worthy but hopelessly out of touch governors, he knew it was futile to argue with them or plead his case.

He preempted the anticipated lecture from the chairperson about how he'd let the school down, let himself down, blah, blah.

'Before you say anything,' he said, 'let me make it easier on you and save us all a lot of time. I'm handing in my resignation, effective immediately.' He looked at the faces before him. Nobody rushed to refuse his resignation, he observed with amusement. That's saved them one unpleasant task, he thought. (He wasn't to know it, but the man who had been nominated to give him the bad news was quite disappointed. He had been bullied by other people, including his wife, all his life and was looking forward to dishing out some misery himself. He would have to take it out on the turnips down at his allotment tonight as usual.)

Chris continued, speaking slowly so that his words would not be misheard. What he had to say was too important to risk garbling.

'But now I'm begging you, pleading with you, not to let this be the thing that closes this school.' There were no reactions on the panel's faces. I've got nothing to lose, Chris told himself, I may as well go for it.

'Forget what I did, if you can,' he said, watching ten pairs of eyebrows all rise together like synchronised swimmers. 'Yes, I know it's hard and I'm not going to bore you with the details but what happened on Saturday was not my fault and it wasn't Dean Ryder's.'

The dubious reactions persuaded him that this would not be a fruitful line to pursue. He hurried on. 'As I say, I won't bore you with what actually happened, but I would ask you to look at the wider picture before you take any final action.'

No response.

'All I ask of you is that you look at the positive results this school has produced. Not in terms of percentages or statistics, I know that they don't make impressive reading, but consider some of the individual success stories.'

No response.

'Look at Ben Carter. He was a habitual offender, destined to move into more and more serious crimes until he came. This was his last chance. And now he's a fully qualified mechanic, working for London Transport.'

Chris looked at the governors and wanted to punch each of them in the face. They were all so-called professional types and were not impressed by a delinquent who ended up a car mechanic. They would have to have known the boy in question to appreciate just what a remarkable achievement his was.

'And Stephen Laird. Arrested thirty-six times before he was eleven. He's training to be a chef. He works sixty hours a week for the minimum wage and his eyes are shining with hope for the future. We gave that to him.'

It was hopeless, Chris knew, but he kept trying. 'And we've had three boys this year go off to sixth-form college voluntarily. And they're all taking NVQs. They'll all get good jobs. We've saved them.'

There was nothing left for him to try. He knew that unless he could present boys who were going to Cambridge and becoming MPs, these soulless bureaucrats would find no merit in making menial workers out of young criminals. Not at an average cost of over £25,000 a year per child.

'I don't suppose you'd be interested to know that, if you shut this school, ninety per cent of these kids will be in jail within a year. None of them will complete their education.'

He was right. They weren't interested.

The chairperson picked up the piece of paper in front of him. 'It has been decided that the school will close on Friday. You can work out your notice until then, if you choose, and after that your contract with this department will be terminated. Your arrest will, of course, go on your record and may affect subsequent job applications.'

Chris swallowed. It had been a long time since he'd been so ritually humiliated and it wasn't easy to take. 'And what about Dean Ryder?'

'Already been transferred to Northview,' the man said flatly.

Chris felt sick at the image of Dean among the hardened tendency he'd meet at Northview. 'That seems harsh,' he said quietly. 'The fight wasn't his fault.'

'Maybe not, but he knew the conditions. He was, by all accounts, spoiling for a fight even if this wasn't the fight he had in mind.'

The fact that this was true didn't make it any less irritating. Chris stood up to leave.

'Do we take it that you will be staying on until the end of the week, Mr Fallon?'

Chris nodded. And left.

Stella answered the phone on the first ring. 'Hello?'

'Hello, Stella, it's Chris, I was wondering if Pete was in?'

Stella was surprised. The trip back from Manchester had been very strained and she'd got the impression that Pete couldn't wait to get Chris out of the car and out of his life.

'He shouldn't be long, Chris. Shall I get him to call you back?'

'Don't bother. I was just looking for someone to have a drink with but I think I'll give it a miss myself. I'm just going to unplug the phone and get quietly drunk in front of the box.'

'What's happened? Oh God, I forgot, did the school catch up with you?'

'They certainly did. I mean I knew they would but it still hurt when it came down to it.'

'That's such bloody bad luck,' Stella said.

'Yeah. Oh well, *c'est la vie*. Bye.'

Stella put the phone down and turned to see Pete standing in the doorway. 'Who was that on the phone?' he asked.

'Oh, it was Chris,' Stella replied.

'What did he want?' Pete said suspiciously.

'He wanted to speak to you as a matter of fact,' she said, bustling around the kitchen.

'Really?' Pete said. 'I'll call him back then.' He went to pick up the phone but Stella stopped him.

'There's no point. He said he was unplugging the phone.'

'How convenient,' Pete observed.

Stella stared at him. 'What's that supposed to mean?'

Pete returned her stare. 'You tell me, Stella.'

Stella shrugged and got on with whatever she was doing. 'I haven't got time for this. I'm fed up with all your moods and silences. If you've got something to say, then say it. If you're not going to tell me what's on your mind, then stay out of my way. I'm too busy to try and psychoanalyse you right now.'

'What are you doing?' Pete asked, momentarily distracted by her frenetic bustling.

'I'm cooking lunch for tomorrow. Beth's coming over and I want you to be there.'

'I'm sorry but I can't just run home and have lunch with my wife and her chums every time you give me an order.'

Stella didn't stop bustling. 'Yes you can. I spoke to your secretary and she told me you had no appointments. You will find when you get to the office tomorrow that lunch at home is scheduled into the diary.'

Pete couldn't hide his fury. 'How dare you manipulate me like that! What the hell makes you think that I would want to have lunch with you and Beth anyway? It's bad enough that I have to suffer your endless dinner parties but now you're going to encroach on my lunchtimes as well?'

Stella whipped round to face him. 'I don't care what you want. This is about what I want. Something is going on in that head of yours that you refuse to share with me. I happen to think, no I happen to know, that Beth is part of this. And tomorrow, we're going to have it out. That's the end of the subject. It's not optional. Don't say another word. Now, I've got an onion tart to make so I'd appreciate it if you left me in peace.'

And Pete left her in peace as instructed. He wished that someone could order him some peace. It was in short supply in his life at the moment.

His head was a soup of conflicting emotions, niggling worries and stabbing doubts. The thought of this lunch bothered the hell out of him. Stella had been behaving strangely for a few days and she was not famous for acting out of character. Sticking to predictable responses was her usual way of dealing with unpredictable events. But this?

He didn't know what Stella was planning and he didn't want to know. Tomorrow would come soon enough.

Chapter 17

'Come on Izzy,' Lauren said, 'why don't you call it a day now?' It was gone seven o'clock and Izzy hadn't left the computer since sitting down at nine o'clock this morning.

'I just want to finish some figures for the Ambleside shop,' she said, not moving her eyes from the screen.

Lauren watched her new protégée with fond amusement. She had underestimated Izzy's capacity for this kind of work. While she had been right that she was bright, methodical and capable of absorbing complex instructions with ease, she hadn't anticipated that Izzy would be so fired with enthusiasm.

'This is great!' she'd said as she typed figures into the database and applied various functions to them.

'What's so great about it?' Lauren had asked. The task she'd given Izzy was painstaking and laborious.

'You don't understand,' Izzy had said, her fingers flicking quickly and accurately over the keys. 'I've never done a job that required any kind of thought.'

This seemed incredible to Lauren. 'I know you did a lot of silly jobs but there must have been others, surely. You've got a degree, haven't you?' She vaguely recollected Izzy mentioning university during their drunken evening.

'Yes. Physics.'

Lauren gasped. 'Physics? You're joking, aren't you?'

'No. Why does everyone think a degree in physics is so unlikely for me? You've reacted just like everyone else I've ever told.'

Lauren was cautious about how she answered this. After their mutual soul-baring on Friday night, she knew how sensitive Izzy was to any comments about her appearance.

'It's a compliment really. I've always thought of science graduates as being rather unimaginative' (good choice of word, she congratulated herself) 'and uncreative. Nobody could ever accuse you of that.'

'Thanks, Lauren, but I know that what you were trying to say was that I don't look intelligent enough to have a degree in physics. You were being kind, for which I am grateful.'

She seemed so at ease in front of the computer, so relaxed, that Lauren decided to be bold. 'You're right to a certain extent. But, Izzy, what I don't get is why you've allowed yourself to be misjudged all your life.'

Izzy took her fingers off the keyboard. 'But I explained on Friday . . .'

'No. You explained why you dress and make yourself up in such extreme styles. And that sort of makes sense although I think you underestimate your own qualities. I think a decent hairdresser and make-up artist could make you look stunning without scaring off small children.'

Izzy permitted herself a small smile. 'Maybe. It's doubtful, but possible.'

'Fair enough,' Lauren said. 'But that doesn't explain why you've wasted your entire adult life in dead-end jobs.

Who can blame people for thinking that you are probably only doing them because you're not bright enough to do something more challenging?'

'The simple answer to that is I've never known what I want to do. I know what I've wanted apart from that, to blend in, find a place where I don't stand out, friends and lovers, work colleagues, who don't do a double-take when they see me.'

'I've got news for you. That's what most of us want. And as for not knowing what you want to do, do you think I woke up one morning and thought: "Golly, I really wish I could go into multinational corporations and facilitate communications between their offices through the application of the latest telecommunications technology"?'

Izzy chuckled. 'It doesn't sound very appealing when you put it like that. So what brought you into this career?'

'That's easy. I got my degree, filled in application forms for the top five hundred companies in the UK. I got six interviews and one job offer. That was with a phone company. I was taken on as what they called a "graduate trainee". What that means is that you haven't got a clue what you're going to do. And neither do they. Somewhere down the line, the company started developing new technical products and I was the only graduate who could add three numbers together. That made me the technical expert. And the rest . . .'

'But you must have had dreams?'

'Grow up, Izzy. Dreams are for people who have the time and money to afford them. If you've got bills to pay, you put your career dreams on hold and get a job. If you want to live in the material world, you put your idealism on hold and play by the material world's rules. And if you want a family, with a decent man who'll love you and respect you and not let you down . . .'

'Then what?' Izzy asked, waiting for the final clue to finding the ultimate philosopher's stone.

'Then you find someone who's got it and ask them how they did it,' Lauren said. 'And then you tell me.'

The moment was broken. Gone. Izzy had come so close to learning the secrets of surviving and conforming and, at the last minute, Lauren had backed down.

But for now Izzy was enjoying her first taste of contentment. She'd found something she was good at, something that others would respect, that would not be met with derision at parties, something of substance that would supersede her looks in terms of what explained her.

And as Lauren watched her, finally free from the paranoia about people mocking her, she saw herself twenty years ago. She might not have had such dramatic hang-ups but she had felt overwhelmed by her failings. Because she had been the victim of her father's undiscerning admiration and, when that was taken away, she felt that she had to look for a replacement before she could continue with her life.

She'd had crushes on teachers, futile love affairs with men who despised her the more she tried to win their approval. She'd had to come to terms with the fact that you can't make anybody feel the way you want them to. You can just find a self that you are comfortable with and hope that maybe, one day, someone else might feel comfortable with your self as well.

And it never came. Or it hadn't seemed to so far. And she hadn't been surprised or disappointed. She'd long believed herself to be an underachiever. From her early twenties she'd given up competing with those lucky, lucky women who seemed free of neurosis. She didn't bother going for the jobs in advertising and PR where the girls with the easy charm and unrehearsed smiles always won through. She didn't go for the nice men with kind eyes who would surely see through her unblemished skin to her untidy mind, lumpy with emotional scar tissue.

She found a job that didn't sound exciting and men who nobody else wanted and here she was. Until a couple of weeks ago, she would have said that she was reasonably happy the way she was. And now she wasn't. She didn't like comparing herself to Izzy even if they were now worlds apart in how far they'd moved on. She didn't like being someone who lied about a necklace to make a man like her a bit more.

And she was not a bit happy about the way she kept finding herself staring at Richard when he wasn't aware of it. She kept looking to see if he brought back memories of her father. No memories returned, which caused her to wonder what it was about Richard that was so compelling.

But yet again the issue had to be put on hold. Something more immediately pressing had come up. She'd phoned her mum today to check that she wasn't still offended after their last call. And a man had answered.

'What did you answer the phone for?' Maureen had screamed at Eddie.

'Because I thought it might be for me. I was expecting a call from up north and, when I saw the number on the

300

display, it looked as if it might be from the right area. So I answered it, OK?'

It wasn't OK. Maureen was frantic. 'But what will Lauren think?'

Eddie kept his voice as calm as he could. 'She will probably think that her mother has a boyfriend. And since her father has been dead for over thirty years, she will probably be very happy for you.'

'Oh, you don't understand! It's easy for you, you're not a mother.'

'Believe it or not, I feel that I am a mother. A mother to your bloody daughter. Because the girl is always here between us. When you're on the phone to her, you don't look at me. When she comes round, I have to go out. When we go out to dinner and she turns up, I have to stand in the pouring rain until I develop a chest infection.' He started to cough again.

Maureen rushed to get him a glass of water. 'Drink it slowly. There you go. Only another couple of days of antibiotics. You'll be feeling the benefit soon.'

Eddie glared at her. 'I shouldn't have to wait a couple of days. If you'd told Lauren about us when you said you were going to, then I wouldn't be ill now.'

'Love, I explained why I couldn't.'

Eddie snorted. 'Oh, that's right, I forgot. She'd had a bit of a tiff with the man she'd met the week before so you couldn't tell her. And what happens if, on Saturday, she turns up and says she's got a verruca? Or she's having a bad hair day? Or her video's broken? Are you going to decide again that you can't tell her and pass me off as the hired help?'

'Now you're being silly. It's because you're not feeling

301

very well,' Maureen said, patting his hand. 'I'll get you a hot toddy, that'll make you feel better.'

He pulled his hand away harshly. 'No it won't. The only thing that will make me feel better is if you call up your daughter right now and tell her about me.'

'I can't do that, Eddie.'

'Fine. Well that's that then.'

'No, you don't understand. I physically can't do that. She's thrown her mobile phone in a lake and I haven't got a number I can call her on in the Lake District. She calls me from her client's private phone when he's not using the office, but I can't call her on it. It wouldn't be professional.'

Eddie's coughing abated. 'It's Wednesday today. On Saturday, when you open the door to your daughter, I am going to be standing by your side leaving her in no doubt as to who I am. If you even hint that I should stand in the background or start fiddling with the gas meter or other such nonsense, then I will walk out of this house and never come back.'

Maureen went white at his firmness. She knew that she had been unfair on him but she had felt torn in two. It would have been different if she had been any kind of mother to Lauren when she was growing up, but she'd more or less abandoned her, and if she were to announce that she had a new partner so soon after their reconciliation it might look like a second abandonment.

This complete misreading of her daughter's feelings came about because she didn't know her, and she didn't have the confidence to ask Lauren's permission to get to know her. She didn't have the right. All she felt entitled to do was to phone a lot, turn up a lot, buy her nice things and hope that, eventually, Lauren might ask her back into her life.

And Lauren wanted to ask her mother in but didn't dare. Because if someone rejects you once, it takes a bucketload of courage to ask again. So they tiptoed around each other, Maureen trying too hard, Lauren firing the occasional well-aimed barb, both wanting nothing more than to sit on a sofa and giggle over *Hello!* magazine. Or go to Sainsbury's together. Or swap money-off coupons for products that one knew the other used. All the easy, familiar stuff that had been denied them in the absence of a continuous relationship for twenty years.

But it would get easier, Maureen was sure. In time. With patience. Except Eddie was running out of both. So it was with the utmost care that she asked her next question. 'Darling, sweetie, what did you say to Lauren on the phone? Precisely?'

'He said what?'

Lauren repeated the exact words to Izzy. 'He said: "She's taking a bath." And you know what that means, don't you?'

Izzy had no idea. She could simultaneously translate German opera into English but she was lost when it came to the relevance of references to baths in the context of mothers with dead husbands.

'Sorry,' she said, wanting to be of use and failing.

'It means that he's sleeping with her. With my mother.'

Wow. Izzy was impressed. 'How long do I have to do your job before I get to understand subtext like you?'

'Are you being sarcastic?' Lauren asked.

303

'No. Well, maybe a little.' Izzy was playing for time. She was uncomfortable at holding back information from Lauren. Not only did she know that Lauren's mother certainly did have a boyfriend, she'd even seen him at the sushi restaurant. She couldn't face Lauren's anger at having this fact concealed from her so she decided to feign ignorance. 'I mean, how can you jump to that sort of conclusion?'

'Think about it. Can you think of any occasion when you might have a bath while there was a man in your house?'

Izzy obediently thought about it. 'I often have a bath while Tris is around.'

'He's your brother. My mum hasn't got a brother. Try again.'

'If a man was doing a really big job that was going to take all day and I was very dirty because, say, I'd been fixing my car, then I'd take a bath rather than wait until he had finished and left. Because I have a lock on my bathroom door. Has your mother got a lock on her bathroom door?'

'I don't know,' Lauren said. She then squandered twenty precious minutes of her life trying to visualise her mother's bathroom, but she couldn't get beyond the jade toilet-roll holder in the shape of a dolphin. Then she jumped up.

'I must be going round the bend. You've got me going along with your crazy hypothesis.' Lauren began pacing. 'No, he's sleeping with her.'

Izzy closed the computer down irritably. She couldn't concentrate while Lauren was pacing.

'I thought I was supposed to be the weird one but

you are acting very strangely, if you don't mind me saying so.'

'I do mind. I would be failing in my responsibility as a daughter if I wasn't concerned about her seeing men, sleeping with men.'

'Then phone her up and ask her,' Izzy blurted out in exasperation. 'For God's sake, you are getting on my nerves. Call her up and ask her. Now.'

'Hello?' Eddie answered the phone aggressively, convinced it was Maureen grovelling again.

Lauren put her hand over the mouthpiece. 'It's him again,' she hissed to Izzy. 'What should I say?'

'Ask him if your mother is there,' Izzy whispered back.

'Erm, I'm sorry to bother you, but is Maureen Connor there?' (And are you sleeping with my mother?)

'She's just popped down to the shops. Can I give her a message?' (Why don't you just come out and ask me if I'm sleeping with your mother?)

'Well, this is her daughter and I was phoning to check that everything is all right for Saturday. She's throwing me a birthday lunch.' (Which you will know about if you're sleeping with my mother.)

'Yes, I know.' (Of course I know, I'm sleeping with your mother.)

'AHA!' Lauren yelled, making Eddie and Izzy jump in shock.

'I'm sorry?' Eddie said.

Lauren calmed down. 'No, I'm sorry. Look, this is silly. The reason I called, well the reason I called the first time was to check that everything was all right for Saturday but then you answered the phone and said that my mother was in the bath so the second time I phoned, this time, was to . . .'

'Find out who the hell I am, what I am doing with your mother and what my intentions are?'

'No, no, not at all.' She paused. 'I mean, yes, that's exactly what I wanted to know.'

Eddie laughed. It was a nice sound. Unmenacing, gentle, not mocking. 'Of course you do. She's your mum. You'd be an odd daughter if you didn't want to know who she was seeing.'

'Thank you,' Lauren said gratefully.

'My name is Eddie Knight. I'm a salesman, I've been seeing your mum for about fourteen months, living with her for six months, I don't beat her or tell her that she talks too much, I carry her bags to every singing engagement in whatever godforsaken part of the South-East she should choose, I applaud when she hits the top notes as well as when she misses them, I bring her a cup of tea in bed every morning and run her a bath when she curls her toes up and down because I know that's a sign her legs are aching. I love her.'

Lauren was speechless. 'What is he saying?' Izzy was hissing in her ear.

'That he loves her,' she whispered falteringly.

'Oh, how beautiful!' Izzy sighed.

Lauren agreed. But she pulled herself together. She had a job to do. Assuming her most professional interrogator's voice, she continued. 'Did I hear you right? You've been living with my mother for six months?'

'That's right,' Eddie said, 'and seeing her for fourteen months.'

'I don't believe this! Why didn't she tell me? Is there

something wrong with you? Are you married? Have you got tattoos all over your face? A criminal record? She must have a reason for keeping you hidden away from me.'

'She has indeed but it's not one that I can explain since I don't understand it. She has this notion that you would be upset about her having a new companion, that you would see it as a betrayal of your father's memory. That's what she tells me.'

'But that's nonsense. I don't think we have ever talked about Dad, certainly not in the last few years since she came back into my life. She must think I'm a terrible monster if I don't want her to be happy.'

Eddie could hear her anger growing. 'Don't be too hard on your mum, Lauren. She's very nervous about you and her. She feels she's got to make up for all the time she wasn't around. And she's terrified to put a foot wrong in case you tell her to get lost.'

'This is unbelievable!' Lauren said. 'What was she planning to do? Keep buying me Jaffa Cakes until she's eighty years old and then, when she's pushing her Zimmer frame out of the door, mention that she's had a gentleman friend for the last thirty years?'

'Like I said, don't be too hard on her. I tried to tell her that she was being foolish but she wouldn't listen. She loves you too much to risk losing you.'

Lauren hadn't known that her mother loved her. She knew that Maureen had once resented her, effortlessly abandoned her, grown to miss her and finally needed her forgiveness. But love hadn't been mentioned. It seemed funny that she should learn of her mother's love from this stranger.

'So when *was* she planning to tell me about you?' she asked, now comfortable chatting with this man.

'Well, she was supposed to tell you a week or so ago, when she came to your flat. But something cropped up and she didn't feel the time was right.'

Lauren groaned as she recalled the something that had cropped up.

'Then we were at the sushi restaurant on Friday when you pulled up in the taxi and I thought it might be a nice natural occasion on which to introduce us.'

'But I didn't see anyone with Mum,' Lauren commented.

'That's because your mum didn't agree with me. She thought it would be better if I sneaked out the door and hid so that you wouldn't see me.'

Lauren thought back to the night. 'Where did you go? It was pouring with rain.'

'I know. I stood in that pouring rain while your mum chatted to you.'

'Oh Mum, Mum!' At least now Lauren knew where her self-destructive tendencies came from. It was comforting to have someone to blame rather than have to live with the belief that you have spawned your own faults.

'So what was supposed to happen on Saturday if it rained? At my lunch?'

'Ah, well, Saturday is supposed to be the big day. The big revelation. The day I jump out of my cupboard and get recognition.'

'I am really going to give my mum some stick over this,' Lauren said.

'No you mustn't!' Eddie cried. Now it was Lauren's turn to jump.

'What do you mean?'

'You mum will go berserk if she knows I've talked to you. She'll say that I could have ruined everything.'

'But you haven't ruined everything. Quite the opposite. I'm really happy with the news. So she should be happy too.'

Eddie breathed deeply. 'You don't know your mum very well, do you? It's got nothing to do with the outcome but everything to do with the alternative outcomes, the ones that might have been, the awful outcomes where you said that you didn't want to see her again or jumped off the Clifton Suspension Bridge leaving a note addressed to Robert Kilroy-Silk saying that it was all down to your mother's betrayal of your father, that sort of thing.'

God, I'm glad I'm not irrational like her, Lauren thought. This provided God with his first good laugh of the day.

'Are you certain that this is my mother we're talking about?' Lauren asked. 'I don't understand the first thing about her.'

'Then get to know her, love, for both your sakes, get to know her,' he pleaded. 'But please, you mustn't let her know we've talked. She'll never forgive me, I know she won't.'

'But what am I supposed to do on Saturday? Act as if we've never spoken?'

'Yes, that's it. It'll only be awkward for a short while. Then, once the introductions are over and done with, we can chat away like we're old friends – which, incidentally, I am looking forward to becoming.'

'I'm not a very good actress,' Lauren warned him.

'That's not what I've heard,' Eddie replied.

'Ouch,' Lauren said. 'I can see I'm going to have to watch what I say with you.'

'Perhaps your life would be easier if you always did that, Lauren. And on that note, I have to go. Your mother is on her way up the drive. Until Saturday. And remember, mum's the word!'

She might laugh at the joke once she'd got through Saturday but, for now, she had two immediate problems. The first was shameful to confess. But she realised that she would now be the only person not partnered off with anybody. It hadn't mattered when her mother was going to be by herself. But now it did. Birthdays were supposed to be occasions when you reflected on your achievements over the year. And turning up at your own party without an escort was particularly pathetic.

This led her to her second problem. Richard. She'd lined him up for her mother but now he was redundant. She couldn't withdraw the invitation so she'd have to think of someone else for him.

It beggars belief that Lauren, whose work entailed lateral approaches to the most intricate problems, did not make the obvious link and spot that she and Richard together added up to a pair. But it was a big conclusion and one she had to arrive at after a lot of self-analysis. Unfortunately she had neither the time nor the ability for that to happen. A few more days and some firm verbal nudges from Richard and she might have got there, but none of us can schedule the rest of the world's events to fit in with our own emotional journeys.

So Richard was still a loose end, and so was she. Therefore she came up with two less than ideal solutions.

She would reinvite Chris to the party. They would be

310

in company. There would be less stress. Nothing could go wrong. Maybe it might even go right. Then there was Richard. The answer to that one was right in front of her: Izzy. Not for romantic reasons but just to even out the numbers.

And so Izzy received her second invitation to Lauren's party.

Chapter 18

'We're through here, darling!' Stella called. Pete dropped his briefcase on the floor and checked his reflection in the mirror. What am I doing? he thought. It doesn't matter what I look like.

He breathed in and out three or four times and then strolled into the kitchen. He made a deliberate effort to go across to Stella and kiss her affectionately before registering Beth's position in the room.

Stella shooed him away. 'Careful! This is hot and if I stop stirring it, it'll end up with a skin. Be a love and pour Beth a drink. She's only just got here and I haven't been able to leave the stove.'

'What can I get you, Beth?' Pete asked, his voice sounding a little too cheerful. Both Beth and Stella heard this.

'Just something soft. I've got some paperwork to get on with later. Orange juice? Mineral water? Anything like that.'

'Right,' Pete said, rubbing his hands together like a jovial pub landlord. 'Orange juice or mineral water. No problem.'

Stella muttered something under her breath.

Pete and Beth both turned to see what she was saying.

She felt their eyes on her, stopped stirring and looked up. Her face was so red from the heat of her soup that it was impossible to tell if she was blushing. 'Sorry, I was just talking to myself. Needs more seasoning, I was saying, the soup.'

She returned to her stirring, Pete returned to his pouring and Beth returned to sitting on a stool wishing she was having her toenails pulled out or anything apart from this. She couldn't look at Pete and he was not handling this much better. When he handed her the glass of orange juice he almost dropped it, so careful was he being not to let his fingers brush against Beth's.

'Right!' Stella announced abruptly. Beth and Pete both stood up, not quite sure why but feeling that action was in order. 'OK,' Stella went on. 'The soup is ready to serve. The onion tart is in the Aga just warming through and there's a chocolate mousse in the fridge. I've set the small table in the living room. I'm going back to work. Bill and Ann have gone home so you've got the house to yourselves. Pete, you sort out whatever is going on in your head or your body or wherever the problem lies. Beth, I know you have professional rules about confidentiality and all that, but you are not to leave here until you have ascertained if anything is wrong with Pete and, if there is, persuaded him to get it dealt with. When I come home, I want to know exactly what has been decided. Those are the rules. *Bon appetit*!'

And with that she swept out of the door, leaving the faintest trace of Rive Gauche behind her.

'She used to wear Rive Gauche when we first met as students,' Pete mused, still watching the door after it had closed and Stella's car had driven off. 'Her brothers had

313

clubbed together to buy her a bottle as a present for doing so well in her A levels. It was the first proper present they'd ever bought her. Normally, their mum would buy some talc or bubble bath and stick the boys' names on the label. But they chose this for her and paid for it with their own money. They only did it the once. She was thrilled that they'd thought of her. She wouldn't let anyone buy her another bottle when it was gone. Not ever. I think she was waiting for one of them to repeat the gift.'

Beth sank back on to the stool. 'Is that supposed to be significant? Is it something to do with all this, Pete?' She waved her arm around the kitchen at the expanse of food that Stella had prepared for them.

Pete sat down two stools away. 'I don't know. It was just the smell. It took me back. Maybe that's what she wanted to achieve. Like I said, I don't know.'

'Then do you know what any of this is all about?'

There were long pauses between everything they said. They hoped that, if they concentrated hard, then it would all come clear.

'Not really. You?'

Beth had gone over that last phone call with Stella. 'This may sound crazy, but I got the impression that she thinks you're ill. And that I can help.'

Pete frowned. 'Where would she get that idea from? I haven't said anything to make her think I'm ill.' But as he spoke, little phrases that Stella had used, fleeting glances of concern, came back to him. 'I should have guessed that myself, knowing what Stella is like.'

'In what way?' Beth asked.

'Stella's always liked the idea of illness.' Beth's curi-ous look led him to explain himself. 'If someone acts out of character, Stella likes to think that they're under the weather. It probably sounds bizarre to you but I sort of understand it.'

'No, I've known people like that myself, but what *is* bizarre is that Stella is a psychology graduate, so you'd think she'd love analysing motivations and second-guessing her friends' thoughts and actions.'

Pete topped up her orange juice. 'Oh, she does. For example, she enjoyed nothing better than to spend hours trying to understand your relationship with Chris. I used to switch off, it got so tedious. She never considered him good enough for you.'

Beth looked affronted. 'I know I should be flattered but I'm rather insulted. It shows that she never really listened to me when I spoke about Chris or she would have seen that I owed a great deal to him. He found me at a time when I'd pretty much given up on having a normal existence and he gently eased me to the position where I took normality for granted.'

'That would explain why Stella felt the way she did. She doesn't rate normality very highly. She likes a guest who can contribute something to her parties either by being a great raconteur or having an interesting job. Helping someone to feel normal doesn't make the best pudding chat.'

'I've always known that,' Beth said.

Pete went on. 'There isn't a single person who hasn't come through this house and then been subjected to a rigorous psychoanalysis for days afterwards. You see, Stella loves all that. As long as there are no ramifications for her own life. As soon as her own status quo comes under threat, her analytical skills close down and she looks for justifications that don't make her anxious, solutions that can be remedied by pills. It's a mechanism she acquired early. When her brothers were treating her shabbily, or just ignoring her, she chose to believe it was because of a hormone imbalance brought on by puberty.'

'Maybe it was,' Beth suggested.

'She was using the same excuse when they were in their twenties. And whenever she and I have fights, she always asks how I'm feeling for a few days afterwards, as if I've been acting strangely because I was coming down with a virus. And the pathetic thing is, that I've gone along with this. I find myself conspicuously taking mega-doses of vitamins in front of her as if to justify her accusations, to give closure to the matter. Her eyes relax when I do it and then I can relax. And relaxing has been as good as it gets for me for a long time.'

'You can hardly hold it against her if you've gone along with it, Pete. Anyway, why did you?'

Pete didn't want to answer this. He had never formulated the words before. They were too dangerous. 'Because she was right to be afraid of the truth. She was right to avoid asking me if anything was really wrong. Because something was wrong and has been for a very long time. And now, when she is terrified because she thinks I might have cancer, that her future with me is in jeopardy, she's not so far off. Because it is serious. Her future is looking distinctly shaky from where I sit. I don't think I love her any more.'

There. He'd said it. And for a man who'd spent a long marriage not saying things, he appreciated the magnitude of declarations like this. In the coming weeks he was to ask himself if things might have been different had Stella let him air his feelings when they were still potentially fixable. But right now he was moving on to a different what-if journey.

'Oh Pete.' Beth was not cruel enough to exult in this news. But she knew what it meant. It opened a door for her, one that she had thought was welded shut this morning.

'There you go,' Pete said meaninglessly, to fill the silence.

'What are you thinking?' Beth asked.

Pete was struck by the question and how he'd heard men say that this was the most intensely annoying question that a woman could ask – and frequently did. Yet for years he had longed for Stella to say those words. And now, when Beth asked it, he was touched, not irritated. He wanted her to want to know what he was thinking.

But this was not the answer he gave her. He was pretty certain that it was ungrammatical, for one thing. And it was too grabby. Too forward. 'I was thinking that you could be right about Stella's suspicions. I have been a bit distant, difficult recently, so she has probably put two and two together . . .' He left the rest unsaid. Maths had never been Stella's strong point.

'In a way, that's good,' Beth suggested.

'How do you come up with that?' Pete asked. He'd tried and failed to come up with anything good about this.

'Well, because it's an easy misunderstanding to put right. With a clear conscience, we can both tell Stella that there is nothing physically wrong with you and then she can throw another party to celebrate!'

'It doesn't sound right when you mock her,' Pete said.

'I'm sorry,' Beth answered, chastened.

'No I'm sorry, Beth.' Pete got up and moved to the stool next to her.

'Shall we have some soup?'

Beth glanced at the pan bubbling away on the hob. 'I'm not very hungry.'

'Me neither,' Pete echoed.

'You know, I'd resolved never to see you again,' Beth whispered.

'Me too,' Pete echoed.

'And I even tried to say no to Stella, to stop this from happening,' she said.

'Me too,' Pete echoed.

'So it's not our fault, is it?'

This time there was no echo. Because Pete was kissing her.

'What's that smell?' Pete sniffed briskly. 'Can you smell it?'

Beth sat up and sniffed. 'I think it's something burning.'

This observation hung in the air for a moment or two before it hit home. Then Pete leapt out of bed and tore down the stairs, not bothering to put any clothes on. 'Oh my God, it's Stella's soup!'

Beth listened to various clangs and bangs and muttered curses culminating in an almighty roar of pain. She jumped up and put her clothes on before running down to see what was happening. Even when she was alone in her own flat, she didn't run around naked. She couldn't.

'Beth!' Pete yelled.

'I'm on my way!'

She reached the kitchen to find him on the floor clutching his foot in agony. He'd picked up the burning pan without using oven gloves and, having burned his hand, dropped the pan on his foot, burning that as well.

Beth calmly ran to the sink, filled the washing-up bowl with cold water and put it on the floor. She then lifted his foot very gently and placed it in the bowl. She got him to lean forward and put his hand in the bowl as well.

'I hate to say this, Pete, but I think we're going to have to get you to casualty.'

'We hadn't even got to the cigarette,' Pete said wryly.

Despite the awful state of affairs, they were at ease with each other and they both instinctively felt that this was something to feel ashamed of. That what they'd done was wrong and they ought to be feeling grubby or guilty or disloyal. But they didn't. Pete was in too much pain to care about valid moral responses and Beth was worried about Pete's foot, which looked as if it might be fractured.

There were practicalities to be worked out. Since Pete was incapacitated, these were left to Beth. Firstly, she had to get Pete dressed, no easy task with a foot and a hand immersed in a washing-up bowl. Then she had to tidy up the bedroom and make the bed.

That was when she felt grubby.

She removed the onion tart, burned into its tray, from the Aga. Pete groaned. 'Stella will kill me. That's her best baking tin. And that soup pan cost her a fortune in Florence.'

As he tried to think of what he was going to say

319

to Stella, Beth sighed. Pete thought she was laughing. 'What's so funny?' he asked, peeved that she found entertainment value in his sorry condition.

'Oh, it's not funny, not one little bit. It's tragic. There you are petrified at what Stella will say when she finds out you've ruined her pans. Well, have you forgotten what we've just been doing?'

Pete slumped back on the floor, a new pain filling the only part of his self that been unaffected by his accident. His heart ached, truly ached.

'You're right, it's tragic. Because we have ruined Stella's life.'

The two of them sat on the floor waiting for the ambulance, not speaking, just holding hands, both lost in the enormity of what they'd done.

Stella ran into casualty, wanting to see Pete right away, to make sure that he was alive, to solve all their problems in this hospital, patch up their marriage while the doctors patched up his wounds.

She had to plough her way through the hospital admissions system before she eventually tracked Pete down lying on a trolley in a corridor. Beth was standing next to him, holding his hand. Stella saw nothing untoward in this and was struck with a rush of gratitude for Beth's care of her husband. Pete wasn't wearing his glasses and he looked about twelve. Stella wanted to spoon-feed him soup and dab his temples with cotton wool and lavender water. She wanted to do things for him.

'God, Beth, what happened? They wouldn't go into any details on the phone just that Pete had an accident and—'

'Calm down, Stella, Pete is going to be fine.'

Stella looked at Pete, who was asleep despite a cast on his foot and a bandage on his hand.

'He doesn't look fine.'

'The doctors knocked him out while they were setting his foot. He'll be drowsy for a while.'

'When can I take him home, Beth?' Stella asked.

Beth was still holding Pete's hand but Stella thought it might appear churlish to push her out of the way and grab his hand for herself.

'They'll probably keep him in overnight. His burns were quite deep.' She gave him the version of events that she and Pete had agreed on in the ambulance. It was close to the truth, just omitting the bit about the trip upstairs, Pete's nudity during the soup accident, and Pete telling Beth that he loved her shortly before the anaesthetic took effect.

'Right. I don't know how to thank you, Beth. Thank God you were there!'

'I can't accept that compliment, Stella. If you think about it, Pete wouldn't have been at home if I hadn't been there, and then he wouldn't have had the accident.'

Anyone else apart from Stella would have been struck by guilt at this veiled reminder that the whole sorry tale was, therefore, all down to her. Oh to be so thick-skinned, Beth mused.

'Picking up a saucepan like that. I've warned him a million times. He's such an idiot,' Stella whispered, stroking Pete's hair away from his eyes.

Oh no, Beth thought. She still loves him. When she'd been in bed with Pete, he'd told her that whatever Stella felt for him, it wasn't love. Or if it was love then it wasn't the kind that mattered.

'How can you be so sure?' Beth had asked him wanting so badly to be assured that she was not breaking up a good marriage.

Pete stared up at the ceiling. 'I think she's been having an affair.'

Beth laughed out loud. 'Stella! I'm sorry to laugh, Pete, but I can't buy that. Stella wouldn't have the time, apart from anything else. And she's not the type.'

Pete moved on to his side so that he could see her. 'And are you and I the types, then?'

Beth felt cheap. Pete felt mean. 'Sorry, I shouldn't have said that.'

'It is true, though.' Beth was curled up, not allowing Pete to hold her. 'So what makes you think she's having an affair?'

'Someone told me. Someone who saw her with another man.'

'Someone reliable?' Beth asked.

Pete imagined Dean Ryder being driven off to the young offenders' institution and he felt unimaginably sorry for the lad. 'Well, it's not someone you'd want on your side in a courtroom but, yes, reliable enough in this instance.'

'So who is this man?' Beth asked, naturally curious.

Pete completely forgot her past connection as he answered bitterly, 'Chris. Chris Fallon.'

Beth hadn't been convinced by the truth of this rumour, but she'd been winded by the news. Everything to do with Chris was still raw and the transfer of her love from Chris

322

to Pete did not ease the rawness. That surprised her and confused her.

Chris and Stella? It didn't ring true, especially knowing how much Chris had always despised Stella. But Pete seemed certain. She hoped that he wasn't using this as justification for his behaviour. Or even worse, that he was trying to get back at Stella. No, she wouldn't think that way.

But now, seeing Stella next to her husband, she was sure that Pete was wrong. About everything. Because Stella loved Pete the only way there was. Truly and fully. And she could throw dinner parties every night and fill the house with chattering strangers and refuse to talk about her feelings but she would still love Pete. And he didn't know it. So whose was the greatest tragedy?

Beth prayed that it would not be hers.

Pete began to stir. He was very groggy and his eyes were stuck together with a gooey discharge. 'Beth? Is that you, Beth?'

'No, honey, it's me, Stella. Beth is here too. She's been taking good care of you for me. You're going to be fine. Everything is going to be all right.'

'OK Beth,' he mumbled and went back to sleep.

Stella stroked him for a while longer until he started snoring. Then she kissed him on the lips. 'I don't know about you, Beth, but I could murder a cup of tea.'

Beth looked down at her watch a little too obviously. 'I'd love to, Stella, but I can't stay. I want to get on with some reports.'

'I understand. Then why don't I walk with you towards your clinic and I'll find my way to the café afterwards? I just want to talk to you.'

Beth could come up with no reasonable excuse to get out of this so she began to walk very fast to keep the time with Stella to a minimum.

'You're very fit, aren't you?' Stella puffed as she struggled to keep up.

'Doctors are supposed to be,' Beth said without any difficulty.

'I know you're in a hurry so I'll keep it short. Beth, what did Pete tell you about himself?'

Beth stopped still. 'There is absolutely nothing wrong with Pete,' she said firmly.

'Apart from burns and fractures, you mean?' Stella joked.

'Obviously,' Beth said, resuming her brisk pace. Stella thought she detected a note of impatience but she put it down to Beth getting into professional mode.

'So Pete had definitely not got any of the symptoms that we're all told we should look for?' Stella repeated.

Beth spun round. 'You can phrase the question a dozen different ways and the answer will still be the same. Pete does not have cancer, which was, I believe, what you wanted to know. And now, Stella, forgive me but I have patients with real illnesses to see.'

She seems a bit off, Stella thought. I wonder if she's coming down with a bug?

She met Bill and Ann an hour later in the shop downstairs. Ann had a hospital bag with her. Bill was walking half a step behind her looking unhappy. He didn't like hospitals. Particularly ones that had his son in them. And ones that were going to do things to his wife's heart.

'Oh Stella, there you are!' Ann cried. 'We've just

seen Pete but he was still asleep. Your doctor friend was with him.'

'Beth? That's odd. I've just walked with her back to her clinic.' Stella didn't dwell on this. It was a hospital. Beth was a doctor. Why shouldn't she be wandering around?

'So how did it all happen?' Ann answered, watching her daughter-in-law scoot around the shop buying biscuits, cakes, sweets, drinks and magazines. Stella repeated the story Beth had given her, adding a few garnishes to make it more interesting.

'What's in the bag?' she asked Ann.

Ann looked down at the bag. 'Oh sorry! I forgot I even had it! The nurse gave it to me and I said I'd pass them on to you. It's Pete's clothes, the ones he was wearing when he came in.'

'Oh right,' Stella said, not paying much attention. She hadn't bought enough things to satisfy the throbbing ache that was bothering her. 'I may as well throw them out. They're probably ruined anyway.'

'Well, that's what I thought. And I joked with the nurse about it, said that even your German washing machine that washes clothes at the right temperature without you having to programme it, even that wouldn't be able to do much with scorch stains and burned soup.'

Stella opened the bag and pulled out the pair of trousers that had been neatly folded by Ann. They were spotless. That was strange enough. But what was really strange, *X-Files* strange, was that they weren't the trousers Pete was wearing when Stella had left him with Beth.

Chapter 19

'Come to gloat, have you, sir?' Dean walked around the pool table, pretending to take an excessive interest in his next shot. Chris wasn't fooled. In the last twenty-four hours, he'd become an expert at hiding his anger and grief and frustration. He knew the signs.

'No I haven't, Dean. What have I got to gloat about? I'm out of a job. My teaching career is probably over. And because of me, the school is shutting down on Friday.'

Dean demonstrated a flicker of a reaction by slightly lowering his pool cue. He then executed a perfect shot, downing the red as declared. Chris chalked his cue and walked slowly round the table, hoping he didn't look as inept as he felt.

'Oh well, it's probably for the best, sir.'

Chris's shoulders sank in disgust. 'How could it possibly be for the best, Dean? You're in here now and half the school will probably be joining you in the coming months.'

He took his shot, missing the ball and narrowly avoiding tearing a hole in the baize. Some of the other boys came to see what was going on. If he damaged this table, he would be lynched. If he lost the game, he would be humiliated. If he won, Dean's status among the other youths would be compromised. If he abandoned the game, he would look like a coward. 'Whose idea was it to play pool?' he asked, to nobody in particular.

'I think you'll find it was yours, sir. I think you wanted to show me that you're one of the lads, a good bloke and that.'

'Am I that transparent?' he asked drily.

Dean pocketed another red expertly. 'Only to someone who's been manipulated by teachers and social workers and probation officers since they were eight. *Sir.*'

'Sorry. I didn't mean to patronise you.' Chris hoped that his apology would come across as sincere. He meant it sincerely.

'Yes you did. Of course you did. How else are you going to deal with kids you don't understand?' Dean was now knocking the balls down speedily and accurately. His aggression was mounting with each shot. But the aggression was always controlled. Chris had always assumed that lack of control was the main problem with kids like Dean. Now he wasn't so sure.

'Dean, I may not have had the same kind of upbringing as you but that doesn't mean I can't understand you.'

Dean glanced up at him before firing off another perfect shot. 'Well, I happen to think it does mean that.'

Chris was exasperated. 'So that means that the only teachers you could ever have any respect for are teachers who've grown up on rundown council estates, had a broken home and nicked their first Toyota before the age of seven?'

'That's about it, sir,' Dean replied coolly.

Chris tapped his cue on the floor impatiently. 'Well, I don't buy that. I've helped some kids out of this way of life. There are boys like you in good jobs now, earning their own money, in their own places. We must have been doing something right.'

Dean curled his lip. 'If you want to take the credit, then go ahead, but don't expect a medal.'

Chris was getting nowhere. It might have helped if he'd known what he'd hoped to achieve from this visit. There was one thing he'd wanted to say and it wasn't easy.

'Dean, the main reason I came here was to say that I'm sorry.'

Dean looked surprised. He hadn't been on the receiving end of many apologies in his life. Perhaps that was why he himself didn't dish them out too often. No familiarity with the concept. 'Why? What have you done?'

'What have I done? It's because of me that you're in here! If I hadn't asked you for those tickets to that football match, then none of this would have happened!'

'Do you really believe that, sir?' Dean was staring at Chris as if he was an alien.

'Of course I do. Because it's a fact.'

Dean shrugged. 'Then you really are a tosspot. You don't get it at all. If it hadn't been last Saturday, it would have been next Saturday or the Saturday after that. I was always going to end up in here. As for you, if you think you would never have made a mistake at any other time in your life if you hadn't gone to that match, then you're more stupid than I am. That's the thing about mistakes. If you had to plan them, you'd never make them.'

'I make mistakes all the time,' Chris said defensively. He thought of Beth. And of Lauren. In that order. No matter how hard he tried to get Lauren out of his head, she kept nudging her way back in. It was the thought of this party coming up on Saturday. He couldn't decide whether he should go or not. He'd received a map in the post this morning from Lauren although he couldn't imagine how she had got his address. Only Izzy and Beth knew it.

He hadn't spoken to Lauren for ten days since leaving her flat after *Pravda* and sushi. He was alarmed to note that he wasn't absolutely certain what she looked like. All he could remember was the necklace that had been the cause of all the trouble. But, no, he couldn't picture her now.

Dean coughed loudly. 'It's your turn, some time in the next hour, sir.'

Chris lined up his cue again, his hands shaking under the pressure of being watched. 'And sir,' Dean said, just as Chris pulled back the cue.

'What?' Chris said crossly, sure he had been about to perform a magnificent shot.

'Apologising for mistakes doesn't change anything. Apart from making you feel better. Unless you can do something about it, then you may as well write it off to experience.'

Chris missed the shot completely. This wasn't going well. He was being thrashed at pool by a boy less than half his age and he wasn't feeling redeemed.

'That doesn't alter the fact that this particular mistake was down to me. And I want to do something about it. I want to do something for you.'

Dean potted the last ball to some grudging applause from the other boys. 'You can help me, actually, sir?'

'What can I do?' Chris asked, relieved that the visit was ending on a positive note.

'You can bring me twenty Marlboro next time you

329

come.' And with that he walked out of the room, followed by two younger boys who had elected themselves his acolytes.

He could hear the sniggering as he walked through the heavily fortified doors leading to the exit. He turned to the man who locked the door. He was a big, muscular man, who jangled the massive ring of keys on his belt like a status symbol.

'How long have you worked here?' Chris asked him.

'Three years. And I deserve a knighthood for it.'

Chris searched the man's face for a glimmer of humanity. There was some, trying to pop its head round the hard, straight mouth and cold eyes. But it didn't stay out for long. 'Why do you do it, if you don't mind my asking?'

'I know you won't believe me, you're probably one of those types who thinks we're fascists, thrashing all the life out of these kids, but I came here thinking I could make a difference.'

Chris knew that feeling. And he also knew how the man felt now, when the futility of this goal had sunk in, when the rare successful result was outweighed by the vast majority of failures, the repeat offenders.

'But you have these boys here twenty-four hours a day. That must give you lots of opportunities to influence them in different ways, through their schooling, training, leisure activities, sport and the rest?'

The warder gave Chris a pitying smile. 'Come and work here for a while and then see what these kids do with your opportunities.'

It was his last word on the subject as Chris left the building. But it was the first time that Chris had reason to feel positive about his future since Saturday. It gave him a possible new goal.

And Dean had helped him to see something else more clearly. He could either write Lauren off as an error of judgement or he could have one more go at seeing where she might lead him. But he wasn't going to apologise to himself or to anyone else any more.

Either way, he was going to the party.

Richard had felt Lauren watching him for a few days now. He'd given up trying to interpret her expression. She didn't want him to know that she was watching him, of that much he was sure. But that could mean anything.

It could mean that he was developing a bald patch on the back of his head of which he was unaware but which was very comical to any onlooker. Or she could be wondering how to get away from this job as fast as possible after their experience in the mountains on Sunday night.

He'd thought that the ordeal had brought her closer to him. He couldn't have felt any closer to her. She hadn't seemed awkward about it. In fact, they were laughing about it all the way home in the ambulance.

Then her odd friend turned up. Of course Lauren had told him that Izzy would be coming. And he knew that this was a professional arrangement. He could hardly expect her to carry out the entire project by herself. But things had changed once Izzy arrived. Lauren had become distant, preoccupied. Something had happened and he didn't like to ask what it was, because it had something to do with him.

He decided to be brave. As soon as he felt the warmth of Lauren's eyes on his back, he spun round. 'Gotcha!' he said, clicking an imaginary camera towards her.

Lauren jumped and started pressing random keys on her terminal. But Richard wasn't going to give up. He was due to meet Lauren's mother on Saturday. He wanted the atmosphere between him and Lauren to be resolved by then.

'It's no use pretending that you were working. You were watching me. And not for the first time. So come on, out with it! Is it my dandruff? Have I developed a hump? Or am I displaying builder's bottom? Please. I can take it!'

Lauren smiled. She liked him so much. But she didn't know why she'd been watching him. At least he'd only just noticed it. She was thankfully unaware that he'd known about her fascination for the last few days.

There was no point in waffling on about funny feelings that she didn't understand. And telling him that she'd been thinking about her dad for the first time in years. Too messy. Too insubstantial.

'I was thinking about the party on Saturday,' she said, 'and how much I'm looking forward to you meeting my mum.'

Really? thought Richard. I don't think so. But if that's what you want me to believe, then I'll let you off. For now. 'Oh yes, your famous mother, with a line in Ethel Merman songs and a taste for Bacardi Breezers. I can't wait to meet her!'

And this reminded Lauren that her mum no longer needed to tone down her attire on Richard's account. She could go for the full Lily Savage look if she wanted. But there was no way of conveying this to her mum without giving the game away about speaking to Eddie.

She had spoken to Eddie once more since that first time. She'd called her mum to let her know that Izzy would be coming to lunch and, once more, Eddie had answered. 'We can't go on not meeting like this!' he said warmly.

They chatted happily for a few minutes before the inevitable approaching steps of Maureen brought the call to a premature end.

'Before you go, can you give Mum a message? Tell her it was left on the answering machine or something? Say I'll be bringing someone else to lunch on Saturday. Her name's Izzy.'

'Lizzie? Righty-ho. Must dash. She's opening the door. See you Saturday!'

And he'd hung up before she could correct him. Not that she was worried. It wasn't important.

'Who was that on the phone, love?' Maureen called from the hall.

'Just a wrong number. Before I forget, your Lauren left a message on the answerphone. Said there's one more for the party. Someone called Lizzie.'

Maureen frowned. 'She's never talked about anyone called Lizzie before. Oh well. That's a good sign. Shows she's making lots of new friends. I'll have to rejig the seating plan for an extra guest.'

Izzy had to make a speedy decision. Should she tell Lauren that she was already going to the party or not? She hesitated too long and then the chance had gone. Like Lauren she had been taught the harsh lesson that

333

not saying the right thing could lead to as many problems as saying the wrong thing.

Still, it would be OK. She'd grab Maureen when she got through the door, give her some excuse about not wanting to spoil the surprise. And that was the excuse she would give Lauren when the time came.

Except it wasn't the truth. In the time she'd come to know Lauren, Izzy'd learned how much she hated deceit and dishonesty. Yes, this also struck Izzy as being a bit rich under the circumstances, but that was why Lauren had been so unnerved by her own little deception.

Lauren knew what it was like to be on the receiving end of other people's lies, harmless or otherwise. She didn't like it. And she didn't like being used or manipulated. Not that anybody does, but she had always tried to avoid inflicting the same damage on anyone else – failing miserably in Chris Fallon's case. And she didn't know the full extent of the fallout.

Izzy was very worried about what her new friend would think of her if she knew about Izzy's little intervention in her brother's – and subsequently Lauren's – life. At the time of her action, she couldn't have guessed that, within days, they would be friends and business colleagues. But she hated the idea that Lauren would despise her for this earlier interference. No. It was best to say nothing.

Ann looked at Bill. 'I think we should say nothing. Not with him in hospital.'

Bill was sitting stiffly on a kitchen chair in their family home. 'But we have to say something. This isn't just about money any more. It's about your health.'

They were both shell-shocked after a grim few hours

at the hospital. There had been a lot of hanging about in between Ann's various tests. They'd read the *Daily Mirror* from cover to cover, Ann holding the paper and Bill turning the pages, the way they'd always done it. Then the smiling face of the consultant who looked young enough to be their son. Or even grandson.

They'd read an article recently that said you should always write everything down when a doctor gives you a diagnosis, because patients commonly didn't take in the details of what they were being told. They thought they did but, when they got home, they would find themselves having conversations much like Ann and Bill's.

'So what did he say it was called again, Ann?'

'Cardio-something. And it had a "p" in it, I know that. And an "s".'

'I think it ended in "itis" or "ina" as well,' Bill offered.

'I think you're right,' Ann said.

Then they made a cup of tea. Ann put the kettle on and Bill got the cups out. Ann poured the water into the teapot, Bill poured the milk into the cups. Ann carried the cups through to the living room, Bill carried the biscuits. They achieved this without speaking and without knocking into each other in the tiny kitchen. They were like Torvill and Dean as they separated, came together, separated, came together. It had taken years of practice to achieve this harmony. And they never spilled a drop.

'So what did he say he was going to have to do, Ann?' Bill asked, breaking his digestive biscuit in two, passing half to Ann, which she accepted wordlessly, and dunking his half in his tea.

Ann screwed up her face to concentrate. 'Something

about taking a bit of vein from my leg and putting it in my heart or near it.'

Bill nodded. That's what he'd understood as well. There was only one part of the consultation for which they hadn't needed clarification. The part where the doctor talked about the waiting list, the six months or more before they could get round to Ann. The danger that her heart could deteriorate in that time leading to the risk of a heart attack. And the look of hope on his face when he asked them about their finances, and whether they might consider going private. And the sum of eighteen thousand pounds being bandied about.

Bill's own heart had started pounding rapidly at the mention of the figure. Look on the bright side, he told himself, if my own heart is going to pack up, I couldn't be in a better place.

Eighteen thousand pounds. No, they didn't need to ask each other about that bit, it was all they'd talked about on the way home. If this had happened six months ago, they could have gone to the building society, written out a cheque and Ann could have had the operation the following week.

But this was now. The bulk of their savings was now tied up in a monstrous house that would take years to make habitable. The only way they could get their money back was if Pete and Stella sold it and recouped the equity. But that could take months in the house's present condition.

'We could always remortgage this house,' Bill suggested.

Ann straightened her back. 'Never. This is our home

and our children's inheritance. We will never sell it. There has to be another way.'

But they couldn't think of one. Unless Pete's meeting with his board of directors was to go better than he expected tomorrow.

Bill understood a little of what might happen to Pete. He could be asked to stay but in a lower position on a lower salary. Or he could be offered redundancy. And he would have to make up his mind on the spot if he was to get the best deal.

That's why Bill decided that Pete had to know the facts about his mother's operation before he made that decision. And that was why he went to visit Pete in hospital. Without Ann.

'They're finally going to let me out this evening,' Pete said, stroking Beth's face with his unburned hand.

'That's good,' Beth said tenderly.

They were enjoying the time together in the knowledge that Stella was at work. Pete was taking some heavy doses of painkillers to counteract the constant throbbing in his hand and foot. But he was glad of the pain. He felt he deserved it for being so happy at the cost of Stella's unhappiness.

Beth had spent the night asleep in a chair next to his bed. Stella had offered to do so, but Pete had dissuaded her. 'Go home,' he'd told her. 'You look tired. I'll be zonked out from sleeping pills anyway, so you'd just have to put up with my snoring all night.'

'Funnily enough, I missed your snoring last Friday when you were in Manchester. I couldn't sleep. I've turned into a right old married woman, haven't I?'

The knife twisted in his heart as he heard the words that she didn't say. 'We *are* all right, aren't we?' she wanted to ask, but didn't. 'We can get back to normal, can't we, to how it used to be?'

She kissed Pete with more tenderness than usual. Probably because I'm in hospital, Pete assumed. But that wasn't it at all. Stella felt more tender towards him because he had suddenly become precious. Precious, rare and endangered. She'd stuffed the bag of his clothes into her briefcase and felt its weight dragging her hand down. She was going to ask him, in a light and jocular fashion, about why he'd changed his trousers and why they didn't have any soup spilled on them. But she didn't. Too scared. Too many things to think about before she faced that one. So she kissed him while there was still hope that it might all turn out fine in the end. And she left.

Pete watched her leave, her briefcase more stuffed than normal. I thought she was going to say something, he'd thought. Then Beth had arrived and he'd forgotten all about Stella.

They'd spent twelve glorious hours together. Pete drifted in and out of sleep, waking suddenly, afraid that Beth would have gone, then soothed by her sleeping presence next to him. The nurses had come by to administer medicines and change the bandages on his hand. They all knew who Beth was and they knew that Pete had a wife. But they didn't judge. Actually they did judge. They talked of little else while they opened their twentieth box of Celebrations bought by a grateful patient. But they kept their opinions to themselves.

And Beth and Pete did look right together.

The following day, Beth had her own rounds to do but

she popped in regularly just to see how he was, make sure he still loved her, that sort of thing. Late in the afternoon he felt strong enough to sit up. 'Come here,' he'd beckoned impishly.

And Beth had sat on the edge of his bed and manoeuvred herself into his arms, avoiding his hand and foot. They kissed carefully and just looked at each other. Pete looked away first; the expression on his face led Beth to pull away to see what had caught his eye.

'Hello Dad,' he'd said.

Bill's face was made of granite. He didn't so much as glance at Beth and he didn't speak at first but the long glare he saved for his son spoke of a father's disappointment.

Pete went to speak but his dad put up his hand to stop him. 'I don't want to know. I'm not interested. I just want to establish one thing – does Stella know about this?'

Stella had got home the night before to survey the damage in the kitchen. There was water splashed all over the floor from Beth's first aid and the saucepan and baking tray were piled in the sink. Ruined. She picked them up sadly. She'd loved these things. Everybody loves some material objects but Stella was one of those unusual women who was unashamed of her attachment to her possessions. They gave her firm links to her past and offered a foundation for her future. Measurable continuity, that's what her belongings guaranteed.

And now Pete had ruined them. She couldn't understand. When she'd left, the soup was simmering gently. Even if they'd left it for ten or fifteen minutes, it wouldn't have boiled dry like that. That must have taken over an hour. And the pie had frazzled to carbon. She checked the fridge. The dessert was still there. The bread and salad on the table were untouched. They hadn't eaten a thing.

She threw the bakeware away and cleared up the remaining food and crockery. She picked up her briefcase to put it in the shoe cupboard, then felt its extra weight. Taking the clothes out, she felt the wave of panic wash over her again.

Very slowly, she climbed up the stairs to the bedroom. As she opened the door, she knew that something was not right. The duvet was neatly spread across the bed. But it was pulled right to the top of the bed, whereas Stella always left the pillows uncovered. And behind the door, she found what she was looking for. Pete's suit trousers were sitting on a hanger, folded perfectly along the crease.

Pete always hung up his trousers and the hook behind the door was the only place available until they had some new wardrobes. Stella took the trousers that Pete had worn to hospital and put them back where she'd left them the day before. On the back of the chair, ready for Pete to change into when he wanted to get on with some DIY.

Beth must have panicked and grabbed the first pair of trousers that she could find, not paying any attention to what they looked like. No wonder they were so clean. He hadn't been wearing them when he had the accident. She looked in the empty laundry basket in the corner of the room. He couldn't have been wearing anything.

And that was when her knees buckled and she crumpled to the floor.

Chapter 20

'So what's the plan of action for tomorrow?' Richard asked. Izzy had been dispatched to Ambleside to try and woo Auntie Joan.

Izzy had frozen when her mission had been explained to her. 'But I can't. She's already told you that she won't work with any newfangled machines or phones. When she sees me, she'll think you've sent me to scare her into submission. She'll hurl garlic at me or something.'

Lauren sighed. 'Trust me on this, Izzy. Once Joan sees you walk into her shop with a computer under your arm, she won't take a blind bit of notice of what you look like. She's a cunning old bat. She'll turn on the charm, make you tea, bring out the shortbread then, as soon as you try and get down to business, she'll have too much work to do to listen. You can't do any worse than me.'

Richard came in while Lauren was saying this. 'She's right about that, Izzy. I spoke to Auntie Joan the day after Lauren's visit. "Lovely girl," she said, "but if she comes back here with her gadgets, I'll set my Barney on her." And in case you're wondering, Barney is her rabbit. He's got a nasty nip on him, but I think you can risk leaving off the body armour.'

'Don't worry, children and small animals are all scared of me,' Izzy said gloomily, packing the equipment into

Lauren's car. 'But if I'm not back by dinnertime, send reinforcements.'

Both Lauren and Richard had felt the mood lift when she left. It wasn't Izzy's fault, she had been great company and she was taking more and more work off Lauren with each passing day. But Lauren had rather enjoyed it when it was just her and Richard. And so had he.

They recovered the ease that had disappeared temporarily and were now spending all their time together. They were cramped in Richard's small office where he always seemed to have things to do whenever Lauren did. 'You can't get enough of me!' Lauren teased, in the way someone does when they have no idea that this is exactly the case.

Richard brushed it off smoothly each time. 'I just know that if I sit here long enough, you'll put the kettle on.'

And Lauren always fell for it, but she made a point of cuffing Richard gently on the head as she went past.

'The plan of action for tomorrow,' Lauren said. 'Well, I suggest we leave about six. That should get us there by lunchtime, even allowing for nuclear attacks on the M1. Also Izzy and I can share the driving.'

'Ah yes, Izzy,' Richard said quietly.

'Is there a problem with Izzy coming? I thought you two got on well?' Lauren was perturbed by Richard's tone. It was heavy with meaning of some kind but she couldn't fathom what.

'I think she's great. I just thought it might have been nice for us to travel up by ourselves. We could have stopped off on the way back if it wasn't too late, find a spot to sit and drink in the air, that's all. Since walking is out of the question.'

That seemed a really attractive idea to Lauren and she was sorry that she'd invited Izzy now. 'We could always ask Izzy if she'd like to come and sit with us,' Lauren said dubiously.

The idea of Izzy sitting still and doing nothing for any length of time struck them at the same time as being hysterically funny.

'Maybe not,' they said simultaneously and burst out laughing again.

They calmed down and Lauren thought of Izzy again. 'She was a bit funny with me when I asked her to come. I think she finds parties or any gatherings a bit difficult. Maybe I shouldn't have pushed her into it.'

'Why did you push so hard if she wasn't that keen?' Richard asked.

'Well, it's a long story but I found out that my mum has got a boyfriend except that, now I've told you, you have to forget I've told you and not look surprised when I look surprised and pretend that I didn't know when my mum introduces me. OK, so far?'

It wasn't OK, far from it, and it didn't get any more OK as the saga continued. But Richard gleaned enough information to grasp the important bit – Chris was going to be there. Chris, the dolt who said 'astrology' in a funny way. Chris, who liked French films and sushi, both of which Lauren hated. Chris, who hadn't been mentioned in over a week and who Richard had merrily written off. Chris, who was no doubt younger than Richard, more sophisticated than Richard and who had evidently appeared so attractive to Lauren that she'd lied to keep his attention. She'd never accurately explained to Richard why she'd lied, largely because she didn't know.

343

It was just a careless slip of the tongue. But Richard had assumed it was because she was very attracted to Chris and was desperate to win his approval.

Lauren had never lied to Richard and now he wanted her to. Just to prove that she thought he was worth lying to.

But Lauren had nothing more to say. She was thinking about Richard and her original plan to pair him off with her mother. The very idea now seemed nonsensical. But she didn't feel stupid for having ever imagined that it was a good plan. All she felt was utter relief.

She didn't understand why. She tried reasoning it through. Maybe the confirmed knowledge that her mum had a boyfriend was exactly what she'd been waiting for to enable her to make her big decision. Maureen might not even have got on with Richard, although the notion of anyone not getting on with Richard was unthinkable to Lauren.

So she could go to New York now if she wanted to. She wouldn't have to worry about her mum. That's good, isn't it? she told herself.

But it didn't feel good.

Chris emptied his locker into his rucksack. The other teachers were doing the same. None of them were talking to him. They blamed him for the school closing down and for losing them their jobs. He wasn't going to argue with them. He blamed himself.

'Look, I know I've said it a hundred times already but let me say it just once more. I'm sorry. I actually believe that, even if I hadn't been so stupid, the school wouldn't have survived more than few weeks but that's irrelevant.

It's my fault it's happening now and I'm truly sorry. I don't know if any of you are interested but I'm buying drinks down at the Nag's Head this evening so I hope I'll see some of you later.'

He didn't wait for the humiliation of being told that nobody would be joining him. He quickly left the staff room and began his final journey through the school. The classrooms were all empty. Desks and chairs had been upturned, graffiti had been sprayed over the walls. And who could blame the kids? He envied them the lack of inhibition it took to vandalise.

Dean had been right. Chris couldn't possibly understand kids like him. It wasn't just his middle-class upbringing and his two dotty, but not neglectful, parents that barred him from participating in Dean's world. There was a bottomless mental chasm of fear between them.

Even Chris's private school had produced its fair share of misfits, the rebels, the tearaways. The only difference was that they had well-off parents to buy their kids out of trouble. Chris had faced his big moment of truth, of commitment, when he was twelve. He was with two friends in the local sweet shop. The challenge was to get the shopkeeper to go into the back to look for something and then, while he was out of the way, Chris had to steal a KitKat.

There were no CCTVs in those days, no neighbourhood watch, not even any computerised stock control to let the poor shopkeeper know he'd been robbed. So it was completely risk-free. The other boys had already done it and Chris envied them the sense of exhilaration they'd demonstrated when they'd charged out of the shop, booty in hand.

But when it was Chris's turn, he couldn't do it. He confessed this to Beth and she had theorised that he possessed a higher moral ceiling which didn't permit him to steal, that he was innately honest. He hadn't argued with her because he hadn't wanted her to know the truth: that he would not have lost a minute of sleep worrying about the moral implications. In reality he was terrified of being caught. That was it. Fear of capture. Yet there was no chance of failure. It was so easy. And he so wanted to do it, to make these boys admire him. But he didn't.

So, all through his career, as he dedicated his life to rescuing youngsters from an unstoppable descent into criminal life, he never lost that pang of envy as he watched them pinching cars, smashing windows and spraying misspelt words on derelict buildings. Because they weren't afraid although they, of all people, had a lot to be afraid of. And this provided one of the less noble motives that led him to work with the troubled youths. Fascination.

He glanced at his watch before getting into his car. He'd have to hurry, his interview was in fifteen minutes.

Pete climbed gingerly out of the taxi fifteen minutes early for his interview with the board. The taxi driver gave him a hand and was rewarded with a large tip. It's probably the last time I'll be able to afford a taxi for some time, Pete thought bleakly.

He planned to spend the fifteen minutes in his office thinking. He had a lot to think about and it was impossible at home where Stella had been acting very oddly.

She'd picked him up from the hospital and had given

346

him a kiss of welcome – she had reverted to the dry-lipped chirpy peck, the tenderness seemed to have gone now that he was out of bed. She helped him into the car, a little impatiently, he thought, but then again he was so heavily drugged that he didn't trust his faculties of judgement.

And then she talked all the way home. Stella had always been a talker, imparting every bit of information to come her way on that particular day, as if to reassure herself that her life was truly full. But she excelled herself today. There was not a single phone conversation with a single client that she didn't relate verbatim to Pete. She told him everything that she'd eaten and drunk down to the single Thornton's chocolate that she'd been offered by the office cleaner whose birthday it was. 'It was a Brazil nut fudge,' she'd said irrelevantly.

It must be the drugs, Pete thought. She seems to have speeded up somehow, fast-forwarded until I feel dizzy just watching and listening to her. But he was happy to let her talk. He was dreading the next few days, acting normally until he and Beth decided what to do next. In the meanwhile, he was going to be gentle and tender with her. If she let him.

Once they got home, Stella upped the pace. 'I got to thinking while you were in hospital, now I bet that's a shock, isn't it, scatty old me thinking, but I do do it occasionally, and I was thinking that we ought to do two things: firstly we should sell this house because I think it was a mistake buying it and secondly I think we should go on holiday. Somewhere in Britain.'

She was waiting with childlike anticipation for his answer. 'Stella,' he said kindly, 'firstly, we can't sell the house, not until we've made it look like somewhere normal people might be able to live, which could take a year; and secondly, you hate holidays in Britain. You hate the weather and the cream teas and trudging round churchyards and the fish 'n' chips.'

'But you love it!' Stella cried. 'And I realised that we haven't had a holiday here for . . .' She tried to calculate when they'd stayed in that terrible B and B in Anglesey.

'Fifteen years,' Pete finished the sentence for her. 'Anglesey.'

Stella shook her head. 'No it can't have been that long ago. Surely not.'

'It was,' Pete said. 'You hated it so much you said that we would never stay anywhere on this godforsaken island again.'

Stella swallowed. For the last fifteen years, she'd chosen all their holidays. Why hadn't he stopped her? She turned to put the kettle on so that he wouldn't be able to see her face.

'All the more reason that we go somewhere you like this time. So what do you think?'

Pete rested his burned hand on the table. 'I don't think we should make any plans just yet. Not with things as they are.'

Stella stopped breathing momentarily, then she recovered gamely. 'Oh that's right, the interview tomorrow. Well, I've been doing some thinking about that as well. Maybe this is all for the best. I mean, it's not as if you've enjoyed your job that much recently.'

How would you know, Stella? You never ask. Another comment best left unsaid.

'So I was thinking, why don't you take your redundancy money and set yourself up in business?'

'Doing what?' Pete said, sharply enough to make Stella flinch. He checked himself and forced an apologetic smile on to his face.

'Whatever you want,' she said weakly.

'That would be great if I knew what I wanted,' Pete said. 'But we have another problem.' Stella held her breath again waiting for what Pete might say. 'It's about Mum.'

Stella exhaled, granted a reprieve once more. 'What about her?' she asked, peeling carrots maniacally.

'You haven't asked how she got on with her tests yesterday,' he said.

Stella slapped her hand against her forehead. 'Oh God, I'm so sorry, it went completely out of my mind. You can't blame me for that, surely. Not with everything that happened.'

Pete softened at the sight of his wife's anxious face. 'No, I don't blame you. Anyway, Dad came in to see me earlier. Without Mum.'

Stella sat down. 'It's not bad news, is it?'

'It's quite serious. Dad isn't sure but it sounds as if Mum is going to have to have a bypass.'

'Oh no, poor Ann.' Her concern touched Pete. Stella had always loved his parents and they had loved her too. This was probably why his dad had been so devastated to see him with Beth. He hoped he would never have to go through anything like that confrontation again. Except he would, with Stella, and that would be a hundred times more painful.

He couldn't shift the image of his dad's face from his mind. Beth had left his bedside, muttering some blanket apologies that Bill had ignored. Following some whispers in the staffroom, a number of nurses were now hovering around Pete's bay, finding unwanted procedures to perform on the hapless patients whose only symptom was being in a bed near to Pete's. This could liven up the day, they'd thought, listening keenly.

'Dad, if you'll just sit down, I'd like to explain . . .'

'Nothing to explain. I'm not interested in your excuses. You're a married man.'

'Dad, I promise I'm not going to make excuses. I just want you to know what is going on, so that you can try and understand.'

Bill lifted his chin and closed his lips tightly together. 'I can tell you right now, I will never understand and neither will your mother.'

'Then just hear me out. And think about what I'm saying. I don't love Stella and I haven't for a long time. What's more, I think you know it.'

Bill grunted but condescended to sit down. 'All this rubbish about love you young people spout. You never talk about commitment or responsibility.'

'That's not fair, Dad. I've stayed in the marriage years longer than I should have. *Because* of my commitment and responsibility.'

'But you're packing it in now. Because you've found someone new. And how would you feel if I said I was leaving your mum for the woman in the wool shop? She's always had her eye on me. Would you say that it's all right as long as I don't love your mum any more?'

Pete smiled. His dad was loosening the leash, ever so slightly. 'The fact is, you wouldn't leave her because you do love her.'

Bill grunted again. He couldn't decide what was worse,

talking about his son's infidelity or talking about love. Neither of the subjects came easily to him. He would far rather be talking about the feature-length *Taggart* that he and Ann had watched last night, holding hands and eating Cherry Bakewells.

'I can't be doing with all this right now and you are not to breathe a word of this to your mother, not in her condition.'

Pete had looked alarmed at this. 'What condition?'

And Bill told him everything that he thought the consultant had said, ending up with the option of the private operation for £18,000. He hadn't needed to say anything more. Pete was devastated. 'I've let you down badly. And that was before all this with Stella. Mum's got to have that operation, Dad. I'll get the money back to you, I swear.'

Bill was now looking small and old as he leaned back in the saggy hospital-issue armchair. 'Do your best, son, that's all I can ask of you.'

Pete gave Stella a heavily censored version of their conversation, although he did throw in the bit about the eavesdropping nurses, hoping to lighten the tension that was oppressing them both. She didn't laugh.

'Eighteen thousand pounds,' Stella whispered. 'Is there any chance you'll get offered that tomorrow?'

Pete took a deep breath. 'I don't know. Do we know anyone religious who can pray for us?' He was joking but Stella had been thinking the same thing. And she hadn't been joking.

'Oh well,' Stella had said finally. 'At least we've got Saturday to look forward to.'

Pete looked blank. 'What's happening on Saturday?'

'It's Lauren's birthday lunch. We always go, I told you about it ages ago.'

Pete shook his head. 'Well I'm not going this year. Phone Lauren's mum up and tell her about my accident. She's bound to understand.'

Stella's voice began to falter. 'Pete, please. I really want to go to this. Lauren's my best friend and it will do us good. I'll drive and you can sit in the back with your leg stretched out. And you can have a drink.'

'Stella, you can go by yourself just this once, can't you?'

And so she had no choice but to beg. '*Please*, Pete. I'm begging you. I want us to go to Lauren's party *together*. To do something normal *together*. Please, Pete. I've never begged for anything like this before. Please!'

Pete was appalled at the state she was in. He didn't know what was going on in her head, what she suspected or what she knew. And he wasn't going to ask. Not yet. He was too weak. But he surprised himself when he quietly agreed to go on Saturday. That just left Friday to get through. Today.

His battered appearance turned out to be an asset. He limped into the meeting on crutches, his face grey with discomfort. Even the hardened faces of the board members looked unsettled by Pete's condition.

'Are you sure you're up to this?' one of the nameless suits asked kindly before assassinating his career.

'Quite sure,' Pete said, wishing he'd taken his tablets sooner. They hadn't taken effect yet, and he was beginning to sweat with pain. 'I just want to get this over with so I can go home and go to bed.'

They were shocked at his honesty. He was the eleventh staff member they'd seen today and they'd met a number of reactions from confrontation to aggression, from tears to abuse. But they were put out by this wounded veteran before them. It threw them off guard.

'Well, this is very delicate for us, Peter, as I'm sure you can imagine . . .' Grey Suit began.

'If I can interrupt. There is every chance that I will throw up quite soon, so if you could just cut to the terms, I'd be most grateful. Now have I got a job or haven't I?'

The suits all exchanged glances. They hated it when their script was preempted. It had taken two executives three days to draw up the packages and write the condescending speeches that were supposed to sweeten the pill. Still, it certainly wasn't unthinkable that this man might throw up in front of them. He could even keel over and die, he looked bad enough. So it was silently agreed to speed up this particular interview.

They cut to the deal. Pete had two choices. He could stay with the newly merged company at a twenty-five per cent pay cut and a reduced job title. Or he could leave immediately and take £15,000 tax free.

Without waiting for them to draw breath, Pete replied. 'I'll leave now and I'll take thirty thousand on the agreement that I won't sue you for discriminating against me because of my physical disability.'

Seven mouths dropped open with satisfying predictability. Some spluttering noises were emitted but no one wanted to say anything specific. He'd used the words 'sue' and 'disability' and, while it seemed highly unlikely that he had a case, not two days after dropping a saucepan on his foot, they couldn't be sure. Every day, the papers would tell of an ever more frivolous lawsuit that had cost the defendants small fortunes. Even if they won their case, the costs alone would be horrific.

One of the blue pinstriped suits spoke coldly. 'I wonder if you could wait outside for a minute while we discuss your offer, Peter.'

Pete restrained himself from punching the man's lights out for calling him Peter when he didn't know him. Since the fight in Manchester, Pete had felt quite belligerent. He wondered if men were like other wild animals who, once they'd tasted blood, developed a craving for it.

He didn't have enough time to expand this philosophical theory before he was called back into the boardroom. The suits were no longer looking bland and smug, they were fizzing with hatred for this man who had got the better of them. Pete didn't bother listening to the platitudes and the legal clauses and warnings and threats. Once he'd heard the words thirty thousand pounds tax free, cheque waiting downstairs, he was up and off.

He was accompanied from the building by a burly security man who had been assigned to ensure that Pete didn't take anything away with him. But the guard had taken pity on Pete, and not only had he helped him empty his drawers into two carrier bags, he'd carried them downstairs and called Pete a taxi. As Pete thanked the guard for his kindness, and closed the taxi door, he thought he heard the man say 'God bless you', but he couldn't be certain.

Izzy sat face to face with Joan. It was *High Noon* meets *The Archers*: a battle of wills. Izzy's computer against

Joan's shortbread. Izzy had formulated a plan. She would drink two cups of tea and then, just as Joan went to brew the obligatory third pot, she would make her move.

In the eight minutes it took Joan to wash up the second lot of teacups and make the tea, Izzy had set up the computer on Joan's table. It couldn't be called a desk, not with crocheted doilies all over it.

Joan walked in with her tea tray, expounding merrily on the importance of taking the pot to the kettle and not the other way round. Before she saw Izzy's triumphant expression, she spotted the machine on top of her doilies. She rushed to put the tray down, except there was nowhere to put it so she had to take it back into the kitchen.

When Joan came back, she had moved on to the predicted second stage in her defence against invasion. 'Well you might have time to sit and play with your computer, but I have work to do.'

'What have you got to do, Joan?' Izzy asked swiftly.

Joan tutted impatiently. 'I've got to go through last year's March sales receipts to work out how many of everything I need to order this year.'

Izzy pointed to the screen. 'Press the button marked F3.'

Joan folded her arms in her best harridan pose. 'I've read about all the radiation that comes out of those things.'

'Don't try all that "daft old dear" stuff with me. You're not daft. Press the button.'

And after some more cajoling, she pressed the button. The screen filled with words and numbers. It didn't take her long to decipher the table. 'These are last year's figures,' she said cautiously, 'where did you get them from?'

Izzy pulled another chair up and patted the seat, encouraging Joan to sit down, which she did. 'I got copies of your sales figures from Richard's files. And then yesterday I keyed them all into the computer. So there you are.'

Joan marvelled at the screen. 'So all I have to do is copy this out on to my order form and that's my stock ordering done?'

Izzy held up a finger to interrupt. 'That's what you have to do today but, once you're linked up to the warehouse, that won't be necessary. Every time you sell something, the cash register will let the warehouse know that your shop is now one short of that particular item. And when it reaches a particular level, it will let *you* know that you are running low.'

Joan folded her arms again. 'Oh I won't be able to do all that,' she said firmly.

Izzy physically unfolded Joan's arms. 'Joan, you pressed the key just now, didn't you?'

'Yes,' Joan replied impatiently.

'That means you have fingers. And you can read, can you?'

'Don't be so cheeky!' Joan said, beginning to fold her arms then changing her mind.

'Then that means you can follow instructions. I GUARANTEE that I will have you using the new till, phones and computer in one day.'

'And what if you can't, what if I'm too old to learn?' Joan asked, smelling a challenge.

Izzy gave this some thought. 'Then I will stay in

this shop until you have taught me to crochet a doily,' she said.

Joan laughed. 'Well, that I'd love to see. OK, lass, we'll give it a go. Now can we have that cup of tea?'

Izzy stuck her tongue out as if she was parched. 'I thought you'd never ask,' she said.

Joan shook a fist at her cheerfully. She walked out towards the kitchen then stopped suddenly. She turned to look frankly at Izzy. 'Do you know what, I liked you the minute I saw you and I was right. But you don't make it easy on yourself, lass. Let me get my daughter, Betty, over.'

'What does Betty do?' Izzy asked curiously.

'She's a hairdresser and beauty therapist,' Joan answered proudly.

Izzy died a quiet inner death at this news.

Chapter 21

'That's wonderful news, Pete! Your mum and dad will be so relieved. I'll get some champagne. Or you can pick up some on the way home.'

'No I don't feel like celebrating. I've just lost my job.' It was a bad connection and Pete sounded as if he was on Mars. He might as well have been. He was distancing himself from Stella as if by light years. Stella wished she could bite her tongue off. She was trying so hard but she was swimming against the tide.

'Oh right. I'm sorry, that was thoughtless of me. Well, I'll see you soon, shall I?' She couldn't keep that desperate plea from her voice. Pete closed his eyes at the sound of her pain.

'I won't be too long. I just have to stop off at the hospital to have my hand looked at.'

She knew what that meant and it took all of her strength to sound cheery and supportive as she said goodbye.

As she put the phone down, she half sat, half collapsed on to the chair by the phone. She didn't know how long she could keep this up. It had seemed a good idea at the time. Ignore his little fling. It was all down to the stress of possible imminent redundancy. It happened to men all the time. The key thing was not to talk about it. Not to say things they couldn't unsay.

So she'd tread water, keep them both afloat until they reached shallower waters again. She would change. And Pete would see that she'd changed and fall in love with her again. They'd move, and Pete would get a new job. It would all be fine. Saturday, they'd be out with people they knew, who saw them as a solid couple. That would remind Pete that they *were* a couple. They'd have fun. And she'd talk to him and ask him things. It would be fine. She just had to hang on until tomorrow. It would all be fine then.

'Absolutely and categorically not,' Beth said, not bothering to lower her voice. They were in the hospital coffee shop and had attracted quite an audience. News of their liaison had spread and there was always good mileage in anything involving a doctor, particularly a female doctor and a patient. All they needed was the wife to come in with a meat cleaver and the drama would be complete.

But that only happened in *Casualty*.

No, in this drama, they were arguing about Pete's request that Beth take up the invitation to Lauren's party.

'Look, how can I go? I barely know Lauren. She's been out with my ex-boyfriend a couple of times. That's hardly going to get me a walk-on in *This Is Your Life* when they do her, is it?'

'Yes, but you've been invited!'

'Only because her mother is certifiable. God only knows where she got my number from.'

'Beth, you've got to come. It will be a nightmare. Stella's practically got us retaking our marriage vows tomorrow. And she's acting as if she's on speed. I won't be able to get through it unless you're there.'

Beth was not moved. Pete borrowed Stella's trump card. 'Beth, I'm begging you. Please. I'm begging.'

It worked. If Pete ever had children, the powerful use of the word 'begging' would be the first piece of advice he handed on.

Beth walked him back down to the hospital entrance where she hailed him a cab. He leaned against her while he waited, loving her unyielding strength, loving her, full stop. If he could only have one wish, it would be that tomorrow was over and that Stella wouldn't be too badly hurt by what he was going to do. Except that was two wishes.

Well, why shouldn't I have two wishes? Pete thought. Is that too much to ask?

Lauren washed her hair and spent extra time on the drying and styling. It wasn't just that it was her birthday, it was the drive up with Richard, meeting her mum's boyfriend. It would herald a fresh beginning. She would wear her necklace unashamedly and make a joke about star signs. If she said the wrong thing, she wouldn't let it bother her. This was her day.

She intended to take a long look at her life as it was presented to her in her mother's flat, as all the disparate elements of her world came together. Then she'd know if she could leave it behind or not.

She was glad that she'd had a chance to prepare for the official introduction to Eddie. She had scoffed when he told her that Maureen was afraid of her own daughter's reaction to this news and that was why she'd kept it a secret. But a little torch of honesty shone inwardly and told Lauren that she might well have been shocked to be presented with this man, without warning.

Because there were feelings to be reconciled here, positive ones to be expressed and negative ones to be faced and buried. She'd needed to work through the facts, come to a conclusion before she opened her big mouth and once more said the wrong thing. Her conclusion was that Eddie was a good man and that her mum deserved him.

She was pleased that Maureen was going to meet Richard even if he was no longer needed for the romantic vacancy. Typical, Lauren thought lightly. My mum goes thirty years without a man and then two come along at once . . .

She made a mental note to ensure that Richard wasn't left in a corner at any time. She knew that her mum would be making non-stop demands on her and Stella would want to repeat to her every conversation she'd had over the last two weeks. And she'd have to talk to Chris as well, although Izzy would be there to keep him company. I'll keep Richard stuck to my side at all times, she decided. If he'll let me, she added as a caution to herself. Unresolved issues still remained.

As Lauren thought of Chris, so he was thinking of her. He had a lot of time to think because nobody had turned up to his farewell drink. Not surprising but he still felt low at the flat end to a career that had meant so much to him. Still, old endings, new beginnings. His interview, which had turned out more of a chat, had gone quite well.

He'd been frank about the business in Manchester but the prison service personnel officer didn't think it would be an insurmountable problem. 'But you wouldn't be doing so much teaching in a young offenders' institution. It's more like being a social worker, probation officer and occupational therapist rolled into one.'

Chris had leaned forward. 'That's what I want to do! I've tried teaching and that wasn't the answer. And I realised it was because these kids didn't expect education to offer them anything. They pull down the shutters as soon as they see a teacher standing in front of them. But they must raise those shutters, lower their guard, at some point. And that's when I want to be there.'

The personnel officer was a jaded woman who'd watched many idealists dive enthusiastically into the prison service only to come out crushed and cynical a few years later. But she knew that this man would not listen to her cautionary tales. He'd have to find out for himself.

There would be retraining, she warned, a cut in salary and status. And not even a guaranteed position at the end of it. None of this put Chris off because he was fired up. He felt the way he'd felt when he first started teaching. A new beginning for him; something he needed after Beth.

But he had tomorrow to look forward to. The anticipation was twice as strong because he had no way of even guessing what might happen. Not after the events of the last two weeks.

Ann phoned Stella at about six o'clock.

'Hello?' Stella sounded a little tense, Ann thought. Not surprising with all that was going on.

'Hello dear, it's Ann.'

'Oh, hello Ann,' Stella said flatly.

Oh dear, thought Ann, she was expecting someone else. 'Is everything OK, Stella?' she asked worriedly. 'Is Pete all right?'

'He's fine,' Stella answered with more effort, remembering that Ann had troubles of her own. 'What about you, how are you feeling?'

'Oh, a bit nervous about the operation, you know how it is. But just very relieved about Pete's news. Not just for us but the extra money will be a help to you as well, won't it? You can decide what you want to do with the house.'

'Yes, it will be a help.' I hope.

'So is Pete there, Stella?'

Stella looked at the clock for the hundredth time. 'No, he, er, had to drop in at the hospital to get his bandages looked at.'

'Really?' Ann said. 'It's a bit late for a hospital appointment.'

Stella didn't want to hear this. She became shorter with Ann, hating herself for being mean but needing to protect herself.

'Whatever. So shall I get him to call you when he comes back?'

Ann dithered. 'I don't know. Oh, well, perhaps you can pass on our apologies.'

'Apologies for what?'

'Bill and I have decided not to come to Lauren's little lunch party tomorrow. I'm sure that if you explain to Lauren's mother about me, she'll understand.'

Stella couldn't help herself shouting. 'But you have to come!'

Ann's eyes widened. What on earth was going on? 'Stella, dear, I didn't think it was that important.'

'It's more than important, it's vital that you come. Pete needs you to be there. I need you. You've got to come. Please!'

It was distressing for Ann to hear Stella like this. 'Stella, sweetheart, what is the matter?'

Stella slowed her speech down. She was getting overexcited and that would just make things worse. If that were possible. 'Sorry, Ann. It's just Pete's accident and all the apprehension we've had about his job. It's got to us both and we hoped that tomorrow we could put it all behind us. And if you're there, then Pete will feel more settled. He's not too keen on going but I think it will do him good. Please, Ann. If you say you're not going, he won't go either. I'm begging you.'

It worked on Ann, too.

'Pull over here please!' The taxi driver swerved across two lines of moving traffic swearing at all the cars he was cutting up. He double-parked, causing an instant tailback on the busy road.

Pete staggered out of the cab as fast as he could, which wasn't very fast at all. He shouted down the street. 'Chris! Chris! Over here!'

Chris turned round, wondering who was calling his name. It was already dark so it was hard to make out the shape waving at him. As far as he could see, it was a hunched creature of not quite human form. As he got closer to the taxi he recognised that it was indeed a man, but a man who'd seen better times. This one was on crutches with a massive bandage on one hand and a plaster cast on one foot. The effect was completed by a pair of crutches that the man was not manipulating very well.

'Good God, is that you, Pete? What the hell has happened to you? Don't tell me you've been brawling in the street again. Don't forget what that nice young police officer said, we wouldn't be let off so lightly next time.'

Pete was not amused. He had dropped change all over the road and the cabbie had accelerated away like a madman, sending a spray of rainwater all over the passenger who had been less than generous with his tip.

Chris ran up to him. 'Here, let me give you a hand.'

Pete let Chris pick up all the loose change. It gave him a few valuable seconds to decide what he wanted to say to Chris or do.

'Pete, you look terrible. And you're soaking wet. Come on, let's get you into the pub and get you a drink.'

Before Pete could protest, Chris had manhandled him into the pub and wedged him into a snug where he wouldn't have drunken punters tripping over his cast. He pushed his way to the bar and returned with two pints. Pete now had a rough idea what it must be like to be permanently disabled. At no point had Chris asked him if he wanted to go into the pub or have a drink. He'd become an appendage that other people felt authorised to coerce into places without consultation.

But he was grateful for the drink and swallowed half the pint. It was all he had needed to refuel his hostility which had grown to a high point at his meeting, bubbled steadily at home with Stella and eventually dwindled while seeing Beth. Now he was simmering again.

Pete gave a bland version of his accident to Chris, leaving out Beth's role in the affair, not even mentioning her in his frame of reference. Chris was predictably staggered by the tale. Also predictably, he laughed at the image of the hot saucepan burning the hand and getting dropped on the foot. 'It's like something straight out of the Marx Brothers,' he said, marvelling at the cartoon-like quality of the episode.

Without asking, Chris refilled Pete's glass. Pete gave a passing thought to his painkillers. He vaguely recollected the pharmacist saying something about avoiding alcohol, but he wanted to drink now so he ignored the warnings.

He's a bit quiet, Chris thought. Must be his injuries. Perhaps he's in a lot of pain. 'I haven't spoken to you since the weekend. I know you weren't too happy about how it all ended.'

That got a response. Good, thought Chris. He's getting some colour back. I'll get him another pint. Alcohol seems to be doing the trick.

As he put the glass down, Chris decided to make Pete feel better by telling him all his bad news. Someone else's misfortune always cheers you up when you're having a run of bad luck.

'So I lost my job, Dean Ryder is in a young offenders' institution and the school is going to close down. Apart from that, everything in the garden is rosy.'

He waited for Pete to show his appreciation of this tale of woe. But instead, he said something that Chris wasn't prepared for.

'I know about you and Stella.' He couldn't believe that the words came out. He'd been thinking them but not intending to give them voice. They were too dangerous and the response was too unpredictable. But it was too late.

Chris regretted having that last pint because he wasn't as sharp as he needed to be to get through this minefield. His last call to Stella had been cut short before he'd had a chance to ascertain if Pete had been informed of Chris's role in the information-gathering operation.

He didn't want to land Stella in it. Not that he owed her anything but he'd felt sorry for her in Manchester. She'd looked so young and exposed without her armour on. If he ever saw her again, he meant to tell her that she looked much better without all the make-up. But he probably wouldn't get the chance.

He trod carefully. 'What do you know?' he asked.

That was all Pete had needed to hear. No immediate denial. Prevarication. Hedging. It all added up to an admission. A confession.

'I know everything now,' he said, 'and I think you're a bastard.' He felt like a ventriloquist's dummy, with someone else putting words into his mouth while he just sat there moving his lips. He could not stop himself.

Chris put his hands up. 'Now hang on a second. I don't know what she's told you, but I was only doing it because she was so worried about you. We were both doing it for you.'

That did it. Pete picked up his glass and threw the beer in Chris's face.

'What did you do that for, you maniac?' Chris spluttered.

'Because you slept with my wife!' The pills were

reacting with the alcohol to make Pete very agitated. Luckily, he was not in a position to grab any more lethal weapons other than some booze-sodden coasters with trivia questions printed on them. Still, they were better than nothing.

He was about to fling them in an action that he remembered was used very effectively by David Carradine in *Kung Fu*, one of his family's favourite programmes on Sunday afternoons in the 70s.

Chris was saved by Pete's mobile phone beginning to ring. It played the theme from *Shaft*, and had been a present from Stella last birthday. He had tried countless times to reprogram the tune to something less 70s. But he suspected that Stella had got Lauren to fiddle with the handset so he could not change the tune. If deliberate then it was a clever ploy because Pete always answered it within two bars to shut the thing up.

'Hello?' Pete was still geared up for finding missiles to throw at Chris and he was fully prepared to begin a separate battle with whoever was calling him. He had enough hostility in him for two fights.

'Pete? It's Stella. Where are you? I've been worried sick.'

'Hah!' He'd never said 'Hah!' before and wished he had. It was so satisfying.

'I didn't hear what you said, Pete. There's a lot of noise in the background. Are you in a pub?'

'I'm in the Nag's Head trying unsuccessfully to beat your boyfriend into a pulp. As I only have one good foot and one mobile hand, I'm reduced to throwing beermats at him. Still, it's making me feel better.'

'What are you talking about, my boyfriend? I haven't got a boyfriend!'

Pete held up the phone towards Chris. 'Did you hear that, Chris? Your girlfriend is denying you. She's turned Judas on you.'

A man passing the table stopped on hearing this. 'If you don't mind my butting in, I think you'll find that it was Peter who denied Jesus in the Bible. Judas betrayed but Peter denied. It is a common mistake.'

Pete stared at the man in disbelief. 'That is the most annoying thing that anyone had said to me for a long time. I think I'm going to have to throw something at you as well.'

The man moved on quickly, realising that his accuser was not in the most rational of moods.

'Pete! Pete! What's going on?' Stella shouted down the phone. 'Oh stuff this, I'm coming down there.' She immediately hung up.

Pete put the phone down and looked around for his drink. Then he saw Chris's wet head and very nervous face before him and remembered what he had done. 'What a waste of beer,' he muttered.

Chris took advantage of the lull in the storm to remove everything from the table including Pete's phone.

'Can we get this straightened out now, please?' he said warily.

'No need, it's all as straight as I need it to be. Now let me see . . .' Pete was looking round for inspiration.

Chris tried to attract his attention back. 'You've got this all wrong, Pete. Nothing is going on between me and Stella—'

Pete interrupted. 'Then how come you were seen in her car, kissing and who knows what else?'

Chris had to really concentrate to work this one out.

Then it came. The school car park. He smiled broadly with recognition. Mistake.

'It's nothing to laugh about! If I could stand up and use my right hand, I'd knock you out cold for that smirk!'

Chris tried his utmost to eliminate all expressions from his face. He thought back to a course he'd taken on how to deal with teenagers in the middle of a paranoid episode. He'd forgotten most of it but he thought he remembered something about smiling. Whether smiling was a good or a bad thing escaped him though.

'I'm not smirking. I know what you're referring to. And I can see how it might have been misinterpreted but we were definitely not kissing. From a certain angle, it would have looked as if we were embracing, whereas I was actually comforting her.'

Pete was listening now. 'Why did she need comforting?'

Chris edged forward. 'She thought you were ill and weren't telling her about it because you were in denial. She wanted me to find out what was wrong with you when we were up in Manchester. She was upset about you, that's why I had to comfort her.'

It took Pete longer than usual to compute all these random facts. The connections in his brain were foggy but enough was trickling through for him to calm down. It didn't sound implausible, he grudgingly conceded.

His foot was itching badly under the plaster and his hand was screaming. He could have wept. Chris was wisely leaving him to his thoughts, having quietly gone to the bar for two more drinks. What an act of faith (or stupidity), Pete thought.

While he was gone, Pete tried to understand why he

was even bothered about the notion of Chris and Stella. He didn't love her any more. That's what he'd said. He didn't want her any more and he didn't want to hurt her. If Chris had been seeing her, it would have done him a big favour.

Oh no. I've turned into that stereotypical, blustering philanderer who doesn't want his woman but doesn't want anyone else to have her either. I've slipped down the food chain when I wasn't concentrating.

But he was being too hard on himself. While his behaviour wasn't untypical, it wasn't totally selfish in motivation. It was because he had loved Stella, did care for her, that he was unable to cut himself off from her so abruptly. This was why Beth felt strange watching Chris with Lauren, and why Chris felt odd watching Beth with Pete at the party.

It was an understandable response and one that would not have generated any ill will had Pete not been mixing pills and beer. But he had and the cocktail was turning him into a fireball of unleashed frustrations and rage.

His head was starting to clear when Chris returned from the bar. Chris sent up a quick prayer of thanks for Pete's evident return to the world of sanity and sat down.

'Are we straight?' he asked, ready to duck if the answer was anything apart from yes. Pete nodded and took a sip from his glass.

'Thank God for that!'

Neither of them knew where to go from there. No doubt they would have finished their drinks and gone home, never to see each other again. Chris would have had a shower. Pete would have taken enough tablets to send him to sleep and the night would have been saved from disaster.

That is, if Stella hadn't burst through the door of the pub like Boadicea ready to conquer all who stood in her way. She spotted Chris and Pete in their corner and rushed across to them, knocking against a table of drinks on the way. The four men whose table it was jumped up furiously as their drinks spilled on to them.

Stella didn't notice. She tore up to Pete. 'Are you OK? You were ranting and raving on the phone, I thought you'd banged your head or something.'

Pete wanted her to go away. She was cranking up the other side of his self again, making his nerve endings throb. But he was calm now so he didn't say that. 'It was nothing. Chris and I had a misunderstanding. He put me right and we're all friends again.'

He raised his glass to his friend in a mock toast. Chris had no knowledge of the tension between Pete and Stella otherwise he would have kept his mouth shut. One likes to think so, anyway.

'It was silly, Stella, somebody saw you on my lap in the car at school last week, do you remember? They told Pete and he put two and two together . . .'

Stella looked unhappy. 'And I thought I was the one who was bad at maths.'

Now Chris felt the tension. 'Why don't I get you a drink, Stella, now that you're here?'

'Oh I don't think so. Come on Pete, let's get you home. You're looking very pale.'

'You didn't say that she was sitting on your lap,' Pete said to Chris ominously.

Oh oh! That tone again. Chris deftly removed the glasses from reach. 'Pete, we've been through this.'

Pete narrowed his eyes. 'No, you said that you comforted her, you didn't say that she was on your lap.' In his altered state, all memory of betraying his wife in the marital bed was consigned to oblivion while he fumed at the outrage of Stella on Chris's lap.

Chris counted to ten silently. 'Pete, she wasn't on my lap as such. She was leaning across the front seat.' He tried to come up with some better way of describing what had happened without using the word 'lap', because this word was upsetting Pete.

'Excuse me.'

Stella, Pete and Chris all looked round at this uninvited interloper. Well, four uninvited interlopers to be more accurate. Big ones.

'Yes?' Chris said, deciding that he was the only one of the three of them who was capable of speaking without sparking off a fight.

'Your wife here just knocked over our drinks. All over our clothes.'

Pete leaned forward. 'She is not his wife, she is my wife. Why does everyone keep assuming that she is his wife?'

The second man sneered. 'We don't care whose wife she is, she's knocked over our drinks. Now what are you going to do about it?'

Pete flicked the new beermat that Chris had provided at the man. It wasn't quite *Kung Fu* but it hit the second man on the nose and made him look silly. Bystanders laughed. Pete laughed too.

'Right, that's it!' the man shouted, lifting the small table and upending it.

'Mind his leg!' Stella screamed, pushing one of the men over and causing a domino effect among all the punters who had gathered round the scene of the action.

Pete, Stella and Chris all gave different accounts of what happened next. Pete claimed credit for tripping up at least two thugs with his bad leg. Chris claimed that he had said and done nothing whatsoever that could be misconstrued as aggression. Stella wept buckets and said, 'I don't know why I bothered, you don't even love me any more.' She said that a lot.

Whatever happened doesn't really matter. They were in the middle of the brawl. They were the cause of it, possibly the instigators. It could only end one way. All three of them were arrested.

As they sat in the back of the police van, Stella looked at Chris and Pete. She shook her head from side to side to side like a nodding dog in a Ford Cortina.

'How did our lives ever get to be this bad?' she asked.

That's what they all wanted to know.

Chapter 22

How did my life ever get to be this good? Lauren asked herself. 'She'll be coming round the mountain when she comes,' she sang, gloriously out of tune but not giving a damn. She couldn't recall a time when she was so uncomplicatedly happy. She felt fantastic and everything was all right with the world.

It was a beautiful March morning and she and Richard had set off during a spectacular sunrise. They were alone in the car. Izzy had called the night before and said that she was staying with Auntie Joan in Ambleside overnight. She was a bit vague as to her reasons.

'You'll know soon enough,' she'd said enigmatically. She was going to drive to Watford in Lauren's car and meet them there. Both Richard and Lauren were pleased at this change of plan but neither of them said so. Richard had woken her up with breakfast in bed.

'Happy birthday,' he'd shouted, yanking open the curtains. Lauren had moaned and pulled the duvet over her head, only to have it pulled straight back again.

'Breakfast in bed for the birthday girl!' Richard had announced. Lauren dragged herself into a sitting position and he put a tray on her lap. She stared at the feast before her.

'What's all this?' she asked in amazement.

Richard perched on the edge of the bed, one foot on the floor for propriety.

'Do you remember the night on the mountains?' he said.

Lauren pretended to rack her brains. 'Not sure. Enlighten me.'

'The night when I broke my foot and it was all your fault.'

Lauren feigned enlightenment. 'Ah, that night. Why didn't you say? I've spent so many nights on mountains with so many men that I need more details to differentiate them.'

'Anyway,' Richard said. 'Do you remember when we told each other all our favourite foods?'

'God yes,' Lauren groaned. 'I was so hungry. And you tortured me by making me list what I would order if I could have anything in the world to eat. And you said you'd have Yorkshire pudding, lamb chops, banana and sugar sandwiches, plain chocolate-covered toffee and clotted cream.'

'And you said,' he announced, pointing to the delicacies laid out on the tray, 'jelly tots, cold rhubarb crumble, Scotch eggs and potato waffles.'

Lauren could only look at the food in astonishment, because the idea of eating any of it at six o'clock in the morning made her very queasy. She grabbed Richard and hugged him. 'This is the nicest thing that anyone has ever done for me,' she said. 'The weirdest but the nicest. And what makes it so special is that you listened to me that night and remembered what I said.'

'But you remembered what I said too.'

Lauren sighed. 'But that's different. I always listen

to what people say. Always have done. I'm a born crowd-pleaser. It never occurred to me that not everyone was like that. My dad . . .' she stopped.

Richard gently urged her on. 'Your dad . . . what?'

Lauren picked up a jelly tot and delicately nibbled off all the sugar. 'Nothing.'

'No, Lauren. Today's your birthday. So why don't we pretend that you're all grown-up now and can talk about your father without anything bad happening?' He was doing a very bad impersonation of Freud.

Lauren scowled at him. 'Very funny. It's nothing like that. I don't talk about my dad because there's nothing to say.'

'Sorry, I don't believe you. The other day, you spoke for an hour about moths. I couldn't shut you up. I was bored rigid but impressed by your staying power.'

Lauren punched him affectionately. 'You should hear me on Broadway musicals. I can keep going for days without drawing breath!'

'Then I'm sure you could squeeze out a couple of sentences on your dad. If you wanted to. So tell me about your father.'

Lauren had to accept that he would not let this go. 'I don't know why you're making such a big deal of it. There's no great family secret to uncover. No abuse or anything melodramatic or sordid. He didn't beat me or anything like that. He didn't come home drunk, at least not after I was born, from what my mum says. He didn't mock me or torment me. He didn't—'

'Yes, thank you for the list of things your dad didn't do, Lauren. But what *did* he do?'

After a painstaking search of her memory, she was

forced to admit that there was only one entry. 'He died,' she said. 'He just died.'

And that's when it struck her. Because, in her living memory, that was all he'd done. Her mum hadn't told her much else apart from how her smile had changed him. He'd never been a real person, not to Lauren, he was a collection of anecdotes, some black-and-white photos and a hazy memory of someone singing 'You'll Never Walk Alone'.

She'd loved *Carousel*, especially the bit where the dead father comes back to earth and gives the daughter a star. Because then the girl can cope with anything, being an outsider and not having a daddy or nice clothes.

It hit her like a mallet. 'Oh God, I've lived my entire life based on one scene in a musical that I saw when I was seven. I've even had dreams about my dad where he looks just like Gordon Macrae in the film. There, the big revelation. So is this all supposed to mean something?'

And now she wasn't joking. The something *she* was thinking about was a someone: Richard. She had finally accepted that she'd erected a barrier in front of Richard, preventing her from looking at him as she should have – not just as a friend but as possibly the one man she wouldn't need to change for. The one man she could never annoy too much. The one who would never leave her. The one. And if the barrier was anything to do with unresolved feelings about her dad, then she was hoping for a dazzling flash of enlightenment to make her next move clear.

Richard stuck out his lower lip to give this some serious thought. 'Well, it either means that you are in need of years of therapy to bring you back down to a more realistic awareness of your life . . .'

'Or?' Lauren prompted.

'Or . . . it means that you're like the rest of us, subconsciously mixing up the bits of our lives that we like with bits that make it seem better. From films, from other people's lives, even from your own imagination. It's normal.'

'So I'm normal. Is that what you're saying?' Lauren wanted this to be the case.

'That's about it.' Richard confirmed his diagnosis.

Lauren tried to imagine herself as a normal person. It was a struggle. 'So why do I say and do so many stupid things?'

'When you're saying and doing all the stupid things, *that's* when you're being normal. All the rest, like running away, changing the subject, that's when you lose it.'

She knew he was referring to New York. She'd refused to discuss the subject all week.

'I'm not running away from anything,' she said quietly.

'You've done it twice,' Richard told her firmly. 'You were originally contemplating moving to the States to run away from your life here and now you're running away from making the decision to stay. Which is what you want to do, isn't it?'

'And your point is?' Lauren could see the point in the distance but she couldn't quite grasp it. She needed one last push.

Richard was happy to provide it. 'The message is: stop trying to please your father. Stop looking for him. Stop letting him get in your way. That father was never real in the first place. Once you've let him go, the other answers should be easy to find. Without my help.'

Richard was a wise man. He knew there was one decision that Lauren had to come to all by herself.

Quite why this should make her sing all the way to Watford wasn't clear.

She mimicked Richard's Freud impersonation. 'I've never sung in public before. Apart from when I was in school plays and even then I used to mime most of the time. Maybe, in my subconscious, I believed that my father didn't like my singing.'

Richard slapped her on the leg. 'I've created a monster! You can forget my amateur analysis now. I probably got it all wrong anyway.'

'Maybe,' Lauren said cheerfully, 'but I prefer your wrong to my right. I'm having a great birthday!'

She then burst into a barely recognisable version of 'Things Can Only Get Better'.

Things were getting marginally better for Pete, Stella and Chris. Beth arrived at the police station at nine o'clock the next morning to bail them out, if necessary, and drive them all home. Pete had given the police her name hoping that, as a doctor, she could persuade them that his actions were entirely due to his physical condition.

In the beginning they refused to do this. Because of Pete's injuries, they'd had to wait for a police doctor to check him over. And on a Friday night, there were a lot of sicker drunks to examine before he could get round to this unhappy trio.

The doctor had not been impressed by Pete's admission that he'd been mixing the painkillers and beer.

'No wonder you were itching for a fight. Shouldn't a grown man like you, an intelligent man on the face of it, know better?'

The police officer interrupted. 'This is the second time in a week that this has happened, doctor. He was involved in a brawl in Manchester last Saturday.'

The doctor tutted annoyingly. Pete wanted to punch him. He suppressed the urge and resolved never to drink again. It might have been psychologically unhealthy for him to repress his negative emotions all these years but, physically, it had probably saved his life. He was down to one good hand already. One more loosening of his inhibitions and he'd be without the use of any of his limbs.

Stella had been released after a few hours. But she decided to wait for Pete. And she felt obliged to wait for Chris too. Although Pete seemed to have been in the pub at his invitation in the first place, she felt responsible for Pete's belligerence towards him which had provided the trigger to the evening's outcome.

Chris was faring the worst. This was now his second arrest and he didn't have any mitigating injuries to explain his involvement. He couldn't afford to be formally charged this time. He was lucky that he was not considered excessively drunk. If he grovelled a lot and made a lot of excuses, he was hoping to be let off again.

All the attention was on Pete. While the police accepted the doctor's statement that the prisoner only had himself to blame after such folly, they had some sympathy towards him. He was in a bad way. He had been the victim of a nasty (but also comical – always useful when you've been arrested) accident and they tended towards the attitude that any man with such injuries would have taken whatever artificial remedies necessary to feel better.

It was touch and go all night. Chris had a stroke of good luck to be interviewed by a sergeant who knew his school (ex-school) well and had supported its aims. Chris had blamed everything on Pete whose aggression had already been officially deemed the result of beer and pills.

In the end, Chris and Pete were let off with a caution. Again. Once more they found themselves outside a police station waiting for a woman to drive them home. Chris wasn't sure why Beth should have turned up. But then again, he wasn't sure of anything. The whole world was mad except him. He was saying nothing in case Pete hit him or Stella yelled at him.

Beth was ignoring him. She was concerned about Pete but Stella seemed uptight about her interest. Chris didn't care. He'd opted out of that little triangle. They could sort it out for themselves. He was never going to get involved in anyone else's marriage again. Not even his own, the way he felt now.

Stella had started talking again. Non-stop chatter about nothing. No one else could get a word in. He found it unnerving. But they'd all been in a police station all night. They were all knackered. Who could say what was a normal way to behave?

Beth had dropped Stella and Pete off first. Stella had jumped out of the car to help Pete out. He'd allowed her to help. He'd leaned on her. He mumbled a 'thank you' at Beth. Stella had said nothing, which Chris thought was bad form. When Beth reached his flat, he wanted to say something appropriate. But try as he might, he couldn't think of a suitable aphorism for that moment when you are thanking your ex-girlfriend for fetching you from jail after a drunken brawl.

'Thank you, Beth,' he said.

'Don't mention it,' she snapped. 'Ever!'

Maureen had been up since seven cleaning the house. She was nervous that she might have forgotten something. This was the largest party she'd ever given. Eddie was sitting in the kitchen peeling vegetables. He found it soothing and it kept him out of Maureen's way. She'd been up till two in the morning icing the cake for Chris and Lauren.

'I'm really not a hundred per cent certain that this is a good idea,' he'd said as she piled pink icing on the sponge.

Maureen dismissed him. 'I've changed my original design. I haven't done hearts. That would have been over the top. No, I'll just do triangles.'

'But what does it mean?' Eddie had said. 'A pink sponge with two triangles with C and L in them?'

'It's what you do when it's a joint birthday. You're driving me nuts with all these questions. Leave the food to me. I know what I'm doing.'

Eddie carried on peeling. Whatever happened today, they would have enough root vegetables to see them through till next Christmas.

He could hear Maureen flapping about with the ironing board. He went to see if she needed a hand. He found her wrestling with some new clothes, trying to tear off unbreakable labels.

'When did you buy those, love?' he asked. 'You've got a spare room full of clothes! You could put on your own production of *My Fair Lady* out of your wardrobes. What's all that for?'

She gave up tugging and thrust the garments into Eddie's hands. He calmly broke the plastic tags then held up the clothes to look at them more closely.

There was a grey skirt with a matching tunic top and a plain black dress. 'Good God, Maureen, has someone died?'

She snatched them back and started to iron them. 'You wouldn't understand, Eddie.'

'Try me,' he said.

Maureen didn't look up from her furious ironing. 'Lauren's ashamed of me, of the way I look. She doesn't want me to show her up.'

'Did she actually say that? In as many words?' Eddie knew the scope for misunderstanding between Maureen and Lauren.

'Yes, she actually did. Well, not in as many words, but practically those.'

Eddie closed his eyes and waited for patience to come. 'My love, you are what you are and, from what you tell me, I can't believe that Lauren would want you to be uncomfortable. Whatever she might have said, I'm sure that she didn't intend for you to dress like Margaret Thatcher.'

Maureen stopped ironing. 'I just want her to love me, Eddie. I want her to be proud of me, to admire me and forgive me. I'll do whatever it takes to have that.'

Eddie put his arms around her. 'Don't try too hard, Mo. That can lead to all kinds of trouble.'

Maureen wriggled away from him. 'Don't talk nonsense. Have you started on the parsnips?'

Eddie slumped back to the kitchen. Maureen in a black dress. It was not going to be an easy day, he could tell.

Chris was almost ready when his doorbell rang. 'Hello sir.'

It was Dean Ryder.

Chris's first thought was: Harbouring an escaped prisoner – if I carry on progressing up the scale of crimes at this rate, I should be burning down petrol stations by Easter.

He opened the door and let the boy in. 'I won't bother asking how you got my address. No, I think I will. What was it? Did you hire someone to follow my car? Put a bug on my shoes? What?'

'You are on the electoral roll. It's at the library, sir.'

'I didn't realise that you knew where the library was. How resourceful of you.'

'And now you're going to say that if I applied my criminal brain to my education, I could go far. I could even be working in B and Q by the time I'm thirty.'

Chris watched the boy wandering round the flat, picking up and examining anything that caught his eye. 'So we both know how smart you are. What are you doing here, Dean?'

'I had to get away. Someone was going to do me tomorrow.'

'Do you? This is something bad, is it?'

'Don't be sarcastic, sir. It isn't a joke.'

'You've got that right. You've escaped from Northview. If . . . when they catch up with you, they'll probably send you to an adult prison.'

'I'm not bothered about that. I just need to get away for a while. Go up north, I've got family there.'

'And you've come to me for a getaway car? Some forged papers? What?'

'A lift somewhere. Preferably out of town. Thanks to you getting the school shut down, most of my mates are locked up somewhere.'

'And what makes you think I won't give you up? Or that I'll actually help you?'

Dean grinned at his former teacher, now twice-arrested streetfighter. 'Because you've had a sheltered life and I'm your last chance at breaking out.'

Chris remembered freezing at the sweet shop petrified of a KitKat. 'Will Watford do?'

Beth got into the car. Stella knows, she repeated to herself. She knows. She wouldn't look at me or at Pete. Her eyes were fixed on a point halfway between us. But she's not going to let on. That's her plan. And it's a good one. According to Pete, she is the queen of diversionary tactics. He could be at home right this minute, drinking Sanatogen, weakly saying that he feels much better now.

She had only been loved by one other man before Pete. And Chris had left her. That gave her a hundred per cent failure rate with men. And now she was going to have to spend the afternoon with them both. Stella will not take her eyes or hands off Pete. In that environment, she will own him. I don't know if he is strong enough to break out.

* * *

386

'So, Bill, you'll have to go over it with me again. What was it that we weren't supposed to tell Stella? I don't want to say the wrong thing.'

Bill switched on the ignition. 'Don't give it a moment's thought. Nothing you might say could cause them any more problems than they already have. Just relax and enjoy yourself.'

Izzy almost crashed the car a dozen times. Whenever she looked into the rear-view mirror, she saw somebody else in the car and panicked. Then she remembered that it was her. The new her. And she panicked again. Either way, it was a stranger and she'd never been confident with strangers.

She would never be able to fathom out why she had permitted Auntie Joan's daughter Betty to take her in hand. Some top hairdressers had begged to be able to do something with her hair and she'd resisted them all. She'd been afraid, although God knows why. Since she had such low self-esteem, one has to wonder what she was afraid of. How much worse did she think she could look?

But she trusted Richard's Auntie Joan. And as she drove down the M1, she worked out why. Because Auntie Joan had liked her. Because she was the first person not to judge her.

In reality, Joan had almost called the police when she'd seen Izzy enter the shop. Richard had prepared her but not well enough. It was fortunate that Joan had spent a lifetime pulling the wool over her family's eyes, pretending to be a sweet, silly little thing when she had the cunning of a wolf.

She'd achieved everything she ever wanted in life by pure sleight of hand and an acting ability that could have taken her all the way to the Old Vic. That was how she had managed to run the shop like her own personal dynasty for so many years, and how she managed to conceal her horror at the arrival of this banshee in her homely emporium.

But whether it was a pretence or otherwise didn't matter. Joan had broken through to Izzy in a way that no one else had managed. She liked Izzy and that was all Izzy had wanted. So if she said that her daughter Betty could work wonders with her, then Izzy believed her.

Stella and Pete sat in the front of their Range Rover waiting for a kindly London driver to let them into the heavy stream of traffic. Stella had stopped talking. It was as if her batteries had run down.

'Let's not be nasty to each other today,' Pete had suggested softly as they'd been getting ready. Stella hadn't answered. She was concentrating on her make-up which she'd been applying with a shaky hand for over twenty minutes.

Pete was tormenting himself with guilt over his behaviour in the pub and afterwards. Blaming it on a biochemical reaction didn't make him feel any better. That had just given him a physical excuse. All the poison that had come flooding out had been there the whole time, as if from a boil just waiting to be lanced.

He had been shocked at his behaviour, having always considered himself a kind man, even when he was facilitating the end of his marriage. He didn't like that part of himself and wanted to bury it once more for all their sakes.

Pete put the car radio on to drown out the silence. 'I will always love you,' Whitney Houston belted out at full volume. Pete and Stella both rushed to the off switch at the same moment.

They smiled a sad little smile at each other. A smile of mutual understanding, almost an in-joke. See, it said, we're not so different after all . . .

Chapter 23

'Which one? The grey or the black?' Maureen held first one and then the other in front of her.

'The gold,' Eddie replied, not lifting his eyes from the parsnips.

'We've had this out! This is Lauren's party and I'm dressing for Lauren.'

'Very well, then. The red with the big stars on the skirt, you know, your Cher dress.'

'If you can't say anything sensible, don't say anything at all,' she sniffed. She stood in front of the mirror with the black, the grey, the black, the grey.

Eddie came up behind her and put his hands round her slowly spreading waist.

'Look at yourself, Mo. You're unhappy. Your clothes are what you are. So wear what you want. It's the only way you can be who you want to be.'

'But Lauren . . .'

'Stop right there. Now you know how I get my feelings?' he asked.

Maureen loved it when he had his feelings. They always came true. In reality they usually didn't, but she only remembered the ones that did.

'Well, I've got this feeling that today is going to be very special for you and Lauren.'

'Oh Eddie, do you really think so? I'm so frightened that she's not going to like you.'

'How can she not like me?' Eddie asked, arms stretched wide. 'I'm a man with feelings – that's every modern woman's idea of the perfect man.'

'I want today to be a success. All of it.'

'Go and put your red dress on. You will be a success. It will all be a success. It's a friendly little lunch party with people who know and love each other. What can go wrong?'

Pete and Stella were the first to arrive. Maureen answered the door to find Stella wearing a loud day dress in gold and black.

'Snap!' the two women cried out, admiring each other's taste in clothes that screamed.

Eddie helped Pete into the flat. 'Come and sit down. Let me get you a drink.'

'Just a Coke for me. I'm not supposed to drink with the pills I'm on.'

'Oh bad luck,' Eddie tutted. 'The party's not going to be much fun without a drink.'

'All the drink in the world would not make today much fun for me,' Pete intoned to Eddie in confidence.

Eddie waited for the witty follow-on line. None came. Pete wasn't joking. He was evidently staking his claim as the Eeyore of the day.

On his way to the kitchen to get the drinks, he made a swift detour to the dining room where he moved Pete's name card to the opposite end of the table to him and Maureen. Well, there was being a good host and there was foolhardy masochism.

Maureen and Stella were chatting animatedly in the hall. 'Aren't you two girls coming through? You're making the place look cluttered out here!' he said. Translation: Don't leave me alone in there with Mr Jolly, please.

He put two strong but gentle hands on their shoulders and led them into the living room where Pete was staring at his Coke and continuously flexing the muscles in his unbandaged hand.

Maureen was gearing up for a spectacular grin to bestow on Pete. Possibly even a bear hug. Eddie saw the signs, the tingling cheek muscles, the quivering upper arms. He had to save her from being bashed over the head with a message of doom.

'So Maureen, aren't you going to introduce us?'

Maureen's hand rushed to her mouth. 'Oh, what an idiot I am! I completely forgot that you don't know anyone. Eddie, this is Stella and this is her husband Pete. They're Lauren's best friends. Known each other for twenty years, the three of them.'

'That's nice,' Eddie said. 'And before she forgets me again, I'm Eddie.'

Maureen stood next to him and held his hand proudly. 'Eddie's my partner. That's what you call them nowadays, isn't it? "Boyfriend" sounds a bit daft for someone as old as me.'

'I don't know anyone who's as young as you, Mo,' Eddie said gallantly, kissing her hand.

'Oh get away with you,' Maureen said fondly.

Stella could have cried at their simple happiness. She longed for Pete to kiss her hand and say something foolish that would make her feel better.

Eddie decided to have a stab at polite conversation in this already taut atmosphere. 'So Stella, how long have you and Pete been married?'

Stella coughed nervously. 'Erm, fifteen years, isn't it Pete?'

'Fifteen years,' Pete repeated evenly. The tone was enough of a clue for Eddie.

'Right,' said Eddie. 'Would you excuse me a second?' He made another trip to the dining room to separate Stella's and Pete's name cards so that they would be able to sit as far away from each other as the table permitted.

The doorbell rang again. 'Thank God,' Eddie muttered under his breath.

'I'll get it!' Maureen chirped. 'You look after our other guests.'

Eddie returned to the living room where Stella was sitting with her back to her husband, at the far end of the sofa. 'I'll put on some music,' he muttered, to himself since Stella and Pete had teleported themselves to somewhere unreachable. Don't come back too soon, he thought uncharitably.

He squatted on the floor to flick through the records. He heard Maureen walking back with another guest. A woman by herself, it sounded like. 'You pop in there and make yourself comfortable while I hang the coats up. Stella, Pete, look who's here! It's Beth. Now you all know each other so I can leave you to your own devices for a minute.'

'What are you doing here?' Stella hissed. 'Can you not stay away from Pete for a single minute? Haven't you done enough damage?'

'Stella sweetheart, don't have a go at her,' Pete said quietly.

'It's OK, Pete, I can take care of myself, I don't need defending. Look, Stella, I didn't want to come, I don't even know why I'm here, except . . .'

'I asked her to be here.' Pete finished Beth's sentence. 'Sorry Stella, you knew I didn't want to come. I couldn't face it by myself.'

'You wouldn't have been by yourself. I am with you.'

'I think I'll go. I shouldn't have come in the first place.' Beth stood up as if to leave.

Stella clenched her jaw and stared at the ceiling. 'You can't do that. Then everyone will want to know why you've left. It will be obvious. All I want is for today to be ordinary. You promised me that, Pete! Just stay out of my way, Beth.' She moved over to where Pete was sitting. 'This was cruel, I didn't think you could be like that.'

Pete was saved from having to find an answer when the booming voice of Howard Keel came thundering out of the speakers. 'Oh what a beautiful morning!' he sang.

Pete, Stella and Beth had all been paralysed by the deafening onslaught before the volume was lowered to a more manageable level. Then Eddie poked his head up from behind the chair where he'd been sorting through the records. The three guests saw his emergence in horror. He must have heard everything they'd said. He sauntered casually out of the lounge and into the dining room. He would need a mathematical genius to handle the computations of this table plan soon, he concluded, as he moved Beth further away from Stella than Pete but far away enough from them both that spitting would be ineffective.

The doorbell rang again. Eddie wanted to scream out: 'DON'T LET THEM IN, WHOEVER THEY ARE!' but Maureen was already there. There was more than one person this time. Not that this was proof of anything. He'd had one couple and one single and they'd all been trouble.

He went into the hall to help Maureen out. Now this was more like it. They looked like a nice normal couple, much like him and Maureen. What a relief! He gave them a particularly warm welcome and chatted to them for a while before deciding it was time to impose the three stooges on them.

'Eddie, this is Bill and Ann, they're Pete's parents,' Maureen had said.

'That's nice,' was all Eddie could force out. I wouldn't let your son near the steak knives, he wanted to say.

'They've been ever so kind to Lauren over the years. This is the first chance I've had of showing them how grateful I am!'

'If you really want to show them how grateful you are, send them away while there's still a chance for them,' Eddie whispered as he hung the coats up.

'Ssh!' Maureen scolded.

The time came when they had to join the others. With an apologetic grimace, he took Bill and Ann through. Eyes darted all over the place. Eddie couldn't keep up. 'So does everyone know each other?' he asked. 'Great!' he continued, not waiting for a reply. 'I've just got to take a peek at the vegetables. Back in two ticks.'

Maureen went into the kitchen to find Eddie crouched on one of the units with his ear to the serving hatch.

'What on earth are you doing, Eddie?'

'Ssh! I can't hear.'

'What's the matter with you?'

Eddie sat back to stretch his back. 'All your guests hate each other, that's what. It's like an Agatha Christie novel in there. If we left them for long enough, half of them would have Capo di Monte ornaments embedded fatally in their skulls by the other half.'

'You're exaggerating,' Maureen said. 'Now stop that and go and chat to them. I'll look after the veg.' She looked at her watch. 'I hope Lauren's here soon. We can't eat without the guest of honour. In you go!'

And she sent Eddie into the other room with a playful whip of the tea towel. Bill was sitting next to Stella. They seemed to like each other. Miracle! Eddie thought. Perhaps we can survive this after all. Quick diversion to the dining room where two name cards could finally be placed together with confidence.

Beth was stuck in the corner. Ann went over to speak to her. Things were looking up. Eddie decided to take a chance and try some mingling. 'So Ann, do you know Beth?' he asked.

Ann smiled pleasantly. 'We've never met but I've heard lots about her from Stella. She always spoke so highly of you.'

'Thank you,' Beth replied, tripping over the words.

'Bill!' Ann called. 'Come and meet Beth! She's Stella's friend, you know, the doctor she's always talking about.'

'I can't right now. I'm talking to Stella,' Bill said in a clipped voice.

'Don't be so silly, bring Stella over too!' She shook her head indulgently. 'Honestly, Eddie, you men have to have the rules of parties explained to you every time! Come on, Bill.'

'We'll be over in a while!' Bill snapped. Ann flinched and became very quiet. She was obviously not used to her husband being so abrupt. This was complicated. Eddie decided not to touch the table until he'd worked out the new group dynamic that Ann and Bill had set off.

They had to listen to two more tracks from *Oklahoma!* before somebody else arrived. Well, two people to be more accurate. It was Chris, the co-guest of honour, and Dean, who hadn't been invited.

Chris took Maureen to one side. 'I hope you didn't mind me inviting Dean in for something to eat. It suddenly began to tip down with rain and he was waiting for a lift to visit his family up north. I couldn't leave him to get soaking wet.'

'Of course, you couldn't, lad, only a heartless monster would do that. He could have caught a chest infection or anything,' Eddie said, glaring straight at Maureen who poked her tongue out in response.

Eddie's confidence was growing with the numbers. Each new arrival increased the possible number of permutations among the guests. Logically, they couldn't *all* hate each other, therefore there were more interchangeable pairs that could be formed. Whether they got on was a separate matter and Eddie had abandoned this golden ideal after the second ring on the doorbell. If no blood was shed, he would be a happy man.

Chris turned out to be a devastating catalyst, disproving Eddie's theory completely. Pete, Stella and Beth all jumped up at the same time. For Pete, it was not such a fluid motion with his physical limitations, but he made it to an upright position eventually. 'What the hell are you doing here?' he said calmly. He didn't want to see Chris. It wasn't that he was still bothered by the affair that never was with Stella. Another dimension to the story claimed his attention. Beth would act differently with Chris there. And maybe Chris would even make moves to try and win her back.

Chris was less upset but bemused by all these familiar faces. 'A better question might be: What are *you* doing here? *I'm* here because Lauren invited me – as did her mother for that matter.' And as he said this, he kicked himself for not even contemplating the possibility that Lauren's oldest friends, Stella and Pete, would be here. They had more right to be present than he did. But hang on a minute, what about Beth? He knew for a fact that she was no old friend of Lauren. But she seemed to be popping up all over the place lately. Then he thought again. All over the place, that is, when Pete is around.

No. Surely not. He couldn't. She couldn't. But one look at their body language gave them away. His first response was rage at Pete. He went up to him and whispered bitterly, 'How dare you have a go at me for some imaginary affair with your wife, when all the time you're cheating on her with my ex-girlfriend!'

Ann could see that Pete was having words with the other young man. They didn't look very friendly.

Pete could see that his mum was going to come over. Bill sent him a warning glare. Pete got the message. 'Look, this isn't the time. Please. I'm sorry about yesterday. I wasn't well.'

'You got that right,' Chris spat. He turned to walk away, not wanting to ruin the party. Although it wasn't what you might call swinging by any means. Then Pete pulled him back. 'Is it my imagination or is that your little hoodlum friend from Manchester over there, casing the joint?'

Chris softened his voice. 'Yes, it is, and I'd appreciate it if you didn't say anything. I feel responsible for him ending up in trouble that Saturday and I'm just doing him a favour to help him out of a fix.'

Pete looked at the boy. He seemed so young among this older crowd. Little more than a child. He wouldn't say anything. But he wouldn't take his eye off him either. And he pushed his wallet deeper down in his trouser pocket.

'Thanks,' Chris said.

'Just try and keep me out of your fights today, will you? My body can't take much more.'

Eddie almost fainted with relief when he saw Pete and Chris shaking hands. He rushed straight back into the dining room.

'Hello Beth.' Chris stood beside her as they surveyed the battleground before them.

'Chris,' she replied coolly.

'This is all unexpected, isn't it?'

'I didn't know I'd be coming until the last minute.'

'That wasn't what I meant, Beth.'

Beth blushed. 'It's none of your business, Chris, not any more.'

'Maybe not, but I can still care about you.'

'Fine, but don't expect me to care that you care.'

'You can't build your happiness on somebody else's unhappiness,' he said suddenly, throwing himself enthusiastically into his new role as begetter of self-righteous clichés.

She looked at him. 'I never wanted to. You're the one who left. I'm just doing the best I can under the circumstances you left me in.'

Chris softened. 'If it makes you feel any better, I'm regretting us splitting up.'

Beth smiled. 'No you're not. You just miss having someone to listen to you, someone comfortable who knows what you like to hear. And I was happy with that because I believed it was the most I could hope for.'

Chris laughed without humour. 'And I suppose Pete is a New Man, making you feel like a real woman, meeting your needs? Your mum and dad will be thrilled! A married man. Or will you hide him away in a tower while you try and find your courage?'

Beth looked at him evenly. 'I already have the courage. It was only you who made me weak. I never introduced you to my parents because I never quite believed that we were right. I always knew, deep down, that you would leave me when I tried to move things along. I always sensed that you were afraid of going that final mile. And I was proved correct, wasn't I?'

Chris said nothing as he thought back to his alarm when Beth had finally agreed to tell her parents about him. She was right, of course. Even Dean had spotted his fundamental fear of risk and challenged him to face it.

'Why, Chris?' she'd asked him over and over on the day he moved out. He'd given her dozens of stock answers ranging from: 'I just need some time to myself' through 'I think we've gone as far as we can go' up to the overused 'It's not you, it's me.' In other words, no answers at all.

Beth was not confident enough or experienced enough

to dare to ask him the question that most bothered her. If she had, she might have forced Chris to acknowledge the true reasons for his decision to leave. It would have left them both less damaged, better equipped to move on, than this messy ending.

But now she was much more confident. And a bit more experienced. 'Why did you leave me *then*?' she asked him suddenly.

Chris looked as if he didn't understand the question. 'I told you at the time. I just wanted . . . you know, it had been five years and . . .'

'Exactly! Five years. So why *then*?' Beth was not going to let this drop. She could be bold now because it no longer mattered. At least not to her. It mattered a lot to Chris and he didn't want to pursue the subject. But he felt bold after rising to Dean's challenge. I can do this, he thought, I can do anything. I am a streetfighter and an abetter of criminals. I am fearless.

He took a deep breath and exhaled silently. 'I suppose I'd persuaded myself that the reason we never got married or talked about children was because you refused to tell your parents about us. It proved to me that you weren't committed to us.'

'Fair enough,' Beth conceded. 'But then when I came to my senses . . .'

Chris looked at her. 'You took away my last excuse. The only excuse. It was down to me. And I realised that . . .'

'That you were the one not committed all along.' Beth nodded as she completed his sentence. 'You'd have left me years earlier if I'd shown the slightest indication that I might be taking things seriously. I must have been the perfect girlfriend for a commitment phobic – someone more afraid of commitment than you.'

Chris smiled weakly. 'Like I said, it was me, not you. If it's any consolation, now that I've had time to myself, I've come to the conclusion that I made a mistake. You took me by surprise. I panicked. If I'd had more time to think about it, I wouldn't have reacted so hastily.'

Beth suddenly pitied him for his appalling sense of timing. 'It's too late now, you know that, don't you. And it's your own stupid fault for being afraid.'

'We're all afraid, Beth,' he said quietly.

Beth shook her head. 'Pete's not,' she said gently. That's when Chris knew, finally knew, that he'd lost her.

Maureen was beginning to be anxious. Lauren was late. She'd tried to call Lauren on her mobile but the line was dead. Eddie reminded her that Lauren had thrown the phone in the lake.

'She clearly didn't inherit my common sense,' Maureen grumbled irritably.

Eddie refrained from commenting on this observation. The man was a saint. 'There must be traffic problems,' he said, 'because the other two girls are late as well, Isolde and Lizzie. I'm sure they'll all be here soon.'

It was another half an hour before Izzy arrived, full of apologies and stories of roadworks, tailbacks and contraflows. 'Lauren and Richard were coming in a separate car, but they're bound to have hit the same trouble spots as me. If they left any later than I did, they could be stuck right in the middle of it all.'

Izzy looked around the room and realised that everyone was staring at her.

'What?' Izzy said. She had forgotten what Auntie Joan's Betty had done to her.

'Izzy!' Chris and Beth cried out at the same time. Izzy's hand rushed to her head defensively.

Chris rushed forwards and spun Izzy round slowly. 'You look absolutely fantastic! I can't believe it! I never knew you could look like that.'

Beth was shaking her head in shock. She forgot all the old bad blood between them. 'Izzy, you look incredible. Your hair! Who did it?'

'Someone in the Lake District,' Izzy replied airily. She decided that there was no need for anyone to know it was a woman called Betty who'd sat her down in Joan's living room and carried out the transformation while not taking her eyes off the television.

It was not what Izzy had been used to. Betty had taken one look at Izzy's face, barely registered a reaction then pulled out a faded orange towel before getting to work. There was none of the West End consultation and general fawning that she'd happily paid £200 for in the past. Without once letting her know what she was doing, Betty had swiftly cut Izzy's hair down to the shortest it had ever been. Then she'd applied a dark brown rinse that looked perfectly natural and set off Izzy's pale skin. With little wisps framing her angular face, she looked feminine, fragile, unspeakably beautiful.

Then Betty began on her face. She had advised very little make-up, just enough to conceal the frown lines, legacies of years of loneliness, and some vibrant lipstick that illuminated her features. The result was breathtaking.

'Come and take your coat off, love,' Maureen said to her, 'and tell me how you got your hair to go like that.' She led Izzy towards the bedroom.

Dean Ryder couldn't take his eyes off her. 'Is she a model?' he whispered to Chris.

'She's my sister,' Chris replied, still stunned by her new look. Then he turned to face Dean. 'And whatever you're thinking – don't.'

Dean held up his hands in mock-innocence. 'You always think the worst of me. Everyone does.'

Chris became serious. 'Why do you think that is, Dean? Could it be because you've had so many chances and you throw them all back? You seem to have a death wish and the rest of us are tired of trying to save you from yourself.'

Dean avoided Chris's eyes. 'Well you won't have to tire yourself much longer.' He glanced out of the window. 'It's drying off now. I'll be on my way soon.'

Chris put his hand on Dean's shoulder. 'I really wish you'd reconsider. You'll have to spend the rest of your life running away. And I might be able to help you. Explain to Northview that you were being threatened.'

Dean smiled and this time it was genuine. 'Nice thought, sir, but not much help to me. Don't worry about me. I'll be fine.'

Chris was unbearably depressed at the realisation that Dean would indeed be fine. He'd done everything wrong but would survive it all. Chris had struggled his whole life through to do the right thing, make a difference, and now he was drowning.

Stella moved over to Pete. 'What are you thinking?' she asked.

Pete managed to stop himself from laughing out loud at Stella's question. Stella couldn't have understood why he found it so funny, how many times he'd longed to hear her ask that.

'I'm watching Chris with that boy.'

'Is he dangerous, do you think?' Stella said.

Pete shook his head. 'I don't think so, not after spending a few hours in a police cell with him. He's just a kid. Messed up, maybe permanently ruined now, but still a kid. But that kid got lucky when he got Chris as his teacher. I just wonder if he'll ever know.'

Stella was encouraged by Pete talking to her, talking properly. She brightened up. 'Have you thought about teaching, yourself? I mean, you got that redundancy money. That would keep us going. We could downsize. You could go and do teacher training. They give grants to mature students, they're desperate for teachers. And you'd be great. You've always been good with kids.'

Pete looked at her affectionately. It was the sort of look a good brother would give to a much-loved sister and it broke her heart. 'I didn't know you'd noticed.'

Stella swallowed. 'Of course I noticed. I notice everything you do. I just didn't want to talk about it. For obvious reasons.'

'Ah yes,' Pete said. 'The obvious reasons.'

Stella hurried before he retreated into silence. 'Yes, and funnily enough, I've been thinking about that too. I know what a selfish cow I am but lots of selfish people have kids and I don't think I'd necessarily make a bad mother—'

Pete took her hand firmly and stopped her before she went any further.

'Don't, Stella, don't say it.'

Stella felt sick. She knew what was coming and he wasn't going to let her preempt him. She wouldn't give up. 'I know what you're going to say, but you don't have to. I know you're not happy with me. So I'll change! I can do it. People do it all the time!'

He put one finger on her lips so gently that it tore her apart. 'Don't,' he repeated. 'It's too late. Much, much too late. And even if you could do it, I don't think it would be right. You shouldn't have to change to suit me. You'd have to spend the rest of your life acting, pretending. What sort of life would that be?'

Stella was having trouble speaking. She was distantly aware of other people in the room and their presence was blunting her reactions. Even when her life was being torn down, she couldn't completely ignore her social obligations. She couldn't scream or hit him or have a tantrum. 'It would be a life with you instead of a life without you,' she said quietly. 'I couldn't bear that.'

Pete couldn't bear any of it. He now knew why he'd stayed married to Stella for all these years. It was because the alternative was this, a searing confrontation that was killing Stella and permanently scarring him. And the only reason he did it now, that he could do it now, was Beth.

'This is all about Beth, isn't it?' Stella said in defeat.

Pete decided to be honest. 'I'm leaving you because of Beth, that's true, but in every other respect, we separated a long time ago. I was always going to go eventually. This has been a non-marriage for years.'

Stella had one last card to play, one that had served her well in the past. 'I'm begging you. Don't leave me. I don't care if it's a non-marriage. I don't care!'

Pete withdrew his hand. 'Well, you should care, Stella. I care. Everyone should care about that.'

Stella's voice became almost inaudible. 'So this is my punishment? I lose you, my home, everything? Because I was prepared to settle for what I had?'

Pete took her hand back, more firmly this time. 'Stella, you'd already lost me. But you won't lose anything else. You can have the rest of my redundancy money and I'll keep up my share of the mortgage until you've got the house into a fit state to sell. You can't pretend you would have wanted to stay there. Not after everything that's happened.'

'And then what?' Stella asked lifelessly. 'I take my half and buy a little one-bedroomed starter home in a Midlands suburb?'

Pete stared at her. 'Stella, why don't you think of life beyond housebuying? Just for once. You'll have a substantial sum of money. You could travel. Start up your own business. Take some chances.'

Stella looked up sharply at this suggestion. 'I don't want to take chances. That's why I married you.'

She surprised herself with this insight. Pete flinched. Although he'd always suspected this to be the case, it still wounded him slightly. *That* surprised *him*. Stella stood up and began to circle the tiny space around Pete's chair. 'Oh, yes! Now it's clear! You know, you married me under false pretences, Pete. Pretending to love me the way I was. Pretending to want the same thing as me. I was the only honest one in this marriage, I realise that now. I didn't change. That was my crime. You did change. That was yours.'

Pete had the grace to look ashamed. 'I'm sorry, Stella.'

This look gave Stella the scrap of dignity she needed to enable her to survive. It wasn't much but it was hers, nobody else's. She knew this was all that was available to her. There was nothing else left to say or do. She got up quietly to leave. She couldn't ruin the party by making a scene. And this proved, oh so bitterly, the impossibility of her desperate promise to Pete – she couldn't change. She could no more become a different sort of wife than she could spoil a party.

But as she walked purposefully towards the door, she didn't look back. She wanted to but she didn't. A newborn instinct in her told her to keep looking ahead. So she listened to the voice and fixed her eyes in front of her, taking the first chance of her new life.

'Where is Stella going?' Ann said to Pete, as she saw the front door. Pete looked across at Bill who knew instantly what had happened. He came straight over and whispered into Ann's ear. 'I think we should make a move, Ann, I'll explain everything on the way home.'

Ann looked mystified. 'But we've only just got here. We haven't even seen Lauren or had anything to eat. We can't just leave. Poor Maureen. She's gone to so much trouble!'

Bill shot a furious glance at Pete, who died a little under the accusing glare. 'Don't worry. I'm sure she'll understand. Pete will explain to her, won't you?'

Pete nodded miserably. Within seconds, Bill had grabbed their coats and guided Ann, who was still protesting, out of the door.

Maureen and Izzy returned, chatting cheerfully. They looked around at the depleted party and stopped talking.

'What's happened? Where's everyone gone?' Maureen asked.

Beth and Chris had watched the entire scene in horror. Dean had thoroughly enjoyed the episode. In later years he would discover a passion for the theatre which he would attribute to his encounters with these dysfunctional but law-abiding people.

Pete realised that it was going to be his responsibility to provide the explanations. He was tempted to jump up and make a run for the door but he had Beth to think of. He would always have Beth to think of from now. And that made him feel indescribably happy rather than trapped.

'The thing is, Maureen, Stella wasn't feeling at all well, so Ann and Bill decided to take her home.' He wasn't an accomplished liar and like all beginners in deceit, he hadn't thought this one through.

'Why didn't *you* take her home?' Maureen asked reasonably.

Pete realised his mistake. 'I thought Lauren would like to see one of us here, so we agreed that I should stay.'

Izzy sensed from the atmosphere that there had been a major incident and nobody was going to do anything to rescue the situation. So she elected herself rescue leader. It must have been the new haircut, she'd never volunteered for anything before. (God bless you, Betty, she thought.)

'Maureen, why don't we all sit down and start lunch before Eddie's vegetables are pulped into juice? Lauren and Richard have obviously got stuck in traffic and I don't think they'd want us to wait for them.'

'Thank you!' Eddie shouted from the kitchen. He'd

heard the whole performance in the living room and, while Maureen was cross-examining Pete, he had efficiently removed three of the name cards from the table and moved the chairs around to fill the gaps. He left Lauren and Richard's (and the mysterious Lizzie's) cards there in case they turned up soon. 'Ah yes,' Izzy had said delicately, 'about Lizzie. I hope you didn't go to too much trouble to accommodate the extra guest because, well . . .'

The only person who was hungry was Dean and so he took the initiative to lead the reluctant guests into the dining room.

Maureen was desolate. Her party was becoming a fiasco. Lauren wasn't even here. The guests were departing within minutes of arriving and the ones that stayed were not looking very festive. Eddie spotted her expression and went over to give her a reassuring kiss and squeeze. 'It'll all be fine, Mo. Keep smiling.'

Lunch was served.

'Haven't you got anything else to eat, Richard?' Lauren asked, groaning. The car hadn't moved for an hour. The number of police cars speeding down the hard shoulder implied to them that this was going to be a long delay. At Richard's suggestion, Lauren had gone into the boot and rummaged through all the walking clothes to see what goodies she could find in the pockets. She found numerous gadgets that were only of use if a mountain stream or the sun or a gullible rabbit were available.

Her total catch consisted of two bars of chocolate, some Polo mints and a slab of the ubiquitous Kendal

410

Mint Cake. 'We should try and stretch it out,' Richard advised, dividing the booty into two. We don't know how long we're going to be stuck here.'

'Good idea,' she said, promptly eating her full half-share in two minutes. 'And if you start that "favourite foods" game, I'll have no choice but to torture you back by singing a selection of popular extracts from Gilbert and Sullivan.'

Richard feigned a painful death before offering Lauren a piece of his chocolate. She accepted gratefully. They sat in the car, Richard shifting occasionally to make his foot comfortable, looking out of the window. There were cars as far as they could see in both directions.

'I hate cars,' Lauren concluded.

'No you don't,' Richard replied placidly. 'You're only saying that because you're in a traffic jam. Once you're back in London, you'll wonder how you could ever have said such a thing. Or in New York.'

Lauren stared at him. 'Why do you keep telling me that I don't know my own mind? First of all, you tell me that I couldn't really want to make a life up there among the lakes and mountains. Now you're telling me that I can't hate cars. What gives you such amazing insight into my mind?'

'What do you think?' Richard asked quietly.

Lauren blushed. Thank God! Richard thought. A reaction! It might not turn out to be the reaction I want but FINALLY she's got the message!

Lauren stared out of the window. She strained to see some green beyond the haze of exhaust fumes that blocked the view. 'Do you know what I'm thinking?' she asked.

'I know what I want you to be thinking,' Richard replied.

'I'm thinking how strange it is to be sitting here with you, in the middle of all this grey and smoke and noise when I can only associate you with green and clouds and silence. You seem different.'

'Is that a good thing or a bad thing?' Richard asked cautiously.

Lauren took a deep breath. 'You seem real to me for the first time since I met you. Isn't that odd? But everything about the last two weeks in Tendale has been unreal. It's been a bolthole to escape to from the mess I was making of things in London. See! I'm even calling it London instead of home, that's how confused I am! And it's been a distraction from having to think about New York.'

Richard took her hand. Lauren acknowledged the gesture by flexing her fingers ever so slightly and then left her hand there. She went on. Richard had no idea where she was heading but if she left her hand where it was, he didn't mind if it took all day.

'And I thought that the reason I liked you, the reason I could talk to you and be honest with you, was that you were nothing to do with my real life. It was as if it didn't matter what I said to you or did with you, there wouldn't be any consequences. None that would matter, anyway. I would either be back in London or the States in a few weeks.'

Richard squeezed her hand. 'So you decided that I was irrelevant and inconsequential. Does this get better or are you softening me up for the crushing finale?' He added a jokey tone to his voice and hoped that he would still be joking once she'd finished.

Lauren turned to face him. 'It gets better,' she said wryly.

'That's a relief,' Richard said, 'especially after giving you the last piece of chocolate.'

'And I think I've realised my mistake for a few days. Maybe I knew all along but I had to work it out for myself.'

'What mistake? Don't go all enigmatic on me. Just because we had a deep and meaningful discussion about your father doesn't mean I enjoy cryptic conversation. That was strictly a one-off.'

Lauren laughed. Thank God she's laughing! thought Richard. While she was just smiling, there was always a chance that I was in trouble.

'My mistake, Richard, was a fundamental one. I got the whole thing the wrong way round. It was all topsy-turvy. As soon as I saw you in Tendale, I assumed that I'd left reality behind me. The party in London, meeting Chris, the sushi bar, all of it, that was my reality. Therefore everything else had to be an illusion, a nice but unattainable dream for a townie. And you were part of the illusion.

'But now I'm sitting here with London or New York in front of me, Tendale behind me and you next to me, I can see that there is only one real thing in my life.'

Richard silently sent up his first-ever prayer. It was a direct challenge to God, the only miracle he had ever asked for or ever would ask for. Let it be me, he prayed. Let it be me.

Chapter 24

'So why do you keep doing it, lad?' Eddie asked Dean. 'I mean, a bright boy like you, what do you want to spend your life in prison for?'

'Because breaking into cars is the only thing I've ever been any good at,' Dean confessed.

'That's a lie,' Chris interrupted. 'You have an amazing gift for maths. You could easily work with computers.'

Dean felt hemmed in by these two men both trying to shape him into the man they felt he should become. 'You seem to think I'm like a junkie. That I want to kick my habit but I can't. What you don't realise is that I love what I do! I love the thrill of getting behind the wheel of a car I've never driven before. I love being chased by the police. Because I've got nothing to lose.'

Chris knew there was no point in mentioning that he did, in fact, have his life to lose. He was a teenager. He knew that he was immortal. It went with the territory.

Eddie refused to be beaten by the boy's stubborn determination to be helped. 'The company I work for, they're always looking for trainees. You'd be good at sales. You've got all the talk, all the cockiness, a head for figures and I don't have to ask if you can drive.'

Dean looked at Eddie with pity. 'You don't get it. Why does nobody listen to anything I say? I don't want to be like you. I don't want a job. I don't want to be reformed. I don't want to change!'

He stood up suddenly and his chair tipped back on to the floor. Everyone stared at him. 'Look, thanks for the food. I'll be off now. Bye. Thanks for the lift, sir.' He grabbed his backpack and was through the door before Chris knew what was happening.

'Aren't you going to go after him?' Eddie asked him, furious that Chris had just let Dean go like that.

Chris went to the window to see Dean swagger down the street, king of the road. 'No. But maybe one day he'll come back.'

'I hope not,' muttered Maureen, whose hospitality had been sorely tested when she caught Dean sneaking a silver photo frame into his bag.

Chris watched the boy become smaller and smaller until he was out of sight. A part of him left with the boy.

Then he turned to face the rest of the sorry-looking faces around the table. Pete and Beth were seated at opposite ends where Eddie had placed them in a futile act of propriety after witnessing the sad humiliation of Stella.

Chris and Dean had sat on either side of Izzy and Maureen had been grateful to find herself next to Eddie. The meal had gone as expected. The vegetables had been horribly overcooked. But everybody finished them after Maureen gave them all a murderous warning to do so while Eddie was in the kitchen dishing up. The chicken dish was edible. That was the best anyone could say about it. But the guests ate that up too. They were too scared of Maureen to do otherwise.

As Lauren had predicted, there was Viennetta for dessert. With a candle. Maureen had wisely decided that the pink cake was not appropriate. 'Why have you put a candle in it?' Izzy asked in surprise. 'Lauren isn't even here.'

Maureen sighed. 'I know, but there's no reason why Chris should miss out.'

Chris had looked baffled at this. Even more so when everybody began to sing 'Happy birthday' to him. Izzy had got up, ostensibly to go the bathroom. On the way, she bent to whisper in Chris's ear. 'I'll explain later. She thinks it's your birthday. Just go along with it.'

Isn't this where it all started? he asked himself. Having to go along with a little fib about birthdays. That was two weeks ago and look at us all now. Well, the ones that are left. The dreadful fallout of friendly fire.

Beth and Pete. They hadn't exchanged a single word since Stella and Pete's parents had left. They'd drifted into the dining room, eaten a large meal without tasting a single bite and managed to sustain polite conversation. It was a heroic achievement. But even with a large table between them, their togetherness was almost tangible. In a matter of days, they had formed a bond stronger and closer than he and Beth had managed to achieve in five years. His failure? His fate? His fear? He couldn't tell. But he was a loser. The loser.

Chris thought of all the pain they'd caused. Could anything positive come out of that level of devastation? Chris doubted it.

Then he looked at Izzy. His sister had changed into someone else entirely. Whether it was this new job, about which he didn't know much, or the haircut, she was born again. For the first time, Chris saw that she had hope. She could allow herself to move forward at last. She finally had direction.

He was happy for her, and he envied her, so much so that he intended to ask her what her secret was. And the day her brother came to her for advice was to be the happiest day of her life.

He'd been staggered to see his sister chatting happily with Beth. The two of them had hated each other when he was living with Beth and now they were getting along like best friends. He was terribly depressed by this, believing that he must have been the cause of five years of animosity. He was wrong.

It was nothing to do with Chris and everything to do with Izzy.

Izzy was not the same person who'd once resented Beth's apparently effortless hold on life. She forgave Beth for being who she was, cool, assured, fulfilled, because finally Izzy had become like that too. And she'd learned what she'd always suspected: that Beth was none of those things, she was just good at acting as if she was. Now Izzy could be that too. They'd always been two of a kind on one level and had never known it. They'd had to find a different level at which they could meet.

Chris wondered if Izzy and Beth would now become friends. Too, too weird, he thought. Still, no less weird than his disastrous attempts to form a friendship with Pete. Maybe the best friendships had to form themselves.

Then there was Dean who'd just left. Chris had dared to believe that Dean was the one. The child every teacher dreams of. The hopeless case he manages to transform into a shining star. The one who makes a whole career worthwhile. Chris had made the mistake of seeing signs where there had been none. He'd regarded the whole incident in Manchester as an omen that he had been thrown together with Dean for the purpose of saving him.

But whatever the purpose was, it hadn't turned out to be that. Unless that had been the purpose and Chris had simply failed. No, he wouldn't accept that. And he wouldn't give up.

Not on Dean. But he would give up on Lauren. He didn't need any more hints to know that the relationship had always been a non-starter.

Then he found the bright side. It had eluded him all day but he found it in the end. He thought of his schoolfriends who had mocked him for his refusal to steal KitKats. He wondered if there had ever been two weeks in their lives when they had been arrested twice as well as abetting a convicted criminal in a daring escape. He doubted it. Hah! And when he walked across the room, it was with an imperceptible swagger.

'Well, Maureen, I'm afraid I'll have to be on my way,' he said.

Maureen looked alarmed. 'But you can't go! Lauren isn't here yet. What will I say to her when she asks where you are?'

Chris smiled sadly. 'She won't mind, trust me. It's been . . . quite a day. Thank you for inviting me.'

He gave Maureen an awkward kiss on the cheek. She was still making half-hearted pleading sounds to encourage him to stay a little longer but Chris wouldn't be persuaded. As she stood by the door, watching him get into his car, she heard whispers and chair-moving in the dining room. When she returned, she saw Izzy, Beth and Pete all on their feet looking like naughty children caught in a prank.

'You're not going too, are you?' she said, only expecting the one answer.

Izzy spoke for them all. 'Sorry. I have to get back to the Lake District. The traffic will probably be horrendous. Thanks ever so much, Maureen. I'm sure we'll meet again. I'm hoping that Lauren and I are going to continue working together in the future.' She thrilled at the words. Lauren had dropped some subtle hints yesterday and, while she said nothing definite, it was clear that an offer of some kind was on the cards.

Perhaps that had been the incentive she needed to let the talented Betty loose on her hair. It was a new beginning and what do all women do when they are about to start something new? They get their hair cut. That's what normal women do, Izzy thought proudly. Like me.

Pete cleared his throat, preparing to say something that might excuse his role in breaking up the party. But Maureen stopped him.

'Don't say it, love. Save your words for the future. You'll need them. I wish you all luck. And that includes your wife. Bye bye, love,' she said to Beth, kissing her briefly on the cheek. Beth said nothing. Emotionally, she was already closing the door on this episode. She would never look back again, or brood over the present. She'd chosen her future, Pete, and she would keep her sights fixed firmly on him.

'Eddie!' Maureen hissed. 'Do the honours!' Eddie,

– who'd had his backside glued to his chair for the last two hours, would have preferred not to move. But an order is an order. He leapt to his feet to collect coats and usher their final guests out of the door with the requisite insistence to come again. He hoped they all realised that he didn't mean it.

As he closed the door, he noticed that Chris was still sitting in his car. 'What's the silly beggar waiting for?' Eddie asked Maureen.

'Oh, I don't know,' Maureen replied irritably. 'Just close the door and let's have a cup of tea.'

An hour later, the doorbell rang. Maureen and Eddie had been watching the M1 traffic jam on the television.

'Lauren! Thank God you're all right, love. We've been worried sick! What were you thinking about, chucking your mobile phone away like that? We've had no way of knowing if anything had happened to you . . .'

Lauren kissed her mother affectionately mid-rant, as she steered Richard past her into the living room. Then Maureen realised it was that moment. She braced herself for the introductions but Lauren beat her to it. She strode up to Eddie, her hand outstretched.

'Hello, I'm Lauren. And you are?' Her performance was sublime.

Eddie shook her hand. 'Eddie. Eddie Knight.' He winked at her so that Maureen wouldn't notice.

Maureen edged forward. 'Er, Eddie is my . . . er, partner.'

Lauren beamed. 'That's nice, Mum. I'm really pleased for you. And this is Richard.'

Maureen was still shocked by the ease with which

Lauren had received Eddie's existence. It was like a miracle. No, it *was* a miracle. 'Sorry, Lauren, I was miles away. This is Richard, you say? Your client?'

He didn't look anything like any of the characters in *Last of the Summer Wine*. More like Harrison Ford. That's eight cans of milk stout wasted, Maureen thought.

'Actually, he's a bit more than a client, Mum.' And Lauren took Richard's hand shyly.

Maureen clasped her hands together. She looked seriously confused. 'But what about—' Eddie developed a major coughing fit which stopped Maureen from saying the unsayable. Maureen took a breath and started again.

'Come and sit down,' she said nervously.

Eddie helped Richard into a chair with practised ease. 'You look as if you've done this before,' Richard observed appreciatively.

Eddie closed his eyes as the whole day flashed before him. 'Not before today. But then today has been somewhat unusual.'

'So,' Maureen said, folding her arms self-consciously in front of her garish dress. 'Is everything all right, Lauren?'

Lauren smiled. 'Everything is more than fine. I've just given up my job.'

Maureen frowned. 'How can you give up your job? You work for yourself.'

'I did work for myself. I've got a new job, now.'

'And it's not in New York,' Richard said in relief.

Maureen was confused. 'Why on earth would you have a job in New York?'

'Exactly what I thought, Mum!' Lauren exclaimed. 'Why would I want a job in New York, running a

421

multinational company division paying a hundred and fifty thousand dollars a year, when I could help Richard sell anoraks for no pay whatsoever?'

Richard raised a finger to correct her. 'Not quite no pay. I did say you could have all the souvenir gift packs of fudge you can eat.'

'That's true,' Lauren acknowledged.

Maureen looked from Lauren to Richard. 'How long were you in that traffic jam? Did you have the heating on? The cold must have got to you, you're not making any sense.'

Lauren took her mum's hand fondly. 'Actually I'm making sense for the first time in my life. I'm handing my company over to Izzy. I can help her find some people to work with her and train her up. I'll still get a small share of the profits. It'll be enough to live on in Cumbria.'

Maureen glowed at the happiness on her daughter's face. It was an expression she'd longed to see for the last three years.

'Oh Lauren! I'm so pleased for you! Well, look at the pair of us! Who would have thought it, eh?'

Richard extended his hand to Eddie. 'I hope you won't mind if I don't call you Dad,' he said drily.

Eddie laughed. 'I don't suppose you fancy some melted Viennetta and some birthday cake?'

'Oh God, that sounds fantastic! We're starving!' Lauren said.

'I'll go and get you something,' Eddie said, disappearing into the kitchen. Lauren had sat down next to her mum on the sofa. 'Mum, look what Richard bought me for my birthday!'

Maureen peered at the little fish brooch. 'It looks almost the same as the necklace I got you.' She felt the quality of the gold. 'Except, oh yes, this is real, isn't it?'

Lauren glanced in amusement at Richard, who was watching her, still amazed and grateful that she was his. 'Pisces is Richard's favourite constellation, that's why he bought it for me.'

The look they exchanged was very private. And as the house filled with chat and shrieks of laughter as photograph albums were being pulled out, the car outside quietly moved away.

Chris had seen what he'd waited to see. He hadn't been able to remember Lauren's face and yet he knew that the face, the woman, had made an impact on him. There'd been something about her smile. So he needed to see her one more time, to file the image away under C for closure.

But as soon as she arrived and he saw her smiling at that older man, he knew his mistake. Too late. Her smile was different to the one he'd remembered, and it was a smile that would haunt him.

Because from that moment on, Chris was to spend the rest of his life looking for someone who would smile at him like that. Just like the rest of us.

Big Girls Don't Cry
Francesca Clementis

Sex, lies and chocolate cake!

Marina has spent most of her adult life going from diet to diet, binge to binge. There isn't a diet she hasn't tried or a type of chocolate she hasn't sampled. But though big girls aren't supposed to cry, in Marina's experience, they don't have much fun either. She's 31, almost fifteen stone and desperate.

Scientist David Sandhurst throws her a lifeline. He's the inventor of a miracle drug – a drug he believes can help people lose weight without dieting or exercise. All he needs to do is prove it...

Enrolled in the year-long test, Marina soon finds herself losing weight and gaining confidence. Soon she's saying goodbye to her hips and hello to her new-improved love-life – and a whole new set of problems! For Marina's about to discover that inside every big woman there's a thin one dying to get out...and eat chocolate!

"Clementis takes humorous chunks out of our skinny-obsessed society"   *Company*

"Incisively funny and terribly sobering... A wickedly funny debut – we can't wait for her next"   *Sunday Post*

"A witty look at our obsession with the battle of the bulge"
Family Circle

Mad About the Girls
Francesca Clementis

All Lorna has ever wanted is a husband and four children. And that's what she now has – except he's somebody else's husband and they're somebody else's children. But Robert Danson and his adorable daughters are practically hers. After all Robert's wife had walked out on him and her family ten years earlier. Having fallen for Robert, Lorna had been only too happy to step into the breach.

Now Lorna has everything a real mother should have (aside from stretch marks). Only Robert's real wife is back. She's beautiful, assured and looking for forgiveness. But is that all she wants? Lorna can't help but feel that this family isn't big enough for the both of them...

A moving and witty novel about a modern relationship under pressure from the bestselling author of *Big Girls Don't Cry*:

'Clementis takes humorous chunks out of our skinny-obsessed society'   *Company*

'A witty look at out obsession with the battle of the bulge'
Family Circle

'Incisively funny and terribly sobering... A wickedly funny debut – we can't wait for her next."   *Sunday Post*